Two Gallant Sons of Devon

A Tale of the Days of Queen Bess

by

Harry Collingwood

Two Gallant Sons of Devon
A Tale of the Days of Queen Bess
by Harry Collingwood

ISBN: 978-93-68095-52-1

Published by

DOUBLE 9 BOOKS

2/13-B, Ansari Road
Daryaganj, New Delhi – 110002
info@double9books.com
www.double9books.com
Tel. 011-40042856

ABOUT THE AUTHOR

Harry Collingwood was the pseudonym of William Joseph Cosens Lancaster (23 May 1843 - 10 June 1922), a British civil engineer and novelist who wrote over 40 boys' adventure tales, the majority of which were set on the sea. Collingwood was the eldest son of master mariner Captain William Lancaster (1813 - (1861 - 1871)) and Anne, née Cosens. According to his birth certificate, he was born on May 23, 1843 at 9:30 a.m. at Concord Place in Weymouth, Dorset. Collingwood was the first of the couple's three children. He was eight years old when his sister Ada Louise was born, and twelve when his sister Sarah Anne (1 June 1853 - 27 December 1941) was born. Both ladies were listed as draper helpers on the 1871 census. Collingwood's father had died by that time, and his mother lived with her daughters until her death. Ada never married and lived with her sister after leaving her family home. Sarah Anne married Mathew Smellie in St Michaels, Toxteth, Liverpool, Lancashire, on June 30, 1880. Harold Ernest Smellie, born on April 11, 1881, died on April 30, 1961. Harold, Collingwood's nephew, registered his death in 1922.

CONTENTS

Chapter One
How Phil Stukely and Dick Chichester
narrowly escaped drowning

It was a little after seven o'clock on June 19 in the year of Our Lord 1577, and business was practically over for the day. The taverns and alehouses were, of course, still open, and would so remain for three or four hours to come, for the evening was then, as it is now, their most busy time; but nearly all the shops in Fore Street of the good town of Devonport were closed, one of the few exceptions being that of Master John Summers, "Apothecary, and Dealer in all sorts of Herbs and Simples", as was announced by the sign which swung over the still open door of the little, low-browed establishment.

The shop was empty of customers for the moment, its only occupants being two persons, both of whom were employees of Master John Summers. One—the tall, thin, dark, dreamy-eyed individual behind the counter who was with much deliberation and care completing the preparation of a prescription—was Philip Stukely, the apothecary's only assistant; while the other was one Colin Dunster, a pallid, raw-boned youth whose business it was to distribute the medicines to his master's customers. He was slouching now, outside the counter, beside a basket three-parts full of bottles, each neatly enwrapped in white paper and inscribed with the name and address of the customer to whom it was to be delivered in due course. Apparently the package then in course of preparation would complete the tale of those to be delivered that night; for as Stukely tied the string and wrote the address in a clear, clerkly hand, the lad Dunster straightened himself up and laid a hand upon the basket, as though suddenly impatient to be gone.

At this moment another youth, with blue-grey eyes, curly, flaxen hair, tall, broad-chested, and with the limbs of a young Hercules, burst into the shop, taking at a stride the two steps which led down into it from the street, as he exclaimed:

"Heyday, Master Phil, how is this? Hast not yet finished compounding thy potions? My day's work ended an hour and more ago; and the evening is a perfect one for a sail upon the Sound."

"Ay, so 'tis, I'll warrant," answered Stukely, as he deposited the package in the basket. "There, Colin, lad," he continued, "that is the last for to-night; and—listen, sirrah! See that thou mix not the parcels, as thou didst but a week agone, lest thou bring sundry of her most glorious Majesty's lieges to an untimely end! There"—as the boy seized the basket and hurried out of the shop—"that completes my day's work. Now I have but to put up the shutters and lock the door; and then, have with thee whither thou wilt. Help me with the shutters, Dick, there's a good lad, so shall I be ready the sooner."

Five minutes sufficed the two to put up the shutters, and for Stukely to wash his hands, discard his apron, change his coat, and lock up the shop; then the two somewhat oddly contrasted friends wended their way quickly down the narrow street on their way to the waterside.

As they go, let us take the opportunity to become better acquainted with them both, for, although they knew it not, they were taking their first steps on the road to many a strange and wild adventure, whither we who also love adventure propose to accompany them.

Philip Stukely, the elder of the two, aged twenty-three and a half years, tall, spare, sallow of complexion, with long, straight, black hair, and dark eyes—the precise colour of which no man precisely knew, for it seemed to change with his varying moods—was, as we have seen, by some strange freak of fortune, an apothecary's assistant. But merely to say that he was an apothecary's assistant very inadequately describes the man; for, in addition to that, he was both a poet and a painter in thought and feeling, if not in actual fact. He was also a voracious reader of everything that treated of adventure, from the story of the Flood, and Jonah's memorable voyage, to Homer's *Iliad* and *Odyssey*, and everything else of a like character that he could lay hands upon. Altogether, he was a very strange fellow, who evidently thought deeply, and originally, and held many very remarkable opinions upon certain subjects.

This it was that made his friendship for and deep attachment to Dick Chichester, and Chichester's equally deep attachment to him, so strange a thing; for the two had not a trait in common. To begin with, Chichester was much younger than Stukely, being just turned seventeen years of age, although this difference in age was much less apparent than usual, for while Stukely, in his more buoyant and expansive moments, seemed considerably younger than his years, Chichester might easily have been, and indeed often was, mistaken for a young man of twenty-one or twenty-two. While Stukely was spare of frame and sallow of complexion, Chichester possessed the frame, stature, and colouring of a young Viking, being already within a quarter of an inch of six feet two inches in height, although he had by no means done growing, broad in proportion, with eyes of steel blue, and a shock of curly hair which his friends would in these latter days have called auburn, while his enemies—if he had possessed any—would have tersely described it as "carrots". In temperament, too, Chichester was the very antithesis of Stukely, for he was absolutely unimaginative and matter-of-fact. Perhaps his occupation may have had something to do with this; for he was apprenticed to a shipwright, and delighted in his work. He was also an orphan; his nearest relative being his uncle Michael Chichester, a merchant of Plymouth, who had adopted him upon the death of his parents, and with whom he now lived.

Not much was said as the strangely assorted pair strode along side by side on their way to the water, for both of them loved boats, and sailing, and all that pertained to the sea life, and both were equally eager to get afloat as quickly as possible, so as not to waste unnecessarily a moment of that glorious evening. At last, however, as Dick turned unexpectedly into a narrow side alley, Stukely pulled up short with:

"Hillo, Master Dick! whither away, my lad? This is not the way to the spot where our boat is moored."

"No," answered Dick, "it is not, I know. But we are not going to take our own boat to-night, Phil; we are going to take Gramfer Heard's lugger. Gramfer is to Tavistock to-night; and he told me this morning that I might use the lugger whenever I pleased, if he did not want her himself. We'll have something like a sail to-night, Phil, for there is enough wind blowing to just suit the lugger, while it and the sea would be rather too much for our own boat."

So saying, Chichester led the way down the alley, and halted at a door in the wall, nearly at its farthest extremity. Then, drawing a key from his pocket, he unlocked the door, flung it open, and Stukely found himself looking in upon Gramfer Heard's shipyard, the scene of Dick Chichester's daily labours. He gazed, for a few seconds, with appreciative eyes at the forms of three goodly hulls in varying stages of progress, inhaled with keen enjoyment the mingled odours of pine chips and Stockholm tar, and then hurried after Dick, who was already busily engaged in unmooring a small skiff, in which to pull off to a handsome five-ton lugger-rigged boat that lay lightly straining at her moorings in the tideway.

A few minutes later they were aboard the lugger, busily engaged in loosing and setting the sails; and presently they were under way, having slipped their moorings and transferred them to the skiff, which they left behind to serve as a buoy to guide them to the moorings upon their return.

The lugger was a beautiful boat, according to the idea of beauty that then prevailed, having been constructed by Mr George Heard—familiarly known as Gramfer Heard—shipbuilder of Devonport, and Dick Chichester's master, as a kind of yacht, for his own especial use and enjoyment. She was a very roomy boat, being entirely open from stem to stern, and was conveniently rigged with two masts, the main and mizzen, upon which were set two standing lugs and a jib, the mizzen sheet being hauled out to the end of a bumpkin; consequently when once her sails were set she could easily be handled by one man.

Stukely, who was the master spirit, took the tiller, quite as a matter of course, while Dick was perfectly content to tend the jib and main sheets; and away they went down the Hamoaze, with the water buzzing and foaming from the boat's lee bow and swirling giddily in her wake as she sped swiftly along under the impulse of a fresh westerly breeze, the full strength of which was however not yet felt, the lugger being under the lee of Mount Edgecumbe, beautiful then as it is to-day. But the prospect which delighted the eyes of the two friends—or of Stukely rather, for Dick Chichester somehow seemed almost entirely to lack the keen sense of beauty with which his friend was so bountifully endowed—was very different from that which greets the eye of the beholder to-day. Devonport and Stonehouse were mere villages; Mount Wise was farm land; where the citadel now stands was a trumpery fort which a modern gunboat would utterly destroy in half an hour; Drake's island was fortified, it is true, but with a battery even more insignificant than the citadel fort; while the Hoe showed a bare half-dozen buildings, chief of which was the inn, afterwards re-named the Pelican Inn, in honour of Drake's ship, famous as the spot behind which, eleven years later, Drake and Hawkins played their never-to-be-forgotten game of bowls.

As the boat slid out from under the lee of Drake's island, however, and headed straight for the Eddystone, she gradually began to feel the full strength of the breeze, and her two occupants settled themselves down to enjoy thoroughly a good long evening's sail, perhaps to be extended into the small hours of the next morning, if the conditions continued favourable. For there was nothing that these two more thoroughly enjoyed than a good tussle, in a well-found boat, against a strong breeze and a heavy sea; and they were like enough to have both to-night, so soon as they cleared the Sound and reached open water. In fact, although probably neither of them had thus far suspected it, both were strongly imbued with the spirit of born adventurers.

An hour's sailing sufficed to carry them to seaward of Penlee Point, when they found that there was just wind and sea enough to make for perfect enjoyment, therefore instead of contenting themselves with a mere sail round the Eddystone and back they determined to make a night of it; and the sheets were accordingly hauled aft for a long stretch to windward, close-hauled, towards the chops of the Channel.

Away sped the boat to the southward and westward, careening gunwale-to, and sending the spray flying in such drenching showers over the weather bow, that presently the water rose above the bottom boards and splashed like a miniature sea in the lee bilge, compelling Dick to abandon the mainsheet to Stukely while he took a bucket and proceeded to bale. But the wind showed a disposition to freshen, careening the boat so steeply that, despite Stukely's utmost care, the water began to slop in over the lee gunwale, as well as over the bows; and at length they decided to take a reef in the mainsail, for Dick had no fancy for spending the rest of the cruise in an ineffectual endeavour to free the boat of water that came in faster than he could throw it out. This was done, and the boat resumed her headlong rush to the southward, until by the time that the sun sank, red and angry, beneath the western wave, the land lay a mere film of grey along the northern board.

Then occurred a thing common enough in the tropics but much less usual in our more temperate climate; the wind suddenly dropped to a stark calm, and then, a few minutes later, came away in a terrific squall from about north-north-east.

So violent was the outfly that there was but one thing to do, namely, to keep the boat away dead before it; and away went the lugger, still heading to the southward and westward, but with the wind now dead aft instead of over the starboard bow. But they had scarcely been scudding five minutes when there occurred a sudden rending crack of timber, and the mainmast, weakened by an unsuspected flaw in the heart of it, snapped, about midway between the heel of it and the sheave, and went over the bows, broaching-to the lugger with the drag of the mainsail in the water, and nearly filling her as she came slowly round head to wind.

The friends were now in a situation of imminent peril, the squall raised a very awkward choppy sea with almost magical rapidity, and, more than half-full of water as the boat now was, she was liable to be swamped out of hand by some unlucky sea pouring in over her bows; the occupants, therefore, set to work with a will to bale her out, Stukely taking the bucket from Dick and handing him the baler instead. But it was both back-breaking and heartbreaking work; for, rendered heavy and sluggish by the large quantity of water in her, the boat frequently failed to rise to the lift of the seas, several of which poured in over her bows from time to time, filling her faster than she could be freed by the joint efforts of her crew; so that at length the unwelcome conviction forced itself upon the two friends that, unless something quite unforeseen happened, the boat must inevitably founder under them.

This conviction caused the toiling pair to cease from their labours for a moment and glance about them anxiously, in the hope that the twilight might reveal to them some craft to which they might signal for assistance. To their great relief, they perceived that there was indeed such a craft within a short two miles to the eastward of them; moreover she was outward-bound, and was heading in such a direction that she would probably pass within half a mile of the waterlogged lugger.

"Thanks be!" devoutly exclaimed Stukely, as his eyes fell upon her. "If we can but attract her attention before the boat founders, we shall escape, after all. Go on with your baling, Dick, while I wave my coat. The thing to do is to catch the eye of somebody aboard that ship and make it understood that we are in distress; then, since we can both swim, it will not greatly matter if the lugger should go down before yonder ship reaches us."

Dick obediently did as he was told, while Stukely, whipping off his coat, sprang upon the mast thwart and, with his left arm flung round the splintered stump to steady himself, proceeded to wave his coat energetically. Luckily for the pair in distress, they were to the westward of the approaching ship, with the evening sky, in which still lingered a pale primrose glow, behind them, and against this background their figures and that of the boat stood out black as silhouettes cut in ebony. It is possible that, even with this advantage, they might have escaped notice, had not Phil thought of waving his coat; but the figure of him standing there, apparently upon nothing—for it was only now and then that a small portion of the hull became visible—waving frantically something big enough to show up strongly, soon attracted attention on board the approaching ship, and Stukely had scarcely been ten minutes engaged on his waving operations when he had the gratification of seeing a flag float out over the rail and go soaring up to the main truck, while the stranger's helm was slightly shifted and she swerved perceptibly toward them.

"Glory be! they have seen us, and are bearing away for us, so it matters little now whether the lugger sinks or swims," exclaimed Stukely, as he sprang off the thwart and resumed his task of baling with renewed zest. "Nevertheless," he continued, "it will be well to keep her afloat as long as we may, since she affords a bigger mark to steer for than would the heads of us two afloat upon the darkling water."

The stranger—a tall and stately ship of some two hundred and forty tons measurement—was now close aboard of the dismasted lugger; and well was it for the occupants of the latter that such was the case; for as the ship cleverly rounded-to, with her topsails lowered, alongside and to windward of the boat, so near was the latter to foundering that the bow wave of the rescuing craft completed the disaster by surging in over the gunwale in sufficient volume to fill her; and down she went, at the precise moment when some half a dozen ropes, hurled by the sailors above, came whirling down about the shoulders of Dick and Stukely.

"Haul away!" shouted the two, with one accord, each grasping the rope's end that came first to hand as they felt the lugger sinking and themselves going down with her; and the next moment they were dragged, dripping wet, up the lee side of the ship and in over her high bulwarks.

"Better late than never; iss, fegs!" exclaimed a stout, burly man of middle height, clad in a crimson doublet of slashed silk, and trunk hose, with a crimson velvet cap, in front of which was stuck a feather of the same hue, secured by a gold brooch, set jauntily upon his head. "But by my faith, my masters, we were only just in time. Mr Bascomb, put up your helm, and hoist away your topsails again. And now, gentles both, who be ye; and how came ye to be in so awkward a scrape as that from which we have just rescued ye?"

This was evidently the captain of the ship; so Stukely, taking the lead as usual, explained in a few brief words the particulars of their mishap, thanked the unknown for his kindness in taking the trouble to pick them up, and concluded by expressing the hope that the individual to whom he was speaking would have the great goodness to stand inshore and land them on the nearest point that he could conveniently fetch.

The captain—for such he proved to be, introducing himself as John Marshall, captain of the good ship *Adventure* of Topsham, westward bound to the Indies in quest of Spanish booty—shook his head good-naturedly but firmly.

"Nay, friend, that I cannot and will not do, for here have we spent the whole of last night and to-day working down channel as far as this, and now that we have at last caught a fair slant of wind I will make the most thereof, not risking the loss of it to land any man, yea, even though he were my own brother! The utmost that I can promise is, that if we should fall in with a coaster, or other ship, bound up-channel, or should sight a fishing boat, I will delay my voyage just long enough to put ye on board, but not a minute longer. And if so be we do not encounter another craft, you will e'en both have to join us, for we have here no room for idlers. And now, hie you both away into the cabin, and take off your wet clothes; Mr Bascomb, the master, will furnish you with dry clothing from the slop chest—though

I misdoubt me," he continued, running his eye dubiously over Chichester's stalwart frame, "whether he will find any ample enough to clothe your friend withal. And when ye have changed, sup with us in the cabin, and we will talk further together."

Marshall then beckoned to Bascomb, and gave the latter instructions to open the slop chest and do his best to provide the newcomers with dry clothes; whereupon the master, in turn, beckoned to Philip and Dick to follow him below, where in due time both were provided with a change of clothing, the resources of the slop chest happily proving fully equal to the strain upon its resources imposed by Chichester's bulky proportions. The change was effected in good time to allow the two friends to join the occupants of the poop cabin at supper, where Captain Marshall made them duly acquainted with his fellow adventurers. These were five in number, consisting respectively of Mr George Lumley and Mr Thomas Winter, Marshall's lieutenants, Mr Walter Dyer and Mr Edmund Harvey, gentlemen adventurers who, with Marshall, had provided the wherewithal for the fitting out of the expedition, and Mr William Bascomb, the master aforesaid. They were all fellow Devonians, a genial and hearty company, in the best of good spirits at the prospect of stirring times before them, with the chance of returning home made men. It is true that—not to put too fine a point upon it—they were pirates, of a sort; but so were Grenvile, Drake, Hawkins, and the rest of their illustrious contemporaries; and piracy was at that time regarded as a quite honourable profession—provided that the piracies were perpetrated solely against the hated Spaniard.

It was by this time dark enough to render necessary the lighting of the great cabin lamp which swung in the skylight; and the apartment, with its long table draped with snowy napery and abundantly furnished with smoking viands flanked with great flagons of foaming ale, presented a particularly cosy and inviting appearance as Dick and Phil, having been introduced in due form to the others, took their seats; the more so, perhaps, from the fact that both of them, having been too eager for their sail to wait for a meal at the conclusion of their day's labours, had tasted neither bite nor sup since midday, and were now each in possession of a truly voracious appetite. Then, the conversation as the meal progressed—the wonderful, almost incredible, stories of past adventure related by Marshall and Bascomb, both of whom had already once visited the Indies, and the confidence with which all anticipated their return to England laden with wealth unimaginable—exercised an almost irresistible fascination over the two newcomers, one at least of whom—Philip Stukely to wit—began to feel, before the meal was over, that he cared not a jot though he should be compelled by force of circumstances to join those daredevil adventurers who

made it clearly understood that, so far as the outside world was concerned, they intended to be a law unto themselves. Marshall's and Bascomb's talk, especially, of cloudless skies of richest blue, out of which the sun darted his flaming rays by day, and in which the stars blazed like jewels at night; of tranquil seas of sapphire in which creatures of strange forms and brilliant hues disported themselves; of tropic shores, coral fringed and clothed with graceful feathery palms backed by noble forest trees of precious woods, made glorious by flowers of every conceivable hue and shape, amid which hovered birds of such gorgeous plumage that they gleamed and shone in the sun like living gems; of rich and luscious fruits to be had for the mere trouble of plucking; of fireflies spangling the velvet darkness with their fairy lamps; and of the gentle Indians who—at least when not brought under the malign influence of the cruel Spaniard—regarded white men as gods; all these appealed with singular force and fascination to Stukely, who sat listening breathlessly and with glowing eyes to everything that the two sailors said about these wonders.

For, singularly enough, although the man had never until now been out of sight of English soil, and although he had never read about them, all these things seemed strangely familiar to him. Times without number, as he had sat meditating over the fire on a winter's night, or had sprawled among the hay or upon the sandy beach on a summer evening, had visions of just such lands and just such enchanting scenes as Marshall and Bascomb described come floating to him like vague and distant but cherished memories.

He awoke, as from a delightful dream, when, the meal being finished, Marshall arose from his chair and invited his guests to accompany him out on deck. It was quite dark when they emerged from the cabin; so dark indeed that for a moment, their eyes being still dazzled by the bright light of the cabin lamp, they groped their way like blind men, and were fain to stand still, clinging to whatsoever their hands happened to find. Then, their sight coming to them again, they followed Marshall up the poop ladder, and stood, staring out upon a night of blusterous wind and faintly phosphorescent, foam-capped sea; of flying clouds amid which the stars twinkled mistily and vanished, to re-appear presently with the tall spars and swelling canvas of the ship swaying dizzily and black among them; a night full of unaccustomed sounds of creaking and groaning timbers, of the splashing and roaring of water under the ship's bows, along her bends, and about her rudder; of strange sighings and moanings aloft; and of the low murmur of men's voices as the watch clustered under the shelter of the towering forecastle, discussing, mayhap, like their superiors aft, the prospects of the voyage.

The Captain peered about him on either side of the ship, anon stooping to send his glances forward into the darkness beyond the heaving bows; then he hailed the lookouts upon the forecastle, demanding in sharp, imperative tones whether there were sail of any kind in sight. The answer was in the negative.

"Well, my masters," said he, turning to Stukely and Chichester, "you see how it is; there is nothing in sight; and every mile that we travel lessens your chance of our falling in with anything into which we can transfer you. If this good breeze holds—as I trust in God that it will—we shall be off Falmouth shortly after midnight, but much too far out to render it at all likely that we shall sight any of its fishing craft; and, once to the westward of Falmouth, your last chance of getting ashore will be gone. Now, what say ye? Will ye, without more ado, up and join us? I talked the matter over with my partners while you were changing your duds before supper, and I can find room in the ship for both of you. We have no surgeon with us, so that berth will fit you finely, Mr Stukely; while, as for you, my young son of Anak," turning to Chichester, "a lad of your thews and sinews can always earn his keep aboard ship. But I can offer ye something better than the berth of ship's boy; we have but one carpenter among us, and I will gladly take you on with the rating of carpenter's mate, if that will suit ye. Iss, fegs, that I will! Now, what say ye? Shall us call it a bargain, and have done wi' it?"

"So far as I am concerned, you certainly may—if Dick will join, too," answered Stukely. "I will not let him go ashore alone to answer for the loss of the boat; for the accident which caused the plight in which you found us was at least as much my fault as his. But I do not believe that we are going to have the chance to get ashore, therefore—what say you, Dick, shall we accept Captain Marshall's very generous offer, and so settle the matter?"

"I am not thinking of the boat—Gramfer Heard is rich enough to bear the loss of her without feeling it—but it is my uncle that I'm troubling about. I am afraid that he will be greatly distressed at my sudden and unaccountable disappearance," answered Dick.

"True," assented Stukely; "doubtless he will. But what about thy aunt, Dick? Will not she rejoice that your worthy uncle's exchequer is relieved of the cost of your maintenance? I have heard that she keeps a tight hold upon her husband's purse strings; and it has been whispered that she begrudges every tester that the good man spends upon thee. Believe me, she will soon find words to console him for thy loss."

"That is true, Phil," returned Dick, with a sigh. "She would sit and watch me eating, like any cat, so that often enough, for very shame, I rose from the table still hungry. But my uncle is not a rich man, and he has three maidens of his own to feed and clothe, so that perhaps it may be just as well that I should take advantage of this opportunity to relieve him of the cost of an extra mouth to fill, and an extra body to cover. But what of Master Summers, Phil? How will he manage without thee?"

"Master Summers must e'en get another dispenser," answered Stukely, with a shrug. "I trow there are plenty of them to be had. But I would that I had my books with me. Not having them, however, I must contrive as best I can to do without them."

"Then," cut in the Captain, somewhat impatiently, "may I understand that you are willing to join us? You will never have another such an opportunity to make your fortunes."

Phil looked enquiringly at Dick, who, after a moment's hesitation, nodded; whereupon Stukely, speaking for both, announced that they were ready to sign the agreement whenever it might be convenient for them to do so.

"No time like the present," asserted Marshall. "You may as well do it now." And, leading the way into the cabin, he produced a parchment setting forth the articles of agreement, which he read over to them. The two friends then took the pen and inscribed their names at the foot of the document, thus forging the last link in a chain which was to drag them into a series of adventures of so extraordinary a character that it is doubtful whether even Stukely, with all his inborn love of adventure, would have been willing to proceed, could he but have foreseen what awaited him in the future.

Chapter Two
How the "Adventure" fought and took the "Santa Clara" off Barbados

And now, at the very outset, almost before the ink of their signatures had fairly dried, a hitch threatened to occur over the matter of berthing the two new recruits. For, Stukely being entered as surgeon, Marshall offered him, as a matter of course, a stateroom aft, while Chichester, being shipped merely as carpenter's mate, was directed to go forward and establish himself in the house abaft the fore hatch, in which were lodged the other petty officers. Dick, to do him justice, was willing enough to accept the lodging assigned to him; but it was Stukely who objected to being separated from his friend. He insisted that Dick, being a gentleman, although merely a shipwright's apprentice, was as much entitled to a cabin aft as he was himself; and when the unreasonableness of this demand was pointed out to him he proposed that he also should be permitted to berth forward. But neither could this be managed, for there was only one spare bunk available in the petty officers' house, namely that assigned to Chichester; therefore the Captain's arrangement had perforce to stand, after all.

"Very well," said Stukely, when at last he was convinced that what he desired was impossible; "let be; you and I, Dick, can at least walk and talk together when we are off duty. And—listen, lad—in an adventure such as this is like to be, many changes are both possible and probable; my advice therefore is that you make friends with Master Bascomb and get him to instruct you in the science of navigation, so that you may be fully qualified to act as pilot, should the occasion arise. You will be no worse a pilot because you happen to be a good shipwright; and your proper place is aft among the gentles, where I hope to see thee soon."

"That's as may be," answered Dick, with a laugh. "Nevertheless thy advice is good, and I will take it."

"And I, for my part, will give friend Bascomb a hint that he is to teach thee all that thou art willing to learn," cut in Marshall. "For the doctor is right; many changes are like to occur among us before we see old England's shores again; and I shall be glad to know that I have one aboard who is

fit to take Bascomb's place, should aught untoward befall him. And now, my masters both, away to your quarters and get a good night's rest. You, doctor, will of course sleep in all night, and be on duty all day; but as for you, Chichester, I will put you in a watch to-morrow morning."

The next day saw the good ship *Adventure* clear of the Channel; for the breeze which had interfered so unceremoniously with the fortunes of Dick and his friend held all through the night and contrary to expectation increased, at the same time hauling gradually round from the north-east, to the great joy of the Captain and Bascomb, who at eight o'clock in the morning shaped a course for the Azores, where it was intended to wood and water the ship, and lay in a goodly stock of fruit and vegetables to stave off the scurvy among the crew for as long a time as might be.

The weather continued fine and the wind fair for four days, during which the ship, with squared yards, made excellent progress; then came a strong breeze from the westward which drove them nearly a hundred miles out of their course. This, in its turn, was followed by light winds and fair weather, with a sun so hot that the pitch began to melt and bubble out of the deck seams, so that the mariners, who had hitherto been going about their duty barefoot, were fain to don shoes to save their feet from being blistered. Finally, after a voyage of twenty-four days, they came to the Azores, where they remained four days, filling up their fresh water, replenishing their stock of wood, and taking in a bounteous supply of vegetables and fruit, especially "limmons"—as Marshall called them—for the prevention of scurvy.

Then, greatly refreshed by their short sojourn, and by the entire change of diet which they enjoyed during their stay, they again set sail, and, making their way to the southward and westward, at length fell in with that beneficent wind which blows permanently from the north-east, and which in after-years came to be known as the Trade Wind. With this blowing steadily behind them day after day, they squared away for the island of Barbados, where, if there happened to be no Spaniards to interfere with them, it was Marshall's intention to lay up for a while, to give his men time to recruit their health, and also to careen the ship and clear her of weed before beginning his great foray along the Spanish Main.

And in due time—on the fiftieth day from that on which Dick and Phil were rescued from the sinking boat, to be precise—with the rising of the sun a faint blue blur, wedge-shaped, with the sharp edge pointing toward the south, appeared upon the horizon, straight ahead, and the joyous shout of "Land ho!" burst from the lips of the man stationed as lookout upon the lofty forecastle. Yes; there it was; land, unmistakably, sharp and clear-cut, with a slate-blue cloud—the only cloud in the sky—hovering over it, from the breast of which vivid lightning flashed for a space, until, having emptied itself of electricity, the cloud-pall passed away, leaving the island refreshed by the shower that had accompanied the storm, gradually to change from soft blue to a vivid green as the *Adventure*, with widespread pinions, rushed toward it before the favouring breeze. And with the cry of the lookout the ship at once awoke to joyous life; the watch below, ay, and even the sick, sprang from their hammocks and rushed—or crawled, as the case might be—on deck to feast their eyes once more upon the sight of a bit of solid earth, green with verdure, and promising all manner of delights to those who had been pent up for so long between wooden bulwarks, and whose eyes had for so many weary days gazed upon naught but sea and sky. It is true that Stukely had never tired of gazing upon that same sea and sky; with the spirit of the artist that dwelt within him he had been able to see ever-changing beauty where others had beheld only monotony; but to the crew at large that wedge of land, growing in bulk and importance as the ship rushed toward it, was more beautiful than the most glorious sunset that had ever presented itself to their wondering eyes.

"What island is that?" demanded Stukely of the master, who was standing halfway up the poop ladder, gazing at the distant land under the foot of the foresail.

"It should be Barbados, unless I am a long way out of my reckoning. But there is no fear of that; besides, I know the look and shape of the place; I have been there before; and it was just so that it looked when I got my last glimpse of it. Yes, that is Barbados; and, please God, we shall all sleep ashore to-night. There is good, safe anchorage round on the other side of that low point, with a snug creek into which the ship, with but a little lightening, may be taken and careened. I pray that there may be no Spaniards there, for there is no better place on God's good earth for landing and recruiting a scurvy-ridden crew."

"Are there any Indians on the island?" asked Stukely.

"There may be; I cannot say; but I never saw any," answered Bascomb. "And if there be," he continued, "they are not likely to interfere with us. Such Indians as I have met have ever been very shy of showing themselves to the whites, and always keep out of their way, if they can. That is to say, they do so among the islands. On the Main, where they have been cruelly ill-treated and enslaved by the Spaniard, they are very different, being cruel and treacherous, and ever ready to attack the whites and destroy them with the poisoned darts which they discharge from blowpipes, and their

poisoned arrows. But, have no fear; the Indians on yonder island—if indeed there be any—will be of a very different temper, and quite gentle."

"Indeed, then, I pray that they may be," returned Stukely. "For though we have been marvellously fortunate, thus far, in the matter of sickness, there are still too many men in the sick bay for my liking; and we ought to have every one of them sound and fit for duty again before we go on with our great adventure. But, look now, what comes yonder? Surely that is a ship's canvas just beginning to show over the land there near the southern end of the island?"

Bascomb shaded his eyes with his hand and looked toward where Stukely pointed. The island was by this time about five miles distant, and the colours of the vegetation were showing up clearly in the brilliant light of the tropic day. But beyond it again, and showing over the tree-tops, there was a faint grey film that was evidently moving, sliding along, as it were, toward the low point. Even as they looked the filmy grey object suddenly became a strong white and assumed a definite form as it emerged from the shadow of a cloud, revealing itself as the upper canvas of a large ship which had either just got under way from the anchorage on the lee side of the point, or—and this seemed to be the more likely of the two—was working up to windward in the smooth water, having sighted the island on her way to the eastward.

"Iss, sure," agreed Bascomb, relapsing into the Devonshire dialect in his excitement; "that's a ship, sure enough, moreover a Spaniard at that, most likely; and, if so, we shall have a fight on our hands afore long. Do 'e see thicky ship t'other side of the island, yonder, Cap'n Marshall?" he continued, addressing himself to the Captain, who was on the poop, conversing earnestly with Messrs Dyer and Harvey, his partners in the adventure.

"Ship, sayest thou? Where then?" demanded Marshall, breaking off his conversation and running forward to the head of the poop ladder.

"Why, there a be, with the sails o' mun just showing over the low point," answered the master. "She'll be clear of the land in another minute or two; and then they'll see us as clearly as we see them. She's a Spaniard, to my thinking, Cap'n; and there may be fine pickings aboard of her—if her don't turn and run so soon's she sees us."

"She'll not do that, Master Bascomb; she be a bigger ship nor we. Besides, how's she to know we baint a Spaniard like herself, if we don't tell her. We'll clear the decks and make all ready before we show our flag, gentles; and see what comes of it. Let the mariners get to work at once, Mr Bascomb."

The excitement aroused by the appearance of land on the horizon, after so many weary weeks of gazing upon sea and sky only, was intensified tenfold when the strange sail—the first they had seen since leaving the Azores—was discovered; and when it was further understood that the chances were in favour of her proving to be a Spaniard, the preparations for a possible fight were entered upon with the utmost eagerness and alacrity. Fortunately, there was not very much that needed to be done; for Marshall, rendered wise by past experience, had consistently made a point of always having the decks kept clear of unnecessary lumber of every kind; but the bulwarks were strengthened and raised, for the purpose of affording the crew as much protection as possible from the enemy's musketry fire; the lower yards were fitted with chain slings, so that the risk of their being shot away, and the ship thus disabled at a critical moment, might be minimised as much as possible; parties of musketrymen were sent aloft into the round tops, with instructions to hamper the enemy as much as possible by their fire, especially by picking off the helmsman and the officers; the powder room was opened, and ammunition sent on deck for the culverins, sakers, and swivels, all of which were loaded; and the men, having armed themselves with cutlass, pistol, bow, and pike, stripped to their waists, bound handkerchiefs round their heads, and took up their several stations by the guns, or at the halliards and sheets. Marshall took command of the ship as a whole; while Lumley and Winter, his lieutenants, assumed charge of the poop and forecastle respectively, Bascomb, the master, taking charge of the main deck. Stukely, with his knives, saws, and bandages, established himself in the cockpit; and Dick Chichester, who had contrived to gain the reputation of being the best helmsman in the ship, was ordered to the tiller.

Meanwhile, the strange ship, having cleared the land, revealed herself as a craft of probably quite a hundred tons bigger than the *Adventure*, and carrying four more pieces of great ordnance than the latter. But this fact by no means dismayed the English; for the stranger was what was called a race ship, and was nearly twice as long as the *Adventure*; Marshall therefore confidently reckoned that, should the two vessels come to blows, the superior nimbleness of his own ship would more than counterbalance the advantage conferred upon the other by her greater weight of metal. The stranger, when she cleared the land, was close-hauled on the larboard tack, heading about south-south-east, and it was judged, from her position relative to the land, that she had not actually touched at the island, but had simply availed herself of its presence to gain a few miles by turning to windward in the smooth water under its lee. The discovery of the presence of the English ship did not appear to have caused any uneasiness to her commander, for he did not deviate a hairbreadth from his course, but stood on, maintaining his luff, the only indication that he had observed the *Adventure* at all being the display of the yellow flag of Spain, which he had hoisted to the head of his ensign staff within five minutes of the time when he cleared the island. Probably he imagined that the *Adventure* was also Spanish.

The English, on their part, took no notice of the stranger, except by gradually edging down toward her, until their preparations for battle were complete; then indeed they hoisted the white flag bearing the crimson cross of Saint George, and hauled their wind sufficiently to enable them to intercept the Spaniard. At this invitation to battle symptoms of alarm and indecision began to manifest themselves on board the latter, for she first put up her helm and kept away, as though about to turn tail and run, but presently came to the wind again and tacked, heading now to the northward.

"Over with the helm, and steer for the northern end of the island," cried Marshall to Dick; "that ought to enable us to intercept him. Thank God, he means to fight instead of running, and the matter will the sooner be settled. Look to that, now; he is stripping for battle, for in comes all his light canvas, and up goes his mainsail. The man who commands that ship is a right valiant cavalier, and will put up a good fight; therefore, let no man put match to culverin or finger to trigger until I give the word. Now, let the waits play up 'The brave men of Devon!'"

Therewith the waits, five in number, stationed on the main deck, between the poop and the mainmast, struck up that favourite and inspiring air with such good effect that before two minutes had passed every man and boy in the ship was singing the song at the top of his voice, and feeling quite ready to fight all the Spaniards who might care to come against them.

A quarter of an hour later the two ships had closed to within musket shot of each other, the *Adventure* having the weather gage, when crash came the whole of the Spaniard's broadside, great guns and small; but so bad was the aim that every shot flew high overhead, and not so much as a rope was touched.

"Good!" ejaculated Marshall. "Now, steersman, up with your helm, and shave past as close under his stern as you can without touching. Starboard gunners, be ready to pour your shot into his stern as we pass! Musketrymen and archers, pick off as many men as you can see, and especially the helmsman! Sail trimmers, to your stations, and be ready to go about!"

Two minutes later the *Adventure* slid square athwart the towering, gilt-bedizened stern of the Spaniard, and one after another, as they were brought to bear, her ordnance belched forth their charges of round and canister, smashing the Spanish gingerbread work to splinters, shivering every pane of glass in the stern windows, and sweeping the decks of the stranger from end to end, the deadly nature of the discharge being evidenced by the outburst of shrieks which instantly followed aboard the stranger.

"Well done, gallants!" cried Marshall, waving his sword. "Now, ready about, and larboard gunners stand by to repeat the dose. Down helm, steersman, and let her come round! Raise fore tack and sheet! Ha! she is falling off, and means to give us her larboard broadside while we are in stays—if she can. Topmen, do your best, now, and pick me off her helmsman before it is too late. Well done!"—as the Spaniard began to come ponderously to the wind again, showing that her helmsman was down—"Let the man who did that come to me by and by, and he shall have a noble for that good shot. Swing the mainyard! Musketrymen, clear the enemy's tops of archers, and shoot down any that may attempt to take their places! Trim aft the head sheets! Swing the foreyard! Starboard gunners, reload your ordnance! We will try that trick again if they will but give us the chance. Now, larboard gunners, be ready, and let her have it as we pass!"

A minute later, and the *Adventure's* broadside again crashed into the Spaniard's stern; and again uprose the hideous answering outburst of shrieks and yells on board the latter as the English ship, with her sails clean full, slid square across her antagonist's stern, the only reply to her broadside being four shot discharged from the enemy's stern ports, not one of which did a groat's worth of damage.

A tall figure completely encased in armour sprang up on the Spanish ship's poop rail and, shaking his naked sword at Marshall, shouted in Spanish:

"You are a coward, señor Englishman! Why do you not fight fair, broadside to broadside, instead of sheltering yourself under my stern, where my shot cannot reach you?"

"Because, señor, I do not happen to be a fool," retorted Marshall in the same language. "But neither am I a coward," he continued, "as I will prove to you within the next five minutes, if you will do me the honour to meet me on your own deck, whither I intend to come without further ado."

"I shall be most happy, señor," was the reply; and down jumped the Spaniard in a hurry, to issue certain orders apparently, for his voice, hollow in his helmet, was heard pealing out in a tone of command as the two ships drew apart.

"Larboard gunners, load your pieces again," commanded Marshall, "and level them so as to take her on the main deck while we are in stays. Luff, helmsman, all you can; I want to get far enough to windward to be able to run down and lay her aboard on the next tack. Boarders, see to the priming of your pistols, and be ready to follow me presently. Now, ready about again, men! Down helm!"

As the *Adventure* hove in stays both ships fired their broadsides simultaneously, one of the English shot entering a port and dismounting a gun, while the rest struck fair in the wake of the deck and went clean through the Spaniard's side, as could clearly be seen; while the Spaniard's shot, as usual, flew overhead, again by great good luck missing everything.

"Now, up helm, steersman, and lay us aboard!" commanded Marshall. "Be ready, men, to throw your grapnels the moment that we touch; and boarders, stand by to follow me into the enemy's main chains!"

As the two ships closed in toward each other for the final grip which was to decide the matter, the Spaniard holding her luff while the English ship bore up and ran down with the wind free, the archers and musketeers on both sides became busy, the Spaniards having a slight advantage because of the superior height of their ship, although this was more than counterbalanced by the greater quickness and accuracy of aim on the part of the English, who shot as coolly as though they had been practising at the butts, and seldom failed to hit their mark. Nevertheless, several Englishmen went down during the ensuing five minutes, and were carried below to Stukely, who now began to find himself surrounded by quite as many patients as he could conveniently attend to. Then the two ships crashed together, the grapnels were thrown, and Marshall, followed by every man whose legs could carry him and whose hands could wield a weapon, sprang into the Spaniard's main rigging, leaving the *Adventure* to take care of herself.

It was a rash thing to do, perhaps; but it succeeded; for the Spaniards were too busily engaged in endeavouring to keep the enemy out of their own ship to think of boarding the other. And most desperate was the fight that ensued, the English being fully determined to force their way aboard the Spaniard, while the Spanish were as fully determined that they should not. The air became thick with flying arrows, and with the smoke of grenades and stinkpots flung down upon the boarders out of the enemy's tops; while swords and pikes flashed in the sun, pistols popped, and men shouted and execrated as they cut and slashed at each other; and the glorious tropic morning was filled with the sounds of deadly strife. Dick Chichester—to let the reader into a secret—had, upon the first appearance of the Spanish ship, been greatly exercised in his mind lest he should fail in courage when the two ships came to blows; but with the discharge of the first shot the queer agitated feeling which he had mistaken for fear completely passed away, and was instantly forgotten; and now, his services being no longer required at the helm, he armed himself with a handspike snatched from the deck, and, watching his opportunity, flung himself from the *Adventure's* poop into the enemy's mizzen chains, climbing thence to the Spaniard's poop, where was no one to oppose him. From thence he made his way down to the main deck, where were gathered all the crew in one spot, crowding together to resist the attack of the English; and upon the rear of these he flung himself with indescribable fury, whirling the terrible handspike with such destructive effect that the astounded Spaniards, thus taken unexpectedly in the rear, went down like ninepins, while their yells of anguish and dismay quickly threw the entire crew into complete disorder. So violent, indeed, was the commotion that the attention of the Spaniards was momentarily distracted from what may be termed the frontal attack, and of this distraction Marshall instantly availed himself to dash in on deck, where, with a few sweeps of his sword, he soon cleared standing room, not only for himself but also for half a dozen of his immediate followers. These in turn cleared the way for others, and thus in the course of a couple of breathless minutes every man of the *Adventure's* crew had gained the deck of the Spaniard, after which the capture of the ship was a foregone conclusion. The rush of Marshall and his party on the one hand, and the onslaught of Dick Chichester with his whirling handspike on the other so utterly distracted and demoralised the Spaniards that they presently broke and fled, flinging away their weapons, and crying out that their foes were a crew of demons who had assumed for the nonce the outward semblance of Englishmen! The hatches were promptly clapped on over the fugitive Spaniards, then Marshall and his followers paused to recover their breath and look about them.

The first thing to claim their attention was the ships themselves. These, being lashed together by means of the grapnels, were grinding and rasping each other's sides so alarmingly, as they rolled and plunged in the sea that was running, that they had already inflicted upon each other an appreciable amount of damage, and threatened to do a great deal more if prompt preventive measures were not taken. Marshall therefore called upon Winter, one of his lieutenants, to take a party of twenty men, and with them return to the *Adventure*, cast her adrift from the prize, and lie off within easy hailing-distance of the latter. This was done at once, Dick Chichester being one of those called upon by Winter to follow him aboard the *Adventure*, and as soon as the two ships were parted an investigation was made into the extent of the damage incurred by each ship. The result of this investigation was the discovery that the *Adventure* was much the greater sufferer of the two, her larboard main channel piece having been wrenched off, and the seams in the immediate neighbourhood opened, while three of the channel plates were broken, thus leaving the mainmast almost entirely unsupported on the larboard side. Water was entering the ship in quite appreciable quantities through the opened seams, and the men were therefore at once sent to the pumps to keep the leak from gaining, while the carpenter and Dick went below to see what could be done toward stopping it.

Meanwhile Marshall, assisted by his co-adventurers Dyer and Harvey, proceeded to overhaul the prize systematically, with the view of determining her value. The first fact ascertained was that the ship was named the *Santa Clara*; the second, that she hailed from Cadiz, in Old Spain; and the third, that she was homeward-bound from Cartagena, from which port she was twenty-two days out. Her cargo, although valuable enough in its way, was not of such a character as to tempt the English to go to the labour of transferring any portion of it to their own vessel. But, apart from the cargo proper, she was taking home ten chests of silver ingots, two chests of bar gold, and a casket of pearls, all of which were quickly transhipped to the *Adventure*, the crew of which thus found themselves the possessors of a fairly rich booty, while still upon the very threshold, as it were, of those seas wherein they hoped to make their fortune. But this was not all; for, in the process of rummaging the captain's cabin, Marshall found certain letters which he unhesitatingly opened and read, and among these was a communication from the governor of Cartagena advising the home authorities of the impending dispatch of a rich plate ship for Cadiz. The probable date of dispatch was given as three months after the departure of the *Santa Clara*, or about ten weeks from the date of that vessel's capture by the English. That letter Marshall thrust into his pocket, together with certain other documents which he thought might possibly prove of value; then, summoning the unhappy Spanish captain to his presence, he informed him that the English having now helped themselves to all that they required, he was at liberty to proceed upon his voyage; and this Marshall recommended him to do with all diligence and alacrity, lest peradventure he should fall into the hands of certain other British buccaneers, at the existence of whom the Englishman darkly hinted, hoping thus to nip in the bud any plan which the Spaniard might have formed for a return to Cartagena with a report of the presence of English corsairs in the Caribbean Sea. The two ships then parted company, the *Santa Clara* steering northward close-hauled against the trade wind, while the *Adventure* bore up for Barbados, shaping a course to pass round its southern extremity. Two hours later the English ship was riding snugly at anchor in what is now known as Carlisle Bay, in five fathoms of water, within four hundred feet of the beach, and the same distance from the mouth of a small river, within which, as Bascomb explained, lay the creek which he had fixed upon in his mind as a suitable spot wherein to careen the ship.

Chapter Three
How they came to Barbados;
and what they did there

The rumbling of the great hempen cable out through the hawse-pipe served as a signal to some dozen or more of poor scurvy-stricken wretches who lay gasping in their hammocks in the stifling forecastle. They had heard the cry of "Land ho!" some hours before, and had groaned with bitter impatience when the subsequent sounds from the deck had made it clear to them that a battle must be fought before they could feast their eyes upon the sight of solid earth and green trees once more, and satisfy their terrible craving for the luscious fruits which they had been given to understand were to be obtained on the delectable island in sight for the mere trouble of plucking. But now at last the time of waiting was over; the sounds and shouts incidental to the taking in of sail, and, still more, the splash of the anchor and the roar of the cable as it rushed through the hawse-pipe told them that the ship had arrived, and with one accord they rolled out of their hammocks—the less heavily stricken helping their weaker fellow sufferers—and made their way on deck, where the business of stowing the ship's canvas was still in full progress. The poor wretches were constantly getting in the way of those who were well and busy, but the latter were themselves just then much too happy to grumble or find fault, so the invalids were good-humouredly assisted up the ladder to the top of the forecastle, where they could enjoy an uninterrupted view of the island, and left there to feast their eyes upon its beauties in peace, until the time should arrive when their shipmates would be ready to man the boats and take them ashore.

And what a glorious sight it was that met their gaze. First of all there was the green and placid water, alive with fish, rippling gently to a narrow beach of golden sand, and beyond that sand nothing but vegetation, rich, green, and luxuriant. Green! yes, but of a hundred different tints, from the tender hue of the young shoots that was almost yellow, to a deep olive that turned to black in the shadows. If the tints of the vegetation were admirable, no less so were its forms; for there were palms of many different kinds, including the coconut palm in thousands, close down to the water's edge. The traveller tree, shaped like a fan made of organ pipes; the banana and plantain, loaded with great bunches of fruit, each bunch a fair load for a man; there were great clumps of feathery bamboo; there were big trees covered with scarlet flowers instead of leaves; there was the flaming bougainvillea in profusion; and, in addition, there were great trailing cables of orchids, of weird shapes and vivid colouring reaching from bough to bough. Yes, there was plenty to see and marvel at, and there would be more when those few yards of rippling water had been spanned and their feet pressed the lush grass of yonder flowery mead close by the river's margin; humming birds, the plumage of which shone in the sun like burnished gold and glowing gems, butterflies as big as sparrows, with wings painted in hues so gorgeous that the painter who should attempt to reproduce them would be driven to despair, enormous dragon-flies flitting hither and thither over the still surface of the river, kingfishers as big as parrots, monkeys in hundreds, agoutis, and, alas!—to strengthen its resemblance to that other Eden— serpents as well, contact with which meant death.

At last! at last! the sails were furled, the ropes coiled neatly down, the decks restored to order, and the word was given to lower the boats. Never, probably, was an order more joyously obeyed. The men rushed to the tackles with shouts and laughter, like schoolboys who have unexpectedly been given a holiday, and in an incredibly short time the boats were all afloat and were being brought one by one to the gangway. Then, under the joint supervision of the Captain and Stukely, the sick were led or carried along the deck and handed gently down over the side, the whole of them being sent ashore in the first boat that left the ship, with Bascomb, the master, in charge, his duty being to see that no unwholesome fruit or poisonous berries were eaten unwittingly. Next, the sick having been temporarily disposed of, there followed the strong and able-bodied, who took ashore with them spars, tackles, and spare sails, with which to rig up temporary tents; and soon the greensward was dotted with busy men, who, in the intervals of their labour, drank coconuts or eagerly devoured bananas, prickly pears, guavas, soursops, grapes, mangoes, and the various other fruits with which the island abounded. By and by, when a certain large tent had been erected beneath the shade of a giant ceiba tree, a boat put off from the shore to the ship, and presently returned bearing nine wounded men—the result of their fight that morning—under the especial care of Philip Stukely. These men, lying in their hammocks as they had been taken out of the ship, were then carried up to the completed tent, when their hammocks were re-slung to stout poles firmly driven into the ground, and where Stukely once more, and at greater leisure, attended to their hurts. But there was one form, lying stark in a laced-up hammock deeply stained with blood, which was not brought up to the tent. It was all that remained of George Lumley, Captain

Marshall's chief lieutenant, who had been shot to death in the very act of boarding the Spaniard, a few hours before; and a grave having been prepared in a small open space on the opposite side of the river, under the shadow of a splendid *bois immortelle* which strewed the ground with its glowing scarlet flowers, a trumpet was blown, calling the crew together. Then, when they were all assembled, they entered the boats, at a sign from Marshall, took in tow the boat containing the body of the officer, with Saint George's Cross at half-mast trailing in the water astern of her, and, having reached the other side, reverently bore the shrouded corpse to its last resting-place, lowered it into the grave, Marshall, meanwhile, reading the burial service, and covered it up with the rich brown earth. This service rendered they returned to the site of the camp, and rapidly proceeded to put up the other tents needed to enable all hands to sleep ashore that night.

The sun was within an hour of setting when at length everything was completed to Marshall's satisfaction, and the men were told that they might cease work and amuse themselves as they pleased, the permission being accompanied by a caution that they were not to wander more than a quarter of a mile from the camp, not to go even as far as that, singly, and not to go unarmed; for although it was assumed that the island was uninhabited, save by themselves, it was recognised as quite possible that a band of Spaniards might be somewhere upon it; and, if so, they would probably have witnessed the arrival of the ship, and might, if strong enough, attempt to surprise and capture both camp and ship. The men therefore made up little parties, and for the most part went off into the woods, either to gather more fruit or to look for gold, some of them seeming to be possessed of a firm conviction that, being now in "the Indies", they must inevitably find the precious metal if they only searched for it with sufficient diligence. As for Dick and Stukely, the latter having by this time done all that he could for his patients, they went off for a stroll together along the beach, in the direction of the southern end of the bay.

"Well, Dick, what think ye of fighting, now that you have had a taste of it?" demanded Stukely, slipping his hand under Chichester's arm as they turned their backs upon the camp. "And, by the way," he continued, without waiting for a reply to his question, "you must permit me to offer the tribute of my most respectful admiration; for I am told that you carried yourself like a right valiant and redoubtable cavalier; indeed the Captain has not hesitated to say that, but for your most furious onslaught upon the Spaniards' rear this morning, while he was leading the attack by way of the main rigging, matters were like enough to have gone very differently with us."

"Oh, that is all nonsense," laughed Dick. "I saw that Marshall wished to reach the deck of the Spaniard; I noticed that the Spanish crew had all congregated together in one place to stop him; and it struck me that I could best help by falling upon them in the rear, which I saw might be done right easily, there being no man to stop me—so—I did it."

"Precisely; with the result that the Spaniards, finding themselves thus suddenly and furiously assailed by one who bore himself like a very Orson, and feeling no desire to have their brains beaten out with so heathenish a weapon as a handspike, incontinently gave way before you and scattered, affording Marshall an opportunity to climb in over the bulwarks. But were ye not afraid, lad, that some proud Spaniard, resenting your interference, might slit your weasand with his long sword?"

"Afraid?" returned Dick. "Not a whit. 'Tis true that when we first sighted the enemy coming out from behind this same island, and I learned that our Captain meant to attack him, I turned suddenly cold, hot as was the morning, and was seized with a plaguy doubt as to whether I should be able to carry myself as an Englishman and a Devon man should in the coming fight; but when the battle began I forgot all about my doubts, and thought no more of them until the fight was over and done with. Indeed, to be quite frank with ye, Phil, I was never happier, nor enjoyed myself more, than during the few minutes that the fight lasted. You know not what it feels like, for you were down in the cockpit, which was your proper place; but you may take my word for it that there is nothing in this world half so exhilarating as a good brisk fight."

Stukely laughed. "True, lad," he said; "I do not know from actual experience what it feels like to be engaged in a life-and-death struggle; for I have never yet taken part in such. Yet I can well believe that it is as you say; for even down in the cockpit I felt the thrill and tingle of it all as I listened to the booming of the ordnance and heard the shouts of the men and the commands of the Captain; nay, I will go even farther than that, and confess that I had much ado to restrain myself from deserting my post and rushing up on deck to take my part in it all. And, a word in your ear, Dick—I believe I should make a far better leader than I am ever like to be a surgeon; for as I stood there, listening to the sounds of the conflict, the strangest feeling of familiarity with it all came to me. I suddenly felt that I had fought many's the time before; fleeting, indistinct visions of contending hosts, strangely armed and arrayed, floated before me; cries in a strange language, which still I seemed to understand, rang in my ears; and for a moment I completely lost sight of my surroundings, being transported to a land of cloudless skies, even as this, clothed with vegetation very similar to what we now behold around us, although the land of my vision was mountainous, with lakes that shone like mirrors embosomed among the mountains and were dotted with islands, some of them palm-crowned, while others bore stately temples of strange but beautiful architecture. And the strangest part of it all was that, while it lasted, it was like a vivid memory of some scene that my eyes had rested upon often enough to grow familiar with, ay, as familiar as I am with the streets of Devonport and Plymouth!"

"Ay; you were ever a fanciful fellow and a dreamer, Phil," replied Dick, who was one of the most matter-of-fact individuals who ever breathed. "I mind me how, many a time, when we have been sailing together outside Plymouth Sound, where a clear view could be had of the setting sun, you used to trace cloudy continents with bays, inlets, harbours, and outlying islands in the western sky; yes, and even ships sailing among them, and cities rearing themselves among the golden edges of the clouds."

"Well, and was that so very wonderful?" retorted Stukely. "Look at yonder sky, for instance. Can you not imagine that great purple mass of cloud to be a vast island set in the midst of the sea represented by the blue-green expanse of sky beyond it? And can you not see how the shape of the cloud lends itself to the fancy of jutting capes and forelands, of gulfs and sounds and estuaries? And look at those small, outlying clouds nearest us; are not they the very image and similitude of islets lying off the coast of the main island? And, as to cities, what can be a more perfect picture of a golden city built along the shore of a landlocked bay than that golden fringe of cloud yonder? And behold the mountains and valleys—ay, and there is a lake opening up now in the very centre of the island. Oh, Dick, my son, if you have not imagination enough to translate these pictures of the evening sky into glimpses of fairy land, and to derive pleasure therefrom, I pity you from my very soul."

"Nay, then, no need to waste your pity on me, Sir Dreamer, for I need it not," retorted Dick. "Doubtless you take joy of your fancies; but realities are good enough for me, at least such realities as these. Look at that bird hovering over yonder flower, for instance; smaller, much smaller, than a wren is he, yet how perfectly shaped and how gloriously plumaged. Look to the colour of him, as rich a purple as that of your sunset cloud, with crest and throat like gold painted green. And then, the long curved beak of him, see how daintily he dips it into the cup of the flower and sips the honey therefrom. And his wings, why they are whirring so quickly that you cannot see but can only hear them! Can any of your fancies touch a thing like that for beauty?"

"That is as may be, Dick," answered Stukely. "The bird is beautiful, undoubtedly, and no less beautiful is the flower from which he sips the honey that constitutes his food; indeed all things are lovely, had we but eyes to perceive their loveliness. But come, the sun has set, and darkness will be upon us in another five minutes; it is time for us to be getting back to the camp."

Despite the croaking of the frogs, the snore of the tree toads, the incessant buzz and chirr of insects, and the multitudinous nocturnal sounds incidental to life upon a tropical island overgrown with vegetation, ay, and despite the mosquitoes, too, all hands slept soundly that night, and awoke next morning refreshed and invigorated, the sick especially exhibiting unmistakable symptoms of improvement already, due doubtless to the large quantities of fruit which they had consumed on the preceding day. The wounded, too, were doing exceedingly well, the coolness of the large tent in which they had passed the night, as compared with the suffocating atmosphere of their confined quarters aboard ship, being all in their favour, to say nothing of the assiduous care which Phil bestowed upon them.

The first thing in order was for all hands who were able to go down to the beach and indulge in a good long swim, shouting at the top of their lungs, and splashing incessantly, in accordance with Marshall's orders, in order to scare away any sharks that might chance to be prowling in the neighbourhood. Then, a spring of clear fresh water having been discovered within about three-quarters of a mile of the camp, one watch was sent off to the ship to bring ashore all the soiled clothing, while the other watch mounted guard over the camp; after which all hands went to breakfast; and then, working watch and watch about, there ensued a general washing of soiled clothes at the spring, and a subsequent drying of them on the grass in the rays of the sun. This done, a gang was sent on board the ship to start the remaining stock of water and pump it out; after which the ship was lightened by the removal of her stores, ammunition, and ordnance, until her draught was reduced to nine feet, when her anchor was hove up and she was towed into the river, where she was moored, bow and stern, immediately abreast of the camp. The completion of this job finished the day's work, at the end of which Marshall, having mustered all hands, proclaimed that in consequence of the lamented death of their gallant shipmate and officer, Mr Lumley, he had decided to promote Mr Winter to the position thus rendered vacant; and further that, as a second lieutenant was still required, he had determined, after the most careful consideration, to promote Mr Richard Chichester to that position, in recognition of the extraordinary valour which he had displayed on the previous day by boarding the Spanish ship and attacking her crew, single-handed, in the rear, thereby distracting the attention of the enemy and contributing in no small measure to their subsequent speedy defeat. This decision on the part of the Captain, strange to say, met with universal and unqualified approval; for Dick's unassuming demeanour and geniality of manner had long since made him popular and a general favourite, while his superior intelligence, his almost instinctive grasp of everything pertaining to a ship and her management, and his dauntless courage, marked him out as in every respect most suitable for the position which he had been chosen to fill.

The next two days were spent in clearing everything movable out of the ship, in preparation for heaving her down; after which she was careened until her keel was out of water, when the grass, weed, and barnacles which had grown upon her bottom during the voyage were effectually removed, her seams were carefully examined, and re-caulked where required, and then her bottom was re-painted. This work was pushed forward with the utmost expedition, lest an enemy should heave in sight and touch at the island while the ship was hove down—for a ship is absolutely helpless and at the mercy of an enemy while careened—and when this part of the work was satisfactorily completed, all necessary repairs made, and the hull re-caulked and re-painted right up to the rail, the masts, spars, rigging, and sails were subjected to a strict overhaul and renovation. This work was done in very leisurely fashion; for Marshall had by this time quite made up his mind to lie in wait for the plate ship which, as he had learned through documents found on board the *Santa Clara*, was loading at Cartagena for Cadiz, and he speedily arrived at the conclusion that a considerable amount of the waiting might as well be done at Barbados as elsewhere. For the climate of the island was healthy, the sick were making excellent progress on the road toward recovery, and it was essential to the success of his enterprise that every man of his crew should be in perfect health; moreover, apart from the crew of the *Santa Clara*—which ship, he had every reason to believe, was daily forcing her way farther toward the heart of the North Atlantic—not a soul knew, or even suspected, the presence of the *Adventure* in those seas; consequently he resolved to remain where he was until the last possible moment. Such work, therefore, as needed to be done was done with the utmost deliberation and nicety; and when at length all was finished there still remained time to spare, which the men were permitted to employ pretty much as they liked, it having by this time been ascertained conclusively that, apart from themselves, the island was absolutely without inhabitants.

At length, however, the time arrived when it became necessary to put to sea again; and on a certain brilliant morning the camp was struck, all their goods and chattels were taken back to the ship; and, with every man once more in the enjoyment of perfect health, with every water cask full to the bung-hole of sweet, crystal-clear water, and with an ample supply of fruit and vegetables on board, the *Adventure* weighed anchor and stood away to tward under easy sail, passing between the islands of Saint Vincent and Becquia with the first of the dawn on the following morning.

Marshall had estimated that the passage from Barbados to Cartagena would occupy eight days; but to provide against unforeseen delays he allowed twelve days for its accomplishment, with the result that, no unforeseen delays having arisen, the *Adventure* arrived off Cartagena just four days before the date upon which, according to the information obtained from the *Santa Clara*, the plate ship was to sail. It was just about midnight when, according to Bascomb's reckoning, the ship reached the latitude of Cartagena, when she was hove-to. But as Marshall had observed the precaution of maintaining a good offing during the entire passage, merely hauling in to the southward sufficiently to sight Point Gallinas in passing, and thus verify his position, it was not surprising that when the daylight came no land was in sight, even from the masthead. This was perfectly satisfactory and as it should be; nevertheless it was important that explicit information should now be at once obtained concerning the plate ship, the progress which she was making toward the completion of her loading, and especially whether she would be ready to sail on the date originally named. Marshall therefore summoned a council of war consisting of, in addition to himself, Bascomb, the master, Winter and Dick Chichester, the lieutenants, and Messrs Dyer and Harvey, the two gentlemen adventurers. The meeting was held in the main cabin; a chart of the coast was produced; and after a considerable amount of discussion it was finally determined to provision, water, and equip the longboat, remain hove-to where they were until nightfall, and then, filling on the ship, work her in toward the land until she was as close inshore as it would be prudent to take her, when the longboat was to be hoisted out and dispatched with a crew of four men, under the command of Marshall himself—who was the only man aboard who could speak Spanish reasonably well. Then, while the *Adventure*, under Bascomb's command, bore up again and regained an offing of some thirty miles due west of Cartagena, the longboat was to proceed inshore, enter the bight between the island of Baru and the mainland, and there remain in concealment while Marshall should attempt to make his way into Cartagena harbour, and, if necessary, even penetrate into the town itself, in an endeavour to secure precise information relative to the movements of the plate ship. It was further arranged that the *Adventure* should remain in the offing during the whole of the succeeding day, working in toward the land again after nightfall, and hoisting two lanterns, one over the other, at her ensign staff as a guide for the longboat—should the latter by that time have accomplished her mission. A bright lookout was to be maintained for the longboat, which was to signal her approach by displaying a single lantern;

but should she be unable for any reason to rejoin the ship on the night agreed upon, the same tactics were to be pursued night after night for six nights; when, if she did not then return, it was to be assumed that she and her crew had fallen into the hands of the Spaniards, and Bascomb was to act as might be determined upon after consultation with the rest of the officers.

This arrangement, then, was adhered to; the *Adventure* remained hove-to in the offing during the whole of that day, filling away and beginning to work in toward the land about half an hour before sunset. Captain Marshall then picked his longboat's crew—which consisted of Dick Chichester, George Burton, Robert Hogan, and Edward Fenner—and directed them to make all necessary preparations for accompanying him; after which they were to turn in and take their rest until they should be summoned on deck.

It was just half-past two o'clock in the morning when Dick, having been aroused from a sound sleep by the cabin boy, presented himself, fully dressed, in the main cabin, where he found Captain Marshall already seated at the table, partaking of an early breakfast, in which, by a wave of the hand, he invited Chichester to join, which the latter promptly did, falling to with a good appetite. A quarter of an hour later, having finished their meal, the pair passed out on deck, where they found the longboat, with six beakers of fresh water in her to serve as ballast, with her locker full of provisions, with her rudder shipped, and oars, masts, and sails lying upon her thwarts already slung and ready for hoisting out.

It was a fine night, the sky clear, excepting for a few small drifting clouds, between which the stars shone brilliantly, the water smooth, the wind a moderate offshore breeze, and the land clearly in view some eight miles to windward; it was in fact a perfectly ideal night for such an expedition as was in contemplation. The task of preparing the longboat had been entrusted to Mr Winter, who now reported her as ready; nevertheless Captain Marshall, like a prudent mariner, subjected her to a very close and careful scrutiny before giving the word to hoist her out. Everything, however, was found to be quite as it should be, therefore, the crew's weapons having also been subjected to a rigid inspection, the order was given to heave the ship to and hoist out the boat. Every preparation having been previously made, this business was soon accomplished; and on the stroke of three, by the ship's clock, the longboat shoved off and, stepping her masts, made sail for the land, being sped on her way by a hearty cheer from all hands aboard the *Adventure*, who had mustered to assist in and witness her departure. Then, the moment that the boat was clear, the ship's helm was put up and she was headed out to sea again under a press of canvas, with the object of running out of sight of the land before the arrival of daylight.

As for the longboat, she was brought close to the wind, on the larboard tack, with Dick at the helm and Marshall sitting beside him, while the three mariners, perceiving that their services were not likely to be required further for some time, stretched themselves out in the bottom of the boat and were soon fast asleep.

For the first hour of their progress the land to windward merely presented the appearance of a black blur, indistinctly seen under the star-spangled indigo of the night sky; but by the end of that time something in the nature of outline began to reveal itself, while, half an hour later, a long tongue of land became distinctly visible broad on their weather bow, with two or three much smaller detached blotches rising out of the sea ahead. Standing up in the stern-sheets, Marshall scrutinised these appearances with the greatest care for several minutes; then, with a sigh of contentment, he sat down again.

"It is all right, Dick," he said; "we have made a most excellent landfall. That long stretch of land yonder is Baru Island, and the small detached blots of blackness are the detached islets at its southernmost extremity which we saw marked on the chart. We must pass to leeward of them, lad, giving them a berth of at least a mile, because, if our chart is correct, there is a reef between us and them which we must avoid. If we can only get up abreast of those islets before the daylight comes I shall be satisfied, because we shall then be hidden from the sight of any fishing canoes which may happen to be outside Cartagena harbour; and, once inside Baru, I think we need not have the slightest fear of discovery. Moreover, I have an idea that we can make our way into the harbour from the back of Baru, without being obliged to go outside again, which will be a great advantage."

"Have you formed any plan of action to be followed after we arrive at the back of the island?" demanded Dick.

"Well, no; I can't say that I have," answered Marshall. "My experience is that, in the case of expeditions of this kind, it is of little use to scheme very far ahead. I have found that the best plan is to trust to luck, and be guided entirely by circumstances. My object, of course, is to penetrate to the town of Cartagena itself, and there pick up all the news that I can get hold of relative to the movements of the plate ship, seeing her, if possible, and so acquainting myself with her build, rig, and general appearance, so that if by any chance she should sail in company with other ships I may know for certain which is the craft that we must single out for attack. It may be possible for us to go up the harbour in the longboat, although I do not regard such a thing as very likely; there would be too much risk in it, I think, to justify such an attempt, at least until all other schemes have failed; and we are not out now in quest of adventure, or to incur unnecessary risks, but to obtain information; the adventure may come later on."

"It is more than likely that it will," returned Dick, dryly; "for I cannot for the life of me see how we are to enter the town without exposing ourselves to very grave risk of discovery."

"Oh, it may be done," asserted Marshall, with far more confidence than Dick thought was justified by the occasion. "Cartagena has a population of several thousands, you know; and I do not suppose it is at all likely that everybody will know everybody else, even by sight; it will be very difficult for anybody to point to anybody else and say, with assured certainty, that he is a stranger who has no right to be there. But, of course, we shall not all enter the town; at least I do not at present contemplate anything so foolhardy. I shall attempt to get into the town alone, leaving the longboat snugly concealed but within easy reach, in case of the necessity for a rapid retreat arising; and you must keep your eyes open to guard against detection, and at the same time maintain a bright lookout for me, and be ready to come to my help, should I be hard pressed. Ah! there is the reef that I spoke of a little while ago; see there, broad off the weather bow; you can see the surf breaking upon it—and there is a small island right ahead of us. Keep her away, lad; up helm and let her go off a point. So! steady as you go; that ought to carry us clear of everything. And, thank God, there is the dawn coming; we shall just get nicely in before it grows light enough for anybody to see us."

The longboat had by this time drawn close in with the land, the island of Baru looming up black and clear-cut to windward, with the islets and their adjacent reef, now known as Rosario Islands, a short quarter of a mile broad on the weather bow, and a clump of hills on the main beyond, just beginning to outline themselves sharply against the lightening sky behind them. Daylight and darkness come with a rush in those latitudes, and by the time that the Rosario Islands were abeam the eastern sky had paled from indigo to white that, even as one looked, became flushed with a most delicate and ethereal tint of blush rose, which in its turn warmed as rapidly to a tone of rich amber, against which a cluster of mangrove-bordered islands, occupying what looked like the embouchure of a river, suddenly revealed themselves a point or two on the weather bow. Like magic the amber tint spread itself right and left along the horizon and upward toward the zenith, to be pierced, the next moment, by a broad shaft of pure white light which shot upward far into the delicate azure, which was now flooding the heavens and drowning out the stars, one after the other. Then up shot another and another shaft of light, radiating from a point just below the horizon, like the spokes of a wheel. Suddenly a little layer of horizontal clouds, a few degrees above the mangrove tops, became visible, rose-red and gold-edged; and an instant later a spark of molten, palpitating gold flashed and blazed through the ebony-black mangrove branches, dazzling the eye and tipping the ripples with a long line of scintillating gold which stretched clear from the shore to the boat, flooding her and those in her with primrose light. Quickly the golden spark grew and brightened until, before one could draw breath a dozen times, it had expanded into the upper edge of a great throbbing, burning, golden disk, flooding land and sea with its golden radiance—and it was day. The sea changed from purple to a clear translucent green; the vegetation ashore, still black immediately under the sun, merged by a thousand subtle gradations, right and left, into olive-green of every imaginable tint, and finally into a delicate rosy grey in the extreme distance; a multitude of trivial details of outline and contour, tree and rock, suddenly leapt into distinctness, a flock of pelicans rose from among the cluster of islands inshore and went flapping heavily and solemnly out to seaward; the dorsal fin of a shark drifted lazily past the boat—and the full extent of the bight behind the island of Baru swept suddenly into view.

"Just in time," exclaimed Marshall, with a sigh of relief, as he rose and stretched himself. "Round with her, lad, and head her up the bight while the wind lasts. It will be a flat calm here in half an hour from now."

"I hope not," said Dick, "for this bight is quite twelve miles long, by the look of it, and it will be no joke for four of us to be obliged to pull this heavy boat the greater part of that distance."

"There will be no need," said Marshall. "We are not in such a desperate hurry as that amounts to. Take the boat close in under the shore of the island, and when the wind fails us we will anchor and have breakfast. The calm will probably last no longer than about an hour; then will come the sea breeze, which, I should say, from the trend of the coast just here, will probably draw right up the bight, and be a fair wind for us."

Thus it proved; the force of the land breeze rapidly declined, until, in the course of half an hour, the boat scarcely retained steerage way. But during that half-hour she had progressed about two miles up the bight, while Dick had hugged the eastern shore of the island of Baru as closely as the depth of water would permit; and when at length the wind failed he took advantage of its last expiring breath to run the boat in behind a small rocky, tree-crowned bluff, where she was not only completely hidden from sight, but where her crew enjoyed the further advantage of being sheltered from the too ardent rays of the sun. Here, having lowered their sails and moored the boat to a rock, they breakfasted comfortably and at their leisure upon fish caught during their progress up the bight, and which they broiled over a fire kindled by means of a pocket lens which Marshall made a point of carrying with him constantly. The Captain was also pretty nearly correct in his estimate of the duration of the calm, for they had little more than finished their meal when the first cat's-paws heralding the approach of the sea breeze were seen playing here and there upon the surface of the water, and five minutes later the wind was roaring with the strength of half a gale over the top of the island, and whipping the surface of the bight into small, choppy, foam-capped seas. Of this fine breeze they at once took advantage by casting off from the rock and hoisting their canvas, when away they went bowling merrily up the bight, at the head of which they arrived about an hour and a half later.

The shape of the bight proved to be, roughly speaking, triangular, measuring about twelve miles long by about four miles wide at its entrance, narrowing at its upper end to a channel about twelve hundred feet wide, separating Baru from the mainland. They passed through this channel before they fully realised where they were going, and upon issuing from its northern extremity suddenly found themselves in a broad sheet of water some eight miles long by about half that width—Cartagena harbour, without a doubt! That would never do, at least in broad daylight; therefore, hastily putting the boat about, they ran back into the channel which they had just quitted, and beached the boat upon the shore of Baru, where, leaving the craft in charge of the three men, Marshall and Dick landed to reconnoitre. The part of the island upon which they landed was quite low, and bordered with mangroves, of which fact they took advantage by concealing themselves among the trees, and from that secure hiding-place examining the harbour at leisure.

They found that they were on the north-eastern extremity of the island of Baru, with the whole of the harbour of Cartagena before them, the roofs and spires of the town just showing waveringly, in a sort of mirage, over the low land which forms the easternmost extremity of the island of Tierra Bomba. It is this same island of Tierra Bomba, by the way, which converts what would otherwise be an open roadstead into a landlocked harbour, for it forms the western side of the harbour, and serves as a natural breakwater, sheltering the roadstead very effectually when the wind happens to blow from the westward. Also, being roughly triangular in shape, its eastern and western sides each measuring about four miles long, and its northern side about three miles, it divides the entire harbour into two parts, namely, the upper and the lower bay. The upper bay in its turn is divided into the inner and the outer harbour by two irregularly shaped spits of low land, the western spit jutting out south and east in a sort of elbow from the promontory on which the city is built, while the eastern spit is divided from the mainland by a narrow channel, and is called Manzanillo Island.

The foregoing is a brief and rough description of Cartagena harbour, given for the information of the reader and to enable him the better to understand what follows; but comparatively few of the above details were apparent to the two Englishmen lurking among the mangroves on the north-eastern extremity of Baru, for the island of Tierra Bomba, the most prominent object in sight, shut out much of the upper bay. They obtained, however, a good view of the Boca Chica, or harbour entrance, and took careful note of the fact that it was effectually commanded, at its narrowest and most difficult point, by a battery built on the very beach itself, and a fort, or castle, crowning the crest of a hill immediately above. They both agreed that if this was the only entrance to the harbour, and if the garrisons of those forts maintained a proper lookout, it should be quite impossible for a ship to enter or leave Cartagena harbour, except with the full permission of the authorities.

"Well," exclaimed Marshall at last, when they had both familiarised themselves with everything that there was to see from their viewpoint, "this is all very well, and we have already learned quite enough to repay us for all our trouble in taking this trip. But I have not yet seen nearly all that I want to see; therefore, by hook or by crook, I must get ashore upon that island yonder"—pointing to Tierra Bomba. "That hill at its north-eastern angle ought to command a view of the whole harbour and town, and I must get up there. Now, how is it best to be done?"

"It appears to me," said Dick, "that there is an opening of some sort— either a creek or the mouth of a small river—immediately opposite us, just to the right of that bay, and also to the right of those two hills, one of which is showing just clear of the other. There are two small islets standing in the mouth of it—"

"Yes, yes; I see what you mean," interrupted Marshall. "Well, what is your suggestion?"

"My suggestion," answered Dick, "is that we remain concealed until nightfall, and then that we should take the boat and explore that creek, or whatever it is; and if it proves to be a suitable hiding-place, well and good. We will conceal the boat and her crew there, and to-morrow morning you and I can climb to the top of that hill and make all the observations we need, even, perhaps, to the extent of drawing a rough chart of the place. It will cost us twenty-four hours of time; but I believe that the information which we shall thus obtain will more than repay us."

"I am sure of it," answered Marshall, heartily; "and we'll do it, my lad. Meanwhile, the mosquitoes are becoming something more than troublesome; so, as we have now seen all that it is possible for us to see from here, we'll get away back to the boat, or the men will begin to think that something has happened to us."

Chapter Four
How Marshall and Dick entered
Cartagena Harbour in the longboat

As Marshall had anticipated, the men were beginning to feel distinctly alarmed at the prolonged absence of their officers, admitting, indeed, that they were seriously debating the advisability of leaving the boat and instituting a search at the moment when Marshall and Dick reappeared. This admission drew forth a sharp rebuke from the Captain, who there and then gave them strict orders that under no circumstances were they ever to dream of doing such a thing. "For instance," said he, "what a pretty pickle should we all be in if, being discovered and pursued hotfoot by the enemy, we were to retreat to the boat and find that you men had left her. It would mean that Mr Chichester and I would be obliged to shove off without you; and that in turn would mean that sooner or later you would inevitably fall into the hands of the enemy. And let me tell you, men, that to fall into the hands of the Spaniards here means being clapt into the Inquisition. And of those who get into the Inquisition not one in a hundred ever gets out again. Therefore, never leave your boat, under any circumstances whatsoever, except at the express command of your officers."

It was by this time considerably past noon; the food was therefore produced, and all hands partook of a meal, after which there was nothing to be done until the evening; the men therefore disposed themselves in the bottom of the boat and took such snatches of sleep as the mosquitoes permitted, while Marshall and Dick sat in the stern-sheets and discussed plans for the morrow.

At length, however, after an interval of waiting that soon grew terribly wearisome, the sun went down, darkness fell, and they pushed off the boat and got under way. There was now a young moon of about four days old, and before she too set she afforded them light enough to make their way across the lower bay, a distance of about three and a half miles, to the island of Tierra Bomba, and to find the indentation to which Dick had directed Marshall's attention earlier in the day. It proved to be a particularly snug little cove, about half a mile long by perhaps a quarter of a mile wide, with thickly wooded hills sloping down toward it on either side at its upper extremity. Two small islets pretty effectually masked its entrance; and a dry sandbank in the middle of it occupied more than half its area, leaving a narrow channel all round it, the water in which was only just deep enough to afford unimpeded passage to the boat. It was stark calm inside the cove, they were, therefore, obliged to lower the sails, strike the masts, and use the oars to reach the head of the creek; but when they arrived there they found a steep bank so completely overhung with trees and bushes that, when once the boat had been forced in underneath the branches, she might remain there for days with little or no fear of discovery.

In this exceedingly snug berth it seemed almost ridiculous to think of keeping a watch; yet, being in the enemy's territory, they decided to do so; Marshall undertaking to stand the first watch of two hours, while Dick agreed to take the second.

When, at ten o'clock, Marshall aroused Dick, in order that the latter might stand his watch, the Captain whispered:

"I've been thinking about a good many things while I have been sitting here these two hours agone in the stern-sheets of this boat. And, among other matters, I have thought that it might be very useful to know something more than we do about those two batteries that we took notice of while we were on the point yonder to-day. Now, I'm not a bit sleepy. I don't believe I could get to sleep if I tried—also the night is delightfully cool; and, although the moon has gone down, the stars give quite enough light for my purpose, therefore, I am going to take a little walk along the shore to that battery on the beach. It can't be very much more than two miles away; and night is the only time when it will be possible to examine the forts without running too much risk. If I do not feel too tired I'll take that fort on the top of the hill on my way back; so if I do not return until close before daybreak you need not be unduly alarmed."

"Very well, sir," answered Dick. "We will keep a bright lookout. And if by any chance things should go amiss, and you should be pursued, if you will fire two pistol shots, one close after the other, I will come, with one of the men, to meet you, provided, of course, that we are within hearing of the shots."

"Yes; you may do that—if you hear the signal shots," agreed Marshall. "But," he added, "I shall need to be very hard pressed indeed to fire my pistols. For shots at night-time anywhere near a battery would be certain to put everybody on the alert, and probably bring a bigger hornet's nest about my ears than you and all hands could beat off. Still, if I want help very badly I shall know what to do. And now, I'll be off. Keep a sharp lookout, and don't allow yourself to be surprised. Good night!" As Dick murmured an answering "Good night" the Captain turned and disappeared in the darkness.

All through the night a careful watch was maintained, but nothing in the slightest degree alarming occurred; and about an hour before daybreak Captain Marshall returned, having accomplished his mission to his own complete satisfaction.

"I had no difficulty whatever," he explained to Dick, "nor did I encounter a single soul; indeed I am strongly of opinion that the island, or at least the southern half of it, is uninhabited, except for the garrisons of the fort and battery. I tackled the battery first, making my way to it by passing round the base of the hill until I reached the shore-line of the next bay, which I then followed for the remainder of the distance. And heavy walking I found it, with a murrain on it; for the sand was loose and deep, except where I came upon mangroves, and there the mud was even deeper than the sand, while, as for the mosquitoes, they were as eager for my blood as the Spaniards themselves would be if they but knew what my business is here. However, I was not to be turned back by the mosquitoes, even though they assailed me in legions; and after trudging through the heavy sand for a full hour or more I found myself beneath the walls of the battery.

"It is planned like a triangle, one face, mounting four guns, commanding the seaward end of the Boca, while the second face commands its inner extremity, the third face being turned toward the land and containing the entrance gate. The point or apex of the triangle juts out into the water; I was therefore unable to walk completely round it; nevertheless I examined both sides by walking past the back of it. The faces of the walls are quite smooth, and about twelve feet high; but the angles are set with rough quoin stones, up which, there being no lights in the battery, and no sign of a sentinel, I essayed to climb, accomplishing the ascent with no greater difficulty or hurt than the wearing of the soles off my stockings—for I took off my shoes for the sake of quietness and to gain a better foothold. Having gained the parapet, I found two sentries sitting there, with their backs against the wall, fast asleep, with their matchlocks beside them. Gently lifting their weapons in my hand, I shook out the priming—lest perchance they should awake and, seeing me, open fire upon me before I could get away—and then, replacing the weapons as I had found them, passed quietly on to examine the ordnance. The guns are very formidable, of a pattern such as I have never before seen, being a good twenty foot in length, and of a bigness to take a shot the size of a man's head, as I learned by passing my hands over the topmost shot of a pile which stood beside each gun. There are eight of these pieces of great ordnance, besides falcons and swivels which I did not stay to count, the heavy ordnance being all that caused me any anxiety. And even now they do not greatly trouble me; for if they keep no better watch there on other nights than they did on this, it would be easy for a couple of resolute men to enter the place, even as I did, bind and gag the sentinels, and spike all eight of the guns, and never a man of them any the wiser until they came to put fire to their pieces.

"Then, having seen all that I desired, I left the battery as I had entered it, and made my way up the hill to the castle on the top. Here, however, I was less fortunate, there being no way of entering the building, save by walking in through the gate, or climbing the walls with the help of a scaling ladder. The place is much more formidable looking than the battery, being in appearance a strong castle, with dry ditch, drawbridge, and portcullis to the main and, so far as I could see, the only entrance. In plan it is shaped like the letter L, with the angle turned harbour-ward; and it must mount about thirty pieces of ordnance, for I managed to count that number of embrasures on its two faces. But of sentinels I saw none; so, if they set a watch, I presume that, like those in the battery, the rascals are in the habit of sleeping their watch through; which is so much the better for freebooters like ourselves. For the dry ditch is not difficult to cross, and I estimate that, once on the other side, a ladder of twenty foot in length should enable a party of half a dozen to reach the top; and, once on the parapet, they should be able to spike the whole thirty of those footy ordnance in ten minutes. And all this means, friend Dick, that with the whole of the heavy ordnance spiked, in castle and in battery, there is nothing to prevent the *Adventure* from sailing into the harbour, coming to an anchor, storming and blowing up both defences, and then holding the town to ransom, as well as capturing the galleon! For, as my soul liveth, I firmly believe that the castle and the battery constitute the entire defences of Cartagena! And then, hey for old England again; for, with the ransom of the town and the booty from the galleon, there ought to be enough to make us all rich for life."

"And if there is not, it ought not to be very difficult for us to play the same game with two or three other towns," remarked Dick. "For I suppose it is safe to reckon that all the towns along the Main are wealthy enough to pay for looting?"

"Ay; no doubt there are good pickings to be had out of every one of them," answered Marshall. "But 'one thing at a time' is a good maxim in such a business as ours, my lad; and we will see what Cartagena yields before we begin to think seriously about any of the other towns. And now, here comes the dawn at last, for which thanks be; for I am as hungry as if I had spent all night to the top of Dartymoor, and want my breakfast."

An hour later the meal had been prepared and eaten; after which Marshall and Dick, having provided themselves with food and water sufficient to last them until nightfall, if necessary, and having given the crew of the longboat most precise instructions as to how to act in the event of certain contingencies arising, cautiously emerged from their place of concealment, and, carrying the boat compass with them for the purpose of enabling them to take such bearings as might be required, set out upon their way to the top of the hill which dominated the north-east corner of the island. The going was exceedingly difficult, for the slope was rough and steep, also it was so thickly overgrown with vegetation that for a good part of the distance they had literally to cut a way for themselves; therefore, although the distance which they had to traverse was little more than a mile it was well on toward noon when at length they reached the summit. But, when there, they were fain to admit that their labour had been well spent; for as they topped the last rise the vegetation suddenly became much thinner, so that they found themselves able to force a way through it without being obliged to have recourse to their hangers; and presently they emerged upon the bare hilltop, and beheld, spread out at their feet, a magnificent panorama embracing a view of the whole upper bay and inner harbour, with the town of Cartagena a bare four miles distant. And there, in the midst of a whole fleet of smaller craft, they also beheld a tall and stately ship, a single glance at which sufficed to assure them that she could be none other than the plate ship which was the great object of their quest.

"There she be!" exclaimed Marshall, pointing. "All of seven hundred ton, or more; and deep in the water, too. She must have pretty nearly, or quite, finished loading. Seems to me that we're only just in time. Now, Dick, my lad, this is your opportunity to make the chart that you were talking about. Come along, and let's get about it; I'll help you. To-night we must make our way into the city, somehow, and find out by hook or by crook exactly when she is to sail. Now, how do we begin upon the chart?"

"Well," said Dick, "to be of any use it must be tolerably accurate, and drawn to scale; and the top of this hill is admirably adapted for our purpose. Our first business must be to measure off as correctly as possible the longest line we can get—and, with a little management, I think we ought to be able to make that line a mile in length, which will be long enough for our purpose. Then, having measured off our line, and taken its compass bearing, all that will remain to be done will be to take, from each end of the line, the compass bearing of as many objects as we require; and where the several bearings intersect will be the correct positions of those objects. Then we can complete the chart accurately enough for our purpose by sketching in the details between the objects, the positions of which we have determined. See, this is the sort of thing I mean." And, drawing a scrap of paper from his pocket, Chichester rapidly sketched a diagram illustrating his meaning.

Marshall took the sketch and considered it attentively. "Yes," he said at length, "that ought to be near enough for our purpose. But how are you going to measure your line?"

"Quite easily," answered Dick. "When I learned that I was to accompany you, the idea of drawing a chart of the harbour at once occurred to me, and I thought out the plan that I have just explained to you. I also borrowed from the carpenter a ball of fine cord, which I then proceeded to knot very carefully at every foot, measured with the carpenter's rule. Here it is, just one hundred feet long; and with the help of it we ought to have no difficulty in measuring our line."

Nor had they: for the hilltop was quite level enough for their purpose. They measured it twice, going and returning, in order to ensure the greater accuracy, and, laying down their work on paper to scale as they proceeded, managed before dark to secure an exceedingly useful and tolerably complete chart of the upper bay and inner harbour, with the help of which they felt that they ought to be able to find their way to the town, even on the darkest night. Of course they were not able to ascertain the depth of water by this means; but the even colour of it seemed to indicate that there were no hidden dangers to guard against anywhere except just inside the entrance of the inner harbour, where the presence of a shoal obstructing the fairway was clearly indicated by a certain glassiness of surface, which was duly recorded upon the chart.

The preparation of this chart served to familiarise them with the principal features of the harbour in a really wonderful manner, and to fix in their memories the relative positions of them one with another. But that was not all; for while they were at work their eyes were busy noting various details, one of which was that a small fishing village existed at the base of the hill upon which they were at work, and not more than half a mile from the spot where the longboat lay concealed. This was a discovery of some importance to them, for it at once suggested the possibility of "borrowing" a canoe from the village, after dark, and proceeding in her to the city; by which plan they would run much less risk of detection than if they attempted to reach the city with the longboat.

They completed their labours and set out to walk down the hill on their way to the boat while the sun was still nearly an hour above the horizon, and were safely aboard her again ere darkness fell. Then, having partaken of a meal, Marshall and Dick stretched themselves along in the stern-sheets of the boat, in order to snatch an hour or two of sleep before embarking upon by far the most hazardous part of their enterprise, namely, their excursion to the city of Cartagena.

Marshall had given instructions that he and Dick were to be called punctually at eight o'clock; but when that hour arrived and the man who had the watch proceeded to arouse them, it appeared that the Captain was already awake, not having been to sleep at all, in fact; and as Dick seemed to be fast locked in the arms of slumber, Marshall softly whispered to the man who was about to arouse him, that he was to be permitted to sleep on, at the same time composing himself to rest and giving fresh instructions that both were to be called at midnight. From which it was evident that in the interim he had modified his original plan.

When at length midnight arrived and the pair were duly awakened Marshall remarked with a grin which the darkness effectually concealed:

"Well, lad, hast had a good sleep?"

"Excellent," answered Dick. "I feel as fresh as a lark, and can scarcely realise that I have only been asleep two hours."

"Two hours!" retorted Marshall, with a laugh. "Thou hast had six hours of good, honest sleep; and 'tis midnight instead of eight o'clock. The fact is," he continued in more serious tones, "I could not sleep when I first attempted to do so. My thoughts were busy with the task that lay before me; and I could not see how it was to be done in the time that I had allowed myself. The way that I looked at the matter was this: I had arranged that we were to start from here at eight o'clock. By the time that we had found our way round to the village where we hoped to get a canoe, it would be nearly or quite nine; and by the time that we reached Cartagena it would be ten o'clock, or after; there would be no work doing, and most of the good folk would be abed; thus I should stand a very poor chance of gaining any information worth having. The proper time for me to be ashore, there, is during the day, when everybody is astir, when there are plenty of people about to talk to and ask questions of, and when they will be too busy to take particular note of me, and wonder who I am and where I came from. So I altered my plan, deferring our departure until now, which will afford me plenty of time to get into the city before daylight. Then I shall have the whole day before me, if I find that I require it, in which to look about me and make a few discreet enquiries; and as soon after dark as it is safe to return I will come back; reaching the boat, if all be well, in time to go out and rejoin the *Adventure* to-morrow night about this time. Now, I shall want you to go with me as far as the village, to help me, if need be, to secure a canoe; and when I have done that, and am fairly under way, you can come back here to the boat, and wait for me; for the work that I have to do can best be done single-handed. Now, if you have any questions to ask, ask them; but if not, we may as well be off, for I want to allow myself plenty of time to make my way into the town."

Dick intimated that he believed he quite understood the scheme which the Captain had outlined, and that he had only one question to ask, namely, how long the boat was to remain where she was in the event of Marshall being detained in Cartagena longer than he anticipated.

"How long?" repeated Marshall. "Let me see. This will make the second complete night that we have been absent from the ship—although it seems very much longer. Stay here, if necessary, for four days and nights longer, as arranged with Bascomb; and if I am not back by midnight of the fourth night my orders are that you are to rejoin the ship, report to Winter and Bascomb all that we have done and learned; and say it is my wish that they shall act as may seem to them best, and without any reference at all to what may have become of me; for if I do not return to you by the time that I have named it will be because I cannot, having fallen into the hands of the Spaniards. And now, if you are ready, let us be going."

Silently, and with the observance of every precaution to prevent betrayal of the longboat's hiding-place to any chance wanderer in the neighbourhood, the pair forced a way through their leafy bower and up the steep bank until they emerged upon clear ground, when, bearing away to the eastward round the foot of the hill which they had that day ascended, they groped their way cautiously over the unfamiliar ground until, in the course of about half an hour, they caught the dim shimmer of starlight upon water, and, between them and it, a group of dark, shapeless blotches which, upon their nearer approach, they identified as the hovels constituting the fishing village which they had seen during the day from the top of the hill.

Circling round these, they presently reached the water's edge, where, as they had fully anticipated, they found a dozen or more canoes of various sizes hauled up on the beach, most of them with their nets piled up in their sterns. They looked about for the smallest canoe they could find, and having overhauled her as carefully as the light would allow, and satisfied themselves as to her seaworthiness, removed the nets from her to the craft nearest at hand and, lifting her by her two ends, carried her down to the water, and set her afloat. Then, with a quick hand-clasp and a low-murmured "Goodbye, lad, and take care of yourself and the men," Marshall stepped softly into the crank little craft, seated himself in the stern, and with a vigorous thrust of the paddle sent himself off into deep water, where a few minutes later he was swallowed up by the darkness. Dick stood by the water's edge, watching the small black blur which represented man and canoe as it receded from the shore until it vanished; and then turned slowly away to retrace his steps to the longboat, happily unconscious that he had looked his last upon his gallant leader.

Returning safely and without difficulty to the longboat, Dick Chichester whispered to the man who was keeping watch that thus far all was well; and then bestowed himself in the stern-sheets to snatch another hour or two of sleep. Then, after a somewhat late breakfast, he emerged cautiously from his leafy refuge and climbed to the top of the hill again, ensconcing himself well within the shadow of a thick bush, from beneath which he commanded an uninterrupted view of the entire upper bay and harbour. Not that he expected to see much, or, indeed, anything in particular; but he thought it well to keep a watchful eye upon things in general and, if anything particular should happen ashore, take care to be where he might perchance be able to detect some indication of it. But he saw nothing at all to indicate that anything unusual had taken place, or was taking place, in Cartagena, the only occurrence of a noticeable character that came under his observation that day being a violent quarrel among certain of the inhabitants of the fishing village below, which quarrel, he shrewdly conjectured, might possibly have something to do with a missing canoe.

He remained on the hill the whole of that day, allowing himself only just daylight enough to find his way back to the longboat, and then, having partaken of a meal, disposed himself to secure a good long uninterrupted night's rest, warning the men, however, to be alert during their watch, so that if the Captain should return during the night and need assistance, they might be prepared to render it quickly.

But Captain Marshall did not return during that night; therefore after an early breakfast the next morning Dick again ascended the hill to keep watch upon the town and harbour, thinking that mayhap he might thus catch an early glimpse of Marshall returning; and if haply he should chance to be pursued, learn the fact in time to go to his assistance. But this day, too, passed uneventfully away, the galleon, with the great golden flag of Spain flaunting at her stern, showing no visible sign of an early departure.

Dick felt so firmly convinced that the Captain would return some time during the ensuing night that he sat up, waiting for him, and taking watch after watch as it came round. But the morning dawned with still no sign of Marshall; and then the young officer began to feel seriously apprehensive; for he could not imagine that his leader should spend two whole days in Cartagena without learning all that he desired to know upon a matter which must be so widely discussed as the departure of an exceptionally rich treasure ship for Old Spain. Yet of course there was the chance that Marshall might be voluntarily prolonging his stay for the purpose of obtaining some especially valuable item of information; meanwhile, the four days having not yet expired, his duty was to remain where he was, and keep a sharp lookout. So again Dick wended his way to the top of the hill, and ensconced himself in his now familiar hiding-place beneath the bush.

And on this day his vigilance was rewarded by signs of activity on board the galleon, to wit, a slow and very deliberate bending of her sails; so slow and deliberate, indeed, that at the end of the day only about half her canvas had been secured to the yards. This of course indicated that the date of her sailing was drawing nigh; and he comforted himself with the reflection that possibly this date had not yet been definitely fixed—the Spaniards were notoriously dilatory in this respect, thinking nothing of a fortnight's, or even a month's delay—and it might perhaps be that Marshall was patiently awaiting the fixing of this date before rejoining them, knowing that the boat would be awaiting him whenever he might find it convenient to return to her.

Thinking and reasoning thus, Dick at length succeeded in so completely convincing himself that Marshall's delay was entirely voluntary, that the anxiety which had gradually been growing upon him passed away; so completely, indeed, that he composed himself to rest with the absolute conviction that the Captain would return sometime during the night; the only orders which he deemed it necessary to give the men being, that they were to maintain a sharp lookout, and awake him immediately upon their general's arrival.

But the night passed; and day—the fourth day since Marshall had left them, and the last of their prescribed sojourn where they were—dawned without sign of the absentee; and when at length Dick Chichester awakened and this fact was borne in upon him, all his former apprehensions returned with redoubled force. Something had gone wrong with the Captain; he was convinced of it; Marshall would never deliberately tarry so long in a town, every man, woman, and child in which was an enemy; his identity as an Englishman had been discovered, and he had been taken, without a doubt. Yet, with a sudden revulsion of feeling, Dick remembered that one trait of his Captain's character was a certain daredevil recklessness which made peril, or rather the overcoming of it, a joy and a delight, and caused him actually to court danger for the pleasurable excitement which the evasion of it afforded him. Might it not be, then, that Marshall, knowing the fate that awaited him in the event of detection, was deliberately lingering in Cartagena in order that he might enjoy to the fullest possible extent the gratification of hoodwinking his enemies and moving freely among them unsuspected?

Swayed thus between hope and fear, the harassed young lieutenant once more, and for the last time, mounted the hill and resumed his anxious watch of the town and harbour. But no indication of any happening of an unusual character, either in the town or in the harbour, was perceptible; everything seemed to be going forward precisely as usual; the only occurrence that in the slightest degree interested the watcher being that the crew of the galleon resumed their occupation of bending sails, which operation, proceeding with the same deliberation as before, they contrived to complete about half an hour before sunset; when Dick, unutterably weary and discouraged with his long and fruitless watch, arose and made his way down the hill to the place where the longboat lay hidden.

Chapter Five
How they disarmed the Batteries on Tierra Bomba

As Chichester neared the now familiar spot where he had left the longboat, he suffered himself to indulge in a returning feeling of elation, for the notion somehow came to him that he would find Marshall in the boat calmly awaiting his return; and this feeling presently grew so strong within him that he could scarcely credit his eyes when, upon passing through the screen of concealing foliage, he saw only the three seamen curled up in the boat. They roused themselves from their semi-somnolent condition and sat up to receive him, with glances of mute enquiry in their eyes.

For a few moments Dick remained silent, absolutely speechless with disappointment. Then he remarked:

"What, lads, has the Captain not yet returned, then?"

"No, sir," they answered in chorus. "We have seen naught of him, or indeed of anybody else, since you left us this morning."

"Then," said Dick, "I greatly fear that evil has befallen him and that he has been discovered and taken by the Spaniards. For this is the last day of our stay here; and his orders to me were that if he returns not by midnight we are to proceed to sea and rejoin the ship; for his failure to return will be due to the fact of his having been captured. Still, there are six hours to run yet before midnight, and he may return even at the very last moment. Let us hope that he will. And now, men, give me some supper, for I have eaten nothing since I left you this morning."

The time between then and midnight was passed by Dick in a state of feverish suspense, that toward the end became almost unendurable, causing him to start and jump at every trivial sound that reached his ear. A dozen times at least he sprang to his feet with the joyous exclamation of "Here he is!" when the flutter of a dry leaf falling from its parent bough, the soft rustle of foliage in the night wind, or the movement of some restless bird broke the silence of that secluded spot; but he was always mistaken. The Captain came not; and at length his watch informed him that the time was half an hour after midnight. Then he rose to his feet with a sigh of bitter disappointment and said:

"It is no good, lads; we must not delay our departure any longer; we have allowed the Captain half an hour's grace, and if he could have come he would have been with us before now. Without doubt he is a prisoner, and we can best serve him now by returning to the ship with all speed and reporting the fact of his capture to the others, who must then decide whether or not we shall sail into the harbour, attack the town, and endeavour to rescue him. Cast off the painter, and let us be moving without further delay."

Almost careless now whether or not they attracted attention, they hauled the boat out from her place of concealment and, stepping the masts, hoisted their sails and got under way, the wind just permitting them to lay their course down past the sand spit and out through the entrance of the cove into the lower bay without breaking tacks. Then, to save time, Dick determined to risk the passage of the Boca Chica, the usual harbour entrance, instead of taking the longer route out to sea behind the island of Baru, relying upon the indifferent lookout of the sentinels as reported by Marshall to enable the boat to pass undetected. In this they were completely successful, the occupants of the batteries giving no sign that the passage of the boat had been observed; and half an hour after emerging from their place of concealment they found themselves safely clear of everything and out at sea.

The night was dark but clear, with a fresh land breeze blowing, and a sky heavily flecked with fast-scurrying clouds, between which the stars and moon blinked down upon them intermittently. They were no sooner clear of the land than they began to look about them for the ship, and within a few minutes they caught sight of her signal lanterns about eight miles distant, dead to leeward. After that everything went quite smoothly; they hoisted their own signal lamp, and bore away dead before the wind, leaving it to the ship to pick them up, which she did about an hour later.

Their shipmates manifested the utmost interest in their return, all hands mustering on deck to see the boat come alongside and hear the news. When, upon the boat being brought to the lee gangway, Dick led the way up the side, he was met at the entrance port by Bascomb, Winter, Dyer, and Harvey, each of whom at the same instant fired at him the question:

"Where is the Captain?"

"Lost—taken, I fear," answered Dick. "He left us four nights ago, intending to make his way into the city of Cartagena, for the purpose of learning precisely when the galleon is to sail, together with any other information which he might be able to pick up. His instructions were that

I was to await his return until midnight to-night, and if he then failed to return it would be because something untoward had happened to him, in which case I was to rejoin the ship at once and report to you, when you would act according to your discretion after consulting together."

For a moment there was a dead silence; then Bascomb turned to his fellow officers, and said:

"My masters, this loss of our general is a very serious matter, and needs looking into. Let us all, therefore, retire to the cabin and hear what Mr Chichester has to tell us about it; after which, as was arranged when Captain Marshall left us six nights ago, we must all consult together and decide what our next step is to be. Come then, gentlemen, to the cabin. Mr Chichester, you will be pleased to accompany us."

Therewith the three principal officers of the ship and the two gentlemen adventurers retired to the great cabin, where, seated upon the lockers, and with Dick occupying a chair in front of them, the tale was told of all that had befallen the boat and its crew, from the moment of her departure to that of her return, including the several expeditions to the top of the hill on Tierra Bomba, and the drawing of the chart.

"And where is that chart now?" demanded Bascomb. "Have you it, or did Captain Marshall take it with him?"

"I have it," answered Dick, "and here it is," producing the sketch. "Fortunately the Captain left it with me, not needing it himself, since all the information required to enable him to make his way to Cartagena he could carry in his head."

The four who were sitting on the opposite side of the table bent over the document, examining it closely for several minutes. At length Bascomb looked up and said:

"My masters, if this chart be reliable—and it should be, judging from the pains taken by our Captain and Mr Chichester—it should suffice to enable us to take the ship right up to Cartagena and lay her alongside the galleon. And if that ship can be taken by surprise and without loss on our part, as I think she may, what is to hinder us from taking the town and demanding a good heavy ransom for it, part of which ransom shall consist in the return to us, sound and unhurt, of our Captain? And if they refuse, or are unable to return our Captain to us in the condition specified, what say you to sacking the place and giving it to the flames? Depend upon it, by so doing we shall soon learn the fate of Captain Marshall, and where he is to be found, for there will be a hundred who will be only too ready to curry favour with us by telling us all that they know, in the hope that thereby we may be induced to spare their property."

"Ay, that will they, I warrant," answered Winter. "And woe betide the city and all in it if aught of evil has been done to our Captain! We will find every man who has been in anywise responsible for that evil, and will hang him before his own door for all men to see how dangerous a thing it is for a Spaniard to lay violent hands upon an Englishman! Now, what say ye, gentles, shall we go in at once and do the work while our blood is hot within us?"

"Nay, sirs," answered Dick; "that may scarcely be. For if our Captain be indeed taken, as I greatly fear me he is, depend upon it the authorities will have identified him as an Englishman, in despite of any tale that he may have told them, and will, in consequence, suspect the presence of an English ship somewhere in the neighbourhood. And, following that suspicion, their first act would be to warn those in the forts on Tierra Bomba to be on the watch for that ship's appearance. And once seen it will, according to the Captain's own account, be impossible for us to force our way into the harbour unless the guns in those forts be first spiked. Now, gentles, I am the youngest of you all, but I have been inside and seen the place. Moreover, I have been privileged to discuss with the Captain this very question of taking the ship up to the town, from which discussion arose my determination to make that chart; and my advice is, that we defer our attempt until to-morrow night, and that in the meantime I be permitted to return in the longboat to our former hiding-place, provided with hammers and nails for the spiking of the guns and such other necessaries as I may require, together with a crew of six of our best men. We can get back to our place of concealment before daylight, and there remain in hiding until midnight or later, when we will sally forth, steal into those two forts, overpower and gag the sentinels, and spike the guns, after which we will signal the ship by the burning of portfires where they cannot be seen from the town, when you will sail in, I meeting you outside and piloting you in. We can then land a party, destroy both batteries by blowing them up, capture the galleon and the town, and sail out to sea again, unscathed, when we have finished our business with the Spaniards."

"Thy plan sounds promising, young sir," answered Bascomb presently, after considering the matter a little; "but there is one weak point in it, which is this. If, as you seem to think, the Spaniards have taken our Captain, and thereby are led to suspect the presence of an English ship in the neighbourhood; and, suspecting such presence, should warn the garrisons of those two forts to be on the lookout for her—all of which I grant to be more than likely—what hope have you of being able to surprise those forts and spike their guns?"

"The task will be a difficult one, I admit," answered Dick, with a shrug of the shoulders; "but, with all submission, sirs, my plan is the only one offering a chance of success. For—and this is the fundamental fact governing all else—the guns must be spiked and the forts destroyed before this ship can enter Cartagena harbour or, having entered, get out again. But the forts once in our possession the whole town and harbour, with all within them, will be at our mercy. The important matter, therefore, to be determined is: By what means can we ensure obtaining possession of the forts with the minimum of loss to ourselves?"

"Yes," agreed Bascomb, "that is undoubtedly the point. Now, gentles, let us have your opinions. Has any one of you a better plan to offer than that of our junior lieutenant?"

At this moment a stateroom door opened and Stukely emerged from the smaller room. Approaching the table, he stood and looked smilingly down upon the company assembled.

"Your pardon, fair sirs," he said, "for thrusting myself uninvited into your counsels. The surgeon is supposed to know but little of warfare beyond the healing of such hurts as may be received therein, but I happened to be lying awake in my cabin when this conference began, and I could not avoid hearing all that has passed, and I am of opinion that I can help you. As my friend, Chichester, here has put it, the problem which confronts you is that of securing possession of the forts without suffering loss of men. Now, the chief danger, to my mind, arises from the difficulty of entering the forts without attracting the attention of the sentinels, thus causing them to raise the alarm and bring the entire garrison about our ears. Is not that so?"

The party at the table signified that it was.

"Very good, then," resumed Stukely. "Now we can go on. Though you are probably not aware of it, my chief delight is research, the investigation of, among other things, the properties and action upon the human system of the juices of herbs. Now, while we were at Barbados I spent much time in the collection of the leaves, roots, seeds, and fruits of several plants; and since then I have been diligently experimenting with them, with the result that I have evolved from one of them a liquor, one inhalation of the odour of which will plunge a man into a state of such complete insensibility that, as I believe, a limb might be removed from him without his feeling it or being any the wiser. My suggestion, therefore," continued Stukely, ignoring the expressions of wonder evoked by his statement, "is that I be permitted to go in the boat with Chichester, taking a vial of the liquor with me, and upon our arrival ashore I will enter the forts with him, subject the sleeping sentinels—I humbly trust that they may be sleeping—to the stupefying influence of the decoction, whereby they may be bound and gagged without difficulty or the raising of an alarm which would put their fellow soldiers on the alert; and then between us the guns can be spiked at our leisure. The remaining details I leave to your riper judgment and experience, gallant sirs."

"But, doctor," demanded Bascomb, "are you quite sure that this elixir or essence of yours may be depended upon to produce the effect stated?"

"I am," answered Stukely, with a smile, "for I have already tested it upon myself—no matter how—and the effect is everything that can possibly be desired."

"Then—what say you, gentles—shall we allow the surgeon to go with Mr Chichester and further test the efficacy of his decoction upon the Spanish sentinels?" asked the master.

"'Twould be folly in us if we did not avail ourselves of the virtues of Mr Stukely's most fortunate discovery," said Winter; "and I for one am in favour of acceding to his proposal."

"And I, also," agreed Dick, in response to a glance from Bascomb.

The two gentlemen adventurers, when appealed to for their opinion, at once agreed that the experiment was quite worth trying; and Bascomb's proposal was accordingly agreed to *nem. con.*

"That matter, then, is disposed of," remarked Bascomb. "Now, the next thing which we have to decide is this—assuming that Mr Chichester succeeds in spiking the guns of the forts—what is to be our next step? Are we to take the ship boldly into the harbour and proceed with our business of capturing the galleon and the town, trusting that Dame Fortune will so far favour us as to permit of our getting out again before the soldiers can unspike their guns; or should we anchor, as soon as inside, land a strong party, and capture and destroy the forts before attempting anything else? It is the guns, and they only, not the forts, which we have to fear; and if we could but permanently disable those guns, the forts and their garrisons might go hang, so far as we are concerned."

"Certainly, sir," cut in Dick, before anyone else could speak. "You have hit the nail on the head. We need trouble about naught except the ordnance, and them we must destroy. And I know how to do it, too. We will take with us enough powder to double charge each gun; having done which we will seal their muzzles with clay. I know where to find as much clay as we shall need; and then we will prime each piece, lay a quick match from priming to priming, light the match, and run for our lives. The guns will burst, and we can then do what we please with the galleon and the town. But in order to ensure complete success, the ordnance in both batteries must be fired as nearly as possible at the same moment; therefore a resolute man must be left in the lower battery to fire the match upon the instant that he hears the explosion of the guns in the upper battery, after which he must run for his life. I can see exactly how the thing is to be done, sirs; and if you approve of my plan we will be starting at once, with your good leave; for it is already late, and we shall have none too much time for the work which is to be done."

"You are right, young sir," agreed Bascomb; "time is so valuable now that we dare waste no more in further discussion; therefore your plan, which is an excellent one, must serve. I would that I could go in your stead, for you appear to be already worn-out with fatigue and lack of sleep; but you have been over the ground already, and know it, therefore weary though you may be I fear that you must needs go. So pick your men, sir, as many as you need, remembering that your party must be strong enough to carry the powder up to the forts; procure from the gunner all that you require; and get you gone. And may God go with you! Amen."

Half an hour later the longboat, under Dick's command, and with Stukely sitting in the stern-sheets beside him, was once more under way and beating in toward the land under a press of sail, while the *Adventure*, with all lights out, lay to in the offing, awaiting the signal of the explosion of the ordnance in the forts to fill away and stand boldly in toward the harbour. So sorely were they pressed for time that Dick dared not waste any in the attempt to elude observation by creeping in, as on the first occasion, behind the island of Baru; he headed as straight as the wind would allow for the Boca Chica, trusting that he might be fortunate enough to slip through unobserved in the darkness, especially as it was now past three o'clock in the morning—and if the sentinels slept at all at their posts, after the warning to hold themselves on the alert which they might be supposed to have received from the authorities, they might be expected to be asleep now. His hope appeared to be justified; for the longboat slid past the smaller battery down on the beach, unchallenged, and some five minutes later, grounded on the sand about a quarter of a mile farther in. Then, silently as ghosts, the men lowered the sails, leaving the masts standing, and stepped out on the sand, each bearing his appointed load of powder upon his shoulder, while Dick and Stukely, with swords drawn, and the former carrying a coil of quick match wound round his waist, led the way.

They directed their steps southward toward the battery which they had sailed past a few minutes earlier, and which could just be distinguished as a darker blur against the blackness of the night. Not a light of any description showed about the building, nor was there a sound to be heard save the soft lap and splash of the water on the margin of the beach to the left of them, and the sough of the land breeze among the trees and bushes on their right. Noiseless as drifting shadows, the party sped forward, and within some five minutes of their landing arrived beneath the walls of the fort. Here Dick, Stukely, and a man named Barker removed their shoes and, walking to the northward angle of the fort, examined it to ascertain what means of ascent it afforded. They found, as Marshall had said, that although the walls were so smooth as to be quite unclimbable, the angles of the building were set with quoin stones of so rough a surface that an ascent by means of them might be made easily; accordingly Stukely, who by virtue of his discovery of the anaesthetic now claimed to take the lead, at once began to climb the angle, closely followed by Dick and Barker. In less than two minutes the trio had accomplished the ascent and found themselves standing on the platform which constituted the flat roof of the battery. The eight pieces of heavy ordnance, their muzzles projecting far over the low parapet, were easily distinguishable, as were also the great piles of shot, notwithstanding the darkness of the night; but for the moment no sentinels were visible. Whispering his companions to remain where they were, Stukely moved away with noiseless tread, swiftly making the circuit of the gun platform; and presently he rejoined the other two.

"It is all right," he whispered. "I found the rascals sound asleep, even as the Captain did, and, withdrawing the stopper from my vial, allowed them to inhale the vapour for a moment. They are now insensible, and will remain so for at least half an hour, therefore you may now do your share of the work, Barker. Come with me, and I will show you where they lie."

The two moved away together, Barker uncoiling a long length of fine line from his waist as he did so; while Dick, leaning over the parapet, dropped a small pebble down among the group below, as a signal that all was well and they might now safely make the ascent without fear of detection. All arrangements having been previously made, every man of the party knew exactly what he had to do; and within five minutes the platform was alive with English seamen, some of whom were engaged in hauling up powder and clay from below, while others were employed in silently loading the guns with heavy charges of powder, upon the top of which they tightly rammed down stiff clay, with which they filled each gun to its very muzzle. Then, when each piece had been similarly treated, the whole were very carefully primed, after which a length of quick match, long enough to allow of the safe retreat of the man who should ignite it, was securely inserted among the priming; the two insensible sentinels, bound hand and foot, and effectually gagged, were lowered to the ground, and the entire party retreated as they had come, with the exception of one man who volunteered to remain and ignite the length of match immediately that he saw a portfire burned from the wall of the castle which stood on the top of the adjacent hill. The whole business had occupied scarcely twenty minutes, and when it was finished there was nothing to show that the garrison had become aware of what was happening above their heads.

Once more assembled on the ground beneath the walls of the battery, the party was rapidly counted by Dick, to ascertain that all were present, save the man left above on the gun platform; and this formality having been quickly gone through, the unconscious sentinels were picked up and carried away to a distance of about a hundred yards from the battery, where they were effectually concealed in a thick clump of bushes, after which the Englishmen rapidly pushed forward up the hill. Arrived near the top, Dick halted them for a moment near a clump of bamboo, two long stout stalks of which were quickly cut down, and, without waiting to strip them of their leaves, converted into a light ladder by lashing cross-pieces of bamboo to them. Then, with this improvised ladder carried by two men, the party resumed its way, arriving about a quarter of an hour later beneath the frowning walls of the castle, which, like the battery below, was found to be in total darkness, at least so far as the face fronting them was concerned. They crossed the dry ditch without difficulty, and once on the other side, reared their ladder against the wall, finding it amply long enough for their purpose.

Here again Stukely took the lead, being the first to ascend the ladder. But as he reached the top and peered cautiously over the parapet he was disconcerted at the discovery that here at least the sentinels did not sleep; for the first object that met his gaze was a man standing at the extreme end of the parapet, apparently gazing steadfastly out to sea, while his crossed hands rested upon the muzzle of his grounded matchlock. Luckily for the English, the man's back was turned toward the spot where Stukely stood staring at him. In an instant the latter had made up his mind what to do, and, cautiously climbing in through the embrasure before him, stole noiselessly toward the unconscious man. A few breathless seconds and Stukely had crept close up behind his intended victim; and the next instant, as he knocked the man's hat off with one hand, he dealt him with the other a blow on the head with the heavy butt of his pistol, which felled the unfortunate fellow as a butcher fells an ox. Quickly bending over the prostrate body, he now held his unstopperd vial to the man's nostrils for three or four seconds, then rose cautiously to his feet. He could see no other sentinels posted anywhere on the parapet, but passed quickly round it in order to make quite sure. Then, finding that only the one sentinel had been posted here, he gave the signal for the rest of the party to ascend; and a few minutes later the scene of a short while before was being re-enacted on the parapet of this much more important structure. They worked silently but with strenuous haste, for although the heavens as yet gave no sign of the approaching dawn, the sudden comparative coolness of the atmosphere and the twitterings of a few early morning birds told them that it could not now be very far off; indeed they had scarcely finished their preparations when a faint brightening of the eastern horizon told them that a new day was at hand.

"Now, are we all ready?" asked Dick, as he personally put the last finishing touches to the preparations. "Then down you all go except the five men who are to help me with the firing of the quick matches. You go last, Phil, and when you are down ignite the portfire which is to be the signal to that man in the battery yonder; I and the five who are remaining with me will see to the rest of the business up here. Now, off you go quickly, for the daylight will be upon us in five minutes."

Dick watched his friend as the latter slid out through the embrasure and descended the ladder; and when at length Stukely reached the ground and was preparing to ignite the portfire, Chichester sprang back among the five men who were awaiting his word, and whispered "Now!" Instantly the six darted to their respective stations, and each man at once proceeded rapidly, yet with the nicest care, to ignite the five ends of quick match which were his especial care. It was swiftly done, the lighting of the whole occupying less than half a minute; yet before the last five were ignited the still air was heavily charged with the fumes of gunpowder and there was a sound of hissing and sizzling suggestive of a whole army of angry snakes.

"Smartly, men; smartly!" urged Dick; "the matches are burning much more rapidly than I anticipated; and if we are not pretty lively we shall be caught by the first explosions. That's your sort; that will do, Parsons, don't stand there fiddling with that match, it is burning all right. Now, lads, away you go; over with you; I go last."

Thus exhorted they stood not upon the order of their going, but went, Chichester bringing up the rear; and the latter was still in the very act of descending the ladder when six crashing explosions, occurring almost simultaneously on the parapet above, shattered the early morning stillness, the sounds being instantly followed by a great rush of wings and an outburst of startled screams that issued from the throats of the affrighted birds in the immediate neighbourhood of the castle, who, thus rudely awakened, dashed away in every direction, loudly proclaiming their terror. An answering explosion almost instantly roared out from the battery on the beach; then when half a dozen further explosions on the parapet pealed out, the little party of precipitately retreating Englishmen heard heavy thuds all round them as fragments of the burst ordnance came showering to the ground. And in between the shattering reports of bursting cannon which were now almost continuous they faintly caught the sounds of human outcry as the astounded garrison, awakened by the reports, sprang from their beds and rushed hither and thither in blind panic, each man demanding of every other an explanation of the extraordinary happenings that were taking place overhead. But long before the bravest of the Spaniards had summoned up courage enough to ascend to the parapet, and ascertain for himself the source of those terrific reports and crashing blows which were causing the castle to tremble to its very foundations, the last of the Englishmen—who happened to be Dick—had vanished over the brow of the hill and was racing down the steep slope toward the spot where the longboat had been left in hiding, urging those ahead of him to redoubled efforts, lest the Spaniards, rallying from their first surprise and panic, should sally forth and attempt to cut off the fugitives.

The disturbance was all over in less than a minute; the echo of the last explosion died away along the mangrove-bordered shore; the thud of the last falling piece of fractured ordnance, as it crashed through the boughs of the trees, had faintly reached the ears of the flying Englishmen; and the birds were rapidly beginning to persuade themselves that the whole thing had been no more than a peculiarly weird and startling dream, when the whole party—which had been joined on the way by the man from the lower battery—reached the boat and pulled up for a moment to listen and recover their breath. But there was neither sight nor sound of pursuit; and presently, after Dick had counted his party and found that all were present and perfectly sound, the order was given to get the boat afloat and shove off. This was done in a perfectly quiet and orderly manner; and five minutes later, with the beams of the rising sun brilliantly gilding her sails, the little craft slid down the harbour entrance on her way to seaward, passing close under the walls of the beach battery, the bewildered garrison of which had by this time summoned up the courage necessary to enable them to go up on the gun platform, to ascertain precisely what had happened. Most of them were gazing earnestly out to seaward as the longboat slid past, consequently they did not see her until it was too late, when, with loud outcries, they seized their calivers and poured a hot but absolutely ineffective fire after the bold adventurers. Two minutes later the boat swept round the low point which forms the southern extremity of Tierra Bomba Island; and then her occupants saw what it was that had so strongly attracted the attention of the Spaniards; for, scarcely three miles away, they beheld the *Adventure* beating up toward the Boca Chica under a heavy press of canvas. Bascomb had seen and interpreted aright the explosions in the two batteries on Tierra Bomba, and was now fearlessly working the ship in toward the land, knowing that, the guns in those two batteries having been destroyed, there was now nothing to restrain him from sailing right into Cartagena harbour itself and demanding the restoration of their Captain, safe and sound. And he meant to do it, too!

Chapter Six
How they took the great Galleon
and a vast Treasure

There was no enthusiasm, no cheering, nothing in the nature of hysterical exultation displayed by the crew of the *Adventure*, when the longboat ran alongside and those who had performed the audacious feat of rendering two powerful batteries innocuous rejoined their shipmates; everything was accepted as a matter of course. It was fully realised by all hands that the deed was one, the successful accomplishment of which required the display of nerve and courage of superlative character, but it was understood that the entire expedition, from start to finish, from its departure from Topsham to its return thither, demanded the constant exhibition of these same qualities—and would receive it. Therefore a murmur or two of approval and satisfaction from Bascomb, when Dick made his report, was all that was said in the way of commendation.

"And now, sirs," said the master, dismissing the topic of the disarmament of the batteries, "Cartagena and the galleon are at our mercy; and the sooner that the Spaniard can be brought to understand this, the better is it like to be for our general. Therefore we will enter the harbour forthwith, lay the galleon aboard and take her, and then open negotiations with the authorities for the ransom of the town and the deliverance of Captain Marshall. Mr Chichester, you know more about the harbour than any of the rest of us. It must be your duty, therefore, to pilot the ship alongside the galleon; the others I will ask to go straight to their fighting stations and prepare the ship for battle, after which, if there be time, we will take breakfast. If not—well, we must e'en fight fasting, and eat after the galleon is taken."

So Dick went up on the poop and, stationing himself to windward, conned the ship as she beat in toward the Boca Chica against the fast-failing land breeze. But, good ship as the *Adventure* was, her progress was exasperatingly slow, as was that of all ships of that date when they attempted to beat up against a foul wind; for neither the form of the hull nor the cut of the sails was at that day favourable to such a manoeuvre, and the ship was still a good mile from the harbour's mouth when the land breeze suddenly failed, and she was left helplessly wallowing upon the oily swell outside.

This, of course, was exasperating enough; for when deeds of desperate emprise are toward it is well to carry them through before the enthusiasm has time to cool. But it could not be helped, the wind was dead, and the ship could not be handled now until the sea breeze sprang up; and, after all, the delay was not an unmitigated misfortune, for it ensured to the crew time enough to complete their preparations for the coming fight and take breakfast afterward; and even at that day it was fully recognised that an Englishman fights best when his hunger has been satisfied. So they finished the work upon which they were engaged, and then went quietly to breakfast, which meal they were able to dispose of comfortably before a cry from the deck apprised them of the arrival of the sea breeze.

Yes; there it came, far away in the offing, ruling the horizon as a band of dark blue that grew lighter and lighter still along its landward edge, until it stopped short at a distance of about two miles from the shore, blowing fresh right up to a certain well-defined point, between which and the land all was gleaming, glassy swell, unruffled by even so much as a cat's-paw. But the boundary line which divided breeze from calm was not stationary by any means, on the contrary, it was creeping nearer rapidly. When Bascomb came up on the poop he merely glanced at it for a moment and then called to the seamen to trim the yards in readiness to meet it. By the time that this had been done the line of demarcation was so near that the musical tinkling of the advancing ripples could be distinctly heard, although the sails still hung limp, idly flapping to the roll of the ship. Another minute, however, sufficed, then with a gentle preliminary rustling the canvas filled, the blue ripples reached the ship, passed inshore of her, and she began to draw slowly through the water and her helm was put up to keep her away for the narrow harbour entrance.

"Starboard you may," said Dick to the helmsman, when the ship had presently fallen square off before the fast-freshening breeze; "we must shave that low point on the left quite closely, for that is where the channel runs, and there is a small shoal right in the mouth of the fairway which we must avoid. So! that will do; now, steady as you go. Mr Bascomb, you see that dark object just opening out over the southernmost end of Tierra Bomba? Well, that is the shore battery, and as it possesses certain small ordnance, such as falconets and swivels, which we could not spare the time to destroy, I would recommend that, as we must pass it close, the men be instructed to lie down behind the bulwarks as we sail by, lest haply any of them be hit; for I make no doubt that they will discharge at us every piece they have as we pass."

"Say you so?" returned Bascomb. "Then, by the Lord Harry, we will be beforehand with them. Ho, there! Load the larboard broadside of ordnance, great and small, and train your pieces to sweep the top of yonder battery as we pass. We cannot afford to risk the loss of any of our number through a mistaken sense of magnanimity."

With swelling sails distended by the ever-freshening sea breeze, the *Adventure* now swept boldly in for the mouth of the Boca Chica, and presently a curl of white water revealed the presence of the shoal of which Dick Chichester had spoken, right in the middle of the fairway. Dick directed the helmsman to steer to the north of this, between it and the island of Tierra Bomba, with its swelling wood-crowned heights. Dick glanced aloft at the castle which crowned the summit of the southernmost hill, but although the golden flag of Spain flaunted itself insolently in the breeze from the flagstaff on its northern turret, not a man was to be seen upon the parapet. Many of the embrasures, one-half of which they could now see, had been destroyed by the bursting of the ordnance, and it soon became clear that none of its garrison intended to make any effort to dispute the passage of the English ship. Whether the garrison of the battery down on the beach would be less prudent still remained to be seen, but one thing was perfectly clear, and that was that the Spanish soldiery were very busy upon the gun platform, their movements being directed by a tall man in a full suit of black armour, the helmet of which was surmounted by a splendid plume of long crimson feathers. The English, however, were not left long in doubt as to the intentions of this individual, who was, doubtless, the commander of the garrison; for as the ship swept along the narrow channel, hugging the northern shore closely, and every moment shortening the distance between the battery and herself, he was seen to draw his sword, which flashed like a white flame in the brilliant sunshine as he waved it above his head, and the next moment a perfect storm of bullets from falcon and falconet, patarero, saker, and swivel, came hurtling from the battery across the narrow water toward the ship. But the gallant cavalier had been just a trifle too eager to display his valour, for most of the missiles fell short, having been fired at rather too long a range, while those which hit were so nearly spent that only a few of them lodged in the solid woodwork of the ship's bulwarks, and not a man on board was hit.

"Now, men," roared Bascomb, "give yonder presumptuous fool a lesson; fire as your guns come to bear, and not before. I want that parapet swept clean!"

And swept clean it was, the English holding their fire and the ship sweeping on in grim, inexorable silence until she was within some two hundred feet of the structure, when all her larboard ordnance, great and small, bellowed and barked back its answer. As the smoke drove away ahead before the wind the wall was seen to crumble into dust under the impact of the heavy iron shot, while the lighter missiles mowed down the soldiers like corn beneath the sickle, until not a man was left standing upon his feet, even the magnifico in armour going down before the hail of iron and lead, to say nothing of the Spanish standard, the staff of which was cut clean in two, so that it toppled over and fell, carrying the flag with it, to the ground at the base of the wall.

"So much for thicky!" exclaimed Bascomb, relapsing into broad Devon for a moment, under the influence of excitement. "If it weren't that we have a long and hot morning's work before us I would anchor the ship, land a party, and blow their footy batteries into the air. But perhaps we may have time to do that when we come back this way. Now, my masters, load again, this time with double charges, consisting of a half-keg of bullets to each culverin, with a chain shot on top, and the smaller ordnance in proportion. We will not fire again, if we can help it, until we run alongside the galleon, and not then until we rub sides with her."

The ship had by this time traversed so much of the Boca that it became necessary for her to shift her helm in order to avoid grounding upon a sandspit that stretched athwart her course, and here the advantage and value of Dick Chichester's previous observations became apparent; for so sharp was the bend, and so little was there to indicate the existence of the shoal, that if Dick had not previously had the opportunity to note its position, the ship would undoubtedly have driven right upon it, under full sail, when she would certainly have been in an exceedingly awkward predicament, and might even have been lost, presuming the Spaniards to have been courageous enough to attack her while placed at so serious a disadvantage. But she was not allowed to get into any such awkward situation; for Dick had noticed everything connected with the dangers of the harbour, while looking out and watching from the summit of the hill on Tierra Bomba, and he carried a complete and perfectly accurate chart of the harbour in his head, in addition to the one which he and Marshall had made together. The helm was, therefore, shifted at the proper moment, and the ship swerved away in a south-easterly direction, making as though for the middle of the lower bay.

The danger did not reveal itself until the ship was actually slipping past it, and in less than five minutes she was clear and the course was again altered, this time to the north-eastward, where the island of Tierra Bomba, thrusting its north-easterly angle inward, divided the upper from the lower bay, narrowing the passage between to a width of less than a mile. Now the ship was fairly inside, and heading for a part of the harbour where Dick remembered to have observed certain other dangers in the shape of rocks and shoals, no sign of which could he perceive from the deck; he therefore mentioned the matter to Bascomb, and obtained that officer's permission to go aloft to the fore topsail-yard and con the ship from there.

In this fashion, then, the *Adventure*, with the red cross of Saint George flying defiantly from her main truck, swept up Cartagena harbour and, rounding the eastern extremity of Tierra Bomba, headed straight for the inner roadstead, where could now be seen, among a small forest of more insignificant masts, the towering spars of the great galleon, with a vast crimson flag bearing a coat of arms floating at her main, and the Spanish flag drooping from the ensign staff reared at her stern. The town being built on low land, the lofty masts of the galleon were at once seen, upon the English ship rounding the point and opening up the city, and a great cry of "There she is!" instantly leapt from every English throat.

"Ay; there she is, men," returned Bascomb. "We can't make any mistake about her, I think; and in halt an hour you shall be alongside her. The rest of the work will be for you to do. I'll tell you my plan, men. We will range up alongside her and lay her aboard, and just before our sides touch we will pour our broadside into her, throw the grapnels and hook on, and then dash aboard in the midst of the smoke and drive her crew below. The secret is to strike hard and often, and keep them on the run. If any man attempts to stand, though only for a moment, run him through at once with a pike. That is all that I have to say, men; you know how to do the trick as well as I."

With Cartagena city and the galleon in plain view, Dick Chichester's work aloft was done, and he, therefore, returned to the deck and the spot upon it from which he had previously been conning the ship, where he resumed his duty as pilot.

As the *Adventure* slid smoothly and rapidly up the harbour, heading straight for the galleon, it was seen that nearly twenty large boats, full of armed men, were pulling off to her from the shore. It was clear, therefore, that the authorities had received notice of the approach of the English, possibly from one or another of the officers in charge of the defences on Tierra Bomba, and, shrewdly guessing that one object, at least, of the unwelcome visit was the galleon, were determined to defend her to the last. But this discovery in nowise disconcerted the sturdy lads of Devon, who had long ago learned to regard themselves as invincible, so far as the Spaniards were concerned; so they continued with the utmost calmness to add here and there some refinement of finish to the preparations which had been completed an hour or more ago. Even the ship's cook, whom nobody regarded as a fighting man, must needs add his little quota to the general preparations, the same

taking the form of several gallons of greasy boiling water with which he had filled his coppers, the which he proposed to employ at such time as might seem to him most suitable. As for Dick, he decided that the handspike which he had used in the fight off Barbados had proved so effective that, regarded as a weapon, it could scarcely be improved upon, and he was on the point of providing himself with another when his eye chanced to fall upon a heavy iron bar which had been brought on deck for some purpose, so, having tested its weight, he at once decided that it was the very thing he needed, and appropriated it accordingly.

The *Adventure* had arrived within about half a mile of the galleon when the latter opened fire with her heavy ordnance, of which she carried two tiers. But whether it was that the Spaniards designed to shoot away the English ship's masts, and so leave her helpless and unmanageable, or whether it was that the pieces were badly aimed, every one of the shot went humming high overhead, leaving the intruder to pass on unscathed and in grim silence; for not one of her guns replied. But Bascomb stepped forward to the front of the poop and issued an order.

"Let every man of you," he said, "take bow or musket, and prepare to discharge a volley upon the deck of yonder galleon when I give the word. Then, that done, return to your ordnance and prepare to fire, for the time will be at hand. Sail trimmers, stand by to let fly all sheets and halliards at the word of command; then be ready to heave the grapnels as we range up alongside."

The English ship, still conned by Dick Chichester, was now steering a course which if persevered in would carry her across the stern of the galleon, at a distance of about twice her own length from that vessel; and it seemed evident, from the uncertain movements of those on board the Spaniard, that they were considerably puzzled as to the intentions of the English. For, having discharged the whole of her starboard broadside at the approaching *Adventure*, the crew of the galleon first began with feverish haste to reload all the guns on that side of their ship; then, seeming suddenly to suspect that their antagonist intended to lay them aboard on their inshore side, they left their starboard broadside only half-loaded and precipitately dashed across the deck to their larboard broadside of ordnance, which they began to clear away hurriedly with the intention of loading. The *Adventure* was at this moment less than twice her own length from the galleon, and Bascomb, standing on the poop, was able to look down from there into the crowded waist of the other ship and clearly see the Spaniards crowding together about the larboard ordnance. The opportunity seemed much too good to be let slip, so calling his bowmen and musketeers up on to the poop, he directed them to discharge a volley into the surging mass of men, which they did instantly, with terribly destructive effect.

"Good!" he exclaimed, as he saw some twenty or thirty Spaniards fall writhing to the deck; "now back to your ordnance, men, and be ready to fire when I give the word. Sail trimmers, let fly all sheets and halliards, and stand by with your grapnels!"

As the sailing master issued these orders Dick signed to the helmsman, who thereupon thrust the ponderous tiller hard down, and the *Adventure* answering her helm perfectly, swept round in a short curve and were gliding up on the starboard side of the galleon.

"Now, gunners all, let fly your ordnance!" roared Bascomb, drawing his sword. And as the bright blade flashed in the air the English artillery, loaded with round, bar, and chain shot, musket balls, spike nails, and every kind of missile that the men had been able to lay hands upon, were discharged when the two vessels were scarcely a fathom apart, and the Spanish ship's upper deck instantly became a shambles, scarcely a man remaining uninjured upon it.

"Throw your grapnels," shouted Bascomb, "and then let every man follow me aboard the Spaniard." As he spoke the *Adventure* crashed alongside the galleon, there was a sound of ripping and rending timber, and a heavy rebound; and then, as the two ships rolled toward each other after the rebound the English crew went swarming over their own bulwarks and down upon the Spanish deck, where they found scarcely half a dozen men to oppose them. But at the head of them stood a very magnificent looking personage in full armour, whom Bascomb took to be the captain of the ship.

"Do you surrender, señor?" demanded Bascomb, speaking in English for the very good reason that he "had" no Spanish.

It is probable that the Spaniard was as destitute of English as Master William Bascomb was of Spanish; but there is a language of intonation and gesture as well as of words, and doubtless that of the Englishman was intelligible enough, for the Spaniard, by way of reply, grasped his sword by the point and offered it to the sturdy Devonshire seaman who confronted him, and who accepted it with a very fair imitation of the bow with which the Spaniard had tendered it.

"That's well, so far," commented Bascomb. "Now"—looking about him and noticing Dick standing near, grasping his iron bar—"that ends the trouble up here. But what about down below, Mr Chichester? You had better take a dozen men and this gentleman down with you; and perhaps he will explain to those of his people who are on the main deck that he

has surrendered. If they will lay down their arms, well and good; if they won't—well, you will just have to make 'em, that's all. Now go; and report to me here when you've gained complete possession of the ship."

Dick took his dozen men and, insinuating his hand in the crook of the Spanish captain's arm, led that individual below to the main deck, where they found a few Spanish seamen still hanging about between the great culverins, apparently quite uncertain what to do, or whether they ought to do anything. The Spanish captain spoke sharply to them; apparently he was very much surprised and disappointed to find so few men there, and seemed to be asking them where the rest were, for by way of reply the seamen said something and pointed to the hatchways. The Spanish captain relieved his feelings by stamping on the deck, grinding his teeth, and indulging in a good deal of Castilian profanity; after which he seemed to give certain instructions, the result of which was that the men laid down their arms and went up on deck, one of their number having previously gone to the main hatchway and shouted something down it which caused the remainder of the crew to come up from below and surrender their weapons.

It took Dick and his party about half an hour to explore thoroughly the interior of the galleon—which they discovered was named the *Santa Margaretta*—and satisfy themselves that none of the Spanish crew were lurking below in hiding; and when at length they returned to the upper deck to report, they found that Bascomb and Winter had mustered the surviving Spaniards forward on the fore deck, under a strong guard, while the English had lowered one of the galleon's boats and in her had boarded and captured a small coasting felucca, which they were at that moment towing alongside their bigger prize. This, Bascomb explained, he had done with the object of getting rid of his Spanish prisoners, whom he proposed to send ashore in the felucca, having no fancy for keeping them aboard the prize, where they would need a strong body of the English to maintain an efficient guard over them. And, with the released prisoners, he proposed to send ashore a letter to the Governor of the city, demanding the immediate surrender of Captain Marshall, safe and sound, together with payment of the sum of five hundred thousand ducats ransom for the city, failure of either condition to be followed by the sack and destruction of the place.

"But," objected Dick, "you can neither speak nor write Spanish; and it may very well be that there will be nobody in Cartagena who understands English; in that case we shall be at a deadlock, and how will you manage then?"

"That," replied Bascomb, sententiously, "will be their lookout. If they cannot find anyone to translate my letter, so much the worse for them. But

there should be no trouble about that; for if they can find nobody else the captain will make my meaning clear to them."

It was considerably past midday when at length the whole of the Spaniards, together with their dead and wounded, were transferred to the felucca and dispatched to the shore, the Spanish captain being entrusted with the letter to the governor or commandant of the town; and then the English found time to look into their own affairs and take a meal. It was found that by a marvellous stroke of good fortune the galleon had been captured without the loss of a man, or even so much as a single casualty on the English side; and, this being the case, the question arose whether or not they should retain possession of the vessel, dividing the *Adventure's* crew equally between her and the prize. There arose quite a sharp difference of opinion on this point, Bascomb and the two gentlemen adventurers maintaining that the prize was far too valuable to be parted with or destroyed, now that they had her; while Winter and Dick contended that they were far too few in number to justify the proposed division, the effect of which would be to put them in possession of two perilously short-handed ships, instead of one fully manned. Moreover, the *Santa Margaretta* was nearly twice the size of the *Adventure*, the proposal therefore to divide the crew of the latter into two equal parts would hardly meet the case, since a crew of forty men could handle the galleon only in fine weather, while as to fighting her effectually in the event of their falling in with an enemy, it simply could not be done. Winter's proposal, in which Dick backed him up, was that everything of value—or at least as much of it as they could find room for— should be transferred to the *Adventure*, after which a ransom of, say, twenty thousand ducats could be demanded for the ship and what remained of her cargo, failing the payment of which she might be burnt at her anchors as a wholesome example! The dispute at length grew so warm that Stukely, who was present but took no part in it, suggested that the matter should be left for Captain Marshall to decide, upon his return.

The afternoon of that day was busily spent by the English, one party of whom, under the joint leadership of the carpenter and boatswain, devoted themselves to the task of repairing the slight damage sustained by the *Adventure* in running aboard the galleon, while the remainder engaged in the work of thoroughly rummaging the prize and transferring from her to the *Adventure* all the valuables they could find. At first some fear was entertained that the treasure which it was intended the ship should take home had not yet been put on board, for it could be found nowhere; but at length a sort of strong room was discovered, cunningly built in the run of the ship, its entrance hidden by a big pile of sails; and when this was entered, there, sure enough, lay the treasure, consisting of no less than five hundred

gold bricks, each weighing some forty pounds; two thousand bars of silver averaging about fifty pounds each, a chest of pearls the value of which was so great that they made no attempt even to estimate it approximately; and a small chest of uncut precious stones, chiefly emeralds and rubies, which of itself would have sufficed to make every man of them rich for life. The whole of this stupendous treasure they at once proceeded to transfer to the *Adventure*; and so much of it was there that, working watch and watch, one watch mounting guard to render impossible anything in the nature of a surprise attack from the shore, while the other watch carried the treasure from the one ship to the other, it was long past midnight when at length the work was done and the weary men were permitted to snatch a little rest.

The authorities ashore had been given until sunrise of the following morning in which to find someone capable of interpreting Bascomb's letter, and to come to a decision as to whether or not they would accede to the terms of the said letter; and the first light of dawn revealed a large boat putting off from the shore, pulled by twelve oarsmen, and flying a white flag at the stern. This was the first boat that had attempted to approach either of the ships since the appearance of the *Adventure* upon the scene, and her approach was watched with the utmost interest and curiosity. She carried three officials in brilliant uniforms and four other individuals in her stern-sheets, but it was Stukely's keen eyes which were the first to detect the fact that Captain Marshall was not in her; and his announcement of this fact at once raised a storm of indignation among those who had hastily turned out and gone on deck when the approach of the boat had been reported.

"Not in her?" incredulously repeated Bascomb—"Not in her? Then what a plague do the Dons mean by coming off to us at all? Surely I made it plain enough to them all that the surrender of our Captain was the very first article of our demand? Then what—?"

"Nay, nay; let be," interposed Winter, speaking quite calmly, but his lips white, and his eyes glowing sombrely like smouldering fires. "No need to work thyself into a passion, Will Bascomb, until thou hast heard what their lordships have to say. Maybe they have not seen the Captain and know naught of him."

"Not seen him? Know naught of him? Why—why—!" spluttered Bascomb. Then he suddenly calmed down. This was no time for disputatiousness or the display of warm feeling between himself and the man who, if haply anything had gone wrong with the Captain, might become the head of them all. Besides, there was wisdom in that suggestion to wait and hear what the Dons had to say before jumping to a conclusion. Thus the little group of Englishmen on the high poop of the *Adventure* lapsed into sudden silence as the boat drew near; but it was a silence that was ominous, menacing, a silence of set lips and burning eyes, pregnant with dire possibilities for the city and all within it if aught of evil had befallen their Captain therein. For not only was Marshall, rough almost to uncouthness of manner though he was at times, beloved by all there, but also there was the feeling stirring in every breast that it was vitally important to each one of them that the Spaniard must be taught, once and for all, to regard an Englishman's life as sacred, no matter what the circumstances might be under which he might fall into their hands, or however helpless and friendless he might at the moment seem. So it was a very grim-visaged, uncompromising-looking group of Englishmen at whom the newcomers stared upward when the boat arrived within easy hailing-distance and lay upon her oars.

An elderly man, attired in the usual mariner's costume of the period, rose in the stern-sheets of the boat and, doffing his cap, opened the conversation by remarking in English:

"Good morning, gentlemen! I am Gaspar Pacheco, lately a master of mariners, but now retired from the sea; and I am here to-day to act the part of interpreter between yourselves and the illustrious Señors Don Luis Maria Alfonso Calderon, Governor of the city of Cartagena; Don Ricardo Picador Garcia, Alcalde of Cartagena; Don Hermoso Morillo, our Intendant; Don Sebastian Campana; Don Ferdinand Miguel Pavia; and Don Ramon Sylva, merchants of Cartagena." And as each individual was named he rose in the stern-sheets of the boat, bowed deeply, and seated himself again.

"I am instructed by my illustrious fellow townsmen to inform you, señors, that although your cartel was handed to the Governor immediately upon the arrival of your messenger in the town, yesterday, it was not until very late in the day that anyone could be found possessed of a sufficient knowledge of your language to interpret it, the only person possessed of such knowledge being myself, who live not in Cartagena itself but in a small hacienda a few miles north of the city. Then, señors, when I had been found and conveyed to Cartagena, and had translated your letter to the authorities, a difficulty at once arose; for mention is therein made of one Capitan Marshall, who is said to have entered the city five days ago, and whose safe return you demand. Now, neither his Excellency the Governor nor Don Ricardo Garcia, our Alcalde, had ever before heard of such a person as el Capitan Marshall, or indeed of any other stranger, being in the city; and it at once became necessary, before anything else could be done, that enquiries should be set on foot to ascertain whether any such person had been seen, so that his whereabouts might be traced. Those enquiries, señors, were at once instituted, and are still being actively pursued; but we are regretfully obliged to confess that thus far they have been entirely without result. Meanwhile—"

"Stop!" interrupted Bascomb, throwing up his hand with an imperative gesture. "Do you mean to tell me that it is possible for a stranger—and that stranger an Englishman—to be four days and five nights in your city without anyone being the wiser?"

The interpreter shrugged his shoulders and spread his hands abroad deprecatingly.

"It would greatly depend upon the skill, courage, and resourcefulness of the stranger, señor," he answered. "If your Capitan Marshall speaks Spanish fluently, and possesses the knowledge of how to look and act like a Spaniard, it is quite possible that he might do so."

"But," objected Bascomb, "he could not well have been in your city yesterday and have remained in ignorance of what was happening. And I know him well enough to feel certain that were he alive, in good health, and free, he would have rejoined the ship ere now. That he has not done so is evidence conclusive and convincing to us all that something untoward has happened to him, for which we shall hold the entire population of your city, individually and collectively, responsible.

"Now," he continued, turning and addressing his companions on the deck, "that is speaking plainly enough for even a Spaniard to understand, isn't it? But since Captain Marshall's safety and well-being must be our first consideration, I think we ought not to make our conditions so hard as to be impossible of fulfilment; I therefore propose that we allow them a little more time in which to find him, before we proceed to extremities. Let us make it clear to them that he must be found and delivered up to us, safe and sound, within a certain time, say noon to-day; and that failure to comply with this demand will be followed by the bombardment and sack of the town. What say you, gentles?"

"Agreed!" came the answer, as with one voice, from all present.

"Very well, then," concluded Bascomb; and turning toward the boat, he hailed:

"Now, listen to me, Señor Interpreter, and mark well my words. It has come to the ears of us English that the Spaniards of the New World, in their selfish determination to retain in their own hands the whole of the trade of this rich country, are making a practice of seizing every Englishman upon whom they can lay hands, and delivering him over to your so-called Holy Inquisition in order that, while salving your own consciences with the plea of religious zeal, my countrymen may be subjected to fiendish tortures, and so be discouraged from attempting to secure a share of the immeasurable wealth which you enjoy. Now the time has come when your minds must be disabused of this notion. No amount of torture which you can possibly inflict upon solitary, helpless Englishmen will deter their fellow countrymen from striving, by fair means or foul, to secure a share of what they are as much entitled to as yourselves; and they will never rest until they have obtained it! Mark you that. And, further, remember this— that henceforward, for every Englishman who is lost on these shores, and is found to have perished under the hands of your Inquisitors, the English will take a terrible vengeance, exacting the lives of ten of the most distinguished Spaniards upon whom they can lay hands.

"Now, our Captain is somewhere in your city at this moment, and for your own sakes he must be found and brought on board this ship before noon. And when that is done we will talk further with you. But if by noon he is not found and delivered up to us, then I say to you that we will first bombard your town, and afterwards sack and destroy it, as a lesson to you and all Spaniards to beware henceforward how you meddle with Englishmen, even when they seem to be absolutely at your mercy. Now, translate that to the illustrious señors your companions."

The interpreter did so; and as he proceeded the varied emotions of indignation, horror, and fear that were evoked by Bascomb's plain speaking were easily enough discernible upon the countenances of his audience. They flushed and turned pale by turns, they wrung their hands, and once his Excellency the Governor started to his feet and shook his fist savagely at the little group on the *Adventure's* poop, but was instantly dragged down again by his comrades, who evidently feared the English more than they did him. When at length the interpreter had finished and the Governor burst into a torrent of apparently violent language, which he seemed to wish the interpreter to translate to the Englishmen, the others interposed with what appeared to be an emphatic veto. This was followed by a somewhat lengthy and very animated discussion among themselves, during which the boat was kept in place by an occasional stroke of the oars. At length a resolution of some sort seemed to be arrived at, for the alcalde was seen to speak earnestly to the interpreter, who presently rose to his feet and hailed.

"Illustrious señors," he said, "I am desired by Don Ricardo Garcia, our respected Alcalde, to say that every possible effort shall be made to find the missing Capitan; and when found he shall at once be restored to you. But, señors, the time you have allowed us is much too brief for an effective search to be made, and—"

"Did you not say that the search was begun yesterday, and is still being actively prosecuted?" interrupted Bascomb.

"Even so, illustrious General," answered the interpreter.

"Very well, then," retorted the master; "if he is in the city, and is alive and well, he will be found before noon. If he is not found, then it will be because some evil has befallen him, for which Cartagena shall be made to suffer. Look in your Inquisition for him, señor; he is as likely to be there as anywhere. And tell your Inquisitors that if he is not forthcoming by noon, the Inquisition shall be the first building to suffer from our shot. Now, go!"

So they went, with much shaking of heads and wringing of hands.

Chapter Seven
How they set out to rescue
Captain Marshall, and failed

The morning was passed strenuously by the English in preparing both the *Adventure* and her prize for the grim business of bombarding Cartagena, if need were; the hope in every man's heart being that the spectacle of the preparations—which was clearly visible from the water front of the town—would have the effect of breaking down the stubborn wills of the Spaniards, and constraining them to surrender their prisoner. For up to this moment there had never been any real doubt in the mind of any one of the Englishmen that Marshall had been discovered and made a prisoner; and they were steadfastly resolved to secure his freedom, let the cost be what it would.

After carefully considering and discussing the matter together, Bascomb and Winter arrived at the conclusion that it would be possible to effect such a division of the crew as would enable both ships to employ the whole of their heaviest ordnance against the town; and this was accordingly done, the *Adventure* being afterward moved to a berth astern of the galleon, so that neither ship should obstruct the fire of the other.

It wanted about a quarter of an hour of noon, and the preparations aboard both ships were complete, when the boat which had visited them in the morning was observed to be putting out again from the wharf and pulling toward the *Adventure*; but it was soon perceived that on this occasion she carried only one figure, which was presently seen to be that of the interpreter.

"The Captain is not there!" exclaimed Bascomb, when this was recognised. "Now, what a plague do they mean by sending off the boat without him? Are they going to beg for more time, I wonder? And, if so, why? For I will never believe but that they know where he is, but are determined to exhaust every artifice and subterfuge in the endeavour to avoid giving him up!"

The others said nothing, for what was the use of hazarding conjecture when they would soon know for certain? So they held their tongues and watched the approach of the boat with gloomy, louring glances. They were disappointed, and in a savage, dangerous mood, ready to plunge at a word into any desperate enterprise.

The boat ranged up alongside, and the oarsmen rested upon their oars as before.

"Hallo! the boat ahoy!" hailed Bascomb. "What does this mean, señor? Why have you not brought off our Captain? Are the people ashore aware that within five minutes the bombardment of the town will begin?"

"Alas! yes, most illustrious señors," answered the interpreter, "unless I should prove fortunate enough to be successful in the mission that has been entrusted to me—that of pleading with your excellencies for a further extension of time."

"Upon what grounds, señor?" demanded Bascomb. "I have already granted an extension of six hours—without result, it would appear. Why should I grant another moment?"

"Because, Excellency, it is now believed that a clue to the whereabouts of your Capitan has at last been found, and it is hoped that in the course of another hour or two his freedom may be obtained," answered the interpreter.

"Ah!" returned Bascomb, with a sigh of relief. "So our Captain has been found at last, has he? And where is he thought to be?"

"In the Inquisition, señor," answered the interpreter.

"The Inquisition!" interrupted Bascomb. "Odds bodikins! didn't I say so? And how long has he been there, friend?"

"If the clue which has been obtained proves to be a true one, your Capitan will have been there close upon four days," was the reply. "The man whom we believe to be he was noticed in a small posada four evenings ago, and the landlord of the house is of opinion that someone must have suspected and informed upon him, for during the evening four familiars of the Inquisition called at the house and, in spite of his violent resistance, took him and carried him away."

"They did, did they?" retorted Bascomb. "If I can lay my hand upon those four familiars I'll make them wish their hands had withered rather than that they had laid them upon an Englishman! But there seems to be a good deal of uncertainty even now about this story of yours, señor interpreter, and I think our best plan will be to take up and investigate the matter ourselves. What say you, gentles? Four days! Why, they will have had time to maim the man for life in those four days! But if they have—! Well, what say ye, my masters; shall us take a strong party of men, go ashore, make our way to their Inquisition, and see for ourselves whether or not Captain Marshall is there? And if he is there, and they have mis-used him, we shall be able to take vengeance upon the evildoers themselves instead of punishing a lot of innocent men and women by knocking their homes about their ears."

"I say that we ought to do as you propose, without a moment's unnecessary delay," replied Winter. "And I, too," answered each of the others present.

"Then it shall be done," answered Bascomb, determinedly. "My proposal, Mr Winter, is that we make equal division of our force; one-half under my leadership to go ashore and look for our Captain, while the other half under you remains aboard the *Adventure* to take care of her and the prize. Is that agreeable to your worship?"

"Yes," answered Winter; "it is as good a plan as we are like to devise, even though we were to cogitate for the rest of the day. It is true that I would have preferred to lead the landing-party, since if aught should happen to you we shall be left without a navigator."

"Nay, that you need not be," answered Bascomb, "for I will leave young Chichester with you, and he can be your navigator; he has been an apt pupil, and now knows as much about navigation as I do, so that difficulty is soon overcome. Hallo! the boat ahoy!" he continued, directing his conversation once more to the interpreter; "come aboard, señor, will you? We shall require your services anon."

"Have I your word, most illustrious, that no evil shall befall me if I put myself into your hands?" asked the man.

"You have," answered Bascomb. "You may trust yourself to us without fear; indeed you are like to be a great deal more safe with us than elsewhere during the next few hours."

"It is enough," returned the interpreter, and signed to the boatmen to put him alongside, climbing to the deck and stepping in through the gangway without fear when they had done so.

"Now then, Señor Pacheco," said Bascomb, when the Spaniard, peering about him curiously, had joined the party on the poop; "I am about to land a party and march it to the Inquisition, in order that I may ascertain for myself whether or not our Captain is within its walls. Whereabout is the place? Can it be seen from here?"

"Nay, most illustrious, it cannot, for it lies at the back, or northern extremity, of the western half of the town," answered Pacheco. "It lies in the direction of the western tower of the cathedral, but far beyond it."

"Um–m!" commented Bascomb; "then, after all, there would not have been much chance of reaching it with our guns. Is it a strong place? Shall we find it very difficult to force our way in?"

"I have never been inside—the saints be praised—so cannot tell you very much about it," answered Pacheco. "So far as the building itself is concerned, it is a strong place, being built entirely of stone, with high walls, which are said to be nowhere less than three feet thick. But the main entrance is guarded only by a pair of oaken doors—massive, no doubt, but probably fastened only with bolts of ordinary strength; for who would ever dream of attempting to break into the Inquisition? Heaven forgive me for affording information to these heretical English," he muttered under his breath in his native tongue; "but, indeed, if in their fury they should tear the place down, I for one should not be sorry!"

"Are there many troops in the town?" demanded Bascomb.

"About a hundred, illustrious señor," answered Pacheco. "Five hundred are on their way down from the interior, it having been intended to send them home in the galleon, but I have not heard that they have yet arrived."

"If they had arrived, do you think you would have heard of it?" demanded Bascomb.

"I might, señor; but, on the other hand, I might not," answered Pacheco. "If they had arrived and marched into the town openly, doubtless I and every other inhabitant of Cartagena would have been aware of the fact. But, señor, your question has given rise to a doubt in my mind, and I am now wondering whether, in view of your presence in the harbour and your threat to bombard the town, his Excellency the Governor may not have taken steps to have the expected troops intercepted and introduced into the town secretly during the dead of night. If you were to ask my advice, señor, I should recommend you not to trust overmuch to the fact that I have heard nothing of the arrival of those soldiers."

"See here, sirrah!" ejaculated Bascomb, suddenly rounding upon the man, "you are extraordinarily free and glib with your information. Now, are you a traitor to your own people, or is your information false and intended to mislead us?"

"Neither, señor, on my honour as a Spaniard," answered Pacheco. "The fact is," he continued in explanation, "that I have seen much of the English during my business as a seafarer, and have learned to like them, in spite of their overbearing ways and the fact that they are heretics. Moreover, señor, you are about to attack the Inquisition, and good Catholic though I am, it would not grieve me were you to take it and give it to the flames, for I like it not, and that's the truth, the saints forgive me!"

"Now, gentles," said Bascomb, "you have heard what Señor Pacheco has said about the troops, and if it be truth—as I doubt not it is—it behoves us to be careful how we thrust our noses into that city of Cartagena yonder. Yet go I must, and will; for it is not to be thought of that our Captain may be in their accursed Inquisition, perhaps suffering torments unimaginable, and we doing nothing to help him. Therefore, in view of the possibility of those troops having arrived, and having been secreted somewhere in the town, I think we must modify our plans a little, to the extent, that is to say, of making the landing-party as strong as we can at the expense of the party remaining behind. Now, Mr Winter, what is the smallest number of men that you would care to be left with?"

"If I am to defend the ship successfully in the event of a possible attack," said Winter, "I must have at least twenty men. I cannot do with less. Leave me twenty, and you may take all the rest, even including young Chichester, who is like to be a great deal more useful ashore than he would be with me."

"Very well," agreed Bascomb, "twenty be it; you can scarce do with less, for it is more than likely that, while we are busy ashore, they will endeavour to recover possession of the treasure. And now, Señor Pacheco, we shall need you as guide to show us the shortest way to the Inquisition. Art willing to do us that service?"

"I am, most illustrious," answered Pacheco; "but, with your favour, señor, it must be under at least seeming compulsion, for if it were known that I did such a thing save under the fear of instant death, I should never again be able to show my face in Cartagena. Therefore, most valiant Englishman, if I am to lead you, it must be with my hands bound and a pistol held to my head."

"Very well," answered Bascomb. "We will manage that for thee, old sea-horse, as natural as life, so that nobody seeing thee being driven along at the head of us shall guess but that thou'rt quaking in thy shoes at every step thou takest. Take charge of him, Dick; he is to be thy prisoner, remember. Bind his hands behind him so firmly that he cannot get away, and just tightly enough to leave a mark. Put a halter round his neck, and hold the end of it in thy hand, and threaten him with thy drawn pistol at every street corner. And now, gentles, to our preparations. Every man of the shore party shall go armed with hanger on hip, a pair of loaded pistols in his belt, a good bow in his hand, and a quiver full of arrows slung over his shoulder.

We muster on the main deck twenty minutes hence, and the pinnace, with the interpreter's boat, ought to be sufficient to carry us all from the ship to the wharf."

The first half-dozen men who were ready slid down the ship's side into the interpreter's boat so swiftly and silently that they took her astonished crew completely by surprise, and held them in subjection until the rest were ready; then Señor Pacheco, slung in a noose, was lowered down the ship's side, and roughly ordered into the stern-sheets by Dick, who followed him there and kept him in apparent awe with a drawn pistol. Within the twenty minutes all were ready and embarked in the two boats—the pinnace having been lowered in the interim, when they pushed off from the *Adventure*, the attenuated crew of which bade them Godspeed with a hearty cheer—and headed up the harbour toward the north-western half of the town.

The distance which they had to pull, in order to reach the wharf indicated by Pacheco, was about three-quarters of a mile, and as they neared the landing-place they perceived that a good many people had gathered, and were watching them curiously; but of soldiers there was not one to be seen, which Bascomb confessed he regarded as rather a bad sign, as the absence of any visible inclination to resist their landing seemed to him to point to the preparation of a trap somewhere on the road. He asked Pacheco what he thought about it.

"God forgive me! I know not what to think, most illustrious," answered that worthy. "But I like it not, for I think with you that the Governor would never permit you to land unresisted, had he not prepared a warm reception for you at some point where you will be at even greater disadvantage than you would be on the wharf. And yet I do not know how that could be either, for he has had no means of learning your destination, so how could he know where to set his trap? But, lest he should have guessed, I will lead you by the less direct way, for there are two roads by which it is possible to reach the Inquisition."

As the boats ranged up alongside the wharf, and the Englishmen mounted and formed up on the quay, the mob, which consisted of about two hundred wharf labourers, with a small sprinkling of half-breed women and fifty or sixty boys, gave back sullenly and scowlingly with a few low-muttered threats and an occasional hissing gibe of *hereticos*! But there was no attempt at violence except when some half-dozen boys began to throw stones. But the stringing of the Englishmen's bows, and the fitting of a few arrows to the strings, sent the mischievous young urchins to the right-about in double-quick time, and within a minute the landing had been accomplished and the march begun.

Pacheco, with his hands lashed behind him and a halter round his neck, the end of which was in Dick's hand, led the way, marching between Chichester and Stukely, the latter having come ashore in Bascomb's boat, bringing his case of instruments and a pocket case of drugs with him. The road lay, for a short distance, along the water front, and they had not been marching two minutes before they came to a wide and busy street which seemed to run right through the very heart of the town to its farther end.

"That," remarked Pacheco, "is the direct road to the Inquisition, and it is for your excellencies to decide whether you will choose it, or whether you will go on and take the longer and narrower road to the same place."

"Which road do you recommend, señor?" demanded Bascomb.

"Nay, most illustrious, it is not for me to recommend either," answered the Spaniard; "the responsibility is far too great for me—for if disaster were to overtake you after you had accepted my advice, I should be blamed for it. I can only repeat what I have already said, that this is the direct road to the Inquisition, and the road which the authorities will naturally expect you to take if they have any suspicion as to your destination."

"Then in that case," decided Bascomb, "we will take the other one. Forward!"

The march was thereupon resumed, the little band of Englishmen being followed, at a respectful distance, by a rapidly increasing mob which seemed, from its appearance, to be composed of all the ruffians and cut-throats of the city. But they did not offer to molest the invaders, beyond occasionally shouting insulting epithets at them, of which the English took no notice. The mob seemed simply to follow out of curiosity, and possibly with the hope of witnessing some interesting developments later on.

A quarter of a mile farther on they came to another street, not nearly so wide as the first—a street of lofty, more or less dilapidated houses, with narrow, cage-like balconies before the upstairs windows, and small cellars of shops on the ground floor. The street was paved with rough cobble stones, and sloped from each side toward the centre, through which ran a kennel or gutter encumbered with garbage and filth of every description, through which a foul stream of evil-smelling water wound its devious way. The street had apparently at one time been one of some pretensions, but had now fallen upon evil days and become the abode of a number of petty tradesmen, such as cobblers, sellers of fruit and cheap drinks, dealers in second-hand goods of every description, and riffraff generally. It swarmed with dirty, slatternly women, still dirtier half-naked children, lean and hungry-looking dogs, and lazy, hulking men with brass ear-rings in their ears, the rags of tawdry finery upon their bodies, and their sashes perfect batteries of murderous-looking knives. They were a villainous, scowling, criminal-looking lot of ruffians without exception, and low murmurs of anger and astonishment, not unmingled with dismay, passed from one to another when the English suddenly wheeled into the street.

They gradually seemed to acquire courage, however, as they noted the small number of the intruders, and the fact that the latter took no notice of them, and presently, when the mob which had followed the English from the wharf swung into the street and began to explain in response to the questions with which they were eagerly plied, many of the tenants and frequenters of the Calle de Santa Catalina joined the procession, which by this time numbered some three or four hundred and completely blocked up the narrow street in the rear of the English. It was becoming an ugly, dangerous-looking crowd, too, the kind of mob whose courage grows with the consciousness of increasing superiority in numbers, and it now began to flaunt its fearlessness before its admiring women folk by joining vociferously in the insulting epithets which were now being raucously yelled after the little band of strangers. The situation was becoming distinctly threatening, and Bascomb quietly dropped to the rear, for it was in that direction that trouble seemed to loom largest.

He had just joined the rearmost file when one boastful ruffian, egged on by the rest, suddenly ran out in front of the crowd and whipping a long, murderous-looking knife from his sash, hurled it with deadly aim at him. Luckily for the master, he caught the movement out of the corner of his eye, and wheeled round just in time to parry the flying missile with the blade of his sword.

"Halt!" he cried, "and extend yourselves across the street, facing outward!" And at the same instant he whipped a pistol from his belt, levelled it, and fired at the aggressor, who flung up his hands and, with a shriek, fell prostrate in the gutter, with the blood rapidly dyeing purple the dirty white of his shirt. A howl of execration and dismay from the Spaniards immediately followed this act of retaliation, knives were whipped from their sheaths, and for an instant it looked as though the mob were about to charge; but the business-like promptitude with which the English fitted their arrows to their bows, and drew the latter, quelled the courage of their assailants for the moment, who contented themselves by yelling execrations as they lifted the injured man and carried him into the nearest house. Then, satisfied with the effect of their demonstration, the English resumed their march; but the mob continued to hang tenaciously upon their skirts, like a pack of hungry wolves, and it became every moment increasingly evident that it would need but a little encouragement to induce them to attack in deadly earnest.

In this fashion the English proceeded for nearly half a mile when they perceived what appeared to be a square opening out before them; and a moment later, as they debouched into it, they saw that this square was full of soldiers, both cavalry and infantry.

"Back for your lives into the street; you will stand a better chance there!" yelled Stukely, halting and facing the little band who followed him. But it was too late; the street behind them had in some unaccountable fashion also filled with soldiers, and the retreat of the English was cut off. They were trapped as neatly and effectually as their enemies could possibly have desired.

"Did you know anything of this?" demanded Dick of the man who had led them thus far.

"On my soul, no, señor, as I hope for salvation!" fervently answered Pacheco, looking fearlessly into Chichester's eyes.

"I believe you," returned Dick, releasing his grasp upon the halter round the Spaniard's neck. "Go, and save yourself while it is possible. One of your own countrymen will doubtless free your hands; I have no time to do it. Go!"

"My thanks, señor; and may the Blessed Mother and the saints protect you!" And, bending forward, he went at a run, with his hands still bound behind him, toward the soldiers, who, seeing that he was an apparently escaped prisoner, opened out and allowed him to pass through their ranks.

At this moment an officer wearing a full suit of plate armour, and mounted on horseback, advanced, and, lifting the visor of his helmet, demanded, in fairly good English:

"Where is the officer in command of this force?"

"Here," answered Bascomb, pushing his way to the front.

The Spaniard bowed. Then, indicating with a wave of his hand the troops present, which must have numbered some eight hundred at least, he said with a smile:

"Señor, do you need any further argument than these to convince you of the desirability of surrendering at discretion?"

"*A buena querra*?" demanded Bascomb, who had picked up a phrase or two of Spanish during his conversations with Marshall.

"Certainly, señor, if, as I presume to be the case, you hold a commission from your queen."

"I hold no such commission, señor," answered Bascomb, who began to realise that he and his followers were in a very tight place.

"You hold no such commission, eh? Then, is one to assume that you are merely a band of ordinary, commonplace pirates, eh?" demanded the officer.

"You are at liberty to assume what you please," retorted Bascomb. "I repeat that I hold no commission, no authority save that which is conferred by my own sword. And I surrender *à buena querra*, or not at all."

"You surrender at discretion, or not at all, señor pirate. Which is it to be?" was the rejoinder.

"Not at all, then," answered Bascomb. "We will fight to the death, rather than surrender to perish in your hellish Inquisition!"

The Spaniard bowed, closed the visor of his helmet, and reined his horse back very slowly until he had returned to his place at the head of the regiment of cavalry which he commanded; while Bascomb, turning to his followers, shouted:

"Now, dogs of Devon, show these cowardly Spaniards a bit of your quality. Look to the troops, horse and foot, that they've brought against us, eight hundred of 'em to our forty; that's just twenty to one, twenty soldiers that each man of us must kill before we can get back to the ship. For that's where we're going; we can't take the town with all these soldiers against us. But let us get back to the ship and we'll tell 'em another story; all their soldiers and twice as many again won't save 'em from the heavy ordnance of the galleon and the *Adventure*; and half an hour's bombardment will make 'em glad enough to come to terms wi' us. Now, the one half of you charge back along, down the street; the other half will follow, retiring backward and facing the enemy. Now, have at 'em, my hearts, for here they come! Clear the way with your arrows first; and then give 'em the cold steel!"

While Bascomb had been delivering his pithy address, the officer in armour had also been haranguing his troops with much gesticulation and sword nourishing, which he had wound up with a command to charge, himself leading the attack upon the little band of English seamen wedged, so to speak, in the throat of the narrow street. At Bascomb's word to "Have at 'em" the half nearest the street faced quickly about, and the whole party fitted arrows to their bows, drew them to the head, and let fly, half of the arrows winging their way to rake the narrow street, while the other half whistled into the ranks of the soldiers in the square, who had just put spurs to their horses. The range was short, and the aim deadly, consequently every arrow found its mark, some of them indeed twice over, for there were at least a dozen of the cloth yard shafts that passed clean through the body of their first victim to find lodgment in the body of the second. As for Dick, he distinguished himself by sending an arrow neatly between the bars of the visor of the officer on horseback, who thereupon reeled out of his saddle, and crashed down upon the cobbled pavement of the square with a rattle like that of a whole cartload of spilled ironmongery, close to Chichester's feet, who thereupon dashed nimbly in and snatched up the splendid sword that flew from the fallen warrior's grasp. Some twenty soldiers fell to that first discharge; and so great was the dismay occasioned by their fall that their comrades, instead of continuing their charge and riding the Englishmen down, as they might easily have done, reined their horses sharply back upon their haunches, with the result that their comrades in the rear dashed headlong into them, and in an instant the whole of that part of the square which abutted upon the street became a confused medley of plunging, squealing, and fallen horses, and dead and wounded men.

Meanwhile, the other front of the English had been equally successful, their first discharge of arrows having been so deadly that the soldiers drawn up across the end of the street to cut off their retreat, had simply crumpled up and withered away, leaving the street open for the retirement of the English; and the latter had accordingly availed themselves of the opportunity to dash in, and, as they fondly believed, secure protection for their flanks. But although the soldiers had given way before that terrible discharge of arrows, they were by no means beaten; and presently an officer succeeded in rallying about twenty, whom he drew across the street in a double rank, with their matchlocks unslung. Bascomb, however, was quick to see the danger.

"Don't let 'em bring their ordnance into use, or it will be all up with us," he shouted. "Keep 'em moving, lads, keep 'em moving; so long as we does that we'm so good as they be—and better; but once let 'em bring their firearms into play, and we'm done. So, keep 'em moving." And he himself set the example by rushing upon the enemy, sword in hand, and laying about him so shrewdly that the Spanish line was once more broken and forced into full retreat.

And indeed what could the heavily accoutred Spanish soldiers, tightly strapped up in a suffocatingly hot uniform, do against the nimble English, who, for the most part, fought in shirt, breeches, and shoes only, whose arrows flew with such irresistible force that they pierced right through a man's body, flesh, muscle, bones, and all, and who seemed to be governed by no laws of fighting, but instead of observing all the niceties, the rules, and the punctilio of fence, simply rushed in and cut a man down before the poor wretch could guess what they would be at!

For ten minutes the fight raged with unimaginable fury before a single Englishman was hit; and then one poor fellow dropped, with a long knife quivering in his skull, flung from an upper window of one of the houses. The man who did the dastardly deed was seen to withdraw hurriedly from the window; but it was enough; half a dozen of the fallen man's comrades instantly dashed into the house, were gone about half a minute, and then returned with a perfectly satisfied look upon their faces, and once more plunged into the mêlée. No more knives were thrown from that house; but unfortunately the deed, and not the swift retribution which followed, had been seen and thought worthy of imitation, and within five minutes there was scarcely a window within range of the fighting which was not vomiting missiles of one sort or another, with disastrous effect upon the English, who, under this new form of attack, began to fall thick and fast. For now that the populace had the support of several hundred soldiers, their courage became so reckless that they could no longer restrain themselves; and they accordingly engaged in the attack upon the English with avidity—from the comparatively safe position of the upstairs windows of the houses on either side of the street. Stukely and Dick were with the rearguard, making a vigorous and successful stand against the attack of the soldiery, when this new feature in the fighting was introduced, and they knew nothing about it until a great stone, hurled from the attic window of the house in front of which they were fighting, crashed down fair upon young Chichester's head and sent him reeling senseless to the ground.

Chapter Eight
How Phil and Dick escaped from Cartagena

When Dick recovered consciousness it was evening; the street was quiet, and he was lying upon a couch in a darkened room, with Philip Stukely and an elderly woman bending over him; the woman holding a basin of warm water, while Stukely assiduously bathed an ugly scalp wound on the crown of his head. The said head was throbbing and aching most atrociously, and when the young man sat up and attempted to rise to his feet he discovered, to his astonishment and chagrin, that he had no control over himself, the room seemed to be whirling and spinning round with him at bewildering speed, and his legs immediately collapsed under him.

"Now, then, none of that, youngster," exclaimed Stukely, as he flung his arm round Chichester and gently lowered the lad back on the couch. "What a plague induced you to start up like that, all of a sudden, before I was ready for you? You will just have to lie still, young man, until I tell you that you may move. And how do you feel, now that you have seen fit to at last come to your senses?"

"How do I feel?" reiterated Dick, trying to pass his hand over his forehead, and failing, for the member seemed heavier than lead. "Why, I seem to have no more strength than a baby; my head is nothing but one big, atrocious ache; and I don't seem to be able to remember things very well. For instance, I don't in the least know where we are, or how we got here; and—and—who is the—ah—lady, Phil?"

"Don't you worry about the lady, youngster, she is all right, and proved herself to be a friend just when we badly needed one," answered Stukely. "The important thing just now is to find out precisely what is the matter with you; so have the goodness to answer my questions as clearly as possible, will ye?"

And while Stukely is closely questioning his patient the opportunity may be taken to explain, in a very few words, how the two friends came to find themselves where they were. As has already been stated, they were fighting among the party who were defending the rear during the retreat of the English back along the street by which they had come, when Dick was felled to the ground by a great stone hurled from the top story of one of the houses opposite which they were at the moment engaged. Stukely, who was fighting behind him, heard the crash of the stone on Dick's head, saw the lad reel and fall, and instantly stooped to raise him to his feet again. But Dick Chichester was no light weight for a man like Stukely to lift unaided, and before it could be done the whole fight seemed to sweep right over them. Stukely was knocked down and trodden under foot, men locked together in the grip of deadly strife reeled and staggered and stumbled over him, and finally he received a kick in the temple which so nearly robbed him of his senses that he was only very vaguely conscious of what was happening during the next minute or two. The next thing of which he was fully aware being that he was being held by the shoulders and dragged along over uneven ground, then he became suddenly conscious of being inside a building, and of hearing a door closed and barred; and, finally, of finding himself sitting upon the floor of the room where Dick and he now were, with the old lady supporting his head on her knee while a young woman endeavoured to pour *aguardiente* down his throat. Then he fully recovered his senses, to find, to his great joy, that Dick also had been rescued, and was then lying senseless on a couch in the same room. Then, somehow, the young woman had disappeared, and rising to his feet, he had devoted himself to the task of wooing back Dick Chichester's senses. This, however, had proved a far more difficult task than he had at first anticipated; and it was not until the golden quality of the light streaming in through the closed jalousies proclaimed the near approach of sunset that Dick manifested any indication of returning consciousness, with the result already recorded. And now a protracted and careful examination of the wound, coupled with much questioning of his patient, convinced Stukely that his friend Dick had sustained a very serious injury to the head which had so far affected the brain that it would be several days at least before the young man could possibly be moved! Meanwhile, what was happening to the ship and the rest of the crew?

That was a question that could not be answered just then, for the old lady, who, for some mysterious reason, had chosen to play the part of Good Samaritan, could not speak a word of English, while Stukely spoke no Spanish; and as for venturing outside the house in quest of information, that was obviously impossible, for two excellent reasons; the first being that Dick's condition was such that he could not possibly be left, even for so short a time as half an hour; while the other equally good reason was that to venture into the street would be to invite immediate assassination.

Well, Stukely told himself, matters could not be helped; Dick and he were the victims of circumstance, and there was nothing for it but to submit, with the best grace possible. And so far as their future was concerned, that must take care of itself. Sufficient unto the day is the anxiety thereof. So, with the elderly dame's assistance, he devoted himself to the task of doing what he could to relieve and help Dick, philosophically leaving the future to take care of itself.

Presently it became too dark to see, and the old lady went to the door of the room and called. Two female voices replied; and a few minutes later two young women entered, one bearing a lighted oil lamp, while the other carried a tray upon which were set out a bowl of soup, a dish containing some roast ribs of kid, some heads of young Indian corn boiled, a loaf of bread, and a flask of wine. These viands were placed upon a table together with the lamp, and the young women retired again, after indicating by signs that the food was intended for the two Englishmen.

Dick's hurt proved to be very much more serious than was at first supposed; he became delirious; and for a whole week Phil was kept busy, night and day, constantly attending to him, his watch being shared by the old lady and her two daughters, who proved extraordinarily kind and solicitous. Then the patient began to mend, slowly; and the young women—who proved to be twins, named respectively Clara and Dolores— did their best to beguile the time for their two guests by teaching them Spanish. And remarkably efficient teachers they proved to be, too; their pupils making enough progress within the next three weeks to enable them to gather a tolerably correct general idea of what was said to them. Thus, little by little, and by dint of frequent reiteration, accompanied by much laughter and many blushes on the part of their fair instructresses, the two young Englishmen learned that they owed their lives to the compassion of the Señoritas Clara and Dolores; who, watching the fight from their window, had been so greatly impressed by the gallant bearings of Dick and Phil, that when the two were seen to go down in the mêlée, the girls, moved by a common impulse, had dashed out of the house, the moment that a favourable opportunity had presented itself, and had dragged the apparently inanimate bodies indoors unnoticed in the prevailing confusion. And they also learned that, according to common report, some eight or ten survivors of the ill-advised landing-party had succeeded in fighting their way back to the ship, which had thereupon got under way and sailed out of the harbour, leaving the *Santa Margaretta* ablaze from stem to stern.

Thus the time went on until Dick and Phil had been secreted in Cartagena nearly six weeks, by which time the former was so nearly approaching convalescence that the pair had begun to discuss seriously the question of their future. Then, one night, about nine o'clock, the two girls, who had been out taking the air upon the alameda, came rushing home in consternation with the news that somebody had somehow acquired an inkling of the fact that they were harbouring two Englishmen in their house, and that the soldiers might be expected to arrive at any moment to take the whole party prisoners! But, as the girls breathlessly explained, if the Englishmen got away at once—as they must for their own sakes—no harm need be expected to befall their hostesses, as it would then appear that some enemy had been spreading a false and malicious report.

The two young Englishmen hardly liked the idea of going off and leaving their kind entertainers to bear unaided the brunt of a strict and severe cross-examination; but it was obviously the only thing to be done, for it would be far worse for the family if the hated *Ingleses* were actually found in the house, than if their recent presence there were only suspected; they therefore agreed to go at once; and, since they had no belongings to pack, were ready to depart upon the instant. But the girls, who were bitterly distressed at the idea of so sudden and unceremonious a leave-taking, would not let them leave the house alone, to take their chance of finding their way, unmolested, down to the harbour; they insisted upon accompanying them and guiding them by the least-frequented ways; and this they did, following a number of narrow, winding, deserted lanes and alleys which at length brought them out upon the wharf where they had landed on the ill-fated day when they had attempted the rescue of Captain Marshall. Here, after a long, lingering, and tearful parting on the part of the girls, the two young men eventually found themselves alone, about half-past ten o'clock at night; by which hour the wharf was deserted, save for themselves.

Now, the whole thing had been so hurried, and the girls had had so much to say during the journey from the house to the wharf, that the two friends had been quite unable to form anything in the nature of a plan; and even now it was not wise to linger on the wharf, discussing the question of what they should do, for the city guard, or watchmen, might come along at any moment and surprise them. They therefore hastily surveyed such boats and canoes as were moored to the wharf, chose the first useful-looking craft they came to, jumped into her, cut her painter, and pushed off down the harbour on their way to the island of Tierra Bomba, which Dick decided had better be their first halting-place.

The night was, fortunately, fine, with a high and spacious sky of indigo, star-studded, flecked with a few thin, fleecy clouds driving up solemnly out of the eastward, and the moon, in her second quarter, sailing high overhead and affording them all the light that they needed, with perhaps a little to spare. The boat which they had appropriated was a very good craft of her kind, about fifteen feet long, very shallow and beamy, and equipped with a pair of oars, a tiller and rudder, and a mast and sail. The latter they were especially thankful for, as the journey before them was one of about seven miles; and as soon as they were fairly clear of the town and had reached a point at which they could bear away far enough to the southward to permit of setting the sail, they stepped their mast, unfurled their canvas, and went buzzing merrily down the harbour, passing on their way the hulk of the *Santa Margaretta*, which had been burnt to the water's edge before the flames could be extinguished. Their destination was the creek in the eastern shore of Tierra Bomba in which the longboat had lain hidden when Dick and Marshall had reconnoitred the town together; and they reached it about midnight, secreted the boat beneath the well-remembered bushes, and then composed themselves to sleep as well as they could in her stern-sheets.

The sun was a full hour above the horizon when his beams, piercing the thick canopy of foliage which overhung their place of concealment, awakened the two fugitives, who arose from their hard couch refreshed but hungry. A plunge into the shallow waters of the creek washed the lingering remains of sleep out of their eyes, and further refreshed them, when, having allowed their bodies to dry in the brisk warm breeze, they dressed and scrambled ashore to hunt for food. Of this they obtained without difficulty as much as they required; for Tierra Bomba was at that time densely overgrown with trees and bushes of various kinds, among which several fruit-bearing varieties flourished wild, particularly plantains and bananas. Upon these, then, they satisfied their hunger, at the same time taking the precaution to secure a bunch of sufficiently generous dimensions to meet all their needs for several days to come. Then, their immediate wants satisfied, they retreated to their place of concealment and, seating themselves in their boat, proceeded to discuss their plans for the future.

The information respecting the doings of the *Adventure*, communicated to them by their fair friends the Señoritas Clara and Dolores, left little doubt in their minds that the crew, thoroughly discouraged at the disastrous result of their adventure in Cartagena, had decided to rest satisfied with the treasure which they had already acquired—and which, indeed, was considerable enough to satisfy most reasonable people—and had sailed direct for England upon quitting the harbour, too hastily concluding, perhaps, that all the missing were dead; or, if not dead, at least captive beyond all hope of deliverance. This assumption seemed to Stukely and Chichester to be the only one at which they could reasonably arrive; and since its acceptance shut them out from all hope of ever again seeing the *Adventure* and being able to rejoin her, the question that naturally arose in their minds was: What were they to do now?

It was Dick who first put this question into words; and by way of reply Stukely put another question—"Why did we come here at all?"

"Well," retorted plain, matter-of-fact Dick, "because we couldn't help ourselves, I suppose."

"Very well," agreed Stukely, "I will concede that, if you like. We came because we could not help ourselves; because, in other words, after we were picked up by the *Adventure*, no opportunity occurred to land us again, and therefore we had no choice but to remain in the ship. But why did we consent to become members of her crew?"

"Why, in the hope of making our fortunes, of course," returned Dick. "And we did so, too; or should have done so, rather, if thicky stone had not cracked my skull for me."

"Precisely," agreed Stukely. "If your skull had not been cracked, and if we had both contrived to get back to the ship, as some of the others appear to have done. But it is just those little ifs, my dear Dick, that rule the destinies of men. If this, that, or the other thing had, or had not, happened, everything would have been very different. Now, for my own part, I am a great believer in destiny; I do not believe that there is such a thing as accident or chance, but that what we usually call by one or the other of those names is ordered by what some men call Fate, but what I prefer to call Providence. I will not attempt to argue this matter out with you just now, but will simply content myself with the assertion that you and I were destined to be left behind. If you ask, for what purpose, I reply that I do not know; I cannot even guess; but I have no doubt that it will be revealed in due time. If my theory is correct and Providence is indeed interfering in our affairs, we may do as we will, but we shall be guided and governed, in spite of ourselves, until we have accomplished the work which we are destined to do. That being the case, let us leave ourselves in the hands of Destiny, to do as she will with us, watching for such right impulses as she may impart to us, and following them implicitly, under the belief and conviction that she is guiding us.

"Now, why did we come to this Golden West? Was it not to make our fortunes, to acquire a share of the wealth with which the land teems? Of course it was; and since we are here, and cannot get away, I say let us push into the interior and see if we cannot find for ourselves some of the gold, or gems, with which the soil is said to abound. There must be scores, nay, hundreds, of undiscovered mines in the lonely fastnesses to which no man has thus far penetrated; and I can see no reason why we should not find one of them. Now, what say you?"

"Simply, that I agree with every word you have said, Phil, and am quite ready to go to the world's end with you," answered Dick. "Now, when do we start, and which way do we go?"

"Well," returned Stukely, "our first business is to get safely away from Cartagena; and the sooner the better. For it is evident that the authorities have somehow obtained an inkling of the fact that two Englishmen belonging to the band who have wrought them so much damage have been lurking hidden in the city; and if my estimate of the Spanish character be correct I believe they will take a good deal of trouble to find us; and if they find us we may rest assured that they will clap us into the Inquisition, by hook or by crook. Therefore, I say, let us get away to-night, immediately after dark, so that we may have a chance to put as many miles as possible between ourselves and Cartagena before daylight. Then, as to which way we should go, the interior is where we are bound for, and the interior lies to the southward, therefore when we get out to sea, let us steer south, and enter the first river of any importance that we happen to come to, knowing that all rivers lead to the interior."

"Agreed!" exclaimed Dick. "We will leave here as soon as the darkness is deep enough to conceal our movements; and we will begin our voyage by slipping across the bay and going out to sea by way of the channel at the back of the island of Baru, by which means we shall reach the open sea some twenty-five miles south of Cartagena, and so avoid the risk of being seen and informed upon by any of the local fishing boats. I would that I had one of Mr Bascomb's charts with me; but as I haven't we must e'en do without it and trust to memory. I have some recollection of having seen a river of some importance marked on the chart not very far south of this; and if we hug the shore pretty closely we can scarcely fail to find it."

This matter settled, they proceeded to take stock of their possessions, which totalled as follows: a pair of pistols each, the locks of which had fortunately been fitted with new flints immediately before the disastrous attempt to force a way to the Inquisition at Cartagena; two powder horns full of powder; thirty bullets each, together with a considerable quantity of greased rags to serve as wadding; a good, serviceable hanger, each; and last, but not least, the splendid sword which Dick had taken from the Spanish cavalier during the fight in the square. These, the clothes which they stood up in, and the boat in which they had made their escape, were all that they possessed in the world; and thus scantily provided these two young men were calmly about to plunge into the very heart of a hostile country, of which they knew nothing, in search of fortune! Truly was it said of these men and their contemporaries that "they feared God and naught else!" and it was they who laid the foundations of that greatness among the nations of the world which Britain enjoys to-day. May she have the wisdom to retain it!

All day the two fugitives lay in their place of concealment, resting and otherwise preparing for a wakeful and busy night; and when at length the sun plunged down into the western sea in a transient blaze of glory, and the sea breeze began to die away, they cautiously pushed out from underneath their leafy screen and proceeded to paddle quietly down the little cove toward the south bay, which they reached just as the last of the daylight was fading out of the sky and the stars were beginning to twinkle out, one after the other, in swift succession, in the great purple dome of heaven above. The evanescent twilight now shrouded everything in mystery; a few boats could be seen moving about here and there, but only by the lingering golden light in the western sky reflected gleamingly from the ripple of bow or paddle, and the fugitives passed across the bay and entered the narrow channel between the island of Baru and the main, just as the first soft breathings of the land wind began to make themselves felt. To these they gladly spread their sail—for paddling was rather too warm work to be agreeable—and went gliding easily and pleasantly along, closely hugging the weather shore, for the sake of the smooth water and the deep shadow afforded by the mangroves that thickly lined the beach.

They had reached thus along the shore for about an hour and a half when a sudden brightening of the sky to the eastward heralded the rising of the moon; and presently the orb, now nearly at the full, sailed up over the tops of the trees which lined the shore, and flooded the entire scene with her soft orange radiance. And the first thing upon which the eyes of the fugitives fell was a large galley lying at anchor right in the middle of the fairway, scarcely a mile ahead. There were no lights visible on board her; but the frequent flash of the moonlight upon polished steel showed that someone at least, probably a sentinel, was moving and presumably on the watch on board her.

Now arose the question: What was to be done? Should they stand boldly on and take the risk of being challenged; or should they run the boat ashore and take to the woods? Everything depended upon the question of what was the galley's business just there, of all places in the world; and it did not take the Englishmen long to make up their minds that in all probability she had been stationed there to keep a lookout for them, as the passage out at the back of Baru was so obviously the one that would be most likely to be taken by people anxious to escape from Cartagena by water. If that were the case they could not possibly hope to slip past the craft unchallenged, for the moon was every moment soaring higher into the sky and more clearly lighting up the scene, and especially the surface of the water. And if they were challenged and, refusing to reply, attempted to escape, what hope of success had they? Absolutely none! Therefore they put down their helm, hove the boat about, and headed in for the land.

If any doubt remained in their minds as to the character and intentions of the galley, it was speedily dissipated, for they had scarcely got their boat round upon the other tack when a musket was discharged on board the craft, and a hail was faintly heard pealing across the water from her, and some two minutes later a ruddy flash succeeded by a puff of smoke leapt from her forecastle, followed, a second or two later, by the splash of a heavy shot in the water a dozen yards or so astern of the boat. Five breathless minutes followed for the fugitives, and then a whole forest of oars suddenly sprang from the galley's sides, plunged into the water, and she was under way, heading straight after the boat.

"Shall we do it, Dick, think you?" demanded Stukely, as he peered anxiously under the foot of the sail.

"Yes," answered Dick, "if the wind holds. Blow, good breezes, blow!" he murmured, and began to whistle softly. Suddenly he sat more upright in the boat and gazed eagerly ahead.

"Look ahead and all along past our weather bow, Phil," he said. "Is my sight deceiving me, or do I see a number of water channels running into the land there? To me it looks as though there was an indentation of some sort, like—well, like the mouth of a river choked with islands, away ahead of us. And, if so, we are saved, for it will be strange indeed if we cannot dodge the galley among those islands—even if she can get in among them," he added. "For unless I am very greatly mistaken the water shoals close inshore of us. Do you notice how smooth it is?"

"I do," said Stukely. "I humbly hope it may not be too shoal for us as well as for the galley. All right, fire away," he continued, apostrophising the galley; "fire away and waste your powder! You will have to shoot a good deal better than that to hit us." For the people in the galley were loading and firing in feverish haste, evidently anxious to hit the boat before she should reach the shelter of the islands, now less than a quarter of a mile ahead.

Presently the boat shot into the belt of smooth water that Dick's keen eye had detected, and Phil seized a paddle and plunged it over the side, to withdraw it a moment later and inspect it by the light of the moon.

"Four foot of water, with any quantity of soft black mud under it," he announced. "If thicky galley keeps as she is going for another five minutes, Dick, she'll be stuck so hard and fast in that same mud that she'll have something else to think about than chasing us. Ah!" as the boat luffed round a small mangrove-covered island, and the galley was shut out from view, "there goes their last chance of hitting us with their footy ordnance—with a murrain on them!"

The fugitives now suddenly found themselves sailing through a labyrinth of small, mangrove-covered islets intersected by water lanes so narrow and winding that they were only able to sail the boat along them by exercising the utmost care and vigilance. This intricate and difficult navigation continued for nearly three hours, at the end of which time they suddenly emerged from the maze of islets and found themselves in a stream of thick, muddy water, averaging about a quarter of a mile in width, with low banks fringed by mangrove trees, beyond which it was occasionally possible to catch glimpses of more lofty vegetation. The water here was so deep that, except when close to the bank on either side, it was impossible to reach bottom with a six-foot paddle; but when they had traversed the river far enough to enable them to get a vista of a clear mile astern of them there was still no sign of the galley, which they therefore concluded had been unable to pass the mud bar at the entrance of the river.

The course of the stream which they were now following was, approximately, north-north-east, for a distance of about twenty-two miles, which was traversed in a trifle over four hours. Here the river suddenly bent sharply round in a south-easterly direction; the mangroves disappeared, being replaced by a thick fringe of reeds, the banks of the river gradually increased in height, and were covered to the water's edge with a thick tangle of bushes, amid which towered the outposts of a forest of magnificent trees that could be seen stretching away for miles ahead. The fugitives considered that they were now well beyond all likelihood of pursuit, and the thick beds of reeds which fringed the river at frequent intervals afforded them excellent opportunities for concealment; but the wind continued favourable, and the moon afforded them ample light; they therefore determined to press forward so long as the conditions continued favourable, one of them remaining on watch and steering the boat while the other slept.

In this fashion they sped up the stream hour after hour, all through the night, the width of the waterway remaining about the same, but the character of the country ever-changing, the banks in places rising to a height of quite a hundred feet, here in the form of a gentle, tree-clad slope, and there towering precipitously, a rocky face, with overhanging bushes and great clumps of fern springing from every fissure. At length the moon sank beneath the tree-tops on the western bank, and the light became so uncertain that the voyagers were seriously debating the advisability of seeking a suitable spot in which to tie up the boat, when a sudden chilliness in the wind warned them that the dawn was at hand, and a few minutes later the sky to the eastward paled, so that the tops of the trees stood out against the pallor black as though drawn in Indian ink, the stars dimmed and blinked out, one after another, the eastern pallor became suffused with delicate primrose that rapidly warmed into clear amber, a beam of golden light flashed through the branches of the trees on the eastern bank of the river, and in a moment the whole scene changed as if by magic, a thousand lovely tints of green, blue, orange, crimson, and white, leapt into view as daylight flooded the landscape, revealing great masses of flowering shrubs and enormous festoons of queer-shaped and gorgeously coloured orchids; colibris that flashed like living gems darted hither and thither; flocks of gaily plumaged parrots winged their way, screaming discordantly, across the stream; brilliantly painted kingfishers darted like streams of living fire from bough to bough, or perched staring intently down into the water from some overhanging branch; enormous butterflies of exquisite colours, and dragon-flies with transparent rose-tinted wings flitted inconsequently over the surface of the water and were leaped at by fish as brilliantly tinted as themselves—and it was day in the South American forest. Half an hour later, as the boat rounded a low bluff, a break in the forest appeared ahead, beyond which a wide expanse of water was seen sparkling in the rays of the early morning sun; and presently the boat shot out of the stream which she had been traversing all night, and the wanderers found themselves floating upon the bosom of a magnificent river about a mile wide, flowing as nearly as might be due north.

For a few seconds the young Englishmen were silent, lost in admiration at the spaciousness, the grandeur, and the tropical luxuriance and beauty of the scene upon which their gaze rested entranced; then Dick broke the silence by murmuring:

"Now, what river is this, I wonder? Surely it cannot be the Magdalena, of which we have heard so many wonderful stories? And yet, if it is not, I know not what river it can be. The Magdalena lies somewhere in this direction, I believe, and—but what matters the name? It is a superb waterway, however it may be called, the current is not so strong but that we can easily stem it with the help of our sail, and it comes from the direction in which we want to go. What say you, Phil? Which is it to be, north or south?"

"South, of course," answered Stukely; "why ask such a totally unnecessary question?" He spoke with so much irritation of manner that Dick looked at him anxiously, fearing that he might be suffering from a slight touch of fever. But no, there was nothing in Stukely's appearance to suggest that he was suffering either from fever or any other malady; but he was glancing about him keenly, eagerly, yet with a puzzled expression, as though he recognised what he was looking at, but could not understand why he recognised it. And his next words conveyed precisely the same impression, for he murmured, as though speaking to himself:

"Now, this is most extraordinary! This scene is absolutely familiar to me; I seem to have gazed upon it—or upon something precisely similar to it in every respect, thousands of times before. Look at those gigantic ceibas yonder; those long, trailing ropes of purple orchids; see those flamingoes with their scarlet, black-barred wings, their long thin legs, and their curiously twisted beaks; observe those graceful white birds with their handsome crested heads; ay, and even the very monkeys swinging down by the creepers to dip up the water and drink it out of the palms of their hands; it is all much more familiar and homelike to me than ever was the scenery of Devon. Yet I have never been here before, unless indeed it has been in my dreams. But could a dream, or even a series of dreams, impart to me the perfect knowledge that I seem to possess of everything upon which my eye rests? Now, yonder, for instance, is a tree out of which I used to make—I mean that in some strange way I seem to know that splendid bows can be made out of the wood of that particular tree; and there, growing close beneath its shade, in the water, is a clump of rushes which, when dried in the sun, make perfect shafts for arrows. And that reminds me, Dick, that, since we must save our powder and shot for very special occasions, we ought to provide ourselves with bows and a good stock of arrows, if only to enable us to procure game. Now, I know perfectly well, in some mysterious manner, how to make bows and arrows; and since the materials for making both are at this moment before our eyes, we ought to avail ourselves of the opportunity. Don't you think so?"

"Certainly," answered Dick. "Though what you mean by saying that you know what particular kinds of trees make the best bows, and all the rest of it, I confess I don't understand."

"Nor do I," admitted Stukely. "But, all the same, I possess the knowledge, however strange it may appear; and perhaps, later on, understanding will come to me. Now, there is a good place to land, among the reeds; push the boat in through them, Dick; we shall find the bank low just there, with water enough for the boat alongside it."

"Now, how can you possibly know that?" demanded Dick. "Nevertheless," he continued, "we will try, because it will afford an excellent opportunity to test the accuracy of your boasted knowledge." And he put the helm up and headed the boat straight for the reeds, into the midst of which she plunged a minute later, pushing them easily aside as she drove through them, while they closed up again behind her, effectually screening her from view from the river, and as effectually obliterating the track which she had temporarily made through them.

Chapter Nine
How Phil and Dick voyaged up the Magdalena

"There, now, what did I tell you?" demanded Stukely, triumphantly, as the boat slid easily through the reeds and glided alongside a smooth, grassy bank, the top of which was scarcely a foot above the surface of the river. "Now," he continued, "if we lower the sail and unstep the mast, we may remain here as long as we please, undetected."

Indeed the statement was strictly true; for, having lowered the sail and unshipped the mast, they stepped ashore upon a smooth, grassy lawn, of some four acres in extent, completely hidden from the river by the screen of tall reeds, the feathery tops of which rose some ten feet above the water's surface, while inland it was completely encircled by a belt of forest the undergrowth of which was so dense as to be absolutely impenetrable by man without the aid of axes or other hewing implements. The lawn was thickly dotted with trees and shrubs of various kinds, amid which was conspicuous the tree which Stukely had asserted was good for the making of bows; and many of the trees were fruit bearers, among them being bananas, pawpaws, guavas, mangoes, and other excellent varieties.

Dick stared about him in amazement as he stepped ashore, taking the boat's painter with him and making it fast to a sturdy bush which grew conveniently close to the water's edge. "Well," he said, in answer to Stukely's question, "you were perfectly right, however you came by your knowledge. And, as to remaining here—well, I think we might do worse. We ought to accustom ourselves gradually to the outdoor, semi-savage life which will henceforth be ours; and I think we cannot do better than begin here. And that reminds me that I have not yet breakfasted, while yonder I see some bananas that appear to have reached the very pink of perfection. Are you hungry, Phil?"

"I am," answered Stukely, with emphasis; "and we have a full larder, it seems; so help yourself, lad. At present we shall be obliged to content ourselves with an exclusively fruit diet; but in the course of a few days, when we have provided ourselves with bows and arrows, we can vary it a little by adding an occasional venison steak, or a parrot or two. I can assure you, Dick, that parrots are very excellent eating."

"How do you know?" demanded the matter-of-fact Dick. "Have you ever eaten one?"

"Ay, often enough," answered Stukely, impulsively, then he checked himself. "At least," he stammered, "I seem to have done so; and yet, of course, 'tis impossible. Do you believe, as some assert, that a certain number, if not all, of us have lived on this earth once, twice, thrice before this present life, Dick? Because that is exactly how I feel, as though I had spent at least one previous existence here, in this very part of the world, amid such surroundings as those which our eyes now gaze upon. It all seems so absolutely familiar; I feel that I know all that there is to know about everything, except the names of them; ay, and there are even times when strange dim memories of past scenes seem to visit me, and for a moment I picture myself surrounded by all the pomp and grandeur of a civilisation that has long passed away. You will call me a dreamer, as indeed you have often called me already; and perhaps you are right. Yet it is strange that all my dreams should centre round scenes glorious as this, and have been so vivid that I recognise hitherto unseen objects as perfectly familiar when my gaze rests upon them. But this is unprofitable talk; the really important thing is that we are hungry, and are surrounded by food in abundance. Let us to breakfast."

When at length they had satisfied their hunger by feasting upon the several kinds of delicious fruits which abounded in the enclosure, Phil approached the tree which he had asserted was good for making bows from, and, drawing his hanger, proceeded to examine very carefully its several boughs, finally choosing two which were absolutely straight and about twelve feet long. These he hacked off from the parent trunk, without difficulty, using his hanger as an axe; then, handing one to Dick, whom he directed to follow his own example, he sat down in the shadow of a great umbrella tree and proceeded to trim away first the twigs and then the bark. This done, he took the bare, straight branch, and trimmed off the thin end until the wood, which was perfectly round, was about three-quarters of an inch thick. Then he cut away enough of the thick end of the branch to leave a pole about six feet long, which he proceeded to whittle away at the thick end until it also was about the same thickness as the thinner end, leaving the middle part about two inches thick. This he did with his pocket knife, without any difficulty, the wood seeming to be quite soft and yielding itself to the sharp blade with the utmost facility. And as he worked, so did Dick, the latter with a smile of amusement upon his face, for he flattered himself that he knew a thing or two about bows; and to him it seemed ridiculous to suppose that this wood which yielded itself as readily as cheese to the shaping of the knife could ever be of the slightest use as a bow. But he worked steadily on, following Stukely's lead, and shaping his own branch precisely as Stukely shaped his, and after some three hours of by no means arduous work each possessed a perfectly straight, smooth rod, accurately trimmed into the form of a bow about six feet long, with properly notched ends for the string to fit into.

"There," said Stukely at last, as he critically inspected his own and Dick's production, "I do not think we can improve upon either of those, which ought to make really formidable weapons when they are ready for use. Now, the next thing is to hang them up in the shade to dry, and that will take three full days at least, after which they will be ready to use, and will steadily improve in quality until the whole of the sap is completely dried out of them. If they have a fault it will probably be that we shall find them a shade too strong for us at first; but we shall grow accustomed to that in time. We cannot do better than hang them to a bough of this tree, where they will be completely shielded from the rays of the sun, and will dry slowly and evenly. Now, the next thing we need is a string for each bow, and—if we can contrive it—a spare string as a stand by. And"—glancing about him—"I think we ought to find the materials for the manufacture of those strings not very far away."

He hung up the two bows in such a situation that at no time of the day would the rays of the sun get at them, and then wandered round the enclosure, peering up among the branches of the trees, and at length seemed to find what he was seeking, for presently he swung himself up into a particular tree, and climbing some little way up it, plucked two brown balls about the size of oranges, with which he descended.

"Here we are," he exclaimed in accents of satisfaction, as he exhibited the balls to Dick. "These are the cocoons of a certain caterpillar, the name of which I forget, but they spin a kind of silk which is admirably adapted for the making of bowstrings, for it is incredibly strong, does not fray, and is not affected by damp. Now—"

"But how on earth do you come to know all this, Phil?" demanded Dick, as he took one of the cocoons in his hand and examined it curiously.

"I cannot tell you," answered Stukely, rather impatiently; "let it suffice you that I possess the knowledge, in some inscrutable way, ay, and a good deal more, too, of which you are like to reap the benefit in the long run."

He then proceeded to explain and illustrate how the silk was to be unwound—a task which kept them both busy for several hours—and when this was at length done he showed Dick how to spin the fine, tough filament into a thin but immensely strong cord. But the most remarkable part of the whole affair was the perfectly intimate knowledge which he displayed of the various operations, none of which, be it remembered, he had ever performed before. The unwinding of the cocoons and the spinning of the cords—two for each bow—occupied the young men during the remainder of that first day and the whole of the second, for the process was a rather tedious and delicate one, in which Dick at least exhibited all the inaptitude of the novice. The third and fourth days were fully occupied in the cutting of reeds and the conversion of them into arrows; and here again Stukely showed the same weird, incomprehensible knowledge and skill that he had so conspicuously displayed in his choice of the wood for the bows, his working of it to the proper shape, and his manufacture of the bowstrings; for the arrows, when finished, were as nearly perfect as such missiles could possibly be, the shafts being of uniform length, perfectly straight, and each tipped with a strong, hard thorn, sharp as a needle, and growing naturally in the form of a barb. Two dozen arrows for each constituted their initial equipment, but they cut a considerable quantity of spare reeds and thorns, and wound quite a large skein of silk to bind the barbed heads with, as they were quite prepared to lose several of their arrows at the outset, and accordingly made ample provision for their replacement, which could be done at odd moments, while working their way up the river. Their next business was to plait two quivers of palm-leaf fibre, with shoulder straps to support the same; and it was Stukely who had to make these, for when Dick endeavoured to follow his friend's instructions he proved to be so absolutely lacking in the necessary skill that, to save time, Phil undertook to do all the work himself. These several occupations kept them busy for an entire week, during which they saw no sign of human presence on the river; and by the time that all was finished the bows had dried into prime condition, and Dick found, to his amazement, that the wood which, when first cut, had been soft and workable as cheese, had become as hard as iron, tough, elastic, and extraordinarily strong; that it had, in short, become perfect for use as a bow.

Being now equipped with powerful and effective weapons which would enable them to save their powder and ball for special emergencies, and provide them with all the game they might require, the two adventurers resumed their journey, heading up the wide, deep river which they believed to be the Magdalena, sailing when the wind permitted, and paddling when it did not, unless they happened to be within sight of a good camping place when the wind failed them, in which case they very frequently ran in alongside the bank, moored the boat, and rested or hunted, or both, until the wind sprang up again.

They were perfectly happy now, these two; and it is difficult to say which was the happier. The life which they were living was, as nearly as possible, ideal; it was passed in the open air, in the midst of glorious scenery which was constantly revealing new beauties and wonders; they had not a care in the world, for the river and the forest provided them with an ample supply of food, while they had no anxiety with regard to clothing in a climate which rendered clothes a superfluity. In short, their every physical need was abundantly satisfied; they enjoyed perfect health, and if their adventures thus far were of a somewhat tame and commonplace description, well, what mattered it? They had not a doubt that excitement in plenty lay before them, and meanwhile their daily life was insensibly training and preparing them to cope with it. Each of them was happy in his own way; Dick, because all was new and splendid, and Phil, because he was possessed of a wonderful overmastering feeling that after a long period of exile he once more found himself amid scenes that were familiar, and, although he could not say precisely in what way, suggestive of glorious associations.

Late on the second day of their resumed voyage they arrived at a point where the river forked, the stream on their right hand being almost as important as the other; but they decided that the stream on their left was the main stream, and therefore followed it. Although they knew it not at the moment, this decision of theirs to follow the left instead of the right stream was of the utmost import to them; for had they decided differently they would have missed the extraordinary adventure that awaited them among the mountains which lay so far ahead that many a weary mile of river, forest, and plain must be traversed before their peaks should swing into sight.

They camped that night on the point of land where the two rivers united their waters, and had scarcely landed when, without a sound to tell of his coming, a graceful antelope emerged from the brake a few hundred yards away, evidently going to the river to drink. The adventurers were at the moment partly concealed by the reeds among which they had moored their boat, moreover the wind was in their favour, and for nearly half a minute the creature failed to see them. By the time that he did, Stukely had seized his bow, fitted an arrow to the string, and risen cautiously to his feet. Then the antelope appeared to become aware of some unusual feature in the scene, and halted to investigate, whereupon Phil cautiously drew his bowstring, released it with a loud twang, and the arrow, flying straight and true, pierced the creature's heart, so that it fell dead in its tracks, and they had their first deer. And now again Stukely gave fresh evidence of his uncanny knowledge, for although he had never before killed a deer, and might be supposed to know nothing of the verderer's art, he at once set to work to skin and "break up" the animal with all the skill of an adept. So that night they feasted sumptuously upon venison steaks, grilled upon the embers of a fire which, with a further display of his strange knowledge, Phil kindled by the apparently simple but really exceedingly difficult process of rubbing two sticks together! And that night, too, they heard for the first time the roar of the jaguar in the adjacent forest.

For several days—so many, indeed, that they lost count of them—they voyaged steadily up the great river, sailing when the wind permitted, paddling when it did not, passing, at tolerably frequent intervals, points where lesser streams discharged themselves into the main body of water, while by imperceptible degrees the waterway narrowed, and the forest—dense, green, flower-decked, alive and gay with bird and insect life—pressed its foliaged walls in upon them ever closer and closer, except where an occasional break caused by fire or windfall afforded them a momentary glimpse of giant mountain ranges to right and left, at first a delicate purple-grey in the distance, but ever, like the forest, creeping closer in upon them. And now at increasingly frequent intervals, they began to see Indians, at first a solitary "buck" spearing fish from his canoe, but later on in parties of from half a dozen to fifty or more, crossing the river, or, like themselves, using it as a highway. But thus far, much as Stukely desired it, they had never succeeded in getting into touch with the natives, for the latter invariably fled at the mere sight of them.

One of the most surprising circumstances, perhaps, in connection with this voyage up the river, was the rapidity with which the two Englishmen—or Dick, rather—lost the capacity to be astonished. Stukely, indeed, had never manifested the least surprise at any of the wonders that were continually coming under their observation, for, steadfastly adhering to that strange fancy of his that he must have lived in these regions during some former state of existence, he persistently asserted that everything he saw was perfectly familiar to him. But with Dick it was very different; he was as matter-of-fact as Phil was fanciful; and the sight of giant trees between two and three hundred feet in height towering up into the cloudless blue a solid mass of purple, scarlet, or yellow bloom; of graceful clumps of feathery bamboo a hundred feet long; of the lofty forest walls on either hand draped with festoons of orchids of the most extraordinary and undreamed-of shapes and the most gorgeous colours; of birds, insects, ay, and even fish, that flashed and glittered with all the hues of the rainbow; of monkeys who followed their course up the river in troops of a hundred or more; of the lithe and graceful jaguar lying stretched upon some trunk or branch that closely overhung the water, watching with ready paw to seize any unwary fish that might chance to swim past within reach; of alligators that basked log-like on the mud banks—all these things were to Chichester at first a source of utmost wonder and admiration; yet within a month they had become the veriest commonplaces to him, and had entirely ceased to attract his attention. He was far more interested in the sight of a fair breeze stealing up the river after them than he was in the sight of the most beautiful flower, the most gorgeous butterfly, or the most dainty and brilliant colibri, for he knew that all these things he would see again a thousand times or more; but a wind that would relieve them of the labour of paddling in that scorching climate—ah! that was indeed a sight worth seeing.

At length, when they had been journeying up the river in leisurely fashion for about three weeks, meeting with no adventure worthy of record, on a certain hot and steamy afternoon, when the boat, under sail, was doing little more than barely stem the current, they gradually became aware of a low, faint roar, at first scarcely distinguishable above the rustle of the wind in the trees aloft and the buzzing hum of the innumerable insects which swarmed in the forest and hovered in clouds over the surface of the water. But as the boat continued to creep upstream the roar gradually increased in intensity, until at length, as they rounded a bend and entered another reach of the river which extended practically straight for nearly three miles ahead of them, they saw, at a distance of about a mile, a long stretch of foaming, tumbling water, rushing headlong down through a rocky gorge, about three hundred yards wide, over what was evidently a rocky bed, for the brown heads of several rocks were seen protruding above the leaping water in the channel. Rapids! with a fall of nearly thirty feet in about half a mile. This was a formidable obstacle indeed, for it did not seem possible that they could get the boat through them; and if they should be obliged to abandon her, what would then happen? Obviously they would be obliged to walk the rest of the distance—or to build another boat, or canoe, above the rapids; and it was difficult to say which was the more distasteful alternative of the two. Walking, probably, for although their belongings were few and by no means cumbersome to carry, the forest was so dense that, as they had already proved by experience, it was scarcely possible to travel a hundred feet without being faced by the necessity to cut their way.

"Well," said practical Dick, after they had sat staring at the beautiful but tantalising scene for full five minutes, "it's no use meeting trouble halfway, or wondering how we are going to get across the bridge until we come to it; let's push on and get as close up as we can; then we'll get ashore, walk up along, and have a look at the place. Perhaps when we come to it, it will not look so bad as it does from here."

The bank on either hand was so densely overgrown with shrubs that landing seemed out of the question; but, seizing their paddles, the two adventurers drove the boat up against the rapidly strengthening current. Presently a tiny strip of beach, a yard wide by ten or twelve yards long, came into view; and here they beached the boat, making her well fast in order that the current might not sweep her away. The rapids were now less than a hundred feet distant, and the rush of the water brought down with it a cool, spray-laden breeze that was infinitely refreshing after the baking breathlessness of the stream below; but the roar of the chafing waters was so loud that it was almost impossible to make one's voice heard; Phil therefore scrambled up the steep bank, and signed to Dick to follow. Fighting their way through the dense undergrowth, through which they were obliged to cut much of their way with their hangers, they at length came out upon a jutting spur of bare rock which overhung the rapids at a height of some fifty feet, and from this point they were able to obtain a tolerably distinct view of the whole gorge. And, as Dick had suggested, when they came to look at the place from close at hand, it did not appear to be nearly so impracticable as they had at first imagined.

The bed of the channel was badly encumbered with rocks, it is true, but only for about two hundred feet at the lower end; the rest of it, while showing a partially submerged rock here and there, was on the whole remarkably clear, the water rushing over its bed in a swift, glass-smooth stream. Even where the rocks were thickest, it was apparent that there was a very well-defined channel between them, up which a carefully navigated boat might easily pass—if propulsive power enough were applied to her to overcome the downward rush of the stream. But how was that power to be obtained? Certainly not by paddling; the stream was too swift for that. But it was just possible that it might be done by warping if a warp long enough and strong enough could be obtained. Moreover the warp need not be so prodigiously long, for now that they came to look at the rapids at close quarters they saw that their original estimate of their length had been a long way over the mark; it was much nearer a quarter than half a mile long. They glanced about them and saw that the trees were here, as everywhere along the river bank, thickly draped with long, thin, tough lianas, and the same idea flashed into both their minds at the same moment: why should they not twist or plait a warp of lianas? There were plenty of them, and, after all, it merely resolved itself into a question of time, while time, just then, was of less importance to them than labour. There was an alternative, of course, they might abandon the boat and construct a canoe above the rapids; and it was worth considering whether the construction of a canoe or the making of a warp would involve the more labour. To settle the point they decided to go on through the woods until they reached the head of the rapids, and there inspect the trees with the view of ascertaining whether there were any suitable for the construction of a canoe; and having come to this decision, they left the rock and re-entered the forest.

For more than half an hour they were so busily engaged in forcing and hewing their way through the dense, parasitical undergrowth that they had no attention to spare for anything else; but at length they became conscious of certain discordant sounds, reaching their ears above the roar of the rapids, which presently became distinguishable as the beating of drums, mingled with a sort of braying bellow, comparable to nothing that they had ever heard before. As the pair pressed on, the unearthly sounds gradually grew louder, not only because they were approaching the source of them but also because it was evident that the producers of the sounds were becoming more excited, for the tapping of the drums increased in rapidity while the braying as steadily grew in stridency and discord. Another five minutes of strenuous labour then the two Englishmen burst through the last of the undergrowth and emerged upon a cleared space of about a hundred acres on the bank of the river just above the rapids. At this point the river widened out again to about the space of half a mile from bank to bank, the gorge being about a hundred yards below, and the current was again gentle enough to render paddling against it an easy matter. A small strip of shingly beach was dotted with some forty or fifty canoes, each hewn out of a single log; and adjoining the beach, scattered over a space of about five acres of ground, was a native village consisting of about fifty palm-leaf huts, dotted about without the slightest attempt at symmetrical arrangement, except that they were built round an open space. The remainder of the clearing consisted of cultivated ground divided into patches devoted in about equal proportions to cassava and maize, with a little indigo here and there. A whole forest of slender poles, connected with each other by lianas, from which large quantities of fish were suspended, drying in the sun, and which, by the way, gave off a most intolerable odour, indicated that the inhabitants depended as much upon the river as upon the soil for their subsistence.

Apparently some sort of festival or religious ceremony was in process of being observed when Dick and Phil burst in so unceremoniously upon them, for the entire population of the village, men, women, and children, were squatted in a circle round the open space in the middle of the village. Despite the scorching heat a large fire was blazing in the centre of the open space, and round it sat the village band, consisting of four drums, made of sections of trees with the inside cut away, leaving a thin cylinder of wood, over one end of which was tightly strained a skin of some sort which was slapped with the palm of the open hand, and about a dozen flageolet players, their instruments being made of baked clay. It was these last that emitted the unearthly braying, bellowing sounds already mentioned. To this hideous medley of sounds a figure in the middle of the circle was dancing, a figure so queer that for a second or two the young Englishmen scarcely knew what to make of it. But presently they saw that it was a man laced-up in a jaguar skin, with teeth, claws, and tail complete, the face of the man peering out from between the gaping jaws. He was not only dancing vigorously, if indeed dancing it could be called, which consisted in leaping violently into the air and springing from side to side over a bundle, the nature of which the intruders could not at first make out, but also singing, or rather howling, certain words which appeared to be gradually working his audience up into a state of savage excitement; for at intervals one or another of them, apparently moved out of himself, would yell furiously and shake in the air a villainous-looking, triple-barbed spear.

AN INTERRUPTED FESTIVAL.

For nearly a minute the people were so completely absorbed in the movements and words of their piache, or medicine man, or witch doctor, as the man in the jaguar skin proved to be, that they were quite oblivious of the presence of the two Englishmen; but suddenly the piache caught sight of them and stopped short in his leapings and howlings, and glared, open-mouthed, at the strangers for a second or two before, with a yell of dismay, he turned tail and, leaping right through the blazing fire in his panic, dashed into a hut and violently drew across the mat which served as a door. This extraordinary behaviour on the part of the medicine man naturally excited the wonder of his audience, and also aroused in them a feeling of consternation which caused them to spring to their feet and look about them apprehensively. Then they, too, caught sight of the Englishmen, and, like their piache, made a mad dash for their huts, yelling as they went. Thus, in the course of a couple of minutes, the two young Devonians were left in complete, undisputed possession of the village, although they were conscious of being stealthily observed from practically every hut in the place.

"Well," exclaimed Dick, as he stared about him in astonishment, "this beats everything! Men and women, big and little, there must have been close upon two hundred of them, and not one had the courage to stay and face us!"

"They probably took us for Spaniards," answered Stukely, "and may have thought that we were merely the advance guard of a considerable force. Hence their terror. I only hope that when they discover their mistake they may not revenge themselves upon us for the fright which we have given them. I would that one or the other of us possessed a smattering of their lingo, sufficient to make ourselves understood; I am afraid that we shall find our ignorance in that respect a very serious hindrance as we penetrate farther into the interior; and we must do our best to remedy the—hallo! what on earth is in that bundle? Did you see it move?"

Phil referred to the bundle over which the piache had been performing his extraordinary dance when they interrupted him, and which had the appearance of being simply a bundle of ordinary matting. But Stukely's eye happened to have been resting upon it while he spoke, and he had distinctly seen it move.

"No, I didn't," answered Chichester, in reply to his friend's question, "for the simple reason that I wasn't looking at it. But we'll look at it now, if you like." And striding over to where the bundle lay upon the ground, he drew his knife, severed the thongs that bound it, unrolled the matting, and disclosed to his own and his companion's astonished gaze the figure of a little old man, securely bound hand and foot. He was an Indian of some sort, evidently, but not of the same race as the inhabitants of the village, his colour being that of light copper, while that of the others was a very dark brown, nearly approaching to black; also his features were of a totally different and much higher type, his forehead being broad and high, his nose thin and aquiline, and his cheek-bones rather high and prominent; in fact he must, in the days of his youth, have been a decidedly handsome man, with an imposing presence; but now he was old—how old it was rather difficult to guess, but probably not far short of a hundred—shrunken and shrivelled up until he resembled an animated mummy more than anything else. His head and face were clean shaven, and he was naked, except for a sort of petticoat of feathers about his loins, the said petticoat having evidently at one time been an exceedingly handsome garment, though now it was soiled, frayed, and generally very much the worse for wear.

As Dick bent over the old fellow, with his long, keen knife in his hand, to sever his bonds, the creature suddenly cried out some half a dozen words, in a thin, high, piping voice, causing Stukely to start forward and gaze earnestly into the face of the speaker; then, to Dick's stupefaction, Stukely replied in apparently the same tongue, bent over and rapidly loosed the thongs which bound the old fellow's hands and feet together, and proceeded gently to chafe the shrunken limbs.

Chapter Ten
How the Two Adventurers
acquired a Companion

"Why, Phil," exclaimed Dick, in amazement, "what does this mean? Surely you are not pretending that you understand the old chap's lingo?"

"No, Dick, I am not pretending," answered Stukely, regarding Chichester with a dazed expression. "It is a fact—a most extraordinary and unaccountable fact, that I really understand what the poor old chap says, without knowing it, without even previously suspecting it for an instant. I seem to possess a sufficient knowledge of his tongue to be able to comprehend his speech, and even to answer him; and I believe that in the course of a day or two I shall be able to converse freely with him. What he cried out just now was an entreaty that we would spare his life, and I answered that he need not fear us, for we meant him no harm."

"Um–m–m!" commented Dick. "Well, this is the land of marvels, and no mistake! I thought I had grown accustomed to the wonders of it, and that I had no capacity for further astonishment, but I confess that you have contrived to give me one more spasm of surprise. Ask your friend who he is, and where he hails from: I dare swear that he is not a native of this village."

Stukely turned to the old man, who was by this time sitting up and gently chafing his wrists and ankles, and attempted to put to him the question which Dick had suggested. But he found that the words would not come to him; he felt that he knew but could not remember them; and after two or three bungling attempts he was obliged to give it up.

"Now, that is very extraordinary," said he, attempting to explain his failure to Dick; "almost as extraordinary as the fact that I understood the old chap's words, and was able to answer them. But I know his language—I am certain I do—and after I have practised with him a little, it will all come back to me. Meanwhile we must do the best we can. Are you feeling better, 'gramfer'? And what were the Indians going to do to you?" This in English.

The Indian looked up in Stukely's face and spoke for nearly a minute; and when he had finished Stukely was again, to his own and Dick's amazement, able to reply.

"We are getting on," Phil explained. "The old gentleman asked me why I did not address him in his own tongue, since I evidently understand it; and then went on to say that we arrived here just in the nick of time, as the villagers were about to torture him to death, to secure the favour of some god or devil of whom they appear to be particularly afraid. And I said that he might depend upon us to protect him so long as we have the power to do so."

Then he turned again to the old man, and, with a good deal of stammering and hesitation, and many long pauses for consideration, said something else, to which the ancient again replied; whereupon Phil made a further attempt, with the result that ultimately the two had quite a long conversation together, although it must be confessed that the elder man did most of the talking. At length the conversation came to an end, for the moment, and Stukely seized the opportunity to transmit to Dick the information which he had acquired.

"Our friend's story is a very remarkable one," he said. "He tells me that his name is Vilcamapata; that he is a Peruvian; and was once a priest of the Sun, in a temple which stood—and the ruins of which, indeed, still stand—on an island in the midst of a great lake which, lies among the mountains far away to the southward. This was when Peru was at the zenith of its power and glory under an Inca named Atahuallpa, whom the Spaniards under Pizarro decoyed into their power and murdered most shamefully and cruelly; afterward seizing the country and making it their own. Since then 'gramfer' Vilcamapata has been a wanderer and a fugitive, always fleeing from the Spaniards, who, it appears, are doing their utmost to extirpate the Peruvians under the pretence of converting—or trying to convert—them to the Christian faith. Thus it was in the course of his aimless wanderings that he came to this village, three days ago, and was seized by the inhabitants, who, after much deliberation, decided to sacrifice him to one of their demons, and were, indeed, about to do so when we appeared upon the scene and interrupted them."

"Well," said Dick, "it seems to me that he stands a very good chance of being sacrificed still, as soon as these Indians find that there are only two of us to defend him. Pray heaven that they may not take it into their heads to sacrifice us too, with a murrain on them!"

"Oh, I don't think they will do that, or even attempt to take gramfer from us," replied Phil, cheerfully. "It seems that they have a very great respect for white men—except Spaniards—and are ever on the lookout for a paleface named Amalivaca to come across the Great Water and unite all the Indians into one great and powerful nation which shall utterly destroy the Spaniards and restore the country to its original owners."

"I suppose they could not be persuaded to accept us as two of Amalivaca's sons, come over as a sort of advance guard to prepare the Indians for the arrival of the old boy himself?" suggested Dick. "But then the difficulty is that we don't understand their lingo. Does gramfer, think you? If so, he might be induced to act as our interpreter, and inform the Indians that we are their friends. Perhaps if they could be persuaded of that they might be induced to help us to get the boat up above the rapids."

"Yes," agreed Phil, "they might; that is a very good idea, and I'll see what can be done." Therewith he turned to the ancient, and again, with much halting and stammering, contrived to explain what they desired to accomplish.

The Peruvian put several questions to Stukely, seeming not quite to comprehend what the white men required; and Dick noticed that after the ex-priest had spoken a little while with Phil, the latter became much more fluent and certain in his speech, so that, in the course of a further conversation of some ten minutes' duration, he contrived to make Vilcamapata clearly understand what he wanted; whereupon the old man, facing round toward the huts, lifted up his voice and made what seemed to be a long proclamation in a language of which Stukely understood nothing. But if what he said was incomprehensible to the white man, it was evident that it was clearly enough understood by the Indians, who, before the speech was half over, came swarming out of their huts and prostrated themselves before Phil and Dick, grovelling in the dust. Nor did they attempt to interfere further with the Peruvian; on the contrary, they listened with the utmost attention to all that he had to say to them; and when he had finished, about a dozen of them jumped into one of the largest canoes, paddled across to the opposite side of the stream, vanished into the forest, and after an absence of about an hour and a half, reappeared, singing a song of triumph and carrying the white men's boat, with all her gear and contents intact, upon their shoulders, having evidently brought her up past the rapids by a path through the forest, on the opposite side of the river to that by which Phil and Dick had ascended.

It was by this time within half an hour of sunset; and when the boat had been launched in the river above the rapids, towed across to the village side of the stream, and safely moored, the piache again made his appearance and addressed himself at considerable length to Vilcamapata; who, in his turn, addressed himself to Phil, informing the latter that the villagers were profoundly grateful for the honour which the white men had done them in condescending to visit their village, and that they trusted the said white men would, by lodging in the village for that night at least, if not for a much longer time, afford them an opportunity to show their gratitude in a practical way. To which Phil, after consultation with Dick, replied that they were gratified to find that their Indian children duly appreciated the honour which had been done them, and that, as a token of their favour, they would accede to their request to spend the night in the village, provided that a new hut were erected for their accommodation; but that they must depart at sunrise, as they had a long journey before them. Whereupon the Indians, with joyful songs, at once proceeded to erect the new hut on a vacant space somewhat apart from the village, pushing forward the work so rapidly that the hut was completed and ready for occupation by the time that the first stars began to appear in the sky. And no sooner had the two white men installed themselves therein, with a large fire blazing before the hut to afford them light, and drive off the mosquitoes, than several women appeared with baskets on their heads, some of which contained cassava, while the contents of others consisted of the young heads of Indian corn, boiled, and wrapped in plantain leaves, the hind quarter of a kid, roasted, roasted plantains, a quantity of fruit, and a calabash containing a liquid which had a faint, mellow, acid flavour, something like weak cider, exceedingly refreshing as a beverage, but decidedly heady, as they discovered a little later on. The Peruvian, at the joint request of the white men, established himself in a corner of the hut, thankfully accepted such viands as they gave him, and generally comported himself in such a manner as to convey the idea that he regarded himself as under their special protection. Indeed they were glad enough that he should so regard himself, for there could be no doubt that he would be of very great service to them, if only as a guide and interpreter; he having, it appeared, been a wanderer up and down the country for—as Phil understood—nearly forty years.

"The thing that puzzles me most of all," said Dick, when they were discussing the day's doings as they sat at supper that night, "is how you and the Peruvian came to be able to converse together. To me it seems nothing less than a miracle."

"Yes," agreed Stukely, "I have no doubt it does; I can quite understand that it would so appear to you. Indeed, when I come to reflect upon it, it also appears miraculous to me; for why should I be able to understand a language that I have never studied, spoken, or even heard before? It seems impossible, upon the face of it, doesn't it? Yet, although I know that I never was abroad until I came over here in the *Adventure*, I have, from the earliest days of my childhood, had a feeling, amounting sometimes to conviction, that sometime in the past I dwelt in just such another land as this; a sound, an odour, has brought to me vague, elusive memories of a country of vast forests, great, shining rivers, stupendous mountains, and island-dotted lakes crowned with vast buildings constructed in a style of architecture such as these eyes of mine have never beheld in England. Then again I seem to be able to recall gorgeous pageants in which I took a prominent part, and at which, in the presence of an innumerable people, I assisted in the performance of strange rites. Such scenes come to me most vividly in my dreams at night; and there are occasions when those dreams are so realistic that when I awake I am puzzled to decide which is the dream and which the reality. And—strangest thing of all—on all these occasions I have spoken the language which I spoke with Vilcamapata to-day! I recognised him, or rather his type of countenance, the moment I set eyes upon him, for I have beheld many such in my dreams. And ever since I have been in this country I have had the feeling of one who, after a long absence, finds himself again among familiar and homelike surroundings. Those are the facts; but I cannot explain them any more than you can explain to me why that fire throws out heat."

On the following morning the up-river journey was resumed, much to the grief of the villagers, who seemed to have taken a most extraordinary liking for the Englishmen, possibly because of some fancy that the presence of the white men would bring good luck to the village and its inhabitants. But neither Stukely nor Dick was minded to delay their journey, and met the pressing invitation of the Indians to remain with them by repeating their explanation that a long journey lay before them, and that there were urgent reasons for the utmost haste. Whereupon the headman of the village, through Vilcamapata, petitioned that a party might be permitted to accompany the palefaces two days' journey up the river, in order that they might transport their friends' boat past certain rapids and a cataract which would be met with at that distance above the village. This statement as to the existence of the rapids and cataract being confirmed by Vilcamapata, Stukely graciously gave the required permission; and when, after an early breakfast, the little expedition set out, it consisted not only of the two Englishmen and Vilcamapata, but also of twenty Indians in two canoes, who were vastly astonished when, a fresh and favourable breeze happening to be blowing, they saw the white men step their mast, unfurl their sail, and go scudding upstream against the current at a speed which taxed their utmost energies to keep pace with. But the wind died away about noon, and then nothing would satisfy the Indians but that they must take the boat in tow, which they did, with the result that Dick and Stukely were spared a long and hot afternoon's paddling. Moreover, not content with this, when the time came for them to camp for the night, the friendly Indians insisted on building a hut for Dick and Phil to pass the night in, one half of the party undertaking this task while the other half plunged into the woods, to return, some three-quarters of an hour later, loaded with fruit and game of various descriptions, the choicest portions of which they placed in the white men's hut.

The next day's journey was, in all essential particulars, the counterpart of that which preceded it, except that about mid-afternoon they arrived at the foot of the rapids, of the existence of which the Indians had warned them. These rapids were very much more formidable than those which they had first encountered, the channel being considerably narrower and the current consequently far more rapid; also the river bed was here full of enormous rocks and boulders, over and between which the water rushed and leapt and boiled in a turmoil of fury that no boat or canoe could possibly have faced. Furthermore, the rapids were nearly a mile and a half in length, beyond which was about a mile of comparatively quiet water, and then came a cataract of over a hundred feet in perpendicular height, with another half-mile of rapids beyond it, before the river once more widened out sufficiently to be navigable. Had the two adventurers been alone they would certainly have been compelled to abandon their boat at this spot; but the Indians made light of the difficulty, beginning by building a hut for their white friends, as on the day before, on a small open plateau near the foot of the rapids, while half a dozen of their number explored the banks on either side of the river in search of a practicable road, by means of which the boat could be carried up past the rapids and the cataract to the navigable water beyond. This they eventually discovered in time to effect the portage before dark. Then, more fruit having been found, and game taken on the way back, a great fire was kindled, and a farewell feast was held in honour of their paleface friends, which was wound up with some of the most weird and extraordinary singing and dancing that the Englishmen had ever heard or seen.

On the following morning the Indians escorted Phil, Dick, and Vilcamapata to the spot where, beyond the cataract and the upper rapids, their boat, with all its contents intact, rode safely in the placid waters of a little bay where the river widened out and navigation was once more possible. Here at last the kind-hearted natives bade a reluctant and sorrowful farewell to Dick and Stukely; the bitterness of parting being mitigated by a promise on the part of the white men that, in the event of their returning by way of the river, they would not fail to make a stay of at least a week in their friends' village.

Now, with a long stretch of unobstructed navigation before them, they had time to improve their acquaintance with Vilcamapata, who was never tired of expressing his gratitude to Dick and Stukely for having saved him from a terrible death. But it soon became apparent that, for some inexplicable reason, he regarded Stukely as much the more important personage of the two, his devotion to Phil being of such a pronounced character that it almost amounted to worship. This, of course, might have been accounted for to some extent by the fact that Stukely was able to converse with him in his own tongue, and the rapidity with which Phil attained to proficiency in the Peruvian language was a never-ending source of wonderment to Dick. But there was evidently something more than this in it, something which he did not offer to explain, and upon which Stukely did not care to question him, fearing that, if he did so, such an exposure of ignorance on his part might result in a weakening of his influence over the Peruvian, while from this influence he hoped to obtain certain very important advantages. A rather remarkable circumstance, which gradually revealed itself in the course of Phil's conversations with the ex-priest, was that the latter did not seem to be in the least surprised that Stukely should be desirous of penetrating Peru; on the contrary, he appeared to regard it as quite a matter of course; nay, more, it almost appeared as though Stukely's visit had been long expected, and was a thing to be rejoiced over. At least this was the impression which Stukely gathered from remarks and expressions dropped by Vilcamapata from time to time; and he would greatly have liked to have questioned the man upon the subject, and learned precisely what he meant by such references; but forbore for the reasons above stated. When at length Stukely cautiously hinted that the object of his journey was the acquisition of wealth, the ex-priest, far from exhibiting surprise or displeasure, displayed the utmost satisfaction, and eagerly assured Phil that he could place him in possession of all the wealth that he could possibly desire. Upon Phil asking where the wealth was to come from, the Peruvian replied that when the country fell into the hands of the Spaniards an enormous quantity of gold, silver, and uncut gems had been concealed in a secret chamber of the temple of which he had been a priest; that it was there still; and that he was quite prepared to reveal the hiding-place to his English friends, feeling assured that they would use it in the manner which had been intended when it was first concealed. This again was a distinctly cryptic remark, of which neither of the Englishmen could possibly guess the meaning; but Stukely replied that Vilcamapata might rest assured that they would employ it wisely and well; and with that answer the Peruvian seemed perfectly satisfied. But when he was asked to describe the whereabouts of the temple, he could only very vaguely indicate it as being built on an island situated in the midst of a sacred lake; that the lake lay at an immense distance to the southward, under the shadow of a rather remarkable snow-capped mountain; that the way thither was encompassed with dangers from wild animals, hostile Indians, and—worst of all—Spaniards; and that, if they were fortunate, they might possibly reach the place in about four moons of diligent travel. Four moons, or months, of diligent travel! It seemed an immense distance; for "diligent travel" through the virgin forest—and Vilcamapata gave them to understand that a very considerable part of the distance would have to be traversed by land—meant something like an average of fifteen miles a day; and fifteen miles a day for one hundred and twenty days meant a journey of eighteen hundred miles! But they were not dismayed; for by this time they had come to have unlimited confidence in themselves. They were daily becoming more learned in woodcraft, being now able to traverse at least three miles of forest in the time that it had originally taken them to travel one mile; familiarity had caused them to lose completely their original dread of wild animals and noxious reptiles and insects; and as for Indians and Spaniards—well, they believed they could always circumvent either or both of them; while, so far as the length of the journey was concerned, what was four months, if there was a fortune to be gained at the end of it? So with light hearts they pressed forward day after day, always following the river, until at length they were obliged, first to abandon their boat in consequence of the increasing number of rapids and falls, and take to a light canoe instead, which they were easily able to transport overland when necessary; and finally they reached a point where the river was no longer navigable, even for a canoe, and they were obliged to take to the forest.

But although they could no longer travel by water they still clung closely to the river, as it was their only source of supply of drinking water; moreover, it happened to lead pretty nearly in the direction of their route. They were now proceeding up a valley, hemmed in on either side by mountains ranging in height from ten thousand to fifteen thousand feet, yet so dense was the forest through which they were travelling that they seldom caught a glimpse of them, except in one particular instance where they frequently sighted a majestic, snow-capped peak right ahead of them when they encamped in a clearing close to the river.

At length a day came when the noble river, upon the broad bosom of which they had journeyed for so many days, dwindled to a tiny brook brawling over a rocky bed, across which they could leap, the forest grew thin and stunted, degenerated to a few scattered scrub oaks, and finally ceased altogether, and they found themselves confronted by a mountain barrier, the bare rocks of which were interspersed with patches of grass, upon some of which were grazing small flocks of most extraordinary animals, such as they had never seen before, but with which Vilcamapata was evidently quite familiar. There were three distinct species of them, although they all bore a striking resemblance to each other, being about the size of donkeys, but having long necks, heads somewhat like those of sheep, and legs and feet resembling those of camels. Vilcamapata informed the Englishmen that these animals were known respectively as alpacas, llamas, and vicuñas, and that the first were used by his countrymen for food, while their wool was woven into garments; the second were used as beasts of burden, and the third were valuable principally for their hair and hides.

The river was now left behind; but this caused the travellers no inconvenience, for the mountains which they were ascending, were most of them snow-capped, and tiny rivulets of ice-cold water, formed by the melting snow, were frequently met with, so that they were at no loss for water wherewith to quench their thirst. But as they pressed on, climbing ever higher and higher, they began to suffer very severely, first from cold, and next from mountain sickness, due to the steadily increasing rarefaction of the atmosphere. Vilcamapata, however, had a remedy for both evils, for he killed three alpacas and stripped off their skins to serve as wraps for himself and his companions, to protect them from the cold; while, as soon as the first symptoms of mountain sickness declared themselves, he produced from his pouch a quantity of leaves of the marvellous coca, and bade the Englishmen chew them, which they did; whereupon not only did the sickness disappear, but they felt no further need of food, while their strength was restored to them in a manner that seemed absolutely miraculous. It cost them three days of arduous labour to cross this mountain range; but the evening of the third day found them once more encamped in the tropical forest beside a tiny stream that flowed to the southward and eastward, while, on the farther side, the valley sloped away into a still deeper depression.

Six days later, having meanwhile traversed about a hundred miles of stifling tropical forest, travelling all the while in a due southerly direction, and having crossed two important streams running in an easterly direction, to say nothing of numberless rivulets, they came to the bank of a third stream, also running almost due east; and here Vilcamapata announced that it would be necessary to build a canoe, as he now proposed to take to the water again. Upon Stukely pointing out to him that this river, like those others that they had recently crossed, flowed east, whereas he understood that their own route lay to the southward, the Peruvian replied that such was certainly the case; but that although the river which they had now reached ran eastward, it eventually discharged into another, by travelling up which they would in process of time come very near to their destination; and that although the distance which they would have to travel by water was very much greater than the direct overland route, they would be able to accomplish it in a much shorter time, and with considerably more ease and comfort to themselves. With this reply the Englishmen were obliged to be content; accordingly while Dick and the Peruvian proceeded to hunt for a suitable tree out of which to construct a canoe, within a reasonable distance of the river bank, Stukely, taking his bow and arrows, went off into the forest in search of game.

There had been a time when he would have hesitated to go very far into those depths of green shadow alone, for fear of losing himself; but that time was now long past for both the young Englishmen. They had grown quite accustomed to travelling through the pathless forest, to wandering hither and thither in it in pursuit of game, and mechanically to note while doing so a thousand signs, quite imperceptible to the novice, whereby they were enabled to return with certainty to the spot where they had temporarily fixed their camp. Therefore on this occasion, as on many others, Stukely, with a word of explanation to his companions, plunged unhesitatingly into the labyrinth of tangled undergrowth which covered the soil between the boles of the giant trees, instinctively taking the direction in which he would be likely soonest to come upon the track of game.

Yet he might have been excused had he hesitated to enter such a maze as that which reared itself within less than a hundred yards of the spot which the party had fixed upon for their temporary camp, for there was no semblance of a path through it, and the mode of progress consisted simply in entering at the spot where the tangle was thinnest and, still following the line of least resistance, in that way make one's devious way forward. Progressing in such a fashion, it would have been quite possible, nay more, almost inevitable, that one unaccustomed to such a mode of travel should become hopelessly lost within the first five minutes; but not so Stukely or Dick; they had learned to preserve their bearings by noting the moss growing on the trunks of the trees, the direction in which their principal branches pointed, and a hundred other apparently trivial signs. But it was a weird place in which to be alone, for, apart from the green twilight produced by the filtration of the light through the dense canopy of foliage that shut out all view of the sky overhead, the under-brake was so thick that it was seldom possible to see more than a yard or two ahead, and it was impossible to say what strange or thrilling sight might at any moment meet the gaze. Then there was the uncanny silence of the place, the kind of silence that caused an involuntary movement on tiptoe and the holding of the breath for fear of breaking it, yet which was broken at recent intervals by stealthy, unaccountable rustlings, or sudden, violent commotions beginning close at hand and gradually dying away in the distance. These strange, sudden, unaccountable sounds, caused in all probability by a boa-constrictor, a buck, or some other creature startled into quick movement by the scent of a human being, wafted to their nostrils by an errant draught of air, were even more startling to the nerves than the distant roar of the jaguar, or the call of the bell bird which irresistibly suggested the incongruous idea that at no great distance in those gloomy forest depths would be found a church!

But Stukely was thoroughly accustomed to these and the various other strange sounds that so frequently broke the silence of the forest, and if he noted them at all it was merely as a hunter notes sounds that guide him toward his game, or warns him of possible dangers. It was not, however, in such a spot as this that he expected to find game, it was in the open glades that occur here and there, where for some unaccountable reason an acre or so of ground is entirely free from trees, or at all events from undergrowth, and where the soil is covered with thick, rich grass, upon which the deer love to graze, and which they seem capable of scenting for miles. So he pushed forward, worming his way through the tangled brake with an ease and celerity that would have seemed absolutely miraculous to him three months earlier, and ever, as he went, his glances darted hither and thither, searching for the stronger light which should reveal to him the whereabout of one of those open glades, or, incidentally, a venomous snake or other noxious creature lurking in his path.

At length, when he had been thus engaged for about an hour, and had travelled a distance of about two miles, a somewhat stronger light away on his right front conveyed to him the welcome intimation that such an open glade as he sought was at hand; and ten minutes later he emerged from the forest to find himself confronted by a scene of so extraordinary a character that he halted abruptly and rubbed his eyes, uncertain for the moment whether what he beheld was reality or the effect of a disordered imagination.

Chapter Eleven
How Phil encountered a most
marvellous Adventure

The place in which Stukely now found himself was a perfectly open glade of about forty acres in extent, carpeted with rich, luscious grass, such as the antelope loves to feed upon, without a tree or shrub of any kind upon it. It was not this, however, which excited his astonishment, for such glades were by no means uncommon even in the densest parts of the South American forest; nor was it that, immediately facing him, on the opposite side of the glade, towered a bare, vertical stretch of porphyry cliff towering up full three hundred feet into the cloudless blue. But it was the unique spectacle which the face of that cliff afforded that excited the Englishman's admiration and astonishment, for it was sculptured all over, from base to summit, with boldly executed figures of men, women, and animals, which, when his admiration had passed sufficiently to enable him to study them in detail, seemed to Stukely to tell some sort of a story. But what the story was he was quite unable to puzzle out, for there were hunting episodes depicted, and also scenes which seemed to represent some sort of religious ceremonial, while others, again, might be interpreted as representing either a human sacrifice, or, possibly, the execution of a criminal; for they represented a group of men thrusting forward by a long pole another, whose hands were bound behind him, toward a great uncouth-looking monster that was emerging from a pool and advancing ponderously toward the unwilling victim with widely opened, cavernous jaws thickly set with most formidable-looking teeth. The figures were executed in rather high relief, and there was a certain quaintness and stiffness of outline in their delineation that marked them as the work of an untutored artist, yet the action of them was depicted with a spirit and vigour which proved that the sculptor, although untutored, was undoubtedly a keen student of nature. Altogether, it was by far the most surprising thing of its kind that Stukely had ever seen, and he stood for a long time studying the various tableaux, and wondering why in the world anyone should have thought it worth while to spend the best part of a lifetime in carving in the stubborn rock so elaborate a series of pictures, where probably no one but an occasional wandering Indian would ever behold them.

Somewhat to Stukely's surprise, there was no game in the glade, yet it was the one place of all others where he would have expected to find antelope at least. He looked about him to see whether he could discover a cause for the emptiness of the glade, and presently thought he had found it in a cave, the opening of which in the face of the opposite cliff he had already curiously noted while examining the sculptures. Doubtless that was it; a panther or some other evil beast had made its home in the cave, and had preyed upon the game that frequented the glade until it had all been frightened away. He decided to go across and investigate the place; possibly the panther, or whatever it was, might be at home, and, if so, its skin would be very useful, for his clothes were becoming much the worse for wear.

So he walked across the glade, and presently noticed, as he drew near the mouth of the cave, that the soil round about it was damp, and that a small trickle of water was issuing from the opening. By the time that he had advanced a few steps farther he had also noticed that the grass immediately about the entrance of the cave was very nearly all worn away, as though by the feet of many animals, while the damp soil about the opening was trodden into the consistency of thick mud that bore the impress of the feet of many animals, among which he recognised those of antelope, wild pig, monkeys, and a jaguar or two. These last confirmed his theory as to the reason why the glade presented such an utterly forsaken appearance; a pair of jaguars, knowing by instinct that such a spot would be largely frequented by various kinds of game, had no doubt taken up their quarters in the cave, and had fared sumptuously every day until their repeated attacks had driven the game away.

Stringing his bow and drawing an arrow from his quiver, Stukely strode forward until he stood in the mouth of the cave, when he halted and looked in. He now saw that it was a very much larger place than he had at first imagined it to be; for, looking inward, he was able to follow the rough walls for a few yards, as they receded inward, when he lost sight of them in the gloom. Also he became aware of a curious charnel-house kind of stench that now and then issued from the cavern. It was just the kind of odour that one would expect to meet with in the den of a carnivorous beast, and Phil peered keenly into the darkness, more than half-expecting to see the shining eyes of a jaguar or puma glaring at him when his own eyes had become accustomed to the subdued light of the place. But no such sight greeted him, only, as he stood, staring and listening, a sudden faint splash of water reached his ears from within the dark depths of the cavern, and a few seconds later, as a little stream of water came trickling down the slope from the interior, a hot, strong puff of the peculiar effluvium which he had previously noticed, smote him and almost turned him sick.

He retreated hastily to the open air—noticing as he did so that the momentary trickle of water had ceased to flow; he felt that after inhaling that dreadful odour he must get a breath of fresh air; also, if he desired to explore the interior of that cavern, he must provide himself with a torch. Accordingly he retraced his steps across the glade, re-entered the forest, and proceeded to look about him for a few dry branches to serve as torches, some dry moss for tinder, and a couple of pieces of wood suitable for rubbing upon each other when it was desired to kindle a fire. These things were soon found, and Stukely was returning to the open glade with the perfect silence and caution which had now become habitual to him, when, as he parted the last branches of the scrub which shut him in, his quick eyes detected something moving along the base of the cliff toward the cave. A single glance sufficed to assure him that it was one of the large apes, almost as big as a man, which abounded in the forest; and he determined to remain where he was for a few moments and watch the creature; if the brute entered the cave, as seemed to be his intention, Stukely felt he might safely conclude that the jaguars, or whatever they might be, were not at home, and that consequently he might himself enter without the observance of quite so much precaution as he would otherwise have considered necessary.

As he had anticipated, the ape was evidently bound for the interior of the cavern, for upon arriving at the entrance the creature paused for a moment, appeared to sniff the air carefully for a second or two, and then went boldly in, somewhat to Stukely's surprise, for although when he first saw the creature he gathered from its movements that it intended to enter the cave, he could not imagine why it should do so; for he knew perfectly well by this time that that particular species of ape lived in a tree, not in a cave. Then he recollected the water, and immediately came to the conclusion that there must be a spring or pond of some sort inside the cave to which the animals of the neighbourhood were accustomed to resort in order to quench their thirst. Yes, of course, that would be it, he told himself; and it would account in a perfectly natural manner for the many footprints which he had seen in the mud at the entrance. And, if that were the case, of course it would not be the den of a panther or other carnivorous animal at all; for monkeys, pigs, and antelopes would not frequent a spring in a cave which one or more of their most deadly enemies had made their lair. And yet— what about that abominable stench which issued from the cave; how was that to be accounted for? It was a difficult question to answer, and Stukely felt that there was but one way of getting at the truth, namely, by thoroughly examining the interior of the cavern. So, forgetting for the moment that he was out after game, and was not engaged upon an exploring expedition, he passed out through the parted scrub and headed straight for the mouth of the cave.

He had traversed about half the width of the glade when the sound of a sudden, loud splashing of water reached his ears, immediately followed by an outburst of the most appalling shrieks and yells; and a couple of seconds later out dashed the ape at a speed of which Stukely would never have believed the creature capable, had he not beheld it with his own eyes. The ape cleared the mouth of the cave as though he had been shot out of it, and came straight across the glade toward Phil. For an instant the latter thought that the simian had caught sight of him and, transported with rage, intended to attack him; so he halted, dropped his branches and tinder, and prepared to fit an arrow to his bow to repel the attack; but a second glance assured him that he was mistaken, for the monkey was not coming directly toward him, but would pass him at a distance of about a dozen paces. Moreover, it was more than likely that the creature did not even see him, for Phil could now see that the poor brute, as it dashed toward him in great, headlong bounds, with its long, hairy arms and hands stretched out before it, its eyes turned back in its head, and the most hideous shrieks issuing from its foaming jaws, was frantic with terror! In the drawing of half a dozen breaths the terrified beast had come up level with, dashed past him, and plunged headlong into the depths of the forest, where its yells at once raised a tremendous commotion among the parrots and other birds, to say nothing of the monkeys and jaguars that made it their home.

Phil meditatively gathered up the materials wherewith he proposed to illumine the interior of the cavern, and slowly resumed his way across the glade. Evidently there was something in the cavern after all, otherwise that poor ape would not have dashed out of it so precipitately, and in such a ghastly state of terror. But what could it be? It must be something even more formidable than a jaguar or a puma, to have terrified that unhappy monkey to the verge of madness; yet, so far as Phil knew, the jaguar was the most dreaded beast to be found in the South American forest. There was but one way of determining the point satisfactorily. So, completely forgetful now of the errand upon which he had started out, Stukely at once decided to adopt that way, which was, of course, to enter the cavern and see for himself.

Accordingly, having arrived within about thirty feet of the opening in the face of the sculptured rock, the young Englishman looked warily about him and peered into the interior of the cavern to make sure that there was no likelihood of his being attacked unawares; and when at length he had satisfied himself on this head, he laid down his bow and proceeded to arrange his dry moss so that it would kindle readily; then he took his two fire-producing sticks, rubbed them one against the other in the most approved manner, and presently had a little flame which he deftly communicated to the tinder-like moss. When this was fairly ablaze, he ignited the biggest and thickest branch he had with him, and was soon in possession of a brilliantly burning flambeau, holding which in one hand, and his bow and arrow in the other, he at once boldly plunged into the interior of the cavern, glancing keenly about him as he held his torch aloft.

The first thing that Phil noticed was that the fetid, charnel-house odour which had before assailed his nostrils was now, for some reason, not nearly so strong as when he had previously stood in the entrance of the cavern; indeed it was scarcely perceptible. The next thing to attract his attention was the fact that the cavern widened out very considerably as it receded into the interior of the rock, and that the floor slightly rose as he walked forward. Then the shimmer of water ahead in the light of the torch caught his eye, and when he had penetrated about fifty feet he suddenly found himself in a vast rock chamber, so large that the light of his torch could scarcely reach its farther extremity or its roof. And there was a peculiarity about this rock chamber which consisted in the fact that the whole of its interior, from wall to wall, was occupied by a pool of water which brimmed to the level of the highest part of the upward sloping entrance passage—nay, it did even more, for it occasionally slopped over and went trickling away in a tiny stream down the passage into the open, thus moistening the soil at the entrance and creating the mud in which Phil had detected the spoor of numerous different kinds of animals. A further circumstance which at once arrested Phil's attention and caused him again to look sharply about him was that the surface of the pool, instead of being glass-smooth, as one would naturally expect water to be in a place completely sheltered from the wind, was considerably agitated, as though some creature of great bulk had recently been swimming in it. Yet, so far as he could observe, he was himself the only living creature in the cavern, and he could see to its farthest extremity pretty clearly, now that his eyes had become accustomed to the comparatively dim light of the torch. Moreover, upon carefully examining the rocky floor upon which he stood, the only wet footprints visible were those of the ape which had recently beaten so precipitate a retreat from the cavern, and Phil was quite certain that the creature had not been indulging in a swim, for he was prepared to swear that the brute's fur was perfectly dry when it dashed past him on its way across the glade. No, so far as the ape was concerned, the signs indicated that it had waded into the water far enough to bend down and drink, and then had been suddenly and very badly frightened. Again Phil gazed about him, searching the obscurity on the far side of the cave, and now he noticed that there was another passage over there, a roughly circular hole about five feet in diameter, running still farther into the heart of the rock. He thought he would like to get across and explore that hole; but how was he to do so? Of course he might swim across the water; but that idea did not appeal to him, for it meant risking the extinguishment of his torch; also he could not very well carry torch, bow, and arrows in the one hand while swimming with the other, and he was by this time much too wise to go poking about in strange places without his weapons. No, that would certainly not do; rather than be guilty of so foolish an act as to discard his weapons he would leave that hole on the other side unexplored. But that alternative, too, was distinctly distasteful to the young Englishman, and he once more raised his torch and carefully examined the walls of the cavern, to see if he could find a way of getting to the other side without being obliged to swim across. And now that he was definitely looking for it he saw that there was a something in the nature of a narrow ledge running along the left side of the chamber, at a height of about six inches above the water's surface, by means of which, and aided by the roughnesses of the cavern wall, he believed he could scramble over to the other side. He at once determined to make the attempt, noticing at the same time, without attaching any particular significance to the fact, that the agitation of the surface of the pond had so far subsided that there was now but the merest suggestion of a ripple on it.

When Stukely reached the ledge by means of which he proposed to essay the passage to the far side of the cavern he found, to his satisfaction, that it was a quite well-defined projection running the entire length of the wall, and apparently nowhere less than four inches wide, while there were places where it widened out to nearly a foot in breadth, also the surface of the wall was so rough that the irregularities would afford him excellent grip for one hand. Therefore returning to its quiver the arrow which he had thus far been holding in readiness for a sudden emergency, and slinging his bow over his shoulder, so that he might have one hand quite free to cling by, the young man set his foot upon the ledge and began to make his way cautiously across.

"AN ENORMOUS HEAD EMERGED"

He had accomplished rather more than half the distance across when he suddenly felt the water surge up over his feet and ankles, and, upon looking down, saw, to his consternation, that it was once more violently agitated, the swirling eddies upon its surface plainly indicating the presence of some powerful disturbing influence at the bottom of the pool. Then, as Phil continued to gaze, that influence revealed itself as a shapeless fawn-coloured something imperfectly seen through the disturbed water, and the next moment an enormous head emerged, a pair of monstrous jaws gaped widely, and the air of the cavern at once became again surcharged with the disgusting effluvium which Phil had once before observed. As Stukely gazed, fascinated, at the terrifying object which had thus suddenly appeared he became aware that the creature was dazzled and to some extent discomfited by the light of the torch, for the lids of its immense goggle eyes blinked incessantly as it returned Phil's gaze, taking immediate advantage of which the young man thrust his torch toward it as far as he could reach, with the immediate result that the great head again sank out of sight. Only for a few brief seconds, however; but the young Englishman availed himself of those few seconds to scramble along the remainder of the ledge and reach the point for which he was aiming, and which now proved to be a sloping surface of rock about twenty feet broad, leading up from the water to the circular opening which Stukely had been so anxious to explore.

Now that he was there he was ready to execrate his folly for not having retraced his steps along the ledge and made good his escape by way of the mouth of the cavern, instead of continuing his journey, as he had done; for his ill-judged action had resulted in placing him at the wrong end of the cavern, and, to escape, he would be obliged to make his way along the whole of that narrow ledge again, with the possibility that the monster, recovering from its discomfiture, might snatch him off before he had traversed half the distance. No, Phil felt that with such a horrible possibility as that confronting him he simply could not essay the return passage along the ledge.

Indeed he was not afforded the opportunity; for he had scarcely reached the broad slope of rock leading up to the circular tunnel which he had been so anxious to explore, when the surface of the pool again became violently agitated, and the monstrous head again appeared, followed this time by an enormous body, four thick, clumsy legs, and a tail; and with a ponderous rush the creature at once made for the spot where Stukely stood. But Phil, without waiting for further developments, incontinently turned tail, and, stooping, bolted up the tunnel-like opening, the comforting assurance coming to him that so monstrous a beast could not possibly enter so comparatively small a passage. Moreover, he was right, for after running a few feet he looked back over his shoulder and saw that although the beast had thrust its head, as far as its eyes, into the opening, it could advance no farther. Then, summoning all his courage to his aid, he retraced his steps, and, plucking an arrow from his quiver, poised it in his hand for a moment—he could not use his bow, as it was too long to be drawn in so confined a space— and then hurled it with all his strength straight at the beast's left eye. The missile flew true—indeed it could scarcely miss at such exceedingly short range—and buried itself half its length in the great blinking orb; whereupon, with a bellowing roar that echoed and reverberated like thunder in that underground chamber, the monstrous head was suddenly withdrawn, and the next moment a sound of tremendous splashing told the hardy assailant that his enemy had precipitately retreated to the depths of the pool. Then, acting more by instinct than reason, Phil rushed back along the way which he had come, out of the tunnel, on to and along the ledge—heedless of the violent disturbance of the water which told of the convulsive movements of the enormous shape hidden beneath its surface—and so back to the cavern entrance, out of which he rushed almost as precipitately as the ape had done half an hour earlier. "No wonder," thought the young man, "that the poor beast was frightened, if he happened to catch a glimpse of the monster of the pool!" Some two hours later he turned up at the spot where the little party had made their temporary camp beside the river, and nonchalantly flung to the ground the carcass of a Guazu-puti deer which he had chanced to encounter on his way back. He found that Dick and Vilcamapata had made good use of their time during his absence, for they had not only found a splendid tree out of which to fashion a canoe, but had actually felled it; and there it lay, within a couple of hundred feet of the river, ready to be hewn into shape and hollowed out.

"You've been away a long time," remarked Dick; "gramfer here and I were seriously discussing the desirability of starting out to look for you. Have you found the game scarce?"

"Game of the kind that I was after, yes; but game of a very different sort, no," answered Stukely. "The fact is, Dick," he continued, "that I have had quite an interesting afternoon. For I have discovered a cliff carved all over with pictures that there is nobody to look at, and—why, yes, now that I come to think of it, some of those pictures show the very beast itself!"

"My dear Phil," remonstrated Dick, "are you talking to yourself or to me? Because, if the latter, let me remind you that I don't in the least understand what you are referring to."

"No," laughed Stukely, "of course you don't. But all in good time, friend; hurry no man's cattle. Thou wilt understand when I explain. Know, then, O most matter-of-fact Dick, that I have this day seen a sight—or two sights, to be strictly truthful—that will cause thee to open thine eyes in amazement. The first of them is, as I have already said, a cliff pictured all over its face with strange and wonderful sculptures, which doubtless tell a story if one had but the wit to read them; and that reminds me that we ought to take the ancient along with us when we go to see them to-morrow; he may be able to interpret their meaning to us. Now, among those pictures there is one depicting—as I read it—a man being thrown to a huge and monstrous beast; and inside a cave in that same cliff I not only found the beast himself, but narrowly escaped being devoured by him. Fortunately for me, there happened to be a hole in the rock big enough for me to enter, but not big enough for him; and when he would fain have followed me his head got stuck fast in the opening, in which position, he being at my mercy, I drove an arrow into his left eye, and escaped while he was endeavouring to free himself therefrom. But we must all go together to-morrow, Dick, and see these wonders; for they are worth seeing, I warrant thee."

Dick Chichester, however, was not to be satisfied with any such bald and incomplete statement as the foregoing, and accordingly, when they sat down, an hour later, to take their last meal for the day, Stukely gave a full, true, and particular account of his entire afternoon's adventure; and it was agreed, then and there, that the first business of the following day should be a visit to the sculptured rocks and the slaying of the strange and monstrous beast.

Accordingly, on the following morning, immediately after an early breakfast, the trio set out, arriving in due course at the glade which lay at the foot of the cliff. As usual, they approached the open space with the utmost precaution, and were thus enabled to secure an antelope, one of a small herd that happened to be grazing there at the moment of their arrival. They killed the creature, not because they required it for food, but because Phil was of opinion that its carcass might serve as a bait for the enticement of the monster out of the pool, thus enabling them to get a fair shot at him; and having dragged the dead animal to the mouth of the cave, they next proceeded to examine at leisure the sculptured face of the rocks, which Vilcamapata at once unhesitatingly pronounced to be the work of Amalivaca, the wonderful being whom the Indians were looking for from across the Great Water to deliver them from the power of the hated Spaniard, and restore to them the undisputed possession of their own country. But he was unable to interpret the meaning of the sculptures, beyond stating vaguely that they, like many others existing in the country, undoubtedly portrayed certain customs and modes of life peculiar to a race who inhabited the country long before the Indians came into it.

Then, having at length satisfied their curiosity by gazing their fill at the curious scenes set forth in the imperishable porphyry, they entered the cavern and inspected the pool, the surface of which was still agitated, showing that its tenant was restless, as indeed might be expected. Then, returning to where they had left the carcass of the deer, they dragged it far enough into the cavern to enable the monster just to reach it by completely emerging from the pool; and then, stringing their bows, and satisfying themselves that the priming of their pistols was as it should be, calmly sat down to await the issue.

For more than an hour they waited in vain; for beyond an occasional stirring of the water, which caused it to overflow momentarily and trickle down the slope of the approach, nothing happened. Then a troop of small monkeys suddenly approached the cavern, and, seeing its human occupants, bolted, loudly chattering their indignation and fright. Shortly afterward a deer came tripping daintily across the glade, halted suddenly, threw up its head, and after sniffing the air for a few seconds, wheeled smartly round and bounded back into the forest. Another hour passed, and they were discussing in low tones the advisability of adopting some other plan for the enticement of the great beast from his lair, when they heard a sudden rippling and splashing of water in the interior of the cave, followed by a low moan and a gust of the offensive effluvium which Phil had noticed on the previous day, then a still more violent splashing of water, accompanied by a quick rush of overflow, a sound of ponderous movements, and then, looming out of the darkness, there vaguely appeared an enormous shape coming slowly and cautiously toward the carcass of the deer. In another moment it had advanced sufficiently to enable the watchers to observe the shape of its monstrous head, and Phil saw that in some way the creature had managed to free itself of the arrow which he had implanted in its left eye on the preceding day; but the brute had doubtless lost the use of that eye, for it could now be seen that it was closed, and that a small trickle of blood was flowing from between the lids. As it slowly advanced, the beast moaned frequently, while the disgusting odour which it exhaled momentarily became stronger.

It had been agreed that if the beast could be enticed out of the water, all three of the hunters should, at a given signal, discharge an arrow at its right eye, and the trio were now standing, with bows fully bent, awaiting the signal. Another moment, and the brute slightly raised its head and halted, as though suspicious of danger. The slight raising of the head was just what was required to enable a perfect aim to be taken, and Phil at once gave the word "Shoot!"

The loud and practically simultaneous twanging of the three bows was instantly followed by a hideous roar, and in another moment the great beast, bellowing horribly, came charging right out of the cave, all but crushing to death his adventurous enemies as he did so, for the three had only just time to dodge behind a projection of the rock when the monster rushed past them at a lumbering trot, to stumble and roll over, just as it reached the open. For a moment the trio thought that in some unaccountable manner they must have missed their aim, for as the creature passed them they were unable to see any portion of the shafts of their arrows protruding from its remaining eye. But it, too, was now closed, and they presently concluded that, with the momentum imparted to them by their exceedingly powerful bows, the arrows must have completely buried themselves in the monster's eyeball. At all events it was perfectly evident that the missiles had got home somewhere, for the huge creature was now rolling and bellowing in agony, as it clawed frantically at its eyes with its immense feet. It was a distressing sight to see such an enormous animal suffering so intensely, so presently Phil and Dick ran out, put fresh arrows to their bows, and stood at a distance of about a dozen paces from the beast, watching for an opportunity to plant an arrow in its heart. It came after a while, the beast subsiding at last into quiescence, as though exhausted; and upon the instant Dick and Phil drew their bows to their fullest possible extent, the arrows flew straight to their mark, and, with a tremendous convulsive shudder and a last moaning bellow, the enormous brute stretched itself out on the grass dead.

Then they proceeded to examine the creature at their leisure, but at a respectful distance, for the odour which it exhaled was so overpowering that they found it impossible to approach the carcass nearer than within three or four yards. The head was somewhat like that of an alligator, but immensely larger, and its enormous jaws, slightly open, disclosed two rows of huge teeth similar to those of an alligator. This monstrous head was joined to the body by a neck as long, proportionately, as that of a horse; the body was lizard-like in shape, but humpbacked; it had four very thick, lizard-like legs and feet, each terminating in four long toes armed with formidable claws. Its tail was nearly as long as its body, thick, deep, and blunt; and a sort of serrated fin ran the whole length of its body from the nape of its neck to the extremity of its tail. Its total length, from snout to tail, as it lay stretched out on the grass, was just a trifle over twenty-two paces!

When they had at length satisfied their curiosity by exhaustively examining the enormous carcass—which, they agreed, must be that of the identical beast portrayed in the carved pictures on the cliff face, or of one precisely similar—they procured torches, and, having lighted them, proceeded to examine thoroughly the interior of the cavern. In the outer chamber, or that which contained the pool—the surface of which was now perfectly placid and mirrorlike—there was nothing to see beyond what has already been described. After a brief glance round, therefore, they passed over to its far side by means of the rock ledge along the margin of the pool, and entered the tunnel-like passage in which Phil had taken temporary refuge on the previous day. This proved to be about one hundred feet long, and gave access to another chamber of such immense dimensions that, standing just within it, and holding their three torches high above their heads, they were unable to see the opposite wall or the roof. But it was a wonderful cavern, and worth travelling a long distance to see; for upon examination they discovered that its walls, as high up as the light of the torches would enable them to see, were most elaborately sculptured in high relief with figures of men, women, animals, trees, representations of spacious landscapes with buildings, and even the sea, with either the rising or the setting sun partially obscured by clouds. And the remarkable thing about these sculptures was that they were very much more finely and artistically executed than those outside; the representation was much more true to nature; the details of clothing were rendered with the most minute elaboration and exactitude; and there was also evidence of a knowledge and understanding of perspective. For the first quarter of an hour or so of their inspection they were unable to obtain any clue to the purpose to which this enormous chamber had originally been put, or the reason which could induce a person—or, rather, a number of persons, for no single individual could possibly have produced the whole of that work, even if he had devoted an entire lifetime to it—to spend time in laboriously executing such work in a situation where it would seem that it could be seldom or never seen. But by and by, when the explorers arrived at the far end of the chamber, they saw that it was neither more nor less than an immense temple; for there, in the very centre of the wall, was a most beautifully and elaborately sculptured niche, within which was enshrined a lifesize figure, in black marble, of a man, in the carving of which the unknown sculptor seemed to have reached the very summit of perfection of his art. For with the most scrupulous and precise fidelity he had succeeded in reproducing every minutest detail, the texture and wrinkles of the skin, the finger and toe nails, the course of the veins, and even the curls in the long hair, bushy beard, and drooping moustache. The figure had originally been executed nude; but, whether from considerations of modesty, or for the glorification of the idol, it had afterwards been clothed in a most elaborate costume consisting of a tunic, confined to the waist by a belt, a cloak, and sandals. The tunic was made of a kind of fine canvas that crumbled away when touched; the mantle was of feathers of the most gorgeous hues; and the sandals were of some delicate kind of leather dressed with the hair on; and they, as well as the tunic and belt, were encrusted with minute scales of dull, ruddy yellow metal, which proved to be virgin gold. These scales were not only sewn on to the material, but were also sewn to each other; and it was due to this latter fact, no doubt, that the garment had not powdered away long ago. The eyes of the idol consisted of two large green polished stones which looked so much like emeralds—which indeed they were—that, Vilcamapata offering no objection, the two young Englishmen determined to appropriate them, as well as the gold scales; with the result that they left the figure denuded of all its finery, and, from an artistic point of view at least, far more worthy of admiration than it was before.

They spent quite two hours in this wonderful cavern, and when at length they emerged into daylight once more they found that already a whole army of vultures had gathered about the carcass of the strange monstrous beast, and were busily engaged in devouring the malodorous flesh. The trio made a wide circuit so as not to disturb the obscene birds at their disgusting banquet, and in due time found their way back again to their camp, where, after a hearty meal, they set to work in earnest upon the construction of their canoe.

Chapter Twelve
How the Two Adventurers
lost their Companion

To hew and hollow a canoe out of a solid tree trunk is a sufficiently formidable task for two men to undertake when they possess no more suitable tools than their hangers—the hanger being a weapon very similar to the more modern cutlass; and although the two Englishmen had already done a similar piece of work once before, and were therefore not altogether lacking in experience; and although Vilcamapata taught them how to hollow out the hull expeditiously, after it was properly shaped, by the use of fire, it cost Phil and Dick very nearly a month's strenuous labour to get their new craft to their liking. But when she was finished she was a very good canoe, indeed, much more shapely than those made by the Indians, and her hull was so thin that, although she measured about eighteen feet long over all by four feet beam, she was light enough to be carried easily a distance of two or three miles, if need be, by the two Englishmen, Vilcamapata being too old and feeble to be capable of lending assistance in work of that sort.

But at length the work was finished, the craft was taken down to the river, put in the water, and found to float true, and as buoyantly as an eggshell. The trio therefore put their few belongings into her, not forgetting the two fine emeralds and the gold scales taken from the idol, embarked, and resumed their journey.

They were now on the headwaters of a river which had its rise somewhere on the eastern slope of the Andes; and the water was icy cold, being in fact nothing but the drainings from an enormous glacier which could be seen, some forty miles away, clinging to the side of a majestic peak that towered nearly twenty thousand feet into the deep blue of the tropic sky. But that was a blessing rather than otherwise, for although they were not yet down among the plains the weather was intensely hot—they being now immediately under the equator—and the coldness of the water helped somewhat to mitigate the stifling heat between the two great walls of forest which bordered the river on either hand.

No sail was needed, for they were now travelling with the stream, which, being as yet little more than a mountain torrent, ran rapidly, so that a paddle over the stern to keep the craft in midstream was all that was necessary. But although the stream ran at the rate of fully six miles an hour their progress was not by any means as speedy as one might at first suppose, for rapids occurred at frequent intervals, and if these were found to be impassable it became necessary to carry the canoe past them through the forest. This plan, however, was only resorted to in extreme cases, for if, upon examination, it was deemed at all possible to shoot the rapids, they were shot; and as this sometimes happened as often as three or four times a day, the adventurers soon acquired a degree of dexterity in the art that they would have regarded as perfectly amazing at the beginning of their journey.

On the evening of the fifth day of their journey down the river they chanced to camp at a spot which afforded them an exceptionally fine view of the mountain range to the westward; and when on the following morning they rose to prepare for the day's journey they saw that a terrific thunderstorm was raging about halfway up the eastern slope of the range. It was a magnificent sight, the clouds, black as night below, but brilliantly illuminated by the sun above, clinging to the mountain spurs in enormous masses which rolled together, parted, and rolled together again like charging squadrons, while the lightning, keen and vivid as molten steel, incessantly darted from their black breasts like the flashes of a platoon of musketry. And while this elemental warfare was raging furiously up there among the mountains it was brilliant weather where the wanderers were camped, with not a breath of wind to assuage the torrid heat. Stukely happened to make some remark upon the contrast to Vilcamapata, to which the old man replied:

"Yes, it is well for us that we are here rather than there; for such a storm might well mean death for us all. But we must be watchful to-day, lord, for that storm covers many miles of country, and the rain is falling in torrents; and, unless I am greatly mistaken, most of it will find its way into this river. Therefore must we be on our guard against a sudden spate, which may overwhelm us if we are caught unawares."

The Englishmen agreed, and nothing further was said about the matter, for they were busy making their preparations for the day; and in due time they embarked and proceeded on their journey. About midday, in confirmation of the old Peruvian's words, the first of the expected spate revealed itself in a sudden acceleration of the current and a change in the appearance of the water, which became turbid with mud in suspension. Yet although the speed of the current continued to increase gradually, it merely helped the voyagers on their way, for they now seemed to have reached a stretch of the river that was entirely free from rapids, nothing of the kind having been encountered since their start in the early morning. Swiftly the canoe sped down the river, running now at the rate of a good nine miles an hour, and her occupants rejoiced exceedingly, for they were getting over as much ground in a single hour as sometimes cost them a whole day to cover. They began to make light of the precautions which they had observed during the earlier hours of the day, and told each other with glee that if this was the worst a spate could do they would welcome one every day so long as they were bound downstream.

Indeed it was speedy travelling compared with what they had been accustomed to; it was like journeying by postchaise after travelling in a market wagon. The country swept past them at a speed that almost made them giddy as they watched it, while the motion of the canoe was smooth and easy as that of a cradle. Then, as they whirled round a bend they suddenly, and without warning, found themselves sweeping through a gorge with vertical, rocky, fern-grown banks on either hand. Too well they knew what that sort of thing was the prelude to. There were rapids ahead, almost to a dead certainty, and they had missed their chance of inspecting before attempting to shoot them, for there was no landing on either of those vertical banks; while as for returning to a point where landing was possible, they might as well have attempted to fly! Well, there was but one thing for it; if there were indeed rapids ahead they must do their best to shoot them without the usual preliminary inspection; they were growing quite accustomed to that kind of work now, and it ought not to be so very difficult.

Accordingly Dick placed himself in the bow of the canoe and Phil stationed himself amidships, each armed with the long pole which they used to bear the canoe off the rocks when shooting rapids, while the Peruvian perched himself up in the stern with the short steering paddle in his hand. Presently the expected rapids swung into view ahead, and a sufficiently formidable sight they presented. It was difficult, nay impossible, to tell how far they extended, for a bend of the river shut out the view; but there was at least half a mile of them in plain sight, a narrow channel of foaming, leaping water, with the black head of a rock showing occasionally here and there amid the foam. Dick drew his feet up under him and raised himself to his full height in the crank cockleshell of a canoe, in order that he might obtain as extended a view as possible of what lay before him: he was admittedly far the more expert canoeist of the two, especially when it came to shooting rapids, therefore on such occasions his post was always in the bow, which then becomes the post of honour—and of responsibility.

What he saw was by no means reassuring; there was far too much spouting and foaming water for his taste, for such appearances invariably indicated rocks submerged to the extent of a few inches at the utmost, contact with any of which meant at least the destruction of the canoe, if no worse mishap. True, in almost every stretch of rapids there exists what may be termed by courtesy a channel, that is to say, there is a passage, more or less tortuous, between the rocks where the water is deep enough to float a canoe if one can but hit it off in time. This channel or passage is usually distinguishable by the comparative smoothness of the water in it; so that if the navigator can guide his canoe fairly into it by the time that the rapids are actually reached, he stands a very fair chance of accomplishing the run in safety, although even then he must be continually on the alert, since the turns are often so sharp that, unless taken at precisely the right moment, the canoe may be dashed with destructive violence against an obstructing rock; and it was the part of the bowman, or pilot, to look out for such rocks and bear the canoe off them with the long pole which he invariably wielded.

At length Dick believed he saw the beginning of such a channel, close under the right bank of the river, and waved Vilcamapata to steer the canoe toward it. Half a minute more, and the little craft had darted in between two formidable walls of leaping water and was speeding downward at a speed of fully fifteen miles an hour, with Dick and Phil standing upright and thrusting their long poles first to one side and then the other as Chichester's experienced eye detected the signs which mark the presence of dangerous rocks to right or left, and signalled accordingly. To cry out was utterly useless, the roar and hiss of the tortured waters was far too loud to render even the voice of a Stentor audible, and those behind the pilot could but watch his motions, and act accordingly.

Two minutes of strenuous labour brought them to the bend in the river, and this, Dick knew, would be one of the most critical points in the whole run; for it is difficult enough to follow the turns of the channel, even when the course of the river is straight, but when the river as well as the channel bends it is difficult indeed to avoid disaster. Still, Dick remained perfectly cool and self-possessed; the certainty and success with which he had piloted the canoe through that unknown half-mile of chaotic leaping and rushing water had given him more confidence in himself than all the rest of his experience put together, and he felt that unless something quite unexpected and out of the common happened, there was no reason why they should not accomplish the remainder of the run in safety. He held up his hand as a warning to those behind him to be extra vigilant, for they were at what was probably the most dangerous point of the run, and the next instant waved to the Peruvian to swerve the canoe powerfully to the left. The Indian obeyed, to the best of his ability; but he was old, his strength was nothing like what it had been, and the little craft did not swerve quite smartly enough to carry her clear of a rock that lay in her course. Therefore out shot Dick's long pole, and the moment that he felt the jar of it upon the rock he threw his whole weight upon it in the attempt to save the canoe. The shock was tremendous, the canoe was turned violently broadside-on to the current, and at that critical moment Dick's pole snapped clean in two, the recoil sending the youngster headlong into the boiling current, while the next moment the canoe swept up against the submerged rock, was rolled over and over, and her remaining occupants were flung into the swirl.

The moment that Dick felt the pole snap in his hand he knew that a capsize was inevitable, and, with the instinct which belongs to the accomplished swimmer, he at once made up his mind what would be the best thing for him to do. If he could manage to get into the centre of the main current he could probably retain his position there, and so swim the remainder of the distance to the lower end of the rapids in safety, provided that he could avoid the rocks. There was no use in looking out for the others; they were as well able to take care of themselves as he was; besides, they would each stand a better chance apart than together in that mad turmoil. As for the canoe, she must take her chance; probably she would be smashed to splinters; but if so, it would only mean the making of another one. True, it would involve a month's delay, but time of late had seemed to lose its value for them all; they were bound for a definite goal, which they would assuredly reach sooner or later, and the loss of a month or two seemed a mere trifle not worth consideration. Accordingly, the moment that Dick rose to the surface he shook the foam and spray from his eyes, glanced round him, verified his position, and at once struck out powerfully for the comparatively smooth water that indicated the main current, noting, as he did so, that Phil and the Peruvian were both swimming strongly, and that the canoe, full of water, was slowly rolling over and over as she drove along through the worst of the broken water. Five minutes of desperate struggle, during which he had no time to think of anything but his own safety, and during which he had several very narrow escapes of being dashed violently against rocks and sustaining serious injuries, if not being killed outright, and he suddenly found himself in smooth water, with the canoe swinging hither and thither in the eddies, close beside him. To swim to her and proceed to push her before him toward the nearest bank was an instinctive act with Dick; and he presently had the satisfaction of grounding her on a small strip of shingly beach where there was a slight back eddy. Then he looked about for the other two, and presently caught sight of Phil, a little lower down, swimming slowly and supporting Vilcamapata's apparently senseless form. Phil looked as though he were rather in difficulties, so Dick at once plunged in again and swam to his assistance, and ten minutes later all three of them were ashore again, about a mile lower down the river than the spot where the canoe had been beached.

"I'm afraid gramfer, here, is rather badly hurt," gasped Phil, as he and Dick lifted the insensible form of the Peruvian to the top of the low bank. "Evidently he has been dashed against a rock and stunned, if not worse," he continued, pointing to a very ugly jagged wound in the right temple, from which the blood was welling pretty freely. "I noticed, as I drove past, that you had saved the canoe. Do you think you could manage to go back and fetch her down, Dick? My case of medicaments is in her—if the thwart to which it was lashed has not gone adrift—and I should be very glad to have it just now. Dost thou mind; or art too tired?"

"Not a bit of it," answered Dick. "Of course I'll go, with pleasure. And you will be glad to hear that, so far at least as I could see, the craft is not damaged at all. But of course her paddles are lost, except the one that gramfer, there, has stuck to so tenaciously, so I must borrow it from him." And he stooped down and, with some difficulty, loosened the grip of the unconscious man's hand on the steering paddle, which he had, no doubt unconsciously, retained in his grip ever since the capsize. "I'll be back as quickly as possible," concluded Dick, as he struck off into the bush that, just there, bordered the river.

He returned again in about half an hour, with the canoe intact, nothing having been lost but the paddles, which were the only articles that happened to have been loose in her when she capsized. With quick fingers he cast loose the small medicine case which Phil had taken ashore with him on the occasion of the ill-fated landing at Cartagena, and which he had carried about with him ever since, carefully enwrapped, like their powder horns, in portions of their shirts liberally smeared with caoutchouc juice to exclude all moisture. Poor old Vilcamapata was still insensible when Dick returned, and Phil was looking exceedingly anxious about him; but the production of the medicine case soon altered matters; and a few minutes later the old man was sitting up and looking about him dazedly. At first he seemed not to recognise Phil or Dick, or to be able to remember what had happened; but gradually it all came back to him; and when Phil asked him how he felt he replied that he was fatigued and desired to sleep. Accordingly, the young medico bathed the wound with water from the river, applied some healing ointment to it, bound it up with what remained of their shirts; then they made up a temporary couch for the sufferer under the shadow of a bush, and left him to sleep as long as he would, while Dick went off in search of game, and Phil proceeded to carve a pair of new paddles and to cut a couple of new poles.

When Dick returned from his hunting expedition, some two hours later, with a small deer and a brace of guinea fowl, he found that Vilcamapata was still asleep, while Phil was putting the finishing touches to the new paddles. The Peruvian, it appeared, had scarcely moved since he fell asleep; and there was some peculiarity in the manner of his breathing which was causing Stukely a good deal of anxiety.

"I am rather afraid," explained Phil, "that the poor old man has sustained some internal injury, in addition to the wound on his head; and, if so, we may have trouble with him. But we will let him sleep as long as he will; for sleep is a great restorer; and the breathing difficulty may disappear when he awakes and sits up. But when he does, I will subject him to a very careful examination. It was most unfortunate that your pole broke, Dick; but for that I believe we should have shot the rapids in perfect safety."

While Phil completed the paddles, Dick set to work to light a fire, break up the deer, and prepare the guinea fowl for cooking; and still the injured man slept on, his breathing ever growing more laboured and stertorous, until at length the difficulty with which he drew his breath awakened him and, with a groan, he strove to raise himself. In an instant Stukely was by his side and, slipping an arm beneath his shoulders, he raised the old man to a sitting position, with his back supported by the stiff branches of the bush under the shadow of which he had been sleeping. And while he was making the poor old fellow as comfortable as he could he enquired solicitously how he felt; but Vilcamapata only looked at him blankly, and murmured a few words in a tongue that was quite unintelligible to his listener. Then, with gentle touch, Phil began to pass his hand cautiously over his patient's body, searching for possible fractured ribs or some similar injury; but the old man waved him impatiently away, and presently broke forth in a low, crooning sort of chant.

"My days are done," he murmured; "my wanderings are at an end; my Father the Sun and my Mother the Moon call me, and I must depart for those Islands of the Blessed that our Father sometimes deigns to show us floating afar in the serene skies of eventide. My spirit is weary and longs for rest. Full forty years have I been an outcast and a wanderer in the land that once belonged to my people; and during those years no friendly face have I ever beheld, no friendly voice has ever reached mine ear until the day when the two white men saved me from the fire of the Pegwi Indians. And to me have they been since then as sons; nay, more than sons, for there was a time when I dreamed that he whom the fair young giant calls Phil might be our Father Manco Capac returned to earth to deliver his people from the thraldom of the Spaniard. But to-day have mine eyes been opened, and I know of a surety that Manco will never return to earth to deliver his people, whose doom it is to disappear gradually from off the face of the earth, and be known no more. Therefore, listen unto me, O ye who have been as sons to me in the days of my loneliness and old age: Ye crave for gold, and the stones that gleam in the light white and bright as stars, green as the young grass that springs to life after the rains of winter, and red as the heart's blood of a warrior; and in my blindness I dreamed that ye sought them as the means whereby ye might obtain the power to drive out the Spaniard from the fair land of the Incas and restore it to those from whom it was wrongfully taken. And in the days of our great calamity there arose one who prophesied that in the latter days our Father Manco should return to earth and do this thing; therefore was a great treasure of gold and stones secretly gathered together from mines known only to our own people, and securely hidden from the Spaniard, in order that when Manco came he might have an abundance of wealth wherewith to buy arms and food and clothing for his armies. But to-day I know that the prophet who foretold this thing was a false prophet, and that the hidden treasure will never be needed for the accomplishment of the purpose for which it was gathered; also I am the last of those who knew the secret of the hiding-place, and if I pass away, taking the secret with me, the treasure will be lost, wasted, useless, remaining for ever undiscovered.

"Therefore hearken now unto me, O ye who have been to me as sons in these the last days of mine old age. When my spirit leaves this withered shell, as it is about to do, ye shall build a funeral pyre, lay my body thereon, and put fire thereto; for by fire are all things purified, and on the wings of the flames shall my spirit mount and soar away to those Happy Isles where is neither sin, nor sorrow, nor suffering, nor any other evil thing. This shall ye do to-night. And with the rising of to-morrow's sun ye shall resume your journey down the river, and so continue for, it may be, twelve days, until this river flows into a much mightier one. Then ye shall journey up that mightier stream—which flows to the south and west—and, turning neither to the right hand nor to the left, shall follow it to its source beyond Cuzco, until ye sight Sorata's mighty snow-clad crest. And there, under Sorata's morning shadow shall ye find the Sacred Lake. There are islands in that lake: that which lies in the centre of the lake is the island which ye must seek, for on it stands the ruined temple of the Sun, beneath the great marble floor of which lies—lies—the—Yea, great Lord and Father, I come!"

And, sinking back among the branches of the bush which supported him, Vilcamapata, the one-time priest of the Sun, closed his eyes as a torrent of blood gushed from his mouth, and quietly passed away.

"Internal haemorrhage!" exclaimed Stukely, as he lightly laid his fingers upon the pulseless wrist. "I feared it. Yes"—as he passed his hand over the body—"three of his ribs are broken, and the jagged ends have doubtless lacerated some internal organ—the lung, perhaps. Well, he is dead, beyond all question; and now, all that remains for us to do, Dick, is to dispose of his body in accordance with his instructions. But I do not altogether like the idea of building his pyre just here. We must see if we cannot find a suitable spot about a quarter of a mile away."

"I know a perfectly suitable spot about that distance from here," answered Dick; "I passed through it on my way back to camp, about an hour ago. Come, I will show it to you; there is plenty of dry wood there, and there is a path by which we can easily carry the body to it. Better make a litter, perhaps, and take it with us now."

Stukely eagerly concurred in this view, and they at once proceeded to construct a litter of boughs bound together with lianas, upon which, when it was finished, they laid the attenuated form of the old man, and, with measured steps and slow, bore him to the spot where his mortal frame was to undergo its typical purging by fire. The place was one of those perfectly open clearings which are so frequently met with in the South American forest; it was about ten acres in extent, roughly circular in shape, and was carpeted with thick grass which the deer and other grazing animals kept close cropped; consequently it was well adapted for the purpose to which it was about to be put, since by erecting the pyre in the centre of the clearing there would be no risk of setting the adjoining forest ablaze.

Laying the litter and its burden down in a convenient position just within the clearing, the two Englishmen plunged back into the forest, and, using their hangers as axes, vigorously proceeded to hew down all the dry, dead branches and underwood they could find; for the afternoon was waning apace and it was essential that the flames should be kindled in time to allow of their returning to their camping place by daylight. Fortunately there was no lack of suitable material close at hand; and an hour's arduous work sufficed to provide a sufficiency for their purpose. Then they proceeded to build the pyre, laying the smallest branches at the bottom, intermingled with plenty of dry brushwood, and putting the thickest branches on the top. Then, on the top of all, they placed the body; and Phil next proceeded to make fire in the usual way by rubbing two sticks together. This was soon done, the fire was inserted into the heart of the pyre by means of an aperture left for the purpose, and then, when the whole was fairly alight, Phil and Dick bared their heads, fell upon their knees, and with the simple faith which so strongly characterised the religious feeling of the time, humbly commended the soul of Vilcamapata to the mercy of God who gave it. By the time that they had finished their petitions the pile was a mass of flame which roared and crackled fiercely as it shot straight upward in the still evening air; and, with a last parting glance at the body, which could be seen shrivelling in the midst of the flames, they turned and silently wended their way back to their camping place. And thus passed Vilcamapata, the last of the ancient Peruvian priests of the Sun, with two men only, and they of alien blood and alien religion, to perform the last sacred rites for him.

On the following morning, having breakfasted and completed their preparations for immediate departure, the two young Englishmen, feeling strangely lonely, walked over to the spot where the funeral pyre had been built, and inspected what remained of it. They found that it had been completely consumed, to the very last twig; and upon searching among the white ashes they found a calcined skull and a few fragments of the larger bones. These they gathered carefully together and reverently buried; after which, having now done all that was possible to preserve the remains of their late friend from desecration, they returned to the camp, embarked in their canoe, and resumed their voyage down the river.

The following fortnight proved quite uneventful for our two adventurers; they journeyed on down the river at an average rate of about twenty miles a day, and from time to time encountered rapids or cataracts, or both together, shooting most of the former, and, of course, being compelled to carry the canoe down past the latter; but they had by this time become so thoroughly accustomed to the negotiation of rapids and waterfalls that they had long since ceased to regard the passage of one or the other as an adventure. True, they saw a few Indians occasionally; but these generally beat a hasty retreat when the white men appeared, and remained concealed until the canoe and its two occupants, now garbed like savages in the skins of beasts, had disappeared round the next bend in the river.

As foretold by Vilcamapata, they reached the "much mightier river"— the Maranon—on the afternoon of the twelfth day, and there their pleasant journeying with the current ceased; henceforward the current would again be their enemy, instead of their friend as it had been of late, and every inch of progress would have to be won either with the assistance of the sail or by arduous toil with the paddle. Luckily for them, they had had the prescience to bring the sail along with them when they found themselves obliged to abandon the boat, and now they reaped the full reward of their labours, and were glad that they had resisted the often-repeated temptation to leave it behind when they encountered some exceptionally difficult bit of road.

Thanks to the help afforded by a strong breeze from the north-east, the end of their second day's journeying on the Maranon found them some seventy miles above the spot where they had struck the river, and in the territory—had they but known it—of the fierce and warlike Mayubuna Indians. They had seen several parties of these during the latter part of the day, and, contrary to the usual custom of the Indians which they had thus far met with, instead of running away at the first sight of the canoe, the Mayubunas had stood on the river bank and watched their progress, manifesting no fear of the whites, but, on the other hand, displaying no outward signs of hostility, unless, indeed, the fact that about an hour before sunset a large canoe had been manned at the last village which the white men had passed, and had proceeded rapidly up the river ahead of them, might be so construed. Unfortunately for them, they did not so construe it, but regarded it rather as a sporting attempt on the part of a number of Indians, bound up the river, to display the superiority of the paddle over the sail, and were amused accordingly.

But when, upon rounding the next bend of the river, the two Englishmen sighted two large canoes, full of Indians, ahead of them, one canoe paddling along close in with the left bank, while the other as closely hugged the right, they began for the first time to suspect that all was not quite as it should be, and Phil—who was sitting idly amidships, while Dick sailed the canoe— rose to his feet and hailed them in the Indian dialect, which he had picked up from Vilcamapata. No notice, however, was taken of the hail, but it was observed that the sailing canoe was now gaining distinctly upon the others.

Encouraged by this evidence of superior speed, the white men pressed on, anxious to get into communication and establish friendly relations with the Indians before nightfall; and it was not until the two canoes ahead suddenly swerved outward and laid themselves athwart the hawse of the sailing canoe, as though to bar her further progress, that either of the occupants of the latter thought of looking astern. Then they realised that matters were indeed beginning to look serious, for behind them were no less than four large canoes, each containing twenty-one men, which had evidently emerged from a small creek about half a mile lower down, and were now drawing near with unmistakably hostile intentions.

"This looks awkward, Dick," exclaimed Stukely, seizing his bow and arrows. "Surely they cannot seriously intend to try to stop us?"

"If they don't, why are they laying their canoes across our hawse like thicky?" demanded Dick. "Hadn't you better speak to them a bit, Phil?"

"Ay, I'll try," answered Stukely. And, stepping into the bows of the canoe, he ostentatiously laid down his weapons and made the usual signs of amity. The reply was a yell of anger and hatred from the Indians, who were blocking the way, while one of them, springing to his feet, shouted:

"Go back, dogs of Spaniards; go back! This is the land of the Mayubuna, and we will permit no Spaniard to set foot upon its soil. We have no desire to be swallowed up, as Atahuallpa and his people were, after he had welcomed you to his country; therefore go back—or die!"

"They take us for Spaniards," explained Phil to Dick; and, raising his hands, he shouted back:

"People of the Mayubuna, you are mistaken; we are not Spaniards, but are the enemies of the Spaniard, and the friends of all who hate them. We are on our way up the river to fight them, now; and we beg you to give us free passage through your land, and also a little cassava."

A laugh of derision greeted this statement; and the Indian who had just spoken shouted in reply:

"You lie, dog and son of a dog; you are Spaniards, for your skins are light, like theirs, and one of you has a beard." And suddenly raising his bow, the speaker discharged an arrow at Phil, which whizzed past within half an inch of that gentleman's ear.

"Make as though you intended to run down that canoe," ordered Phil. Then, seizing his bow and fitting an arrow to the string, he answered:

"Fools! we are English, I tell you, and the deadly enemies of the Spaniard; therefore let us pass in peace, otherwise must we make a passage for ourselves by force of arms."

The reply to this was another scornful laugh and a flight of arrows from every Indian in the two opposing canoes. By a miracle Phil again escaped unhurt, although no less than five arrows lodged in the puma-skin tunic which he was wearing, and the sail of the canoe was literally riddled with them. He felt that the matter was getting beyond a joke, that the time for fair speaking was past and the time for action had arrived, so, raising his bow, he drew his arrow to its head, and aimed it full at the breast of the Indian who had addressed him so abusively. For a single moment he hesitated, then he released the arrow, and the next moment, with the shaft buried so deep in his body that the point protruded nearly a foot out of his back, the savage flung up his arms, reeled backward, and fell into the water, capsizing the canoe in which he had been standing as he did so.

Chapter Thirteen
How they fell into the Hands of the Mayubuna

A yell, expressive in about equal proportions of amazement at the strength which could drive an arrow very nearly through the body of a man, and fury against the audacious slayers of that man—who happened to be a cacique—immediately arose from the occupants of the companion canoe, to be almost immediately succeeded by loud cries of dismay as a sudden swirl and rush along the surface of the stream toward the spot where the occupants of the capsized canoe were splashing in the water betrayed the presence of a hungry alligator. Paddles were dashed into the water with frantic energy as the occupants of the other canoe, abandoning all attempts to bar the passage of the Englishmen, whirled their craft round and sped to the assistance of their friends. But the alligators were beforehand with them, for before they could reach the spot where the capsized canoe floated, bottom up, surrounded by her crew, two piercing shrieks were followed by the abrupt disappearance of two Indians beneath the surface of the water; and a few seconds later a third Indian vanished in the same terrible manner.

"The caimans are among them!" shouted Stukely to Dick. "This is our chance to get past, lad. Starboard your helm a little. So, steady! Keep her at that. Now, if we were vindictively inclined, we could hamper their efforts very considerably by galling them with our arrows as we slip past. But let be; perhaps the lesson which they have already had will teach them the folly of interfering with Englishmen!"

The Mayubuna, however, had not yet received their full lesson; for when the canoe of the would-be rescuers dashed in among the swimmers the latter, frantic with fear of the alligators, seized her gunwale and made such frenzied and reckless efforts to scramble into her that, despite the warning cries of her occupants, she, too, was instantly capsized. And now blind, senseless panic seized in an instant upon every Indian present; for shriek after shriek told that the alligators were still busy; while the remaining four canoes, which had also been hastening to the rescue, suddenly paused, evidently fearful lest, if they approached the scene of the disaster, they, too, might be involved in it.

Meanwhile, the Englishmen, taking the fullest possible advantage of the situation, slid at a safe distance past the spot where the Indians were all struggling in the water in a vain effort to right their canoes and climb into them, and, favoured by a freshening breeze, pursued their way up the river. But although they had escaped for the moment, Phil and Dick still had plenty of cause for anxiety; for they had by this time been long enough in the wilds to have learned that when Indians are hostile their hostility is very bitter and pertinacious; and they could scarcely hope that, having mistaken them for Spaniards—who at that time were more feared and hated than any other earthly thing by the Indians—the Mayubuna would be satisfied with the issue of their first encounter with the white men. Moreover to add to the difficulties of the said white men, evening was now drawing on apace, the sun had already sunk so low that his beams were unable to pierce the forest on their right hand, while the orange glow which suffused the tree-tops on their left told them as plainly as words that the great luminary was within a brief half-hour of his setting. And, unfortunately, there was no moon just then; while without the light of the moon it was impossible to use the river at night. It would therefore be imperatively necessary for them to seek quickly a place of concealment wherein to pass the night if they wished to avoid being overtaken by darkness on the river; they therefore now proceeded to look anxiously about them for such a place. Eventually, when the brief twilight of the tropics was closing down upon the scene and the fireflies were beginning to appear, they sighted a spot which, while by no means ideal for their purpose, might possibly be made to serve.

It lay about a hundred yards up a small creek branching out of the main stream, and as it was the only spot at all suitable which they had seen since their encounter with the Indians, they really had no choice but to avail themselves of it. It consisted of a little grassy mead of about two acres in extent, lying quite open to view from the main river, the surface of the soil being not more than a foot above that of the water, and with no rushes to form a screen. Therefore, if they were to camp there for the night, as indeed they must, there being apparently no other place for them, they would have to manage as best they could without a fire wherewith to cook their supper. But needs must, under certain circumstances, so, with a glance astern to assure themselves that they were not being followed, the sail was lowered, the canoe was turned into the creek, and a minute later the voyagers were ashore and glancing keenly about them to ascertain the possibilities of the place. These were rather better than a first glance had led the wanderers to hope for, for their first necessity was to find a hiding-place for the canoe, and there, about a hundred and fifty yards away, was a clump of detached bush which would serve admirably for such a purpose. So, availing themselves of the very last of the waning light, they hauled the canoe out of the water, hoisted her upon their shoulders, and, carrying her to the clump of bush, very effectively concealed her therein, afterwards going back over their trail through the grass and carefully obliterating it by means of a leafy branch, in the manner which they had learned from Vilcamapata. Then they looked about them for a spot in which they might themselves pass the night. The place was by no means an ideal one for fugitives to pass the night in, for there was nothing even remotely resembling a hiding-place that they could see; and concealment was just then what they wanted more than anything else. True, there was an enormous ceiba tree growing upon the very edge of the clearing, among the upper branches of which they might possibly be able to conceal themselves; and in the absence of anything more suitable they at length determined to avail themselves of that, braving the perils of possible jaguars, scorpions, snakes, ants, and other undesirable bedfellows. Accordingly, the two friends ascended to the lower branches of the tree by climbing the lianas, hand over hand, which depended conveniently from the boughs, and, working their way aloft as well as they could in the thick darkness created by the luxuriant foliage, at length established themselves quite safely and comfortably in the fork formed by the junction of two enormous branches with the parent stem. They had no food with them, and were possessed of a healthy hunger, for they had eaten nothing since midday; but they were also exceedingly tired; and it was not long before they forgot their hunger in profound sleep.

Probably they would not have slept so soundly had they known that they had unwittingly entered a trap. But they had; for the Indians whom they had encountered shortly before knew that part of the river perfectly, and were fully aware that the difficulties of navigation were such that the fugitives could not possibly proceed very far in the darkness, and they also knew that the spot where Dick and Phil had landed was the only one within many miles where an upstream landing was possible. They therefore conjectured shrewdly that, since the white men would arrive at this spot just about nightfall, they would be certain to land there, and they took their measures accordingly. First of all, to make everything quite sure, they sent a messenger on to the next village, some fifteen miles up the river, to inform the cacique of the presence of the two white men in the neighbourhood, and to request that a watch for them should be kept, with a view to their capture. They requested further, that in the event of the white men being captured, they should be sent back down the river to pay the penalty for having caused the death of seventeen Mayubuna Indians. Then, having by this means ensured the capture of the fugitives, in the event of their succeeding by any chance in forcing their way up the river in the darkness, they launched and manned four canoes, each containing ten men, and these four canoes, spreading themselves right across the river, so that nothing could possibly pass downstream undetected, proceeded to make their way cautiously up the river to the spot where they knew it was morally certain that the white men must and would land. It was nearly eight o'clock at night when the four canoes arrived at the spot for which they were bound, and it was then of course much too dark for them to see anything. They therefore troubled themselves not at all to search for signs of the white men's presence, but assumed that they were there somewhere, and at once, with infinite precaution, proceeded to surround the open plateau, cunningly concealing themselves in the long grass. Half a dozen of them lay immediately beneath the overhanging branches of the ceiba tree; but they arrived there so silently that, even if Dick and Phil had been awake, they would have heard nothing.

Now, there is probably no creature in this world of ours more vindictive than an angry Indian; and these particular Mayubuna Indians considered that they had ample cause for their anger against the two white men whom they were taking so much trouble to capture; for had not those same white men been directly responsible for the loss of seventeen male Mayubuna lives? And among the South American Indians, who, even then, were beginning from a variety of causes to die out, nothing is so valuable as the life of a male—females they care nothing about; they may live or die as they please—therefore those who were responsible for the sacrifice of no less than seventeen men's lives must receive a punishment, the severity of which should be proportionate to the enormity of their crime. Consequently not one of those Indians closed his eyes for a moment throughout the long hours of that night; and with the first hint of approaching dawn, long before either of the occupants of the ceiba were awake, they were keenly looking about them for "sign" of the white men's presence. For some time, however, they looked in vain, for the Englishmen had learned a few of the ways of the wild from Vilcamapata, and had succeeded in obliterating their tracks so completely that even the sharp eyes of the savages failed to detect them. But by and by, when it was broad daylight, one of the Mayubuna who had recognised the possibilities of concealment afforded by the ceiba detected spots here and there on two of the depending lianas where small strips of the bark had been freshly torn off as though somebody had very recently climbed up them, and to this he immediately directed the attention of the rest, with the result that it soon became a practical certainty that the fugitives were somewhere in that tree. This having been determined, certain of the Mayubuna young men of the party, anxious to distinguish themselves, proposed to climb the tree forthwith and bring the white men down, dead or alive; but the cacique in command of the party, who happened to have been in one of the attacking canoes on the preceding night, and had therefore already had experience of the prowess of the hunted men, at once vetoed the plan as being far too dangerous; besides, for certain grim reasons which will in due time appear, he wanted the quarry to be taken alive and unhurt, if possible. Therefore, instead of permitting any of his men to climb the tree, he so disposed them round the base of it that, while far enough away to ensure that they should not be seen by the occupants during their descent, they should be near enough to rush in and effect the capture of the white men the moment that they set foot on the ground.

Meanwhile Stukely and Chichester, absolutely unconscious of the elaborate preparations that were being made for their capture, slept soundly on until the sun was fairly above the horizon, when the cries of the birds in the neighbouring branches of the tree aroused them to the fact that another day had arrived, and that it was high time for them to descend from their lofty hiding-place and proceed with the preparations for the resumption of their journey. Accordingly, they began their descent with the observance of every precaution which their past experience had taught them; but, unfortunately, they had not yet learned that when you ascend a tree in search of concealment, it is always advisable to descend some other, as they might easily have done had they thought of it; for, as is the case almost everywhere in the South American forest, the trees grew so thickly together that they might easily have travelled for miles without descending to the ground, merely by climbing along from branch to branch. But this idea did not occur to them, therefore they proceeded to lower themselves gradually down the giant trunk, carefully inspecting what lay beneath them before attempting to reach the next branch below. For the first fifty feet or so of their descent, however, the foliage of the tree was so dense that it completely shut out all view of the ground beneath; and by the time that an occasional glimpse of the grassy glade below became visible they were so near the ground that, as the cunning cacique had anticipated, it was impossible for them to detect the hiding-places of the concealed Indians.

At length the two adventurers reached the lowest branch of all; and here they paused and very carefully scrutinised the ground beneath them. But if they knew how to obliterate their tracks, so did the Indians, and there was nothing visible to indicate the presence of forty foes lurking in the long grass below, or indeed anywhere within the glade. Therefore, with the assurance begotten of a conviction that they had succeeded in hoodwinking their foes of the preceding evening, they boldly ran out along the great spreading branch, seized a liana each, and slid rapidly to the ground—to find themselves skilfully noosed in a lasso and their arms tightly confined to their sides, the moment that their feet touched the earth. Then, despite their frantic struggles to free themselves from the entangling lassos, they were instantly seized and other ropes of raw-hide were deftly twisted about their limbs and bodies, until in less than a minute they were so tightly and securely trussed up that they could scarcely wag a finger; after which they were each hoisted upon the shoulders of four Indians and borne with songs of triumph and rejoicing to the canoes, into which they were tumbled with scant ceremony. Then, with further songs of triumph, they were swiftly transported back down the river to the village to which their captors belonged.

This village was quite invisible from the river, being approached by means of one of those small, short, winding creeks that so frequently occur on the South American rivers, and the existence of which seems so difficult to account for; but when, upon the canoes rounding a bend, the place swung into view, it was seen to be of quite considerable extent, consisting of fully one hundred palm-leaf huts standing in an open glade of about two hundred acres in extent, part of which was under cultivation, being planted, in almost equal proportion, with bananas, yams, and cassava.

The triumphant songs and shouts of the victorious expedition caused the entire population of the village to turn out and swarm down to the small strip of beach which constituted the landing-place; so when Dick and Phil were lifted out of the canoes they beheld a crowd of some four or five hundred Indians, men, women, and children, crowded together to gaze upon and jeer at them. And jeer at them they did, with all the more gusto when it was seen that so tightly had the bonds been drawn about the prisoners' limbs that when they were set upon their feet they were unable to stand, but sank helplessly to the ground with an involuntary groan. But the Indians had already had enough of carrying their stalwart prisoners, and especially Dick, who towered head and shoulders above the tallest of them; therefore when they saw that it was impossible for the white men to stand, and had fathomed the reason for their helplessness, they loosed the thongs about their prisoners' feet and legs, and allowed them a few minutes pause for the blood to circulate afresh. Those few minutes were surcharged with exquisite suffering for the unfortunate victims, but they bore it with stoical silence and composure; and when at length the cacique gave the order for them to rise and march they at once scrambled to their feet and proceeded, in charge of a dozen Indians, fully armed with pocunas, or blowpipes, bows—the arrows of which were doubtless poisoned with curare—and long spears. In this order, and followed by the entire population, our friends were marched up through the village to a hut situated near its northern extremity, into which they were bundled, while the guards ranged themselves round the hut outside, to frustrate any attempt at escape.

The unfortunate prisoners were by this time suffering so acutely from the tightness of the ligatures which confined their arms to their bodies that they were in no mood for conversation, but just lay upon the earthen floor of the hut in silent torment. But, luckily for them, they were not called upon to endure very much longer; for when they had lain there about half an hour the cacique appeared and gave orders that their bonds were to be loosed, at the same time warning them that the first indication of an attempt to escape would be met by a shower of arrows, the smallest scratch from which would be followed by a death of intolerable agony. Phil replied that under those circumstances the cacique might rest assured that no such attempt would be made, and followed up the assurance by asking why they had been taken prisoners, seeing that they were not Spaniards, but were enemies of the Spaniard and therefore ought to be regarded as friends by all who hated the Spaniard. To which statement the cacique made no reply, but simply turned on his heel and departed. A few minutes later, however, two women appeared bearing food—a portion of roast kid on a plantain leaf, and some cassava bread, together with a small gourd of what looked like sour milk—which they set upon the ground before the prisoners; and Phil and Dick both agreed that in the regards of these women there was more of pity than of hate.

During the whole of that day and the next our friends were kept close prisoners; but on the morning of their third day of captivity they were summoned from their hut almost before they had finished breakfast; and, upon emerging, were conducted to the open space in the middle of the village, where were assembled not only all the inhabitants of the place but some seven or eight hundred more who seemed to be visitors. The crowd generally were densely packed round the sides of the quadrangle, the middle being kept clear by a line of armed men who maintained order by the free use of their heavy clubs, which they unhesitatingly drove into the pit of the stomach of any unauthorised person who displayed an undue eagerness to get a good view of the impending proceedings. In the middle of the clear space sat the cacique of the village, with two men, apparently visitors, on either side of him; and a little apart from these stood two other men, one of whom Phil immediately recognised as having been in one of the canoes which had attempted to bar their progress up the river.

A little murmur of excited expectancy, perhaps mingled with wonder, swept through the crowd as the two prisoners were led forward and halted in front of the cacique; but it quickly died away and an intense silence ensued, which was presently broken by the cacique, who, addressing Stukely, said:

"White man, whence come you, and whither were you going when you strove to force a passage up the river on the evening of the day before last?"

"We come," replied Phil, "from an island far away across the Great Water; so far that we were voyaging a whole moon and more without sight of land; and our business is to fight the Spaniard, who is our enemy, as well as that of the Indian. Twice have we fought him already; once on the Great Water, where we took from him one of his great canoes; and once again in one of his towns, far away to the north, where we took another of his great canoes, with much gold of which he had robbed the Indian. But by a mischance my friend and I were left behind when our comrades sailed away; and for a time we were in danger of falling into the hands of the Spaniard. Then we escaped from them, but, having no canoe big enough to take us across the Great Water, we were obliged to remain in this land; and, having heard that there are many Spaniards in the land lying to the southward, we determined to seek them out and take from them as much as we can get of the gold which they have unrighteously taken from the Indians."

"If that story be true, why did ye not tell it us instead of slaying many of my people, one of them by an arrow from your bow, and the rest by the jaws of the caimans?" demanded the cacique.

"Nay, why ask a question of which you yourself know the answer?" retorted Phil. "For you were in one of the canoes, and saw and heard everything that passed. Did not I make to your leader all the signs of amity and goodwill? But he rejected them; he called us dogs of Spaniards; bade us go back by the way that we had come; and himself shot the arrow which led to all the trouble. Is that the way in which the Mayubuna treat those who come to them as friends?"

"How do I know that ye come as friends?" demanded the cacique. "When the Spaniards first appeared in this land they, too, said that they came as the friends of the Indian; and how have they proved their friendship? By killing the Inca Atahuallpa and seizing his kingdom; by enslaving the Indian and despoiling him of all that he possesses; by ravaging the country with fire and sword! Nay, I believe not your story. If ye are not Spaniards, ye are white-skinned, even as they are; your hearts are evil and full of guile, like theirs; and if we were foolish enough to listen to your lying words you would treat us even as they treated Atahuallpa and his people. But there are only two of you, and you are in our power; moreover ye have slain, or caused to be slain, seventeen men of the Mayubuna; therefore shall ye die; not quickly and easily, but little by little, so that ye shall die not once but a thousand times; and your torments shall be as honey to the friends of those whom ye have slain, and your groans and cries for mercy shall be more pleasant to them than the songs of birds. Go; I have spoken!" And amid tumultuous shouts of rejoicing from the assembled multitude the two Englishmen were conducted back to their prison hut and once more placed under strict guard. For they were trebly valuable now, having been condemned to die by the torture, and it was seldom indeed that an Indian was afforded so delectable a sight as that of a white man suffering the unspeakably hideous torments which, with fiendish cleverness, were designed to inflict the maximum amount of pain which the human frame could possibly endure, and still continue to live. Moreover there were two of them; big, strong men, apparently in the very pink of health and condition; they would linger long and endure unimaginable torments before succumbing; and the sight of their agonies would be one long-drawn-out rapture to those who were privileged to witness them. Oh yes; they must be guarded well, for their escape now would mean lifelong disappointment to the whole village and its guests.

But they must not only be kept safe; their health and strength must be preserved intact; therefore during the remainder of that day an abundant supply of food was provided for them, and they were urged with the utmost solicitude to partake of it freely. Which they did; for as Phil remarked to Dick, their strength was never of such vital importance to them as now; since it was not to be supposed that they were going to submit to be slowly tortured to death without at least making an effort to escape; and for that effort to be successful they must keep well and strong.

The worst of it was that they were quite unable to obtain the slightest inkling of the form which their torture was to take; the men who guarded them were willing enough to converse with them upon general subjects, indeed they were full of curiosity, and asked innumerable questions respecting the past adventures of the Englishmen; but when it came to talking about the forthcoming festivities they at once fell silent; they either could not or would not give the slightest information.

"Well," said Phil, at the conclusion of a long conversation with their jailers, "we are at least unbound; our hands and feet are free; and before I suffer myself to be again tied up a good many of the Mayubuna are going to die."

"I say ditto to that," replied Dick, rising to his feet and stretching his long limbs as though to test their strength, an action which, by the by, at once brought the guard facing round with their spears poised and their bows bent, so alert were they to act upon the slightest thing that seemed to hint at an attempt to escape. Yet that was precisely the problem that was exercising the minds of the two white men all through that day and the succeeding night; and three times during that night did they make tentative efforts to escape the watchfulness of their gaolers, but without success.

One thing, however, was pretty evident, and that was that the torture, whatever might be its nature, was to begin on the morrow; for the village was in a perfect ferment of excitement all day, and all through the night, too, for that matter; people were constantly coming and going in crowds past the hut, merely for the sake, apparently, of getting a casual peep at the prisoners as they passed; and with nightfall great fires were lighted in the square, and singing and dancing went on all through the night as a fitting introduction to the entertainment of the following day.

At length, after a sleepless night of intense anxiety on the part of the prisoners, and, as has been said, more than one unavailing effort to elude the vigilance of their guards, the morning dawned of the day which was to see those prisoners begin to die; and with the rising of the sun the excitement and hilarity of the village became still more pronounced. The crowds grew more dense, the laughter and conversation louder; the people had donned their holiday attire—such as it was—and the children chased each other with joyous shouts in and out of the throng. Then a meal was brought to the prisoners; and while they were partaking of it a sudden clamour of drums and horns arose, and the laughing, chattering crowd seemed to dissolve as suddenly from the vicinity of the prison hut, leaving it plunged in an atmosphere of silence, save for the monotonous banging of the drums, the blare of the horns, and a low, humming murmur which might be that of a multitude of people conversing in low, hushed voices.

"That means that our time has come, I suppose," remarked Stukely, as he set down the food of which he had been partaking. "Well, keep up your courage, lad; and remember that if we are to die we will do so in a fashion which the Mayubuna will never forget, so long as they are a people. There are wives now who will be widows before the sun goes down; for they shall never torture me to death; nor you, either, lad, if I can help it. We have our hands free, and a Devon man can do much with his hands alone, when put to it; but my plan is to watch our chance, and snatch the first weapon that comes to hand, and make play with it. They will no doubt shoot us down with their arrows, rather than let us escape; but that kind of death will be infinitely preferable to one of lingering torture—if die we must."

"Yes," agreed Dick; "and you may depend upon me to—"

He was interrupted by the arrival of a messenger who summoned them and their guards to follow him; whereupon they rose to their feet and, completely hedged in by sixteen fully armed men, were marched toward the centre of the village, ultimately arriving in the square where they had previously been interviewed by the cacique. And a curious sight the square presented on this occasion, for it and the long street which ran through it from end to end of the village were packed with people who had come, in response to an invitation, from all the villages within a radius of twenty miles, to see the two white men die. They were ranged right along what may be called the main street, in a dense crowd some eight or ten deep, for a distance of a quarter of a mile, and were arranged in two compact lines, with a clear lane of about six feet wide between the two lines of people. Through a gap which had evidently been left open in one of these lines for that especial purpose, the two prisoners were conducted into this lane and led to one extremity of it, where upon a raised platform sat the cacique, with five men, presumably the caciques of neighbouring villages, on either side of him. The Englishmen were marched up to this platform and there left face to face with the cacique and his friends, the guards retiring through the gap by which they had entered, which thereupon was immediately closed.

For the space of a full five minutes or more Phil and Dick stood facing the cacique, while a profound and impressive silence fell upon that vast crowd of Indians, broken only by the rustle of the wind in the tree-tops, and a faint rumble caused by the movement of the naked feet of the assembled multitude, who were in the grip of an excitement so intense that they apparently found it impossible to stand quite still, but must needs continually shift the weight of their bodies from one foot to the other.

At length, when the pause had become almost unbearably impressive, the cacique rose to his feet and, lifting his hand to command attention, spoke.

"White men," he said, "ye have told me a story which may or may not be true. Ye have declared yourselves to be the enemy of the Spaniards and the friend of the Indian; but how have ye shown your friendship for us? By causing the death of seventeen men of the Mayubuna, by creating seventeen widows and forty-six fatherless children, for whom the rest of the villagers must now provide food. For this great wrong ye are doomed to die; and it rests with yourselves whether your death shall be quick, or whether it shall be one of long-drawn-out torment.

"Ye see this great lane of people stretching right through the village, and ye will note that each man of the front rank is armed with a club. Now, your doom is this. Ye shall start from where ye now stand, and shall run to the farther end of the lane of people; and as ye run each man on either hand shall smite ye as often as he may with his club. If ye can hold out against the blows which ye will receive, and retain strength enough to reach the other end of the lane without falling by the way, then your death shall be quick; but if ye fall, then he who falls will be tied to a stake and slowly done to death for the pleasure of the spectators. You understand? Then—go!"

During this brief address the two Englishmen had been thinking hard and rapidly. Phil's first thought had been to force his way up on to the platform, seize the cacique, and threaten him with instant death unless the man would consent to give them both immediate liberty; but he instantly discarded the idea, for as the thought flashed through his mind he noticed that the Indians in front of the platform were all fully armed; and for an unarmed man to force a passage through that hedge of deadly spears, ten deep, was a simple impossibility. Then he threw a glance along the lane which he and Dick were to traverse, and which was hedged in on either side by serried ranks of Indians, each armed with a heavy club about three feet long. The Indians were by no means powerfully built, and, individually, looked by no means formidable; and the thought came to him that if he and Dick, instead of starting to race at top speed from end to end of the lane, were each to snatch a club from the nearest man, and then, back to back, fight their way slowly along the lane, they might possibly contrive to reach the end of it without being beaten to the earth, after which who knew what unforeseen possibilities might arise? It was not a particularly hopeful plan, but it was the best that suggested itself on the spur of the moment; moreover, both he and Dick were experts at quarter-staff play, and they would at least be able to make a fight for it, so he hastily communicated his plan to Dick while the cacique was speaking, and received Dick's murmured acceptance of it at the precise moment when the cacique uttered the word "Go!"

Chapter Fourteen
How Phil and Dick were made to run the Gauntlet

"Go!"

As the word left the cacique's lips the two Englishmen faced round, back to back, and each sprang straight at the Indian who happened to be nearest him. A perfect forest of bludgeons whirled in the air on both sides of the human lane, and from one end of it to the other, in savage anticipation of the moment when the two victims should dash past; but the length of the weapons was such that not more than three could reach each victim at any given moment; and of this the two friends had already taken note, deciding with the rapidity of thought that if by skill and quickness of action they could evade those three simultaneous blows, they need not trouble about anything more for the moment; for their progress down the lane would simply be a continuous succession of evasions of three blows aimed at them at the same moment. Their object, therefore, was each to secure a bludgeon before receiving a disabling blow; and this they contrived to do, their sudden spring taking the Indians so completely by surprise that the weapons were wrenched out of their hands without the slightest difficulty. Then, instead of sprinting for their lives down the lane, by which course of action they must have inevitably exposed themselves to the certainty of receiving a sufficient number of violent blows to disable them, and in all probability prevent them from reaching their goal, they placed themselves back to back and, each facing his own particular line of assailants, moved sideways along the length of the lane at ordinary walking pace, contenting themselves with parrying with their bludgeons the blows aimed at them, and not attempting to return those blows excepting when some particular Indian happened to exhibit especial vindictiveness, when, if opportunity offered, they retaliated with such effect that before fifty yards of their course had been traversed at least half a dozen Indians were down with cracked skulls. Now, it would naturally be imagined that a multitude of savages, finding themselves thus baulked of the vengeance to which they had been so eagerly looking forward, would have with one accord broken their ranks and, rushing in upon the two white men in overwhelming numbers, have slain them out of hand. But they did nothing of the sort. On the contrary, the cool, calm courage of the prisoners, their audacity in daring to face such enormously overwhelming odds, the gallant fight that they were putting up, and the extraordinary skill with which they handled their bludgeons, all seemed to appeal to some elementary sporting instinct that must have been lurking dormant and unsuspected in the Mayubuna nature, exciting their admiration to such an extent that several of the Indians who might have struck an unfair blow actually forbore to do so, and presently they even began to utter shouts of admiration when either of the white men achieved a particularly brilliant passage of defence. In short, it seemed gradually to dawn upon them that they were playing a game, and that since the balance of advantage was enormously on their own side they were morally bound to play it fairly. And within certain limits they did, although there were not wanting those whose ferocious passions were so deeply stirred that all they seemed to crave was the life of the white men, and they were willing to go to all lengths to get it. Thus one man aimed so savage a blow at Dick that he smashed his bludgeon to splinters upon that of Chichester as the latter guarded the blow. Then, doubtless enraged at his failure, he sprang out of his place in the ranks and, catching Dick unawares, stabbed at him with the splintered fragment of the weapon that remained in his hand, inflicting quite a painful jagged wound on the young Englishman's shoulder. But it was his last act, for, stung into sudden fury by the smart of the wound, Dick turned upon him and, throwing all his strength and weight into the blow, struck out with his clenched left fist, catching the unfortunate Indian square on the point of the chin. So terrific was the blow that it actually lifted the man clean off his feet and sent him whirling back through the air for a distance of nearly four yards before he fell to the earth dead with a broken neck. A great shout of mingled amazement, admiration, and terror arose at this wonderful exhibition of strength; and thenceforward, influenced either by fear or the spirit of fair play, or, it may be, a combination of both, there were no further attempts made to take an unfair advantage of those two who were making so gallant a fight to save themselves from a fate too hideous to be put into words.

At length the gauntlet was run, the far end of the lane was reached, and the two young Englishmen still stood upon their feet. But not unscathed; very far from it. They had made a gallant fight, and had afforded their savage captors a far more exhilarating spectacle than they had ever before witnessed, although it had been of a very different character from what had been anticipated; and now the two prisoners stood, trembling with exhaustion from their superhuman efforts, cruelly bruised, bleeding, and altogether too dazed and helpless to make that sudden, wild dash for freedom which each had planned in his heart when entering upon the terrible ordeal through which they had just passed. What was to be the next move in this grim game of life or death?

They were not long left in doubt, for the party of armed men who had conducted them on to the ground now forced their way into the lane and, arranging themselves in a circle round the two white men, led them back to where the cacique of the village sat enthroned. And as they passed back along the lane of humanity which they had fought their way through a few minutes previously, many of those whose arms still tingled with the jar of the parried blows which they had aimed at them, now greeted their return with murmurs of commiseration or admiration. Then, almost before they realised where they were, they found themselves, still hemmed in by their armed guards, facing the cacique, who sat for some moments silent, regarding them with an inscrutable countenance. Then, raising his hand for silence, he spoke.

"White men," he said, "ye have not fulfilled the terms of the agreement which I made with you. Ye were to run from this end of the lane to the other, and ye walked. And instead of accepting unresistingly — as was intended — the blows which were aimed at ye, you took by force and superior strength two clubs from my people, wherewith to defend yourselves; and, worst of all, ye have killed outright no less than four, more men of the Mayubuna and maimed five others so that it will be many days before they will again be able to provide food for their wives and children. Therefore, because of all this, and what has gone before, your doom is —"

"Nay, nay; be merciful, O my father!" cried a number of women's voices, "be merciful!" And, forcing their way through the throng, a party of some twenty women of varying ages — from girls of seventeen or eighteen to one withered hag who, from her appearance, might have been a hundred years old — flung themselves upon their knees before the cacique.

"Mercy!" reiterated the cacique, in astonishment. "Who pleads for mercy on behalf of these white men? Surely not you, Insipa, whose only son they have done to death, leaving you desolate in your old age?"

"Yea; I, even I, Insipa," answered the hag above mentioned. "Hearken now, O my father," she continued. "It is a custom among us that if a man be killed, and his slayer be taken alive, if the mother or widow of the slain man claim the slayer as her slave, to provide food for her in the place of the slain man, her demand shall be granted, and the slayer shall be given to her for the rest of her life. Now, behold these two white men and see what mighty men they are. Between them they have slain no less than twenty-one men of the Mayubuna, leaving twenty-one women and many children with none to protect or find food for them. Let them be given as slaves to us, then, that we whom they have thus cruelly bereaved may not suffer from the loss of father, husband, or son. It is our right, and we demand it."

The cacique considered this extraordinary request for several minutes; then he turned to Dick and Phil.

"White men," he said, "ye have heard what this woman asks. Now behold, I give you your choice: will ye become the slaves of these bereaved women, to till their fields, tend their cattle, hunt and fish for them, and generally watch over and protect them and their children in the place of those whom ye have slain? Or will ye go straightway to the stake and pay the penalty of your misdeeds by dying a slow and miserable death?"

"Since we must needs do the one or the other," answered Phil—who alone fully understood the purport of the cacique's speech, and therefore took it upon himself to reply—"we choose to become the slaves of these women who have intervened to save us from death. And we will do our best to fill the places of those whom we have unfortunately slain, tilling their fields, tending their cattle, hunting and fishing for their wives and children, and protecting them from all evil."

"It is well," answered the cacique. Then, turning to the group of women, he said: "Take them; they are yours; I have granted your request. Nevertheless, methinks you would find it easier to tame two full-grown jaguars, fresh from the forest, than to subdue these white men to your will. But that is your affair." And with a wave of his hand he dismissed the party.

"'Subdue them', said he?" muttered the ancient Insipa. "Ha, ha! we shall see; yes, we shall see! These men are truly young and strong and fierce, yea, stronger and fiercer than black jaguars, while Insipa is old and weak; nevertheless—here, take them and bind them for me." She turned suddenly and held out two tough, raw-hide ropes to the armed guard who still surrounded the prisoners; and they, with a coarse jest or two at the old woman's expense, at once proceeded to bind Dick's and Phil's hands behind them, after which they placed the two free ends of the ropes in the beldame's hands and left the way free for her to lead her prisoners away.

"Come, then," cried the old woman, jerking the ropes roughly; "come, sons of mine! Ha, ha! I have lost one son, who was lazy, who cared not for his poor old mother, and often left her for many days without so much as the smallest morsel of deer meat, and let her garden be overrun with weeds. And in his place I have gained two—two who are brave enough to protect me, and strong enough to till my garden and my fields, and to keep my hut well supplied with all that I need. Ha, ha! I have done well; I am a gainer! Come, white men, come, and make old Insipa's declining years pleasant and happy!" And she proceeded to drag her prisoners away, followed by the other women who were—or believed they were—part owners of the bodies of Dick and Phil.

"Now, what does all this mean? What is to be our fate; and what has that withered old mummy to do with us?" grumbled Dick, who had scarcely half-understood what had passed since he and Phil had been led back to the cacique.

Phil explained, adding, "It will probably be unpleasant enough for a time, but we must grin and bear it, lad; and at all events it will be less disagreeable than being lashed to a stake and slowly tortured to death. If we had accepted that fate everything would have been at an end for us within the next two or three days; whereas by choosing the alternative we at least save our lives; and that is the main thing with us at present. There would have been no comfort or satisfaction in being tortured to death by a parcel of savages, after having come so far and done so much. Besides, if we are to hunt and fish for these women we must be free to come and go pretty much as we please. And do you need me to tell you what we shall do as soon as we obtain our freedom?"

"Of course not," answered Dick. "We shall just watch our opportunity and continue our journey."

"Precisely," agreed Phil. "And I must confess I am greatly surprised that our friend the cacique did not foresee such a possibility. Well, then, it seems to me that what we have to do is to be good boys for the present, do everything with a good grace that we have undertaken to do, and, generally, use our utmost endeavours to win the confidence of these people and disarm the suspicion with which they are certain to regard us at the outset, and then our way to escape will soon become clear."

The hut of Insipa was a wretched, neglected hovel of a place, in the very last stages of dirt, neglect, and decay, situated on the outskirts of the village, and to this delectable abode the old crone conducted her two "sons" and inducted them therein. But before she took them inside the hut she carefully examined their hurts; and when at length she had satisfied herself that although these were no doubt painful enough, and, for the moment, so severe as to incapacitate her prisoners for anything but the very lightest of work, there was no serious harm done, she dispatched one of the women who had followed her, and who considered herself as part owner of the prisoners, to the river for water, another for wood to make a fire, while a third was sent into the forest to hunt for certain herbs. Then she took the two men into the hut, released them from their bonds, and graciously gave them permission to lie down upon a heap of dried fern, which they were glad enough to do after the rough and trying experience through which they had so recently passed, and in a few minutes both were fast asleep. They slept soundly for an hour or more; and when they awoke Insipa was ready with hot fomentations for their wounds and bruises, poultices of macerated leaves for application after the fomentations, and finally, food—a piece of roast goat's flesh, cassava bread, and a warm drink of somewhat peculiar but not unpleasant flavour, after partaking of which they both again fell into a profound sleep which lasted until the following morning; for the drink had been medicated. Insipa was anxious that her "sons" should begin to work for her at once, and she knew that, after their hurts had been dressed, sleep was the very best restorative that she could possibly administer to them.

As a matter of fact, when Phil and Dick awoke from their long night's sleep they found, to their astonishment, that the ache and stiffness of their bruises were gone, and that for all practical purposes they were as well as ever, and quite fit to be up and about again. Insipa was delighted with the success which had attended her ministrations, so much so, indeed, that instead of ordering them out to find food for her at once, she went out and borrowed some from a neighbour, on the strength of her new acquisition, brought it home, cooked it, and laid it before them, with the information that it would be the last unearned meat they would get.

This hint, however, did not greatly interfere with the appetite of our friends; for they had already agreed that they were quite well enough to resume their journey up the river, and had decided to do so at the first opportunity, whenever that might occur. And they believed that it might occur at any moment, that very day, perhaps, although they were quite prepared to find that precautions of some sort would be taken, for a little while at least, to see that they did not get away. In this they were not mistaken; for they had scarcely finished their meal when they were summoned to the presence of the cacique, who informed them that he had arranged that one of them should spend the day in hunting, while the other should remain in the village, and, under the direction and supervision of a member of the village council, till the gardens and attend to the cattle of the twenty-one widows whose property they were, and that they might settle between themselves which of the two should be the hunter. Now this at once put an effectual stop to any plans for immediate escape; for although not a word had passed between the two friends on the subject, they were both of one mind that whenever they went it must be together; in fact neither would have dreamed of going off and leaving the other behind. Probably the shrewd old cacique had guessed as much when he arranged the apparently simple but really ingenious scheme whereby at least one of the two white men would always be in the village and under close observation. Of course Dick, being the younger, offered Phil the choice of the two occupations; and Stukely at once unhesitatingly decided that he would undertake the agricultural work, while Dick was to do the hunting; and this arrangement came into force forthwith, Dick's duty being to secure all the game and fish he possibly could, and take the products of his industry to the cacique, who would divide them out equally between the twenty-one widows according to the numbers of their families.

To provide flesh food enough to satisfy more than sixty healthy appetites was no mean task, particularly in the immediate vicinity of a village of five hundred inhabitants, where the whole of the neighbouring country was strenuously hunted day after day; but Dick happened to be a particularly keen and clever hunter; moreover his training during the journey had been of such a character as to develop his speed, strength, and endurance to such a degree that he was able to go farther afield than any of the Indians, and thus reach a district where the game was neither so scarce nor so wild as it was in the immediate neighbourhood of the village; also he soon got to know the spots where game was most likely to be found. Consequently after the first three or four days, during which he was learning the country, he did quite as well as could be reasonably expected, and frequently excited the cacique's admiration by the quantity of meat which he contrived to bring in.

As for Phil, he was a Devon man, and consequently had acquired, almost unconsciously, a considerable amount of knowledge regarding farming matters, so that he found himself more than on a par with the Indians, whose knowledge of agriculture was of the most elementary character; also he understood the full value of system in the arrangement of work, which the Indians did not. Consequently, by working systematically, and making the women do their fair share, he found that he could do the work which had been allotted to him, and still find time for his favourite hobby of research.

It is not necessary to give a detailed description of our friends' doings, day after day, during their sojourn with the Mayubuna Indians; the above indication will enable the reader to picture the uneventful sort of existence which they led; and it is only needful to add that so well did the young Englishmen contrive matters that by the time that they had been three months in the village the suspicion and distrust with which they had at first been regarded had entirely disappeared, and the Indians seemed to have gathered the impression that their white prisoners had quite settled down and were content to spend the remainder of their lives with them.

But it took fully three months to establish matters on this satisfactory basis; and this brought the time on to what may be termed the winter season; that is to say, the period of the year when, after a long-continued spell of fine weather, during which the crops ripen and are gathered in, the season of rain, wind, and violent thunderstorms begins which is to soften, nourish, and invigorate the baked earth and prepare it to bring forth the luxuriant vegetation of another summer. And it was one of those violent thunderstorms which provided our friends with the opportunity to escape for which they had been so long and so patiently waiting.

The day had been unusually hot, to start with; and about noon the sky, which had been clear during the earlier part of the day, had gradually become veiled by a thick haze through which the sun revealed himself with ever-increasing difficulty merely as a shapeless blotch of whiteness in the midst of the haze before vanishing altogether. Then the wind fell, the atmosphere became so oppressively close that the mere act of breathing became difficult, and a great silence fell upon the scene, for the insects and birds, warned by instinct of what was impending, sought shelter in the deepest recesses of the forest, while the Indians, unable or unwilling to labour in the enervating heat, and also knowing from past experience what was coming, retired to their huts and resigned themselves to the overpowering languor which oppressed them. Of all the inhabitants of the village, Dick and Phil were the only two who resisted the enervating influence of the hour, for Dick was away hunting, as usual, while Phil, having set himself a certain task to perform, was not the sort of man who would allow himself to be deterred from its execution by such a trifle as mere oppressiveness of weather.

But as the day wore on and the sky grew ever more lowering and the heat and closeness more pronounced, he found his work growing increasingly difficult and distasteful; and it was with a sigh of deep satisfaction that at last, having finished what he had set himself to do, he wended his way to the hut which he and Dick had been permitted to erect for themselves, and, having laid aside the primitive tools which he had been using, continued his way to the creek where, at the conclusion of each day's labour, he was wont to indulge in the refreshing luxury of a bathe. While he was still in the water he was joined by Dick, who had also done a good day's work, having brought in two deer, which he had duly delivered over to the cacique.

By the time that the pair had sufficiently refreshed themselves the gloom of the departing day was deepening into the darkness of a moonless, starless night; and as they entered their hut the first shimmer of sheet lightning which was the precursor of the coming storm flickered above the tree-tops of the contiguous forest.

"Phew!" exclaimed Dick, as he flung himself upon the heap of dried fern that served him as a bed, "how unbearably hot and close it is, and how tired I am! I doubt if I could walk another mile, if my life depended upon it."

"I am sorry to hear that," gravely returned Phil; "for, unless I am very greatly mistaken, I believe we shall have an opportunity to escape to-night."

"To escape?" reiterated Dick. "How do you mean, old man?"

"Do you know what is going to happen to-night?" demanded Phil.

"I know that we are going to have a pretty severe thunderstorm, if that is what you mean," answered Dick; "but what has that got to do with our escaping?"

"What has it to do?" repeated Phil. "Why, everything, my gentle cuckoo. Dost thou not yet know that Indians generally, and the Mayubuna in particular, have a very wholesome dread and horror of thunderstorms, believing, as they do, that the evil spirits come abroad and hold high revel upon such occasions? If an Indian happens to be struck by lightning, his fellow Indians are firmly convinced that he has been killed by an evil spirit; hence they are extremely reluctant to venture abroad during a thunderstorm. We have observed that reluctance even in the case of the comparatively few unimportant storms that have visited the village since we have been here; but hitherto the Mayubuna have been too suspicious and too watchful to afford us an opportunity to get clear away. Now, however, I think we have at last succeeded in completely lulling their suspicions; they have not been nearly so watchful of us of late; and I am very doubtful whether there is a single Indian in this village, from the cacique downward, including old Mammy Insipa herself, who will be willing to turn out in such a storm as is now brewing, merely for the purpose of watching that we two do not run away."

"Yes," agreed Dick, "I have no doubt you are right. Well, I am quite ready to make the attempt whenever you say the word."

"But what about thy fatigue?" demanded Phil.

"Oh," answered Dick, with a laugh, "I am not so tired but that I dare say I can manage to do whatever may be necessary to secure our escape from this wretched place."

"Very well, then," said Phil; "in that case let us get our supper, make our preparations—Heaven knows they will be few and simple enough—and then lie down and get what rest we can; it will be two or three hours, yet, before it will be safe for us to make the attempt."

The friends were awakened out of a sound sleep by a blaze of lightning that flashed across their closed eyelids with the vividity of noontide sunshine, followed an instant later by a crash of thunder that caused them to start upright from their fern beds in something akin to panic, so appalling was the sharpness and intensity of the sound, followed as it was by a series of deep, heavy, reverberating booms which might have been caused by the broadsides of an entire navy simultaneously discharged, and the concussion of which sent a perceptible tremor through the earth beneath them. The booming sounds seemed to echo back and forth from cloud to cloud, rumbling and growling as though reluctant to cease, but at length it subsided into momentary silence, only to burst forth with even greater violence a few seconds later as a second flash tore across the ink-black sky.

"That is our signal," remarked Phil quietly, as he rose to his feet. "We may safely move now, for the 'bad spirits' are abroad with a vengeance to-night, and every Indian in the place—man, woman, and child—will be cowering with head tightly wrapped in blanket and unable to move for fear of what may be seen. There! listen to that!" as another vivid flash illumined the hut, and low, terrified wails burst forth from all round about them, mingling with the roar and volleying of the thunder—"that gives one some idea of the state of mind that the poor wretches are in. I believe that if the village were to take fire they would remain in their huts and burn rather than turn out and face the lightning. Come along; we must get clear away, if we can, before the rain comes, because when it begins we shall be able to see nothing. Now; have we all our belongings—my medicine case, our pistols and ammunition, swords, bows and arrows? Yes; I think there is nothing missing. Are you ready? Then—march!"

"But where are we going?" demanded Dick, as they groped their way out of the hut in the opaque darkness that followed upon a dazzling flash of lightning.

"First, round to the back of the hut, and then past the rear of the other huts—since, although I believe we might walk straight through the village without being seen, I do not believe in running unnecessary risks. Then, down to the beach," replied Phil.

For the first few minutes of their journey the going was exceedingly difficult, the eyes of the pair being alternately dazzled by the vivid electric flashes and blinded by the Cimmerian darkness that followed them; but by the time that they had groped their way through the village and were approaching the beach, the flash and glimmer of the lightning, both fork and sheet, had become almost continuous, and they were able to see their way for the rest of the distance without difficulty.

"Now," said Phil, when at length they reached the beach and stood among the canoes, "our first business must be to choose a handy canoe for ourselves—I hope we shall not require her for more than an hour—and then send the rest adrift down the river, which will put it out of the power of the villagers to pursue us. It is, of course, a bit hard upon them, but it cannot be helped; and after all, they have kept us enslaved here for three months, so it is not so very unfair an exchange. Now, this is a handy little craft, and ought to serve our purpose very well, even if we cannot find our own canoe again, so help me to haul her up, Dick; and then we must push the others off as quickly as we can. The suck of the current will soon draw them down the creek into the main stream; and when once they are there the Mayubuna may say goodbye to them."

It took them the best part of half an hour to send the whole of the canoes adrift, but they did the job effectually, and by the time that the last canoe had been thrust off into the middle of the creek the first dozen or so were fairly in the main stream and being rapidly sucked out toward the middle by the strong current. Then Dick and Phil, after giving a last look round, and flinging a parting glance toward the silent and apparently deserted village, thrust off the canoe which they had reserved for themselves, sprang lightly into her as she went afloat, seized the paddles, and headed down the creek. Upon reaching the main stream they found that the current was running very strongly, showing that there had been much rain higher up among the hills; but, on the other hand, the storm, which was still raging violently, although it had brought no rain as yet, had bred a strong breeze from the northward which would be of incalculable value to them if they could but recover their own canoe, with her sail; they therefore paddled across to the opposite side of the river, where the current was to a great extent nullified by eddies, and worked their way upstream, close inshore, until they reached the creek near which their own canoe remained—as they hoped—concealed, when, turning into it, they paddled up it until they arrived at their former landing-place, easily recognisable in the light afforded by the incessant lightning flashes. In like manner they had no difficulty in finding the detached clump of bush in which they had hidden their canoe on the evening preceding their capture by the Mayubuna; and toward this they now hurried, eager to learn whether she still remained where they had put her.

As they strode rapidly across the little meadow they noticed that the tall grass all round the clump in which they hoped to find their canoe was much beaten down, as though a number of people had been walking round it, and they also observed several well-defined trails leading away from the clump toward the forest, all of which sent their hopes down to zero, for the signs all pointed to the fact that someone—or something—had made frequent visits to that clump of bush—some of them quite recently; and if those visits had no reference to the hidden canoe, they could not very well guess what their purpose could be. But one thing was evident: that clump of bush must be approached with caution; and accordingly they loosened their hangers in their sheaths, strung their bows, fitted an arrow to the string, and then stole cautiously forward, their figures strongly outlined in the vivid light of the incessantly flashing lightning.

Reaching the spot where a slight thinning of the undergrowth had first suggested to them the idea of hiding the canoe there, Dick suddenly thrust Phil aside and, cautiously parting the bushes, proceeded to insinuate himself into the opening thus made, Phil following him close up, with his drawn hanger in his hand, raised ready to strike a blow if necessary, although, hemmed closely in on every side, as they were, by the tough, elastic stems and boughs of the undergrowth, it was almost as difficult to strike a blow with a sword as it was to effectively draw a bow. Working his way quietly but rapidly forward in the effective manner which he had acquired by several months' practice in the penetration of such growth, Dick at last stretched out his hand and touched what he at once knew was the hull of the canoe.

"All right, Phil," he exclaimed, delightedly, "here she is. Now, if you will stay where you are, and widen the opening a little, so that she will pass out easily, I will go to the other end, and help you to lift her out."

Accordingly, he proceeded to work his way along the length of the canoe, forcing the boughs aside to make a passage for himself, until he had reached to about mid-length of the canoe, when, the darkness in there being almost impenetrable in spite of the continuously flashing lightning, he reached his hand over to ascertain whether the sail and paddles were still in the craft as they had been left. As he did so he became conscious of a strong musky odour, and while he was still pondering what this might portend his hand came in contact with a cold, clammy, scaly body which his touch told him, before he hastily withdrew his hand with a low cry of astonishment and repugnance, must be not far short of as thick as his own body. And the next instant there occurred a sudden rustling that caused the canoe to shake and quiver and the paddles in her to rattle, a huge, dimly-seen shape upraised itself in the canoe, a gust of hot, fetid breath smote Dick in the face, and a loud angry hiss made itself heard even through the heavy booming of the thunder.

Chapter Fifteen
How they escaped one great Danger, only to fall into a greater

There was no need for Dick to ask himself, or his friend, what was the nature of this monstrous, indistinctly seen shape that upreared itself out of the canoe and poised its head within a foot of his face, its two eyes flashing baleful green fires into his as its long forked tongue flickered angrily in and out of its slightly opened jaws; he knew it at once for one of the enormous boas that dispute the sovereignty of the South American forest with the puma, and the black jaguar, that most rare and ferocious of all the cat tribe. And, for an instant, so great was his astonishment at thus unexpectedly finding himself at close quarters—nay, face to face—with a creature big enough to envelop his body half a dozen times over, and strong enough to crush him into a shapeless mass, that he was completely paralysed. He had no fear of the serpent, although he was perfectly aware of the awful danger in which he stood—he knew that in another instant the enormous body might fling its great coils about him and gradually bring into action the tremendous pressure which should crush every bone in his body to splinters—but, on the other hand, it never occurred to him to make the slightest effort to save himself from so hideous a fate. But as he stood there perfectly quiescent for, as it seemed to him, a quarter of an hour or more— the actual length of time did not probably exceed three seconds—a sharp rattling of the dry twigs over his head and a heavy thud met his ears, a little shower of twigs and leaves rained down upon him, and at the same instant a terrific upheaval occurred in the canoe, coil upon coil the vast length of the serpent's body leaped into view, and plunged over the side, there was a violent rustling and crackling of branches for a few seconds as the monster snake writhed its irresistible way through the neighbouring bushes; and then it was gone. And as the last sounds of its hurried retreat died away, Dick Chichester sank helplessly to the ground, violently sick.

PHIL SAVES DICK'S LIFE

For a minute or two the paroxysms of vomiting were simply dreadful, and then the feeling of horrible nausea gradually passed away, and, pulling himself together, Dick struggled to his feet.

"That's right, lad," he heard Stukely's voice say, as he felt his friend's encouraging pat on the shoulder. "Feel better, now? That's capital. Faugh! what a disgusting stench! No wonder it made you sick; I feel almost as bad myself. But I'll bet a trifle that the brute feels a good deal worse than either of us, for I must have hit him pretty hard; indeed if it had not been for the thick growth that baulked me and hindered my stroke I could have cut his head clean off."

"Well, you—you—have—saved my life, Phil, and I—" gasped Dick thickly, as he felt for the other's hand and pressed it convulsively.

"Pooh! nonsense; that's all rubbish, you know," interrupted Phil, patting Dick on the back, "I should have cut at the brute just the same, if thou hadst not been there. And now, if you feel all right again, let us get the canoe out and see what she looks like; a nice mess he will have made of her, I expect, making his lair in her; with a murrain on him!"

"You have put something worse than a murrain on him, or I am no judge," laughed Dick, a trifle hysterically. "The brute will certainly die before morning. Now, then, are you ready? Then—lift!"

With some difficulty they at length extricated the canoe from her hiding-place, to find, a good deal to their surprise, that, apart from two broken paddles, the craft was very little the worse for having been made the lair of a snake so big that he must have practically filled her from end to end. Luckily the mast, yard, and sail had been placed in the bottom of her and so had not been broken, although almost the whole of the boa's ponderous weight must have rested upon them. So when presently they put her into the water, they were rejoiced to find that although she had been lying dry for three months, so completely had she been shielded from the sun's rays that her hull was still intact and that she leaked not a drop. This was far better than they had dared to hope for, so, stepping into her, appropriating the paddles of the other craft, and leaving the latter moored to the bank, they joyfully shoved off, and three minutes later were in the main stream, with the canoe's head pointed up the river.

Meanwhile, the storm still raged as furiously as ever, the flashes of lightning were incessant, the rolling of the thunder was continuous and deafening, and the northerly wind was blowing so fiercely that the surface of the stream was whipped into small, foam-capped waves. But they were not high enough to imperil the safety of the canoe, moreover the wind that roared so savagely aloft among the tree-tops and stripped off the dried leaves and rotten branches in blinding showers was a fair wind for the fugitives, so they stepped their mast, close-reefed their sail, and were presently foaming up the river in midstream—where, although they had a strong current to contend with, they were at least safe from the branches that flew hurtling through the air—as fast as a horse could trot.

Now, all this time the storm had been a dry storm, that is to say, not a drop of rain had fallen from the bosom of the scowling clouds that seemed bursting with it, but it was bound to come, sooner or later, and come it did, with a vengeance, when our friends had been under way about an hour, and just as the canoe had shot into a broad, lagoon-like stretch of the river where it broadened out to about a mile in width, and where consequently the water was shallow and the current scarcely perceptible. And well was it for them that the rain caught them just at that point, for otherwise they must perforce have landed until the worst of it had blown over. For it came down, not in the sober, steady, respectable fashion in which it falls in temperate climates, but literally in sheets, through which it was not possible to see anything more distant than an ordinary boat's length. With it came more wind, so that the canoe, with the gale right behind her and a close-reefed sail set which, in that condition, was not very much bigger than a man's shirt, rushed along with the foam boiling up level with her gunwale, and sometimes even in over it. While this state of affairs prevailed, and nothing could be seen beyond the dripping sail glistening in the flash of the lightning, the Englishmen continued their headlong flight up the river, unable to see where they were steering but keeping the boat steadily dead before the wind, confident, from the glimpse they had had just before the rain came on, that so long as they were able to do this they would be running up the centre line of the river and could not come to very much harm.

The first violence of the rain lasted about twenty minutes, and then it settled to a quiet, steady downpour for about an hour, during which the thunder and lightning gradually subsided until the thunder became a mere muttering in the extreme distance, and finally died away altogether. But the sheet lightning continued to play intermittently, low down on the northern horizon for some time longer, affording light enough for the fugitives to see where they were going, and as the wind still continued to blow strongly they held on, hour after hour, making the most of the splendid opportunity thus afforded them to make good their escape, so that when at length the morning came and the wind died down with the rising of the sun, they were far beyond the reach of pursuit by the Mayubuna.

Now ensued a month of comparative uneventfulness, during which the two dauntless young Englishmen forced their way up that great river which, where it falls into the Amazon, is named the Maranon, while in its higher reaches it is called the Ucayali, and higher still, the Quillabamba. But although their journey up this magnificent stream may be fitly described as comparatively uneventful, it must not be inferred therefrom that they met with no adventures at all; on the contrary, there was scarcely a day when they did not meet with an adventure of some sort, but it was scarcely of a sufficiently notable character to justify amplification in these pages, being merely the sort of occurrence that is inevitable in a river journey through wild country in the tropic zone. For example, there were frequent rapids and cataracts to be negotiated, food to be sought for and obtained, in the course of which search many strange creatures were seen, many curious and wonderful sights witnessed, and occasionally savage animals encountered. Also Indians began to be met with at frequent intervals, some of whom proved friendly while others were hostile and would fain have disputed the right of the white men to be in the country at all—thanks to the tyrannical treatment which they had experienced at the hands of the Spaniard; and once they encountered a tribe of genuine Amazons, women who had turned the usual order of things upside down, having usurped the functions of the men, such as fighting, hunting, and fishing, while their men folk were compelled to cultivate the land, care for the cattle, cook the food, look after the children, and so on! Then there was the gradual change in the nature of the vegetation and the character of the scenery as the travellers worked their way upward from the level of the great plains, or pampas, into the mountainous region toward Cuzco, with the ever-increasing difficulties of the navigation, which at length became so great that the canoe had to be abandoned altogether, and the journey continued by land, although they still followed the course of the river as closely as possible, in order that they might always be able to get water, and also because it served them as a guide.

But it was not until they had been journeying a full month, after their escape from the Mayubuna, that their next really important adventure befell. They had by this time climbed upward out of the low, hot, tropic forest region, and had attained an altitude at which the climate might almost be described as temperate, where, while the days were still distinctly hot, the nights were cool, sometimes even to the extent of sharpness, and where dense morning-fogs were frequent at that particular period of the year. Those fogs were the cause of much inconvenience and delay to the pair; for they could neither hunt nor travel in a fog, the result being that they were frequently obliged to remain in camp until eight or nine o'clock in the morning, instead of resuming their journey at daybreak, as had heretofore been their custom.

Such was the case on the particular morning when the young Englishmen encountered their next important adventure. The sun had been above the horizon nearly two hours when at length the dense fog which had enveloped their camp cleared sufficiently to permit of their proceeding upon their journey, but it still hung about here and there in heavy wreaths, motionless in the still morning air, when they quite unexpectedly came upon one of the old Peruvian roads constructed by the Incas. This road bore evidences of having at one time been a magnificent highway; but under the rule of the Spaniards it had been neglected until now it was little more than a sandy track over which Nature was fast resuming her sway. But it happened to lead in approximately the right direction for the Englishmen, and heavy as was the travelling over it, it was less laborious than toiling over a rough, trackless country, they therefore promptly decided to follow it so long as it ran their way.

About a mile from the spot where our two travellers came upon the road it entered a dense wood; and here the fog still hung thickly. But the friends decided that this was of little consequence, since the road, though its surface was broken up and much overgrown, was still easily distinguishable; accordingly they plunged into the wood without hesitation. A quarter of an hour later, as they rounded a bend in the road, they made the exceedingly unwelcome discovery that they had walked right into the midst of a party of some fifty Spanish soldiers who, having recently partaken of breakfast, were now resting by the roadside until the fog should clear.

The encounter was so sudden, so absolutely unexpected on the part of the Englishmen, that almost before they realised the presence of the Spaniards the latter—who had heard Dick and Phil talking together as they approached—had surrounded them, rendering flight an impossibility, and in a trice the pair were disarmed and, hemmed in by an escort of a dozen armed men, conducted to the spot where the captain—a tall, dark, handsome man, in full armour, but without a helmet—with his horse standing beside him, was reclining against the trunk of an enormous pine.

"Ah, Jorge!" exclaimed this individual, in Spanish, rising to his feet, as the party approached; "what have we here? Prisoners? Who and what are they? Surely not Indians—although they might well be, from their garb."

"Truly, señor Capitan, I know not who or what they are," answered the man addressed as Jorge, and who seemed, from his dress and equipment, to be some sort of inferior officer, possibly a sergeant; "but we heard them approaching along the road, and as their speech was strange I deemed it my duty to seize them; I therefore hastily arranged an ambush, into which they the next moment walked; and—here they are. If they were not so dark in colour I should say that they might possibly be Englishmen."

"Inglés! here!" exclaimed the captain. "But that is impossible! Who are you, pícaros?"

Now, during their six weeks' residence in Cartagena, under the hospitable roof of the señoritas Clara and Dolores, the two Englishmen had, by assiduous study, acquired a sufficient knowledge of Spanish to enable them to understand the nature of the question thus contemptuously addressed to them; and Phil—who, as usual, took the lead whenever any talking was to be done—at once replied:

"Impossible or not, señor, we are Englishmen; but, beyond that bare statement of fact, you must pardon us if we decline to say anything."

"Oh!" retorted the Spaniard. "You decline to say anything, do you? Very good. I am not at all curious to learn the history of such vagabonds as you appear to be. The fact that you are—by your own confession—English, is enough for me. But there are others who may be more interested than I; and, if so, you may rest assured that they will find a way to make you speak. Take them away and secure them, Jorge," he continued, addressing his subordinate; "and take care that they do not give you the slip. I shall hold you responsible for their safekeeping. And as soon as you have secured your prisoners to your satisfaction, let the men fall in, and we will resume our march."

The man to whose charge our friends had been committed saluted, and then gave the signal for the prisoners to be led away, adding to his signal the significant order "Shoot the rascals at once upon the slightest sign of an attempt to escape."

At a spot among the trees, situated about a hundred yards from where the captain had been standing, the little party came to the place where a dozen pack mules had been tethered; and a brief search among the heterogeneous articles which comprised the packs furnished the sergeant with a raw-hide rope, from which he cut off a couple of lengths sufficient to securely bind the hands of Phil and Dick firmly behind their backs, and this operation was at once so effectually performed that anything in the nature of escape by simply breaking away and running for one's life was rendered impossible, quite apart from the sinister and significant order to shoot which had been given to the soldiers. A quarter of an hour later the entire party were on the move, and the two Englishmen had the mortification of finding themselves marched back along the road by which they had come.

Shortly after passing the spot where our friends had struck the road, the path—for it was little more—curved away toward the left, and led along the top of an extensive plateau of rich pasture land, upon which, about midday, they sighted the first herd of cattle that the Englishmen had seen since their escape from the Mayubuna; and during the afternoon they saw other herds in the charge of peons, showing that the party were gradually approaching civilised territory; and about half an hour before sunset they marched into a small village, composed chiefly of adobe huts, where a halt was called for the night, and where our friends were confined in a ramshackle barn of a place in company with the sergeant and ten men. That the sergeant was quite determined not to get into trouble by the neglect of any possible precaution soon became perfectly evident; for when, about half an hour after the arrival of the party at the village, supper was served, the individual in question gave orders that before the hands of the prisoners were released to enable them to convey food to their mouths, their ankles were to be securely bound together; and this was done. Then, after supper was over, without unbinding the ankles of the prisoners their wrists were again bound together behind their backs, after which their ankles and wrists were drawn as closely together as they could be induced to come, and firmly lashed behind them; and in this constrained and exceedingly painful posture they were unceremoniously flung into opposite corners of the hut, where, upon the bare floor, and suffering torments from the vermin with which the place was infested, and from which, in their constrained position, they were helpless to defend themselves, they were left to pass the night as best they might.

A seemingly interminable night of torture for the hapless prisoners came laggingly to an end at last when, about half an hour after daybreak, the lashings which had confined their limbs all through the hours of darkness were loosed, and they were allowed to scramble to their feet and walk to and fro for a few minutes before partaking of breakfast. After breakfast the march was resumed; and—not to dwell at unnecessary length upon this portion of the narrative—about an hour before sundown the entire party marched into a city which one of the soldiers surlily informed Phil was Cuzco; and here the two young Englishmen were at length safely deposited in an underground dungeon of a building which had once been one of the Inca's palaces; escape being rendered impossible by the simple process of chaining them to the wall by means of a heavy iron chain about six feet in length, one end of which was attached to an iron girdle locked round the prisoner's waist while the other end was welded to an iron ringbolt, the shank of which was deeply sunk into the solid masonry of the dungeon wall.

On the morning of the following day they were temporarily released from their loathsome prison—where their bed had consisted merely of a thin layer of damp straw cast upon the stone flags with which the dungeon was paved, and where the only ventilation consisted of a small iron grating let into the masonry above the door—and conducted, under a strong guard, into the presence of the Governor of the city, who questioned them closely concerning their names, nationality, where they had come from, where they were bound for, and why they wished to go there. At first the two Englishmen resolutely refused to answer any of the questions put to them; but when at length the Governor, growing exasperated at their obstinacy, threatened them with the torture of the boot, Phil so far satisfied the man's curiosity as to inform him truthfully of their names and nationality, adding the fictitious information that, having quarrelled with their captain, they had been forcibly put ashore somewhere in the Gulf of Darien, and had since been wandering aimlessly about the country, not knowing where to go or how to escape from it. The story was well enough concocted, considering that it was made up on the spur of the moment; but it was evident that it did not altogether satisfy his Excellency, who finally ordered them to be taken back to their dungeon and kept there pending certain enquiries which he proposed to make. Later in the day, when they once more found themselves alone, and again chained to the dungeon wall, Dick, in his simplicity, ventured to question Phil as to his reasons for resorting to fiction instead of boldly telling the truth, or refusing to say anything at all; to which Phil replied:

"My gentle buzzard, if I had persisted in refusing the Don's request for information, we should have been put to the torture; for when these fellows threaten a thing like that, they usually mean it; or, if they do not actually mean it at the moment, they would unhesitatingly carry out their threat, rather than give themselves the lie; and we should show ourselves singularly deficient in common sense were we to submit to be tormented for hours, and probably maimed for life, rather than impart a little information—so long as that information is of such a nature as to harm nobody. At all costs we must avoid being tortured, if we can; for how could we hope to escape, or, having escaped, hope to carry out our plans, if our bones were broken, or our limbs twisted out of joint. Therefore, as soon as torture was mentioned, I decided that the time had arrived when speech was to be preferred to silence. But I was careful to avoid saying anything which might connect us with the *Adventure*; because sooner or later news of the exploits of that ship is certain to penetrate as far south even as this, and I have a suspicion that the participants in those exploits will not be altogether popular with the dons. Also, we must remember that there was a rumour that two of the crew of that ship had found shelter and succour in a certain house in Cartagena; and if two persons belonging to the *Adventure* should eventually be found at large in this country a certain colour of probability might be imparted to the rumour; in which case our gentle friends Clara and Dolores might get into serious trouble. Therefore I thought it best on all accounts to mingle a little fiction with my facts. And I trust that long before his Excellency's proposed enquiries have borne fruit we shall be far enough away from Cuzco and its Governor."

"Do you think, then, that there is the slightest chance of our effecting our escape?" asked Dick, glancing expressly at the chain which bound him to the wall.

The darkness of the dungeon was too profound for Phil to detect that glance; nevertheless he must have guessed at it, for he replied:

"No, my son, I don't think anything of the sort; I know! Don't ask me how I know, for I cannot tell you; but the knowledge is nevertheless here," tapping his forehead. "Keep up your courage, youngster," he continued. "Those chains are nothing. Neither chains nor stone walls can long hold in restraint the man who is destined to be free; and I tell you that neither you nor I are doomed to die at the hands of the Spaniard. More I cannot tell you; for although I am as certain as I am of my own existence that we shall escape, my foreknowledge is not clear enough to enable me to say how that escape is going to be effected."

"I wish I felt half as confident as you seem to do about it," grumbled Dick. "At present it appears to me that nothing short of a miracle can help us. But—well, we shall see."

The lad's pessimism seemed to be fully justified when, on the following day, the pair were once more released from the chains that confined them to the wall, and were summoned by their jailer to follow him. They obeyed the summons with alacrity, each of them animated by a secret hope that an opportunity might present itself for them to break away from their custodian and effect their escape from the building, and eventually from the city; but this hope was nipped in the bud when, immediately outside the door of the dungeon, an armed guard, consisting of half a dozen soldiers and a corporal, were seen to be awaiting them. Evidently, the moment for escape was not yet.

To the surprise of both, when the prisoners arrived at the top of the flight of stone steps leading from the dungeon they found that, instead of being again conducted along the passage which led to the Governor's quarters, as on the previous day, they were marched along another corridor, and presently they found themselves in the street. But even now there was no encouragement for them to attempt to escape, because, besides being hemmed in by their escort of half a dozen soldiers, the entire party were surrounded by a gaping, scowling, execrating mob of ragged, unwashed ruffians, apparently the scum of the city, who would have effectually frustrated any attempt on the part of the Englishmen to break away from their guard and take to their heels; indeed if one might have judged from the expression of their coarse, brutal features, and the remarks which fell from their lips, nothing would have pleased them better than for the prisoners to have made such an attempt, since it would have afforded the mob a legitimate excuse for hunting the pair to death. Nor were the prisoners permitted to remain very long in suspense with regard to their destination; for when presently the soldiers wheeled their charge into a certain street a loud murmur swept through the accompanying mob of—"Heretics! they are heretics, and are being taken to the Inquisition!"

So indeed it proved; for some five minutes later they arrived before a big, gloomy, jail-like building, constructed of great blocks of stone, and having a number of exceedingly small apertures in the wall, each aperture being guarded by iron bars of quite unnecessary thickness. The entrance to this place was a great gateway some twelve feet wide and nearly twice as high, fitted with a pair of enormously solid wooden doors, so heavy that each leaf was fitted with a roller running upon a quadrant rail let into the pavement to facilitate opening. But it soon became evident that these ponderous gates were only opened on special occasions; for when, having halted the little party, the corporal in charge tugged at a handle attached to a chain which hung down from an aperture in the wall, and a bell was heard to clang somewhere in the far interior of the building, a small wicket cut in one of the big gates was presently thrown open by an individual in the garb of a lay brother, and the soldiers with their prisoners were invited to pass through it.

The party now found themselves in a lofty, vaulted passage, some twenty-five feet in length, the farther end of which opened upon a paved courtyard surrounded by cloisters surmounted by lofty buildings massively constructed of the same dark-grey stone as the building through which they had just passed, and, like it, provided with windows strongly protected by massive iron bars, only instead of being all small, as were the windows in the exterior walls, some of those which looked out upon the courtyard were of very considerable dimensions. At the opposite side of the courtyard, facing the passage through which the party had just passed, was another door, giving admission to what appeared to be the main building, and to this they were now conducted by the lay brother, who, having unlocked the door, threw it open and bade them enter the big, gloomy cavern-like, ill-lighted hall which now stood revealed. Once inside this place, the prisoners were delivered over to the custody of a huge, brawny brute in the shape of a man who, from the fact that he bore a bunch of big keys attached to his belt, was no doubt the jailer of the institution. Then a tall, thin, ascetic-looking man in the garb of a priest stepped forward, scanned the two prisoners attentively, carefully compared their appearance with the description of them contained in a document, which the corporal handed to him, signed the document and returned it to the corporal, dismissed him and his followers, and waved the jailer to lead his charges away, which the fellow immediately did, in morose silence. Their way lay down a long, narrow corridor, having doors opening out of it at intervals on either side; and at the precise moment when the prisoners arrived opposite one of these doors a long-drawn wail, rising to a piercing shriek, rang out from behind it, causing their flesh to creep upon their bones with horror, so eloquent of keen, excruciating, almost unendurable physical anguish was the sound.

The jailer, who was leading the way, glanced over his shoulder at his prisoners with a smile of such gloating, Satanic suggestiveness and cruelty on his heavy features as the cry pealed forth that, on the instant, the feeling of passive repugnance with which the two Englishmen had thus far regarded the fellow was converted into fierce, hot, active, unreasoning hatred; for the fraction of a second they glanced questioningly into each other's eyes, then, each reading in that lightning glance the thought of the other, the pair flung themselves upon the fellow. And while Dick, exerting all his giant strength, pinned the man's arms to his sides, and at the same time, by a deft movement of his left foot, tripped the fellow up so that he crashed violently forward upon his face on the stone pavement of the passage, Phil clasped the man's throat with his two hands, compressing his windpipe in such a vice-like grip that it was utterly impossible for the fellow to utter the slightest sound, and thus locked together, the three went down in a bunch under the impetus of the sudden attack, the jailer being undermost. The hard pavement seemed to fairly ring with the violent impact of the man's skull upon it, and the next instant Dick felt the fellow's tense muscles relax as though the violence of the blow had either partially or wholly stunned him, whereupon the youngster, still acting upon an impulse that seemed to emanate from somewhere outside himself, pushed Phil on one side, flung himself in a kneeling posture upon the prostrate jailer's shoulders, and, grasping the man by the hair with both hands, pulled up the fellow's head and dashed it furiously upon the pavement again thrice, after which the victim lay silent, inert, to all appearance dead.

"Roll him over, quick, and unbuckle his belt; we must have his keys," hissed Phil in Dick's ear, and before five seconds had passed the two Englishmen were on their feet standing over their victim, while Phil rapidly examined the keys, one after the other. Quickly he selected one that showed signs of more frequent wear than the others, and then glanced keenly about him. They were near the far end of the corridor, which ended in a wall lighted by a fair-sized window, and there were only four more doors to be passed, two on either side, before the end of the corridor was reached.

"Stay here until I beckon you, and then bring the man to me," whispered Phil, and darted off to the end of the corridor, leaving Dick to mount guard over the prostrate body of the jailer. Rapidly, yet with the utmost coolness, Phil tried the key which he had selected in the lock of one of the farther doors. It slid in, turned, and the door swung open. A single glance sufficed to assure Phil that the door was that of a cell, and that the cell was unoccupied, whereupon he beckoned Dick, who hoisted the unconscious jailer upon his shoulders, bore him to the cell, and flung him unceremoniously upon the heap of straw which was apparently intended to serve as a bed.

"Now, the belt, quick," whispered Phil, who had followed, gently closing the door behind him; and, rolling the still insensible body over on its face, the pair bent over it and with deft fingers contrived to fasten the ankles and wrists of their victim together in such a fashion, that the more the man struggled the tighter would he draw the ligature. Then using the formidable-looking knife which the man had worn suspended from his belt, they formed a gag by cutting strips from their skin clothing and wrapping it round the largest key of the bunch, which they detached from the chain and inserted in their victim's mouth, thus rendering it as impossible for him to cry out as it was for him to move. Having disposed of the jailer in such a fashion that he would not be likely to give trouble for the next hour or two, the pair left the cell, closed and locked the door behind them, and stood listening intently to ascertain whether the sounds of the recent struggle had attracted attention.

Chapter Sixteen
What happened in the Inquisition at Cuzco

For perhaps half a minute the pair stood outside the cell door, listening with all their ears, but not the slightest sound broke the silence which seemed to pervade the whole of the vast building. Then, from somewhere in the far distance, there came the sound of a door being closed, and almost at the same instant a quavering cry, rising to a long-drawn shriek of agony, again pealed forth from behind that awful door a few paces along the corridor.

"For mercy's sake, what is it?" whispered Dick, with ashen lips. "Surely such sounds can never be human?"

"They are, though!" replied Phil in a low, tense whisper. "They are the cries of some poor soul under the torture—'being put to the question' as these fiends of Inquisitors express it. Oh! if I could but lay my hands upon one of them, I would—but come along, lad; we must not dally here. If we are again taken after what we have done our fate will be—well, something that won't bear thinking of!" Then, seizing Dick by the arm and dragging the lad after him, Stukely proceeded softly on tiptoe along the corridor.

They had arrived within a yard of the door from behind which those dreadful sounds had emanated when it suddenly opened and a tall, dark man emerged, clad in a long black habit girt about his waist with a cord of knotted rope; his features were partially obscured by the hood of the garment, which he wore drawn over his head so that it stood up in a sort of peak, and wearing round his neck a massive gold chain, from which a gold crucifix depended. His back happened to be toward them, and he had closed and latched the door behind him before he turned and saw the two Englishmen within arm's length of him. For a second he stood motionless, regarding the two wild-looking figures with blank amazement; then a look of mingled terror and anger leapt into his eyes, and it was evident that he was about to open his mouth and shout an alarm. But the cry never passed his lips, for in that instant Stukely was upon him with the silent, irresistible bound of a jaguar, and in the next he was dragging wildly at the Englishman's hands to tear them away from his throat. Nevertheless he might as well have striven to force his way through the solid masonry of the adjoining wall as to tear away those two relentless thumbs that were compressing his windpipe and choking the life out of him, and presently he grew black in the face, his eyes rolled upward until only the whites of them were visible, his grip on Phil's wrists relaxed and gave way, his arms fell limp to his sides, his knees yielded, and he sank slowly to the ground, or rather, was lowered to it by Stukely, who still maintained his remorseless grip upon the other's throat, kneeling upon one knee beside the now prostrate body.

Presently, however, Phil rose to his feet, and with his eyes still fixed upon the body of the priest, whispered to Dick:

"I would fain break the fellow's neck, and so in some sort avenge that poor soul in there; but we have no time for vengeance now. We must be clear of this accursed building before that villain revives or our fate is sealed; so come along, lad." Therewith the pair resumed their passage along the corridor.

A few seconds later they found themselves back in the great, gloomy entrance hall of the building, with not a soul in sight in any direction. Phil came to a halt.

"Now, where is that lay brother who admitted us?" he whispered to Dick. "We must have him, or rather, his keys; for without them we cannot get out of the place."

"I believe," whispered Dick in reply, "he went in there" — indicating a door — "after he had let out the corporal and his guard."

"Then," returned Phil, "let us see if he is in there now." Then, crossing to the door, he tried the handle, turned it, flung open the door, and boldly entered the room, closely followed by Dick, who closed the door behind him.

The apartment was empty of human occupants, and otherwise presented a bare and uninviting aspect, the only furniture in it consisting of a table and two chairs. It was imperfectly lighted by a small window looking out upon the cloisters which surrounded the courtyard that the prisoners had crossed a quarter of an hour earlier, and a bell suspended near the ceiling and attached to a chain leading out through a slit in the wall seemed to indicate that it was the room in which the warder of the outer gates was accustomed to sit. But the man was certainly not then in the room, nor was there anything to indicate that he had recently been there. If therefore Dick's belief that he had seen the lay brother enter had been well-founded the man must have left again almost immediately, while the two Englishmen were being conducted to their cell by the now imprisoned jailer. True, he might have passed on to an inner room; for there was another door opposite to that by which Dick and Phil had entered.

After a hurried glance round, the two friends, moved as it might have been by the same impulse, crossed to this door, and, quietly opening it, glanced into the adjoining apartment. A single glance round this room sufficed to show that the man whom they sought was not in it, for it also was empty, so far as human occupants were concerned. It was a room of very considerable size, and was apparently the refectory, for two rows of tables, each capable of seating about fifty persons, ran lengthwise down the hall, and were draped with coarse white cloths upon which were set out an array of platters, water pitchers, knives, and the rest of the paraphernalia used at meals. This room was very much loftier and better lighted than the one which the Englishmen had just left, there being four large windows in the outer wall, overlooking a large and beautifully kept garden in which several people were working, some of them attired in the garb of monks, while others wore the dress of lay brothers. There were two doors in this room, in addition to the one by which our friends had entered, one being at the far end of the room and communicating with the kitchen of the establishment, if the sounds and odours which emanated therefrom were to be trusted, while the other and much larger door occupied the centre of the inner wall and was obviously used by the inmates of the establishment at meal times.

"Now, what can have become of the man?" demanded Phil in an angry whisper, as the pair glanced round the room and noted its deserted appearance. "Are you quite sure that you were not mistaken as to the door by which you saw him enter?"

"No," answered Dick in the same subdued tones, "I am not quite sure; but I believe I am not mistaken all the same. But, Phil," he continued, "is it really necessary that we should find him? Cannot we get out of the building in some other and safer way than by finding that man, knocking him down, and taking his keys from him? Besides, even if the way were free for us to leave here this instant, where could we go? We could not walk half a dozen yards along the street, attired as we now are, without attracting attention and being recognised as strangers. We should inevitably be recaptured within ten minutes!"

"Then, what a plague are we to do?" demanded Phil, impatiently. "To remain here is to court recapture as surely as if we showed ourselves in the streets. Why, even now, at any moment a man may enter this room, see us, and give the alarm."

"Yes," agreed Dick; "that is very true; and no doubt if we remain here long enough that is what will happen. But this Inquisition seems to be a rambling old pile of a place, and I cannot help thinking that it must contain many an obscure, little-used recess or cupboard in which we might find at least temporary safety and concealment until the small hours of the morning, when we might leave the place and make our way out of the city with comparatively little risk."

"You are right, Dick," agreed Stukely; "that is undoubtedly our best plan—if Dame Fortune will but stand by us. But it will be plaguey risky for us to attempt to remain in here until the small hours of the morning. How can we possibly hope to avoid being seen by some prowling priest or lay brother within the next twelve hours? But pish! what is the use of anticipating trouble? Your plan is certainly the right one, and the sooner that we see about carrying it out the better. Now it is quite evident that there is no place of concealment in this room, so there is nothing to be gained by dawdling here. Also, we know that it is useless to retrace our steps; and yonder is obviously the kitchen, and must therefore be avoided. That leaves us with no resource but to try the big door; so come along and let us see how far our luck will hold good."

Without further ado the pair advanced cautiously to the door which Phil had indicated, and the latter laid his hand upon the handle, which he turned gradually and noiselessly as far as it would go; then, having noticed that the door opened inward, he drew it toward him the fraction of an inch and glanced through the slit thus created. Phil now found that he was looking into a long and wide corridor, or passage, imperfectly lighted by two small windows, one at each end. There was no one to be seen in that part of the corridor which came within his somewhat limited range of vision, so, emboldened thereby, he opened the door widely enough to enable him to peer out and take a hasty glance along the full length of the corridor. That glance assured him that, for the moment at least, the passage was empty; and at the same moment he became conscious of the low, sweet notes of an organ being played somewhat toward the far end of the building.

"Good!" he whispered excitedly to Dick. "Do you hear that, lad? It is an organ; which means that the chapel is not very far away; and if we can but gain its interior we shall be reasonably safe; for there is sure to be a dark nook somewhere in it where we may be able to lie concealed for a few hours. Since the coast seems to be clear just now we may as well proceed upon our hunt at once; all hands are probably now engaged upon their regular morning's business, and, if so, we may be lucky enough to go a good way without meeting anybody, whereas later on the whole place will probably be alive with people. So, come along, lad; no time like the present."

Silently as ghosts the pair slid through the open doorway into the corridor, drawing the door to and closing it behind them in the very nick of time; for as Phil released his hold upon the handle he heard the door leading from the kitchen to the refectory open, the hitherto subdued sounds of activity in the kitchen suddenly became greatly intensified, while voices and the sound of shuffling sandals on the stone floor of the refectory came through the door which he had just closed.

"Quick, lad, for your life," whispered Stukely in his companion's ear. "This way, and run; for we are lost if they come into the corridor and find us here!" And, running tiptoe on their bare feet, the two sped down the corridor like mist wreaths driven before the wind.

At the very end of the corridor they came upon a large doorway fitted with folding doors, one leaf of which was ajar, and through the aperture the notes of the organ softly played floated out to them. With the tips of his fingers Phil gently pushed the door a trifle wider open, and, peering in, saw that they were indeed at one of the entrances to the chapel which formed part of the Holy Inquisition of Cuzco. The building of which Phil thus obtained a glimpse was unexpectedly large; so large, indeed, that he instantly jumped to the conclusion that it was intended for the use of the general public as well as for the members of the Order, the accommodation being sufficient for at least four hundred worshippers. The door through which they were peering was situated underneath a gallery, in which was placed the organ loft, for the notes of the instrument floated down to them from immediately overhead. To the right of them stretched away the main body of the church, one half of it—the half nearest them—being fitted with pews, while the other half, toward the great west door, was furnished with common rush-bottomed chairs, evidently intended for the use of casual worshippers and the lower orders generally. To the left lay the chancel, fitted with exquisitely carved and gilded stalls, tall, elaborately worked brass standards for lamps, gaudily painted and gilded statues of various saints, a superb reredos in marble surmounted by a cross bearing a fine lifesize figure of the Redeemer; the whole illuminated by the rainbow tints which streamed in through the beautiful stained glass of the magnificent east window, and a faint odour of incense still clung to the air of the place. The main thing, however, or at least that which chiefly interested the two interlopers, was, that although the west door stood wide open, affording a glimpse of a broad gravel path leading up through a superb garden, beyond which could be seen a road, houses, and the traffic of foot passengers, horsemen, and vehicles, there was not a soul to be seen inside the church, the organist being apparently its only occupant for the moment. Phil therefore wasted no more time, but, pushing the door wide enough open to afford admittance to himself and his companion, slipped through, dragging Dick after him, and pushed to the door again behind him, leaving it ajar as he had found it. Then, advancing a pace or two, but taking care to keep well beneath the shadow of the gallery, the pair made a rapid but comprehensive survey of the building in search of a hiding-place where they might safely lie *perdu* for the next few hours.

They noted several places that looked quite promising, if they could but reach them, only, unfortunately, there was the organist up aloft, and doubtless an assistant to blow the bellows. If either of them should chance to glance down into the body of the church at the moment when the fugitives happened to be making for the chosen spot, all would be lost. For instance, the choir stalls rose in tiers one behind another, and that of course meant that beneath the floor of the rearmost tier there would be a hollow space amply sufficient to conceal a dozen men—if they could but obtain access to it. Then there was the high altar. It was doubtless hollow, and possibly access to its interior might be obtained at the back; but to gain either of those positions it would be necessary to pass over a part of the pavement which Phil conjectured might be seen from the organ loft, and he felt very strongly disinclined to take the risk of being seen after they had thus far so successfully evaded detection. But he fully recognised that he must not waste much time in making up his mind. There was the priest whom they had left senseless outside the door of the torture chamber, to say nothing of the jailer. It was simply marvellous that the one had not yet been found or the other missed. As the thought flashed through his mind a confused sound of shouting and scurrying feet came to his ears, muffled by distance, through the slightly opened door. And he knew in an instant what that meant. The thing which he had all along been fearing, which indeed he knew must very soon happen, had happened; a discovery of some sort had been made. Probably the priest had recovered sufficiently to raise an alarm, and now in a minute or two the whole place would be swarming with searchers, hunting in every possible and impossible place for the missing prisoners. Something must be done, some decision arrived at instantly. There was no more time for indecision, and Phil once more flung a lightning glance about the building. The walls of the chancel on either side of the high altar and up to the level of the sill of the glorious east window were draped with rich tapestry, depicting on a background of gold thread, on the one side the Annunciation, and on the other the Apotheosis of the Blessed Virgin; and Phil noticed that these tapestries were suspended from rings strung upon massive brass rods, which were supported by brass brackets let into the wall. It seemed to him that those brackets were of such a length as to afford space enough for a man to hide between the tapestry—which reached right down to the floor—and the wall. The organ was softly breathing out the notes of the "Agnus Dei" from a Mass which the organist was evidently practising, and the man would probably be intent only upon his music. The organ-blower, Phil decided, must be risked—perhaps he would be behind the organ, or in some part of the loft from which the chancel could not be seen;—and, as the voices outside grew louder and seemed to be drawing nearer, he plucked Dick by the sleeve, beckoned him to follow, and the pair stole softly up the length of the chancel to the altar, dropped on their knees, lifted the bottom edge of the tapestry, crawled underneath it, let it fall behind them, and rose to their feet in the enclosed space between wall and tapestry at the precise moment when a great bell began to peal out its alarm note from some distant part of the building. The organist almost immediately ceased playing, and a minute later the soft pad-pad of his own and another's sandalled feet descending a wooden staircase not far away came, muffled, to the ears of the fugitives; then followed the slam of a door, the turn of a key in a lock, and the two friends knew themselves to be alone in the church, with the west door wide open, affording them the means of instant flight into the outer world, if they chose to avail themselves of it.

But that thought came to them only to be rejected on the instant. They were still clad in the skins of beasts, which had taken the place of their worn-out clothing; they were unkempt, unshaven, and altogether far too conspicuous in every way to justify them in venturing into the streets by daylight, or indeed at any time while the inhabitants were abroad, therefore they must remain in hiding until darkness fell and the people had retired to rest; and both fervently hoped that the citizens of Cuzco kept early hours. Then they began to feel hungry, for it was now several hours since they had tasted food; but they had grown accustomed to such petty discomforts as hunger and thirst long ago. They were as nothing compared with the torture which that poor wretch must have been undergoing in the room yonder; and as Phil thought of the possibility that, even yet, Dick and he might be recaptured and subjected to similar suffering, he worked his way along the foot or two of distance that separated him from the high altar, and proceeded to examine the latter. As he had more than half-expected, the structure proved to be hollow, being built of massive slabs of marble as to the front and sides, but having no back, and for some reason which he was quite unable to divine, but which he was most heartily thankful for, there was a space left between the sides of the structure and the wall of the church just wide enough for him to squeeze through without undue discomfort, and so gain the interior of the altar. This seemed a distinctly safer place to hide in than merely behind the tapestry; there was room for three or four men to bestow themselves comfortably, and they could lie down if they chose, therefore they lost no time in transferring themselves to this new place of concealment; and they had scarcely settled themselves comfortably therein when they heard a door noisily unlocked and thrown open, and the sound of many sandalled feet swarming into the church.

Judging from the sounds alone, the fugitives crouching in the interior of the altar estimated that about a dozen people had entered the church. They seemed to rush forward a few paces and then halt, as though staring about them; then followed a few brief, desultory movements, and silence. Finally, a voice said, in Spanish:

"Well, it is perfectly clear that they are not here."

"From what do you draw that inference, brother?" demanded another voice.

"First, from the fact that the door by which we entered was locked on the other side; and next, because the great west door is wide open," answered the voice which had first spoken.

"True," answered the second voice. "Yet neither of those facts is proof that the fugitives are not lurking somewhere in the church. Do you ask why? I will tell you. First, Brother Gregorio has been here this morning, as usual, practising; and we know that it is a habit of his to leave the door communicating with the domestic part of the establishment unfastened, and very often open, while he practises. Therefore, if he did the same thing to-day—and I happen to know that he did, for I was in the church myself half an hour ago—it would be an easy matter for the fugitives to gain access to this building and conceal themselves somewhere in it. As to the open door yonder, I attach no importance at all to it, for the Englishmen are much too conspicuous in their appearance and attire to venture abroad in the city by daylight; they would be recaptured in less than five minutes if they did so, and I give them credit for being sensible enough to know it. Consequently, I maintain that they are still somewhere within the walls of the establishment, and, as likely as not, may be in this church; therefore let the place be thoroughly searched at once."

Nothing more was said; but sounds of renewed activity immediately followed upon the order to search, the scuffle of footsteps along the aisles and on the steps leading to the organ loft distinctly reaching the lurking pair as they crouched beneath the altar intently listening, to gather, if they might, some indication of the direction in which the search was proceeding. Presently, to their discomfiture, they heard the footsteps of apparently two persons approaching the enclosed space within the altar rails, the pair talking in low tones as they approached.

"For my part," said one, "I entirely disagree with Fray Felipe. I believe the English heretics have escaped, and by that open door; for, if not, where are they? They cannot be in the other part of the establishment, for, if so, they must have been seen by someone—unless, indeed, they are in league with the devil and have the power of disappearing at will. And they are not in this church; because if they had come here they must have seen that open door, and nobody shall persuade me that, seeing it, they would not avail themselves of the opportunity which it offers."

"Nay, brother," answered the other; "I think Fray Felipe is right; and so would you, had you seen the two men. They looked and were dressed like savages, and could never—"

"Pooh!" interrupted the first, impatiently, "that is all nonsense. If they looked as conspicuous as all that what was there to prevent them from entering the vestry and appropriating a couple of the spare habits that are always hanging there? If they did that they could walk out of the church in broad daylight, and nobody would dream of challenging them. Now, if they are in the church at all, it is my belief that they will be found behind this tapestry. You take that side, brother, and I will take this. Just run your hand along the length of the tapestry; and if they are lurking behind it, you will soon find them."

"Ay," grumbled the other, "and, as like as not, be slain by them for my pains. I tell you, brother, that I like it not. No, they are not here," he concluded, as he ran his hand along the tapestry in an exceedingly perfunctory manner without discovering any sign of the missing prisoners. "I am beginning to think, with you, Brother José, that the rascals have escaped."

"Of course they have," agreed the first speaker. "No, they are not on this side either. Ah!"—as a great bell began to toll somewhere aloft—"there is the bell for Mass, thank heaven! and now this foolish search will be brought to an end." Therewith the footsteps retired, much to the relief of the concealed Englishmen, who were momentarily dreading that it might occur to one or the other of the searchers to turn up the tapestry and peep into the opening beneath and behind the altar. But it did not—possibly neither of the worthy brothers was particularly anxious to find himself suddenly face to face with a couple of desperate Englishmen—and presently the sound of retreating footsteps died away in the distance and all was still in the great church.

But not for long; the lurking pair had only time to dispose themselves a little more comfortably on the hard marble pavement when other footsteps were faintly heard, accompanied by the occasional scrape of a chair in the distance, and the fugitives knew that a congregation was assembling. Then the great bell ceased to toll, the organ once more poured forth its sweet and solemn notes, a door opened, measured footsteps were heard approaching, there was a slight momentary bustle as the brethren of the Order filed in and took their places; and then the service began, and the Englishmen, who were both lovers of music, enjoyed an hour of such keen delight as they had not experienced for many a long day.

In due time the solemn service came to an end, the congregation retired, there ensued an opening and closing of doors, the sounds of which echoed and reverberated hollowly along the aisles and among the arches of the sacred building, and then a great silence fell. For a time the fugitives remained huddled up in their hiding-place, silent and listening; but at length, convinced that the church was indeed empty, they began in low, whispered tones to discuss their situation. The two priests who unwittingly came so near to finding them had furnished them with a hint—if they cared to avail themselves of it—as to how they might make good their escape even in broad daylight, and, so far as Dick was concerned, he would have been quite willing to act upon it by raiding the vestry there and then, appropriating one of the habits which Fray José had said were to be found there, and sallying forth into the city without more ado, for his bones were by this time growing sore with lying so long upon the hard, cold marble. But although Phil's bones were aching quite as much as Dick's, the elder of the two was very strongly disinclined to run the slightest unnecessary risk; he argued that, the church having once been subjected to a tolerably thorough search, he and Dick were reasonably safe, so long as they chose to remain where they were, and that, to venture abroad prematurely, even in disguise, for the mere sake of avoiding a few hours of further discomfort, would be the very height of folly. For, how could they tell at what moment a door might open and someone enter the church and discover them—supposing them to be so foolish as to venture out of their place of concealment? And who knew how many more services were to be held during the day? If it happened that there were no more, then indeed it might be safe enough for them to venture out and go in search of the vestry and those spare habits; but not otherwise. Moreover, how could they be sure that the habits, if found, would actually prove to be as effective a disguise as Fray José had asserted they would? Phil knew enough about the Roman Catholic religion to be fully aware that those who professed it were sometimes prompted to stop the first priest they might chance to meet, and discuss with him some spiritual difficulty, or even to invoke his aid in some merely temporal trouble; and what sort of a figure, he asked Dick, would they cut in such a case as that? No; hungry and thirsty as he was, and sore as were his limbs through long contact with the hard pavement, he was all for remaining where they were, at least until nightfall, when probably, if they could procure effective disguises, they might venture to sally forth and essay the attempt to get out of the city. And so cogent were his arguments that at length he succeeded in silencing Dick, if he did not altogether convince him.

Phil's conjecture that there might be further services in the church before the day was over proved to be correct, there being two, the last of which occurred late enough in the evening to necessitate the lighting of the lamps in the building. And it was while the lamps were being lighted that the two Englishmen learned, from the gossip of those engaged in illuminating the grand altar, that much perplexity and uneasiness had resulted from the fact that, despite the most rigorous search of the entire city, no trace of the missing prisoners had thus far been discovered, and that the conclusion had therefore been at length arrived at that they must have got clear away. This knowledge was eminently satisfactory to the two whom it most intimately concerned, for it seemed to indicate that those engaged in the search had at length lost heart, and that if the hunt was still to be maintained it would only be in a more or less perfunctory manner, and that consequently the fugitives might, by the exercise of a proper amount of caution, hope to make good their escape from the city.

At length the last service of the day was over, the lurking pair heard the closing and locking of the various doors by which the general public entered the building, and this was followed by the shuffling of feet here and there as the lamps and candles were extinguished, one after the other, the low murmur of voices gradually died away, and finally there came the loud slamming of a door which, from the direction of the sound, the fugitives conjectured to be the door beneath the organ loft, by which they had entered the church during the morning, then followed the grating of a key in a lock, the rattle which indicated the withdrawal of the key, and—silence. At last, thought the weary pair behind the altar, the church was empty, and closed for the night.

To make assurance doubly sure, however, they agreed to remain where they were for another half-hour; but when at length they judged that period to have elapsed they crept very cautiously out of the place of concealment which had served them so well, and made their way to the choir stalls, upon the soft cushions of which they rested their weary limbs for a short time while their eyes were growing accustomed to the gloom of the place. Then, having agreed that a certain small door, immediately opposite that by which they had found their way into the church, must be the one giving access to the vestry, they stole silently across the pavement, and Phil, having first satisfied himself that the room, or whatever it was that lay beyond, was in darkness, found the handle and proceeded to turn it as cautiously as though he believed the place on the other side to be full of people. The door proved to be unlocked; and a minute later the fugitives found themselves, as they had expected, in the vestry of the church. The room was a small one, but it was lighted by a fairly large window, and as the night happened to be brilliantly fine and starlit, the gloom here was not nearly so intense as it had been in the interior of the church, consequently they were able to distinguish without much difficulty that there were indeed, as Fray José had said, a number of garments of some sort hanging from pegs on one of the walls. Why these garments should be kept there the fugitives never troubled themselves to conjecture, the fact that they were there was sufficient for them; and they lost no time in appropriating and donning two of them. They were long black garments reaching from shoulder to ankle, with large hoods which might be drawn up over the head, almost entirely concealing the features when the wearer was out of doors, and were confined round the waist by a girdle of knotted rope. Attired in these, the pair felt that they might safely brave any but the very closest scrutiny, and they therefore had no scruples about sallying forth into the open forthwith.

The window of the vestry overlooked a portion of the extensive garden, a glimpse of which they had gained through the great west door of the church earlier in the day, and, peering out through it, the two friends saw that there was a thick shrubbery at no great distance that looked as though it might afford them good cover from which to reconnoitre the ground prior to their attempt to gain the street beyond, and they at once decided to make for it in the first instance. Another moment and they were at the outer door, which proved to be locked. But the key was, luckily, in the lock, and on the inner side of the door, that slight difficulty was therefore soon got over; and a minute later the pair drew a great breath of relief as they found themselves once more in the open air—and free.

Chapter Seventeen
How they escaped from the Inquisition

Yes; free—in a sense; yet not wholly so; for they were still within the boundaries of the Holy Inquisition, although outside the building. To have done so much as they had, however; to have evaded capture for the best part of a day, and finally to have won outside the walls, undetected, was no mean achievement; and they felt that, having accomplished so much, the rest ought to be an easy matter.

Standing within the deep shadow of the doorway for a minute or two after they had silently closed the door behind them, the pair searched with their gaze as much of the garden as came within the range of their vision, and nowhere could they detect any sign of human presence within it; indeed they scarcely expected to do so, for it was now altogether too dark for anything in the nature of gardening operations; moreover, they surmised that it was about the hour when everybody connected with the establishment would be at supper. Therefore, feeling that the moment was propitious, they left the shelter of the doorway, and, keeping as closely within the shadow of the building as they could, moved off toward the shrubbery, into the dense obscurity of which they plunged a minute or two later. Here, as they wound their way cautiously among the bushes, they suddenly found themselves close to a long low block of buildings which, being entirely in darkness, they surmised must be sheds devoted to the storage of the gardeners' tools, implements, and paraphernalia generally, and they at once halted and subjected the buildings to careful examination; for, their weapons having been taken away from them by the soldiers who had seized them, weapons of some sort were now a first necessity with them, and they hoped that the sheds might at least afford them a knife apiece, if nothing better. Investigation, however, resulted in the discovery that the sheds were locked; but this difficulty was soon overcome by the simple process of breaking a pane of glass, inserting a hand, unfastening the hasp, and entering through the open window, when their enterprise was eventually rewarded by the discovery of several formidable pruning knives, two of which, together with a couple of short, stout iron bars, and a length of thin, strong rope, they unhesitatingly appropriated.

The two adventurers now felt that, whatever might befall them, they were no longer altogether defenceless, and leaving the sheds behind them, they again plunged into the shrubbery, their object now being to discover a way of escape from the garden into the streets of the city.

The first obstacle which they encountered was a stone wall about fifteen feet high, surmounted by *chevaux de frise*; and deciding that this was rather too formidable to be tackled until they had made a further search, they followed the wall for some distance, and eventually arrived at a stout wicket gate built of wood. Of course, it was locked; but upon examination they soon came to the conclusion that, with the help of their pruning knives and bars, it would not be a difficult matter to burst the lock open. Unfortunately, however, this could not be done without making a considerable amount of noise, and they had already ascertained, while examining the lock, that a good many people were still abroad in the city, for they heard footsteps frequently passing on the other side of the wicket; they therefore decided to seek further before attempting to force a way out, their decision being influenced by the fact that it was evidently still early in the evening, or there would not be so many people moving about, and that consequently it might be wise to delay their final escape until the bulk of the population had retired to rest. Soon afterward, however, while pursuing their investigations, they reached a spot where the wall ended and where the grounds were enclosed for some distance by a lofty iron railing which, despite the fact that it was formidably spiked at the top, they thought might be easily scaled by two men who were accustomed, as they were, to climbing the masts and rigging of a ship. But on the other side of the railing was a wide, open street, along which people were constantly passing to and fro; the adventurers therefore retired to the shelter and concealment of the shrubbery, having come to the resolution not to run any unnecessary risk by undue precipitancy, since they had managed so excellently thus far.

At length, however, the sounds of traffic in the streets began to diminish sensibly, and finally they died away altogether; the good people of Cuzco seemed to have gone home to bed at last; so, throwing off his disguise for the moment, Dick essayed to climb the high railing which was now the only barrier between them and liberty. The task was not at all difficult, except when it came to his clambering over the complicated arrangement of spikes at the top; but a steady head and a little patience were all that were needed; and in about two minutes young Chichester was standing on the pavement outside, once more in his clerical disguise, receiving the few articles that Phil passed through the railings to him before the latter in his turn climbed over the obstacle. As it chanced, they only just accomplished the feat in time, for as Stukely reached the pavement on the right side of the railing, footsteps were heard approaching, and Phil scarcely had time to don his priest's habit, draw the hood well over his head, and conceal his bar and pruning knife in the ample folds of the garment when a belated frequenter of one of the numerous posadas of the city staggered past, humming in maudlin tones the refrain of a bacchanalian song which he cut short when he realised that the two dark figures which he jostled were, as he supposed, connected with the dread institution which lay back there frowning in the distance.

As soon as this roysterer was fairly out of the way the adventurers looked about them to get their bearings. Their purpose was to leave the city by the same way that they had come into it, and then strike eastward until they again came to the river, which, in accordance with Vilcamapata's instructions, they were to follow to its source. Recalling the several twists and turns which they had taken through the building after their encounter with the jailer that morning, they finally decided that they must follow the footsteps of the drunken man until they reached the first street bearing to the right, which would be the street by which they had been conducted to the Inquisition that morning; once arrived in which they were convinced that they could find their way over the remainder of the route. Accordingly they started briskly off, and in the course of a few minutes reached the street which they sought, and which they presently verified as the right one by passing the great entrance gateway by which they had been admitted to the Inquisition building that morning. That morning! It seemed much more like a week ago! Still walking briskly, yet without exhibiting undue haste, and meeting only an occasional wayfarer here and there who took no notice of them except to stand respectfully aside and yield the narrow pavement to them as they passed, the two Englishmen wound hither and thither along the streets, occasionally identifying some building that they remembered to have passed before, until, in a little, narrow street, Phil suddenly halted before a small building which bore across its narrow front a sign reading, in Spanish, of course—"Mateo Cervantes. Armourer. Plate and chain mail. Blades of the finest, imported direct from Toledo in Old Spain; musquets; pistolettes; and ammunition for the same."

"Ah!" ejaculated Phil, with a sigh of satisfaction; "here we are at last. This is the place that I have been looking for. I was beginning to fear that I had missed it."

"And what a plague want ye with it, now that you have found it?" demanded Dick, peevishly; for he was beginning to feel sleepy, and knew that many a weary mile must yet be walked before he could hope to get any rest.

"What want I with it?" reiterated Phil. "My gentle mutton-head, read the sign over the shop; there is light enough for that, surely, though it is but starlight."

Dick read the sign, and his eyes brightened. "Ah!" he said, "of course; I begin to understand. I have been wondering, all along, what we should do without weapons, if we chanced to make good our escape. These bars and pruning knives are well enough in their way, and are better than nothing at all, of course; but they won't help us to get game—"

PHIL AND DICK IN THE ARMOURER'S HOUSE

"Precisely," interrupted Phil. "Therefore, since the Spaniards have seen fit to deprive us of our weapons, I propose to make a Spaniard provide us with others. Now, I am going to knock up our friend Cervantes, and persuade him to supply our needs, so far as the resources of his establishment will allow. And, to make sure that, after we have obtained what we require, the señor shall not prematurely give the alarm and set the soldiers upon our track, we must seize and bind him, or whoever comes to the door. So be ready to pounce as soon as the door is opened." And therewith Phil proceeded to hammer loudly upon Señor Cervantes' door.

Five or six times did he hammer upon the door with his iron bar, gently at first, but with steadily increasing vehemence, before any notice was taken of his summons. At length, however, a thin pencil of light appeared through the shutters of a window over the door, the drawing of bolts became audible, and just as Phil began to hammer afresh the window was thrown open, a figure appeared, and a gruff voice demanded, querulously—

"Hallo, there! who knocks at this untimely hour? Away with you, whoever you are, and leave me in peace, or I will sound my rattle and summon the watch!"

"The watch!" exclaimed Phil, under his breath, "phew! I never thought of that. If we should chance to encounter the watch we may yet have trouble." A sudden inspiration came to him, and, stepping back into the middle of the road, where his hooded figure might be seen from above, he exclaimed, in a deep, solemn voice:

"Mateo Cervantes, in the name of the Holy Inquisition I command you to open!"

"The Holy Inquisition! Ave Maria! What have I done?" ejaculated the figure above, in evident trepidation. "Your pardon, Reverend Father," he continued, "I knew not who you were. I will be down instantly." And the light vanished from the window.

"That was a good idea of mine," remarked Phil, in a whisper. "I thought it would fetch him down. Now, I do not think it will be necessary to seize and bind friend Cervantes immediately that he comes to the door. He will admit us without question, no doubt; and after we are in and the door is closed, we must be guided by circumstances, and act accordingly. Here he comes."

A streak of light showed beneath the door; there was a sound of bolts being drawn; and presently the door opened and a big, burly, elderly man, his touzled hair touched with grey, and his body enveloped in a long white nightgown, appeared; holding a candle above his head. As the light fell upon the two hooded figures he involuntarily drew back with a gasp, whereupon Phil and Dick stepped into the passage, closing the door behind them.

"Holy Fathers," exclaimed Cervantes, dropping on his knees, placing the candle on the floor beside him, and raising his hands in an attitude of supplication, "I swear to you that I have done nothing; I am a good Catholic—"

"Peace!" commanded Phil, raising his hand imperatively. "How many are there in the house with you?"

"How many?" reiterated the trembling man. "I am alone, Reverend Father, quite alone, I give you my solemn word. My workmen do not live here with me; the house is not large enough—"

"It is well," interrupted Phil. "Now, rise to your feet, friend Cervantes, and conduct us to your shop."

"My shop!" echoed the armourer. "I give you my word, Reverend Sirs, that there is nothing in my shop that—"

"The less reason why you should hesitate to lead us thither," interrupted Phil, sternly.

"Of course; of course," agreed the man, anxiously. "Follow me, your Reverences; I have nothing to conceal; nothing to conceal." Then, scrambling to his feet and taking up the candle, the man proceeded a few steps along the passage, flung open a door, raised the candle above his head in such a manner as to throw the light into the room, and stood aside to allow his unwelcome and untimely visitors to enter.

"After you, friend," remarked Phil, waving his hand for the armourer to precede them. "And light a lamp or two," he added, "we must have more light than your candle affords."

The man bowed, entered the room, which was in fact the shop, set the candlestick down upon a bench, and proceeded to light a couple of lamps which stood on wall brackets. While he was doing this his visitors were busily engaged in noting the contents of the shop, so far as the imperfect light afforded by the single candle permitted. The most prominent objects, and those which therefore first arrested their attention, were half a dozen complete suits of very fine armour, two of them being black inlaid with fine gold scroll-work, while the others were perfectly plain, but highly polished. Then there were back and breast pieces, greaves, gauntlets, maces, axes, and sheaves of arrows suspended from the walls, several very fine bows tied up in a bundle in one corner; and last, but by no means least, a large case resting upon a counter, in which were set out a number of swords, daggers, and poniards. There were also three long cases ranged along the base of the side and back walls of the shop, which the two visitors shrewdly suspected contained firearms and ammunition.

"Now, Reverend Sirs," said the armourer as, having lighted the two lamps, he turned and faced the two hooded figures, with a bow, "I am at your service. Be pleased to give me your commands."

"It is well," retorted Phil. "Now, hark ye, friend Cervantes, you are credited with being a man of discretion; see to it, then, that ye justify your reputation by observing the most complete silence regarding this visit. You understand me?"

"Perfectly, Father," replied the armourer. "No word or hint will I breathe to a living soul about it."

"Good!" replied Phil. "You will do well to remember that promise, and keep it. Now, for a reason which does not concern you in the least, we require certain arms, and they must be the very best you have. To begin with, therefore, show me the two best swords in your stock."

"Arms! swords!" ejaculated the astonished Cervantes, looking keenly at his visitors. Then, suddenly seizing the candle and thrusting it forward, he endeavoured to peer into their faces. "Who are ye?" he exclaimed. "Ye are not—ah! I have it. Ye are the two English prisoners who this morning—"

Before he could get any further the pair threw themselves upon him and bore him to the ground; and while Phil gripped the unfortunate man by the throat to prevent him from crying out and raising an alarm, Dick whipped out the rope which he had been carrying beneath his habit, and trussed up the worthy señor so securely that he could move neither hand nor foot. Then they gagged him very effectively by thrusting the hilt of one of his own daggers between his teeth and securing it there.

"Now, hark ye, friend Cervantes," admonished Phil, "it is unfortunate for you that you have penetrated our disguises, since it will necessitate your remaining as you are until the morning, when no doubt someone will arrive to release you. We need certain weapons, and we propose to help ourselves to them; but you need not fear that you are about to be robbed; we will pay you generously for whatever we take. Now, Dick," he continued, turning to Chichester, "pick your weapons, and let us begone, we have none too much time before daylight. I recommend for your choice, a good sword, a musket, a brace of pistols, with a good supply of ammunition for each, a stout dagger, a bow, arrows, and a good strong machete for general purposes. That, I think, will be quite as much as it will be advisable for us to cumber ourselves with."

"So do I," agreed Dick, dryly. "For my own part I am not at all sure that we could not dispense with the musket, which is a heavy, cumbersome thing to carry, and we may never need it. Still, I suppose we may as well take one apiece; we can always throw them away if we find them too troublesome. But how do you propose to pay the man, Phil? You know that we have no money."

"True," assented Phil; "but we have still the two emerald eyes of the idol which we found in that cave where we slew the monstrous beast: we will give him one of those in payment; and handsome payment it will be, too."

"Ay, that it will," agreed Dick. "I had entirely forgotten about those emeralds. Give him one of them, by all means; we can then help ourselves, with a clear conscience, to the best the shop affords."

Swiftly, yet with the greatest care, the two Englishmen selected the weapons which they required, together with as much ammunition as they considered it wise to cumber themselves with; after which Phil extracted from a pocket in his puma-skin tunic one of the emeralds which he had mentioned, and holding it close to the eyes of the prostrate armourer, said:

"You see that, my friend? It is an emerald; and its value is about one hundred times that of what we have taken from you. Nevertheless, I am going to leave it with you for payment. See, there it is." And he placed the stone on the floor where Cervantes could see it. "And now, listen to me," continued Phil. "You probably have it in your mind to go to the authorities to-morrow, as soon as you are released, and inform them of this visit of ours to you. Isn't that so? Yes, I can see by the expression of your eyes that I have guessed aright. Well, friend, be advised by me: Don't do it. Remember that we have escaped from the Inquisition; and if the Head of that institution should learn that we have been here, he will certainly hold you responsible for our escape from the town; and it will be useless for you to say that you could not help yourself, that we surprised and overpowered you, and helped ourselves to some of your property; he will simply reply that you ought not to have allowed yourself to be surprised and overpowered, that you knew two prisoners had escaped, and that you should have had wit enough to have seen through our disguise and given the alarm before we had time or opportunity to overpower you. And I suppose I need not remind you of what your fate will be in that case. Therefore, think well over the matter, and do nothing that you may afterward regret. You should be easily able to concoct a story to account for your present plight that should satisfy those who may find you in the morning, without referring to us. And now we will leave you. Farewell!"

Therewith the two friends extinguished the lamps, and, taking the candle, retired from the shop, quietly closing the door behind them. The light of the candle enabled them easily to unfasten the outer door; and, this done, they blew out the light, silently opened the door, and cautiously peered out into the street. It was silent and deserted, therefore, without further ado, they tiptoed down the steps, closing the door behind them as they went, and, keeping within the shadows as much as possible, hastened in the direction which would take them out of the city. An hour later they were clear of Cuzco, and using the stars as their guide, were speeding along a fairly good road which led in a south-easterly direction, intending to strike off to the eastward in search of the river some twenty or thirty miles farther on, since they suspected that the high road would be the last place where their pursuers would be likely to look for them. But about ten o'clock the next morning—having encountered meanwhile only a troop of some thirty loaded llamas with their attendant drivers, whom, having sighted them at a distance, they easily avoided by concealing themselves until the whole had passed—they unexpectedly came upon the river again where a bend brought it close to the road; they therefore deserted the latter at this point, and, although the going was by no means so easy, thenceforward followed the river until at length they reached its source high up among the Andes of Carabaya.

And now ensued a period of incredible hardship and suffering for the adventurous pair; for they were now among the most lofty of those stupendous peaks which run in an almost unbroken chain from one end of the continent to the other, from the Sierra Nevada de Santa Marta in the north to within little more than one hundred miles from the Strait of Magellan in the south; and their way lay over boundless snowfields, across enormous glaciers gashed with unfathomable crevasses, up and down stupendous precipices, and along narrow, ice-clad ledges, where a single false step must have hurled them to death thousands of feet below. To journey amid such surroundings was of course bad enough in itself; but the hardship of it was increased tenfold for the two Englishmen, from the fact that they came new to it and without experience, after months of life in the torrid lowlands had thinned their blood and rendered them peculiarly sensitive to the piercing cold of those high altitudes, which was further intensified by the icy winds which seemed to rage continuously about the peaks and come howling at them through the ravines. Add to this the difficulty of obtaining food—for there was no life among those mountain solitudes, save an occasional llama or guanaco, so wild as to be scarcely approachable, and a condor or two soaring aloft at such a height as to be scarcely distinguishable to the unaided eye—and the impossibility of making a fire, and the reader will be able to form some faint idea of what Phil and Dick were called upon to endure while making that awful passage over the mountains. Fortunately for them, it lasted only five days; had it been prolonged to six they must inevitably have perished. Fortunately, also, for them, they had acquired from the Indians a knowledge of the wonderful, almost miraculous, virtue that lay in the coca leaf—with a bountiful supply of which they had been careful to provide themselves—otherwise even their indomitable hardihood and courage must have succumbed to the frightful toil, privation, and exposure which they were obliged to undergo. A detailed description of that five days' journey over the mountains would of itself suffice to fill a book, for it would be a record of continuous adventure and hairbreadth escapes from avalanches that were constantly threatening to overwhelm them; of treacherous snow-bridges that crumbled away beneath their feet; of furious, icy winds that, seeming to be imbued with demoniac intelligence and malignity, always assailed them in some especially perilous situation, and sought to buffet them from their precarious hold; and of long hours of intolerable suffering when, during the hours of darkness, they were compelled to camp on some snow-patch and build themselves a snow-hut as a partial protection from the howling, marrow-piercing, snow-laden gale. Such a narrative, however, exciting as it might be in its earlier pages, would soon grow wearisome from the rapidity with which one adventure would tread upon the heels of another, and can therefore only be hinted at here. Suffice it to say that early in the afternoon of the fourth day, upon surmounting the crest of a long ridge of ice-encased rock, at a moment when the demon of the mountain had temporarily withdrawn himself elsewhere, and the atmosphere was for a brief space calm and clear, the two weary and exhausted adventurers caught a brief but entrancing glimpse of a long green valley stretching away ahead of them between the two mountain ranges, with an island-dotted lake in the far distance, and Sorata's dominating ice-clad peak piercing the blue sky to the left of it. At last, at last, their goal was in sight; and incontinently they flung themselves down, gasping, upon the iron-hard rock, and gazed entranced upon the glorious vision—thrice glorious to them after all that they had suffered—until another great snow-cloud evolved itself out of nothing and swooped down upon them in a final effort at destruction.

The gale and snowstorm lasted less than an hour, however, and when at length the atmosphere again cleared the two friends, who had been crouching under the sheltering lee of a great shoulder of rock, rose to their feet and again looked forth toward the land of promise. A vast snowfield, corrugated by the wind as the sand of the seashore is by the rippling advance of the tide, but otherwise smooth of surface, and gently sloping downward, offered them an easy road for the first two miles of their descent; and, weary though they were, they traversed it in half an hour. Then came an almost perpendicular descent of some five hundred feet to another snowfield, where, in a deep recess that might almost have been termed a cave in a great spur of rock, they camped comfortably for the night and enjoyed the sweetest rest that they had known for many a long day.

When they arose on the following morning, rested and refreshed by their long night's sheltered sleep, but weak and famished with hunger which even their coca leaves could now but partially relieve, nature was again kind to them, for the air was still and so crystalline clear that they were able to determine accurately their road for many miles ahead; while, most welcome sight of all, in a little sheltered valley, some six miles away, on a small patch of green, they perceived a flock of some twenty vicuña grazing. Here, at last was food for them once more, if they could but reach within bowshot without alarming the animals; and to this task they bent all their energies, with such success that three hours later they were gorging themselves to repletion on the raw flesh of one of the animals, being still without the materials wherewith to kindle a fire. But this marked the end of their troubles; for before the night again closed down upon them they had not only passed below the snow-line, but were also fortunate enough to encounter an Indian who was herding a flock of llama; and upon Phil addressing the man in his own language—of which, it will be remembered, Stukely had acquired a knowledge in some extraordinary and quite incomprehensible manner—the fellow received them with open arms, conducted them to his hut, fed them as they had not been fed since they had fallen into the hands of the Spaniards, and not only lodged them for the night, but gave them minute instructions how they were to proceed during the following day. Four days later they arrived at the northern extremity of the Sacred Lake.

They reached its margin at the precise moment that the sun sank beyond the long line of lofty, rugged, snow-clad peaks that ran parallel to the lake on its western side. The evening was perfectly calm and cloudless, save in the west, where an agglomeration of delicate rosy-purple streaks and patches of vapour lay softly upon a clear background of palest blue-green sky, forming the picture of a fairy archipelago of thickly clustering islands, intersected by a bewildering maze of channels winding hither and thither, with the thin sickle of the young moon, gleaming softly silver-white, hanging just above the whole. It was one of those skies that set the imaginative dreamer's fancy free to wander afar into the realms of fairyland and to picture all sorts of strange, unreal happenings; the sort of sky that probably suggested to the simple mind of the Indian the poetic idea that when gazing upon it he was vouchsafed a vision of the Isles of the Blessed where dwell the souls of the departed in everlasting bliss; and for full five minutes after the two Englishmen had halted by the margin of the lake, the smooth, unruffled surface of which repeated the picture as in a mirror, they stood gazing, entranced, upon the loveliness of the scene that lay spread out before them.

In front of them and almost at their feet lay the placid waters of the lake, bordered with reeds and rushes just where they happened to stand, its glassy, mirrorlike surface faithfully reproducing every soft, delicate tint of the overarching sky, the bank of rosy clouds in the west, the cold, pure blue of the snow-capped sierras on their right, the ruddy blush of the peaks on their left—upon the summits of which the last rays of the vanished sun still lingered, to change to purest white even as they gazed—and every clump of sombre olive vegetation between. To the right and left of them, a few miles apart, two streams, having their sources in the neighbouring mountains, discharged into the lake; and so perfectly still was the air that the murmur of their waters came faint but clear to the ears of the two comrades who had travelled so many hundreds of miles with that scene as their goal. To right and left of them the shores of the lake swept away in many a curve and bay and indentation clear to the horizon, and far beyond it; and in the whole of that fair landscape never a sign of life, human or animal! Yet, stay; what was that dark film, like a tiny cloud, that came sweeping down toward them from far up the lake? Dick, the practical, was the first to catch sight of it, for Phil was standing like one in a trance gazing at the scene with a retrospective look in his eyes that seemed to say his thoughts were far away. As Dick watched the approaching cloud-like film it resolved itself into a flock of wild ducks, making, as it seemed, directly for the patch of rushes near which the two were standing, and, with the momentous question of supper looming large in his mind, Chichester plucked his companion by the sleeve, pointed to the approaching wild ducks, and suggested the propriety of immediately seeking some hiding-place until the birds had settled.

"A murrain on you and your ducks, Dick!" exclaimed Stukely, in a tone half-pettish, half-playful; "you have jolted me out of a reverie in which I was endeavouring to account for the extraordinary feeling that sometime in the past I have beheld this very scene, even as I behold it now. Of course I know that it is only a fancy; I know that I have never before stood on the soil which my feet are pressing at this moment; yet, believe me or not, as you please, all this"—he waved his right hand before him to right and left—"is absolutely familiar to me, as familiar as though I had lived here all my life! Nothing is changed, except that the clumps of bush seem to have approached a little closer to the margin of the lake, and—yes, you see that low bluff yonder? Well, when I last looked upon it—oh, well! never mind; you are laughing at me, and I have no right to be surprised that you should do so; but, all the same, I know exactly where we are now; I know that there are islands out there on the lake, beyond the horizon, and I know which of them it is that we must visit—I shall recognise it instantly when I see it; remember my words. And now, come along, and let us see whether we can get one or two of those ducks; they seem to be making for the reeds yonder."

The pair crept down to the margin of the patch of reeds, and concealed themselves therein; and scarcely had they done so when the flock came sweeping along with a great rush of wings, wheeled, and finally settled, with loud quacks—probably of satisfaction that their day's work was over, and that they were once more back in their haven of rest. Then the two muskets—which the wanderers had tenaciously retained throughout their perilous journey across the mountains—barked out their death message simultaneously, and the flock rose again with loud squawks of alarm, leaving a round dozen of their number, either dead or badly wounded, behind them. Ten minutes later, as the brief twilight was rapidly deepening into night, the nude figures of the two Englishmen scrambled out of the water, each bearing his quota of dead wild duck, and, laying their spoils upon the ground, nonchalantly proceeded to resume the quaint garments of skins that now constituted their only clothing.

Long into the night sat the pair, crouching over their camp fire, for though the days were hot the nights were bitterly cold, even in that valley between the two ranges of mountains; and while Dick gazed abstractedly aloft into the velvet blackness at the innumerable stars that glittered above him through the frosty atmosphere, Phil spoke of the strange dreams—which he persisted, half-jestingly and half in earnest, in regarding as memories—that visited him so frequently, of curious scenes that he had witnessed and remarkable deeds that he had done in the far past, either in imagination or reality, he could not possibly say which. And while he talked and Dick listened, vacillating between amusement and conviction, some twenty stalwart figures, thin and aquiline of feature, copper-hued of skin, and strangely clothed, came creeping up out of the darkness until they reached a clump of bush within earshot of the pair, where they lurked, waiting patiently until the audacious intruders upon their most sacred territory should resign themselves to sleep—and to a captivity which, as planned by the chief figure of the group, was to be of but brief duration, ending in a death of unspeakable horror.

Chapter Eighteen
How they found an enormous Treasure, and took it Home

It was past midnight, and the camp fire, which Dick had bountifully replenished with stout branches from the neighbouring clump of bush, the last thing before stretching himself out to sleep, had dwindled to a mass of dull red smouldering embers, when the white-clad figure of an elderly man, copper-hued, bald-headed, and clean shaven, approached with stealthy footsteps the recumbent bodies of the two slumbering Englishmen. Bending over first one and then the other, he held a saturated cloth toward their nostrils in such a manner that the sleepers were permitted to inhale, for about a minute each, the faint, fragrant fumes that emanated from it; then, abandoning all further caution, he withdrew from the fire a half-consumed branch and waved it in the air until the smouldering stump was fanned afresh into flame; when, the torch having served its purpose as a signal, he flung it back upon the almost extinguished fire. A couple of minutes later those to whom this man had signalled approached the camp fire, and while two parties of four each raised the recumbent and now unconscious figures of the Englishmen to their shoulders, the remainder carefully gathered together and took possession of the weapons and other belongings of their prisoners, after which, at a signal from their leader the entire party moved off, marching inland away from the lake. Relieving each other at frequent intervals, for they found their unconscious burdens heavy—especially those who were told off to carry Dick—the party marched a distance of nearly eight miles, until, in a sequestered valley among the hills, they reached the ruins of what had evidently at one time been a city of considerable importance, built equally on both sides of an ice-cold mountain stream. Most of the buildings were in ruins; many, indeed, had been razed almost to their foundations—possibly to provide material for the maintenance in repair of those that remained intact, but there were sufficient of the latter to afford accommodation for fully three thousand people, and all of these were inhabited. Many of the inhabited buildings were of considerable size, but, with one solitary exception, architectural grace and beauty were conspicuously absent, the buildings being, with the exception mentioned, constructed of large blocks of stone so perfectly worked that the joints of the masonry were scarcely perceptible, but without ornament or adornment of any kind whatever, and roughly roofed with thatch. The exception was in the case of the temple, which, like so many in ancient Peru, was dedicated to the Sun. This structure was erected upon the summit of a low mound, scarcely important enough in height to be termed a hill, yet high enough to allow the building to dominate all the rest of the town, and was built of a beautiful white, fine-grained stone, very much resembling alabaster. Also, in startling contrast to all the other buildings in the town, it was admirably proportioned, and elaborately ornamented with bold mouldings, cornices, and other architectural ornaments which, although somewhat barbaric in design, were nevertheless exceedingly effective. But its chief glory lay in the pair of immense bronze doors of its main entrance, the entire surface of which was most exquisitely engraved with a series of pictures representing the ceremonial of sun worship. The building stood upon an immense quadrangular base of massive masonry, the sides of which were worked into steps; and some idea of the age of the structure could be gained from the fact that immediately opposite the main entrance the steps were worn away to a depth of nearly three inches by the innumerable multitudes of worshippers who had passed up and down them. The pavement of the interior was of marble of various colours, worked into an elaborate pattern; and beneath this pavement there were chambers for the confinement of prisoners, and other and more sinister purposes.

It was in one of these subterranean chambers that our friends Phil and Dick recovered consciousness on the morning following their arrival at the shore of the Sacred Lake; and their amazement at awaking to find themselves bound hand and foot on the cold stone floor of a dimly lighted dungeon, whereas they had fallen asleep in the open, may be readily imagined. Their first and most natural impression was that they had again fallen into the hands of the Spaniards; but they were disabused of this idea when, an hour or two later, four stalwart copper-hued, sharp-featured men, with long, straight black hair, clean shaven, clad in white, sleeveless tunics, with sandals on their feet, and each armed with a short, broad-bladed sword of copper, entered the cell, leaving two coarse earthenware basins liberally filled with what looked like stiff porridge, and two jars containing water. Placing these upon the floor, two of the four proceeded to unbind the hands of the prisoners, while the other two drew their copper swords and stationed themselves at the door of the cell, with the evident purpose of frustrating any attempt at escape which the prisoners might be ill-advised enough to make. Then Phil, inspired by that knowledge which he had so mysteriously acquired, at once recognised that he and his companion had fallen into the hands of a body of aboriginal Peruvians, and his face cleared.

"We are all right, Dick," he exclaimed, joyously; "these fellows are evidently a surviving remnant of the original inhabitants of the country, of whose existence Vilcamapata told me, and whose language I speak. It will only be necessary for me to tell them who we are, and they will free us at once." But when he addressed first one and then another of the quartette, they paid no attention whatever to what he said, contenting themselves with signing to the prisoners to eat and drink. Instead of obeying, however, Phil continued to talk to them, alternately explaining, ordering, and finally threatening the men; and it was not until, some twenty minutes later, when they proceeded to bind the hands of both behind their backs again, that Stukely realised, too late, that the quartette were evidently deaf and dumb. Thus Phil missed his breakfast that morning, while Dick, the practical one of the two, secured his, having fully availed himself of the opportunity afforded by his unbound hands to eat and drink.

In this eminently unsatisfactory and comfortless fashion the hapless prisoners passed the ensuing ten days, seeing nobody but the four deaf mutes, who twice daily brought them food and water, and stood over them while they ate and drank, afterward securely binding them again; although this seemed to be an altogether unnecessary act of cruelty; since so strongly constructed was their place of confinement—even the door being a massive slab of stone—that, had they been entirely unbound, they could not possibly have forced their way out.

At length, however, on the twelfth day of their captivity, some two hours after their morning meal had been served to them, they were quite unexpectedly visited by their four deaf-and-dumb jailers, who, having unbound their ankles, signed to them that they were to leave the noisome hole where they had hitherto been confined; and when the pair passed through the stone door they found themselves in a long passage, where they were immediately surrounded by an escort of a dozen soldiers armed with sword, spear, and shield, all of bronze, and wearing breastplates and helmets of polished bronze, the latter adorned with the tail feathers of some bird that gleamed with a brilliant metallic golden lustre. Hemmed in by these, the prisoners were marched along the passage until they reached a flight of stone steps which the party ascended, finding themselves, at the top, in a long, spacious, lofty corridor, lighted at intervals by circular openings high up under the flat stone ceiling. Along this corridor also the prisoners were marched until they reached a doorway closed by two bronze doors, at which the officer of the party first knocked, and immediately afterwards thrust open, revealing a room in which were congregated some thirty men attired in a garb that Phil at least instantly recognised to be priestly. By these the pair were at once taken over from the armed guard; who thereupon retired and were no more seen. At one end of the room stood a table upon which lay heaped a quantity of flowers, and two stalwart priests having taken possession of each of the prisoners, the latter were led to the table, and the flowers, which had been arranged in the form of two long festoons, were thrown round their necks, crossed over their breasts, passed round their waists, and finally tied in front, with the long ends drooping almost to their feet. They were evidently being decked as the victims of some sort of sacrifice!

Then Phil suddenly wrenched himself free from the hands of the two priests who were putting the finishing touches to his adornment, and spoke in a low voice to the assembled concourse of priests. What he said was wholly incomprehensible to Dick, for it was in a tongue of which young Chichester had no knowledge, but it had a most extraordinary effect upon the priests, who first seemed stricken dumb with amazement, and finally overwhelmed with paralysing fear. For several minutes, while Phil spoke, in accents of mingled indignation and reproach, the priests stood silent and motionless, with many mingled emotions displaying themselves upon their expressive countenances; but when at length he concluded his tirade by pronouncing certain words in an unmistakably threatening tone of voice, the whole assemblage, as though moved by the same impulse, threw up their hands with an action that clearly expressed the deepest profundity of horror, and then incontinently with one accord prostrated themselves on the marble floor at the feet of the two prisoners, uttering howls of sorrow and abject entreaty. For perhaps five minutes Phil permitted them to remain in this posture; then suddenly he shouted a single word which had the instant effect of reducing the prostrate ones to silence, when he again addressed them, this time in gentler tones; and when he at length concluded, the party rose slowly and humbly to their feet, after which two of them stepped forward and, with every appearance of the deepest reverence, proceeded to untwine the garlands of flowers and release the pair from their bonds. Finally, the erstwhile prisoners were taken in charge by two of the priests, who first conducted them to an apartment wherein were all the requisites for a bath, together with a complete change of clothing, and afterward to another room, very luxuriously furnished, in which they found not only a choice though evidently hastily provided meal, but likewise all their weapons, ammunition, and other belongings. While this was being done the remainder of the priesthood filed into the temple—where a vast congregation had assembled to take part in a specially arranged festival in honour of the full moon, to be accompanied by a sacrifice—to explain, as best they could, to the assembled multitude that an unfortunate and most regrettable mistake had been made; and that, consequently, although the festival would proceed, no sacrifice beyond that of a pair of goats would be offered!

To Dick Chichester this sudden and extraordinary change in the fortune of himself and his friend was utterly incomprehensible; and no sooner were they once more alone than he turned to Phil and demanded an explanation. But, to his great surprise, Stukely, for almost the first time since that memorable night when they had escaped from Cartagena together, seemed inclined to be reticent; he professed himself not to understand wholly the sudden and remarkable turn which affairs had taken, appeared thoughtful, and inclined to be silent; and would only say that the Peruvians had mistaken them for a couple of Spaniards, and that they had consequently escaped a terrible death by the very skin of their teeth. And when Dick further pressed him with several very obvious questions, the only reply which he could extort was, that in the excitement of the moment certain words, the meaning of which he did not in the least understand, had involuntarily escaped his lips, and that it was undoubtedly those mysterious words which had wrought the singular change in the priests' attitude toward them; of which change he had felt himself justified in taking the utmost advantage immediately that it became apparent. He added that, although danger seemed for the moment to be past, the situation was still exceedingly difficult and delicate, demanding the utmost care and circumspection in handling; and he wound up with an earnest request to Dick to cease from questioning him further, as he wished to think the matter out and decide upon the plan of action which it would be best to pursue under the circumstances.

A week ensued during which Dick and Phil saw very little of each other, for the latter was engaged during practically the whole of each day in conference with either the chief priest or the authorities who governed the town, and sometimes with both together; while at night Stukely manifested an unmistakable desire to be left alone to puzzle out some problem that seemed to be worrying him.

But at length, when they had been exactly a week in the town, Phil returned late in the evening to the quarters which he and Dick had been jointly occupying in the temple; and it was at once apparent to the younger of the two that the troubles and difficulties with which Stukely had been wrestling were at an end, for he was once more his former self, frank, genial, self-reliant, and in exuberant spirits.

"It is all right at last, Dick," he exclaimed, flinging himself down upon a couch; "I have straightened everything out; and to-morrow we start for the Sacred Island, with labourers, tools, provisions, and in short, everything that we require. And, as things have turned out, it was very fortunate for us that we fell into the hands of these people; for otherwise we should never have succeeded in penetrating to the hiding-place of the treasure and getting safely away again. Now, however, we are going there with their full knowledge and approval—they have even insisted on furnishing us with all the help we may require—consequently we shall have nothing to fear from those who are guarding the island, and who, had we approached as strangers, would certainly have destroyed us."

"In that case," said Dick, "I suppose we ought to congratulate ourselves upon what has happened, although I do not hesitate to acknowledge now that I thought it was all up with us when we were hauled up before the priests, last week, and decorated with flowers. But what has happened to bring about this fortunate turn in our affairs? Don't you think that you may as well explain the whole affair to me?"

"Certainly I will," agreed Stukely, "indeed it is necessary that you should understand the situation, in order that you may know how to comport yourself in the presence of the people.

"First of all, then, this town is called Huancane. It was a place of very considerable importance in the time of the Incas, being, in fact, one of the places to which the Inca was in the habit of resorting during the period of the extreme summer heat, both on account of its proximity to the lake, and also because of the exceptional salubrity of the climate. Now, at the time of the conquest of the country, a few Spaniards settled here; upon which the Peruvians, in accordance with a pre-arranged policy, entirely abandoned the town and retired to certain secret hiding-places among the mountains, believing that the Spaniards could not possibly contrive to exist here, if left entirely to themselves. But, to the astonishment of the Peruvians, the Spaniards not only contrived to exist, but they steadily increased and multiplied to such an extent that there were some three hundred of them settled here, and supporting themselves entirely upon the products of the valley. Then came a change respecting which the Peruvians of to-day are exceedingly reticent, but one thing is certain, Huancane developed a remarkable and mysterious unhealthiness of climate that rapidly cleared it of every Spaniard, so that for two or three years the town was uninhabited and fell rapidly into decay; after which the Peruvians returned to it, and have been here ever since. So much for the history of Huancane.

"Ever since that time the Peruvians have been very jealously on the watch against any return of the Spaniards to this part of the country; a watch for them has always been maintained; and when, from time to time, small parties have appeared in the neighbourhood they have—well—vanished. Our friends here are very reticent about these disappearances, too.

"Now, it seems that on the day of our arrival at the margin of the lake we were seen and watched all day, under the impression that we were Spaniards; and when night came and we slept, a party stole upon us, stupefied us in some fashion—they did not explain how—and brought us eight miles or so from our camp to the town, where, as I understand, rather elaborate preparations were subsequently made for our dispatch from this world to the next.

"That plan, as you know, fell through in consequence of certain remarks which the exigencies of the situation prompted me to make. I somehow had an idea that we were being mistaken for Spaniards; and the decorating of us with those wreaths of flowers also seemed to me a sinister sign; I therefore concluded that the moment for an explanation had arrived; and I began by informing them that we were not Spaniards, but were such inveterate enemies of them that we had sailed across the Black Water in a great canoe for a whole moon and more with the express object of fighting them. Then, suddenly, that story of Vilcamapata's came into my head, and I hinted that there was more than met the eye in the fact of our presence in this country. I suddenly assumed a high and mighty demeanour, reproached them for their blindness and inability to recognise the friends who stood before them, and finally, moved by some impulse for which I am wholly unable to account, rapped out certain words that flashed into my mind, of which I knew not the meaning, but which I somehow seemed to understand were words of power. And they were, too; for, from what has since transpired, I understand that they were the mysterious words the utterance of which by a complete stranger was to be the sign to the Peruvians that Manco Capac, the first of the Incas, had returned to earth to free them from the hated Spanish yoke!

"Now, of course, I know that the utterance of those magic words at what was, for us, a most critical moment, was a very extraordinary, almost a miraculous thing; but I have had very little time to dwell upon it thus far; for when I saw the astonishing result of the words which I had spoken, my mind was at once exercised with the task of turning the utterance to the best possible account. But here I was met by a great difficulty, for while the attitude of the priests became instantly changed from relentless hostility to submissiveness so complete as to be absolutely servile, I was without the knowledge which would have supplied the key to the situation, and I therefore had to conduct myself with the utmost circumspection lest I should say or do something which would nullify the good effect which I had unwittingly produced. By adopting an attitude of extreme reticence, however, and allowing the others to do all the talking, I gradually attained to the knowledge that I am regarded as the reincarnated Manco; and now our copper-coloured friends are all on fire with eagerness for me to initiate the operations which shall eventuate in the expulsion of the Spaniard from this wonderful country. Many of them are desirous that I shall at once assume the style and title of Inca, make Huancane my headquarters, and send forth a summons to all the Peruvians scattered throughout the country to come in and enrol themselves under my standard—I understand that, even now, there remain enough of them to sweep the Spaniards into the sea, if properly led. And Dick, my lad, the idea is not without attractiveness, by any means. I assure you that I have quite seriously considered it—tried to picture myself as Inca—with you as Lord High Admiral of my fleet, and Generalissimo of my army—and the prospect appeals to me very strongly, so strongly, indeed, that I intend to give it much further consideration. For, somehow, I feel that the position would exactly suit me, and that I should suit the position. The task of driving out the Spaniard and restoring the country to its position of former power and splendour would provide us both with many years of strenuous work and wild adventure, eh? Meanwhile, however, there are several formidable obstacles in the way of an immediate adoption of the proposal, and these obstacles I have laid before the chief priests and the half-dozen nobles who govern this place, and they have recognised the reasonableness of my contention, and are willing to leave everything in my hands. We arrived at a complete understanding and agreement upon this matter to-day; and I thereupon boldly informed them that the first step which I proposed to take was to secure possession of certain treasure, the existence and situation of which has been revealed to me; and that I demanded their assistance in the task of its recovery. There were one or two of them who were shrewd enough to enquire in what way I proposed to employ the treasure when I had secured it; but that question I refused to answer, hinting that, in the present position of affairs, the less they knew about my plans the better it would be for everybody concerned; and with that rather ambiguous assertion they have been obliged to remain content. The outcome of the whole affair, however, is that to-morrow we start for the Sacred Island, accompanied by a gang of thirty labourers provided with the necessary tools; so now I think I may say that, with one very important exception, all our troubles are over."

"And pray what is that one important exception?" demanded Dick.

"The question of how we are going to convey the treasure home when we have secured possession of it," answered Phil.

"Ah!" responded Dick, emphatically, "yes; that is going to be a puzzler. For there are only us two; and—"

"Quite so," interrupted Phil, "there are only us two, as you say. Nevertheless, I am not going to worry myself unduly over it, for I have no doubt that the problem will solve itself, as all the others have during our wonderful journey. And Dick, my son, the resolution which has brought us two, all alone, from Cartagena to this spot, will not fail us when the time comes for us to decide how we will transport our treasure to England; so don't you worry either, lad. And now, good night; I am tired to death, for I have scarcely slept a wink during the last five or six nights."

The expedition which set out from Huancane on the following morning was unexpectedly imposing from the point of view of the two Englishmen; for, in addition to the thirty labourers promised by the authorities, there were half a dozen llamas, four of which were harnessed to a couple of vehicles somewhat resembling hammocks suspended from long poles, these being intended for the accommodation of the Englishmen, while the other two were loaded with food for the expedition, each labourer carrying his own tools. Each llama had its own driver; the expedition therefore consisted of thirty-eight people, all told, including the two white men. Its route lay along the eastern side of the lake; and it covered a distance of twenty-five miles before camping for the night. On the following day, when the afternoon was well advanced, the party arrived at a point where at a distance of some three miles from the shore, a small islet rose out of the bosom of the lake, the highest point of which was crowned with a group of extensive and very imposing-looking ruins. This islet the guide in charge of the expedition declared to be the Sacred Isle; and Phil, strong in the assurance springing from the knowledge of which he was so mysteriously possessed, agreed with him.

The next question was, how to reach the islet, for there were no boats or craft of any kind upon the lake; but that difficulty was quickly met by the labourers, who at once set to work to cut a large quantity of reeds, which they bound together in such a fashion that they formed a commodious and exceedingly buoyant raft, upon which the entire party, with the exception of the llamas and their drivers, crossed over the first thing on the following morning.

The passage of the raft from the mainland to the island, propelled as she was by paddles only, occupied about an hour and a half; and as the unwieldy craft gradually approached her destination the two white passengers on board her began to realise that the island ahead was considerably larger than they had first imagined, being fully a hundred acres in extent; while the character of the ruins made it clear that not only had the island been chosen, for some inexplicable reason, as the site upon which to erect a vast and very magnificent temple dedicated to the worship of the Sun, but that a monastic establishment of corresponding importance had also been founded there. Now, however, the whole of the buildings were roofless and in ruins; yet, even so, they were sufficiently imposing to imbue Dick at least with several new and startling ideas regarding the extent of the civilisation to which the Peruvians had attained under the rule of the Incas. As for Phil, he seemed to have undergone a complete yet subtle transformation during that short journey across the waters of the lake; his eyes blazed with eagerness, his nostrils dilated as though after a prolonged absence he was once more breathing his native air; he carried himself with a new and kingly dignity that somehow seemed to render him unapproachable; he gave his orders with the calm finality of tone of an absolute monarch; his knowledge of the place which he was approaching was so intimate as to be positively uncanny, as was evidenced when the raft drew near the island: those in charge would have run her ashore at the nearest point, but as soon as Stukely perceived what they would be at he turned to them and said rebukingly:

"Not there; not there! bear away to the south. Do you not know that there is a bay on that side of the island, with a wharf at which we can land comfortably and conveniently?"

Apparently the Peruvians did not know; yet when the balsa rounded the point, there was the bay, and there the stone pier or wharf of which Phil had spoken!

The first thing to be done, upon their arrival, was to instal the party in as comfortable quarters as the ruins afforded; and this was accomplished more easily than had seemed possible at the first glance. For although, as viewed from the lake, not only the temple but also all the other buildings had appeared to be roofless, a closer inspection revealed the fact that one of the small chambers which formed a part of the main building of the temple was still intact, even to its coved roof of solid masonry; and this Phil at once ordered to be cleared out and prepared for the reception of Dick and himself; while, as for the rest, a building was soon found which, with the aid of a few branches cut from the neighbouring grove of trees, and a quantity of rushes, which grew abundantly along the margin of the bay, could be quickly covered in sufficiently to render it habitable. These preparations kept the Peruvians busy for the remainder of that day; and while they were thus employed Phil and Dick devoted themselves to a minute inspection of the temple proper.

This had evidently at one time been a magnificent building, probably the finest of its kind in the entire country; but now it was in a state of utter ruin, its beautiful roof and walls having been stripped entirely of the massive hammered and engraved gold and silver plates which, Phil asserted, had once adorned them, while its marble pavement was heaped high with immense fragments of masonry, some of which were evidently portions of a boldly moulded cornice that had once adorned the inner walls of the structure, while others bore upon their faces signs of having been exquisitely sculptured in alto or basso rilievo. It was a melancholy sight, even to the unimpressionable Dick, this irreparable ruin of a once noble and surpassingly beautiful building; but Phil, as he gazed round him in silence, was so deeply moved that, for the moment, he seemed to have entirely forgotten the object of his visit to the place; seeing which, Dick at length wandered away and left his friend to himself and his own mysterious self-communings.

Later on, when they again met to partake together of the evening meal which had been prepared for them, Phil, who, though still in a somewhat melancholy mood, seemed to have become once more almost his normal self, endeavoured to explain to Dick the emotions which had swayed him all through the day.

"It was one of my strange fits, again, that overcame me," he said. "You know, Dick, that I have been subject to them, off and on, as far back in my life as I can remember. They come upon me without previous warning or apparent cause, sometimes in the form of extraordinarily vivid dreams, and sometimes as more or less vague memories, awakened by a chance sound, or sight, or odour. Either of these apparently slight causes has sufficed, at times, to recall scenes in which I seem to have been an actor far back in the past; so far back, indeed, that if they really occurred at all it must have been long before I—that is to say, my present body—was born. Now, don't laugh at me, lad; no doubt, when I talk thus, I must seem to you to be stating absurdities, impossibilities; for you have often told me that you have never experienced the curious sensations of which I speak; but let me tell you that, however extraordinary they may seem to you, to me they appear the most natural thing in the world, because they occur to me so frequently, and because they began to come to me when I was still too young to recognise their extraordinary character. The most remarkable thing about them, to my mind, is that they all seem to bear a close relationship to each other; they all appear to refer to the same period of time, and the same locality; that locality being this country of South America, and especially Peru. Is it not a strange thing that I should have dreamed of being associated with a people, one of whom I instantly recognised in the person of Vilcamapata? And is it not equally strange that in my dreams I should have acquired a knowledge of the language spoken by him and these people who are now with us? Yet you know that such was actually the case. And now I tell you, Dick, that when I stood among the ruins of this once splendid temple to-day, the feeling was strong upon me that I was not standing within its walls for the first time! I could shut my eyes and recall a dim and tantalising vision of it in all its pristine glory; I seemed to again see those ruined walls standing erect and perfect, with their decoration of gold and silver plates and ornaments, their sculptured panels, their heavy cornice, and the magnificent golden roof surmounting all. Oh, it is tantalising to remember so much and yet so little; to have these memories flash athwart one's mind only to vanish again before one has time to fix and identify them! Why do they not come to me perfectly—if they must come at all? These fleeting memories puzzle and perplex me; nay, more, they worry me; for I cannot help thinking that they must have a purpose; if I could but know what it is.

"And now, to turn from generalities to particularities. I am worried as to the locality of the hidden treasure. You will remember that Vilcamapata's last words to us were that something—which I have always believed to be the treasure—lies beneath the great marble floor of this temple; and until to-day I have believed that I had but to come here and straightway find the entrance giving access to the vaults in which the treasure lies hidden. Yet I have spent the whole day in wandering among the ruins in search of that entrance—without success; I have been quite unable to find any opening which promises to lead to the underground part of the structure. And all day, too, I have been haunted by an elusive memory of some secret connected with, the hiding of the treasure, which memory continually seems to be on the point of becoming clear and illuminating, only to fade away into nothing again. We are here, however; that is the great point; and I swear that I will not go away again without the treasure, even though it should be necessary to raze the temple to its foundations, stone by stone, in order to find it!"

For a time it seemed that nothing short of such drastic measures would serve the purpose of the two adventurers; for, search as they would, they could find no door or opening of any description giving access to the chambers which Vilcamapata had given them to understand existed beneath the floor of the main building; indeed, so far as their discoveries went, there might have been no such chambers at all, although Phil was most positive as to their existence. But they made a beginning of a kind, by setting the labouring gang to work to clear away all the débris and rubbish which lay piled high upon the temple floor; and in the course of a fortnight sufficient progress had been made to lay bare about one-fourth of the marble floor at the eastern end of the building, including the once beautiful but now sadly damaged altar dedicated to sacrifices to the Sun. And then the secret which had so persistently eluded Phil was revealed; for one of the rear corners of the altar had been broken away by the fall of a heavy mass of masonry from the roof, exposing the interior of the structure, which, it now appeared, was hollow. But it revealed more than that; it revealed the fact that the massive slab which formed the rear of the lower portion of the altar was movable, being pivoted on stone hinges at one end, so that by applying pressure in a certain way to the other end it could be made to swing inward, giving access to a flight of steps leading downward. The hinges, it is true, had become stiff from long non-usage, so that it now needed the united strength of half a dozen men to revolve the slab, but when once it was forced open it remained so, and there was no further trouble in that respect. Yet, even then, it was found to be impossible to penetrate to the subterranean chambers at once, for when an attempt was made to do so, the torches which the would-be explorers carried refused to burn in the mephitic atmosphere; and time therefore had to be allowed for the exterior air to penetrate and displace the poisonous vapours which had accumulated in the chambers during the many years that they had remained hermetically sealed.

At length, however, after the process of ventilation had been permitted to proceed for nearly a week, the air in the subterranean passages was found to be fresh enough to be breathed without much difficulty, and to allow of the torches burning in it with scarcely diminished luminosity, and the search for the treasure chamber was resumed. And now it was discovered that the labyrinth of passages and chambers extended far beyond the area covered by the superstructure, many of the chambers having evidently been used as prison cells, in some at least of which the unhappy prisoners had been interned and apparently left to perish of hunger and thirst; for, upon being broken open, they were found to still contain the mummified bodies of the unfortunate wretches; while others seemed to have been used by the priests as places of retirement and meditation. One exceptionally large chamber, too, had been used as the place of interment for the successive chief priests of the temple; for their bodies also, withered and shrunken in the dry atmosphere of the place, were found ranged round the walls of the mausoleum, clad in their sacerdotal vestments, and enthroned in bronze chairs of very beautiful and elaborate workmanship.

Finally, after the two Englishmen had been exploring this elaborate system of underground chambers for nearly three hours, they came upon the object of their search—and stood for awhile breathless and dumb in the presence of apparently incalculable wealth!

The chamber was by far the largest that the pair had thus far entered; so large indeed was it that the light of the torches which they carried was not nearly powerful enough to illuminate the entire chamber. But even what they beheld at the first glance was enough to take their breath away; for upon forcing open the door they found themselves confronted by an enormous mass of dull white, frosty-looking metal which, upon closer inspection, proved to be composed entirely of bricks—hundreds, thousands of them—of pure silver, each brick weighing about thirty pounds, or just as much as a man could conveniently lift with one hand. For several minutes the pair stood gazing enraptured at this enormous mass of precious metal, experiencing such sensations as it is given to few men to feel—for it must be remembered that both had been brought up amid such conditions that the possession of a few hundred pounds would be regarded by them as wealth! Then, as if moved by the same impulse, they turned to each other and burst into a torrent of mutual congratulation, mingled with expressions of amazement that there should be so vast a quantity of wealth in the world. For a few joyous minutes they could scarcely speak rationally to each other, so intense was their delight; but presently they pulled themselves together and proceeded with their investigations. Passing round the enormous pile of silver they were again brought to a stand by a pile of metal of almost equal size, but this time it was dull ruddy yellow in colour—in fact, gold! Gold, piled up like the silver in a solid mass also composed of bricks a trifle larger than those of the less valuable metal, being actually of such a weight that a brick was as much as one man could conveniently lift with both hands. But this was not all; for beyond this pile of gold bricks they came upon row after row of great leather sacks which, upon being opened, were found to contain more gold, either in the form of rough nuggets, just as they had been taken from the mine, or dust which had evidently been washed out of the sand of some river. The sight came near to driving them demented, for there were tons of the precious metal; far more of it indeed than they could possibly hope to ever carry away. But even this was not all; for at the far end of the chamber they came upon three great bronze coffers of elaborate and exquisitely beautiful workmanship, which, upon being opened, were found to be more than half-full of crystals—diamonds, rubies, and emeralds—that reflected the light of their torches in a perfect blaze of vari-coloured effulgence so dazzlingly brilliant that for the moment they could scarcely credit the evidence of their eyes. And with all this at the end of their journey, they had been jealously hoarding and guarding first the pair and latterly the remaining one of the emeralds that had formed the eyes of the idol, and the few gold scales that had decorated its clothing! The idea seemed so absurd, so supremely ridiculous, that when it occurred to Phil and he mentioned it to Dick, the pair of them burst into peal after peal of laughter that soon became hysterical; indeed the pair were very much nearer to being driven crazy than either of them dreamed of, by the sudden sight of such incalculable wealth. Fortunately for them, however, they were in the pink of health and condition, thanks to their long, arduous journey through the wilderness and their continuous life in the open air; and since a sound mind goes with a sound body, their mental processes were in the best possible condition for withstanding the shock, thus suddenly brought to bear upon them; and eventually after their hysterical outburst of joy had spent itself, they once more became rational beings, and fell to discussing the momentous question of how all this treasure was to be transported to England. They soon came to the conclusion that to transport it all to England—or rather to the coast, for, once there, the rest should be easy—would be an impossibility; and they finally decided to take the gems, and as much of the gold as they could find means of conveyance for. This last, namely, the means of conveyance to the coast, was the problem that now confronted them; and they eventually agreed that there was only one way of solving it, and that was by returning to Huancane and enlisting the services of the high priest and the other authorities of the town in their favour. Accordingly, with that object in view, they closed the door of the treasure chamber again, and made it temporarily secure; after which they returned to the upper air and electrified their Peruvian followers by directing them to make immediate preparations for a return to Huancane; and such was the energy which they contrived to infuse into the natives that they not only crossed to the mainland but also accomplished a very satisfactory return march before sunset, that night.

The return of the adventurers to Huancane with the news that the secret hiding-place of the treasure had been discovered caused the utmost rejoicing among the inhabitants, for somehow the idea that the elder of the two strangers was the reincarnated Manco Capac had got abroad, and what is more, had found general acceptance; and now every native in the place, and for miles round, was in a perfect fever of impatience that operations for the recovery of the country from the Spaniards should be pressed forward with all possible speed. Therefore when Phil intimated that he required a strong transport train to assist in the conveyance of the treasure to the coast, nobody thought of demanding his reasons for the conveyance of the treasure out of the country; they simply, one and all, devoted their energies to the collection of the train and the armed guard which Phil declared would also be necessary. And when Stukely, determined to avail himself to the utmost of their obliging mood, further intimated that he would also need at least thirty Peruvians to man the ship which he intended to capture, the said Peruvians of course to proceed across the Great Water with him, he met with no difficulty in securing as many volunteers as he needed. But the formation and equipment of such an expedition as Phil had demanded was not to be accomplished in a day, or even a week; therefore while men, animals, and arms were being got together at Huancane, a messenger, armed with the necessary authority, was sent forward along the route which would be followed by the caravan, with instructions to the natives all along the route to collect a certain quantity of food for the men and fodder for the animals, in order that the passage of the expedition to the coast might be expedited as much as possible. While this was being done, Phil and Dick, having taken formal leave of the Huancane authorities, returned to the Sacred Island, and, assisted by a dozen Peruvians, proceeded to transport to the mainland as much of the treasure as they thought they would be able to convey to the coast. This, of course, was soon done, and then all that remained to them was to wait patiently for the transport train, without which they could do nothing really worth the doing.

At length, after they had been idly waiting for nearly three weeks, the train duly arrived. But what a train it was! Two hundred llamas, with a driver for every ten beasts; two hundred and fifty armed men to protect the caravan from possible—but not very probable—attack by the Spaniards; and forty men, every one of whom were prepared to follow Phil to the world's end and back, if need be. Ten of the llamas were intended for the transport of provisions on the march from one village to another, and were already loaded to the full extent of their capacity; four were harnessed to the curious hammock-like arrangements which had been provided for the accommodation of Phil and his friend on the march; and the remaining hundred and eighty-six animals, as well as the forty volunteers for sea service, were available for the transportation of treasure, each llama being provided with a pair of saddle bags the broad connecting band of which sank so deeply into the wool of the creature that there was not the slightest fear of the bags slipping.

This transport train was so very much stronger than the Englishmen had dared to hope for that they instantly recognised the possibility of carrying away nearly twice the quantity of gold which they had originally arranged for; and the day following the arrival of the train was accordingly devoted to the transport of further gold bricks from the island to the mainland, until a full load was provided for every animal, including those which were harnessed to the hammocks, Phil and Dick preferring to make the journey on foot.

On the following morning, however, the imposing caravan started, with the first light of day, upon its journey toward the coast, winding its way along the eastern margin of the Sacred Lake until it reached its southern extremity, when it swerved away to the south-westward across the valley in which the lake lay embosomed, toward the towering snow-peaks of the western cordillera of the Andes. The first three days of the journey were quite pleasant and uneventful, for during that time the caravan was winding its slow way across the mountain valley; but on the fourth day the train entered a mountain pass which the Peruvians asserted was known only to themselves—and which they had chosen in order to avoid the possibility of collision with the armed forces of the Spaniards; and thenceforward, for four full days, the train wound its perilous way along narrow pathways bounded on the one hand by towering, inaccessible, rocky cliffs, and on the other by ghastly precipices, of such awful depth that their bases were frequently hidden by the wreaths of mountain mist floating far below; across frail swing bridges stretched from side to side of those awful, fathomless rifts called *barrancas* which seem to be peculiar to the Andes; or up and down steep, rugged, almost precipitous slopes where a single false step or a loose stone would send man or beast whirling away down to death a thousand feet below. But the llamas seemed to be more sure-footed than mountain goats, and despite their loads they scrambled up and down apparently inaccessible places, or plodded sedately along the narrowest and most dizzy ledges without accident, while the Peruvians seemed to be absolutely at home among the peaks and precipices.

But at length, after four full days of incessant peril, the train emerged from the last mountain pass and found itself upon a sloping, grassy plateau on the western slope of the Andes, with the limitless Pacific stretching away into the infinite distance, and the perils and hardships of the journey were at an end; for thenceforward the road wound its serpentine way downward through a series of ravines that, wild and savage enough at first, gradually widened out into gentle, grassy, tree-clad slopes that led down to the sandy plains which lie between the lower spurs of the Andes and the ocean. It took the train two days to cross these plains, which, under the neglect of the Spaniards, were fast returning to the desert state from which, under the wise rule of the Incas, they had been reclaimed; and finally, on the seventeenth day of the journey the entire train arrived safely at the little Peruvian village on the site of which the important port of Arica now stands. And thanks to the precautions adopted by the guide of the party, not a Spaniard had been encountered on any part of the journey.

But the good luck of the party did not end here; for on the very night of their arrival a small Spanish coasting craft of about seventy tons was sighted by the light of the full moon, becalmed in the offing; and manning four fishing canoes with the forty Peruvian volunteers, Dick and Phil paddled off and took her without the slightest difficulty, towing her safely into the bay before sunrise, where they brought her to an anchor. Her crew of fifteen Spaniards were easily disposed of by the return train, who took them far enough up into the mountains to render it impossible for them to do any harm, and then turned them adrift. The craft herself—named *El Ciudad de Lima*—proved, upon examination, to be a very fine, stanch little vessel, nearly new, in ballast; she therefore required nothing to be done to her to prepare her for her long voyage, save the storage of a sufficient quantity of water and provisions; and this, with the assistance of the Peruvians, was soon obtained. Before sailing, however, Phil, at Dick's suggestion, had her completely emptied of all her ballast and stores of every description, and then hauled close in to the beach, in a sheltered position, and careened, so that her bottom might be carefully examined, and all weed removed from it. Then, when this was done, the gold bricks were stowed right down alongside her keelson, upon plenty of dunnage, and on top of them was stowed the gems, packed in strong wooden boxes, the joints of which were afterward caulked and well paid with pitch, the boxes finally being thickly coated all over with pitch. Then, on top of and all round the gold and the boxes of gems, a sufficient quantity of sand to ensure ample stability was placed; and on top of that again the water and provisions were stowed. To do all this to Dick's satisfaction demanded nearly a month's strenuous labour; but when it was all finished and the little craft—re-christened *Elisabeth*—was finally ready for sea, Dick pronounced her fit to face the heaviest weather and the longest voyage. As she was only a small craft, the pair decided that twenty of the forty Peruvian volunteers would suffice as a crew, and these twenty were selected because of their superior fitness for the work of sailors, as exemplified during the preparation of the little ship for sea.

At length, everything being ready, the little craft hove up her anchor and sailed out of the bay on her long voyage round the southern extremity of America and up through the vast Atlantic ocean. To say that this voyage, undertaken in so small a vessel, and with a crew of men who had never before looked upon the sea, was an adventurous one, full of peril, and marked by countless hairbreadth escapes from capture and shipwreck, seems superfluous; indeed so full of adventure was it that a detailed description of what the little vessel and her crew went through would require a larger volume than the present for its adequate recital. It must suffice therefore to state that the adventurers ultimately arrived safely and with their precious cargo intact in Plymouth Sound, some six months after her departure from the Peruvian fishing village, to the unbounded astonishment and delight of those who had long given up Phil and Dick for dead. The meeting with old friends—and relatives, so far as Dick was concerned—the landing and eventual disposal of the gems and gold, with every necessary precaution, must be left for the reader to picture in detail; but it may be mentioned that while Dick purchased a big estate and built himself thereon a magnificent mansion not far from Plymouth, speedily becoming one of Plymouth's most important citizens, using his enormous wealth wisely and well, and ultimately earning his knighthood for his valiant conduct in assisting to disperse the Spanish Armada, Phil Stukely was so enamoured of the idea of returning to Peru, becoming its Inca, and driving out the Spaniards, that he actually fitted out an expedition with that intent. How he fared and what ultimately became of him it may perhaps be the privilege of the present historian some day to relate.

Postscript

My story of the great and wonderful adventure of Philip Stukely and Dick Chichester is ended; yet upon reading the pages which I have with so much labour compiled I am conscious of a certain sense of incompleteness, conscious that something still remains untold. I feel that to let the narrative go forth to the world without offering some sort of an explanation of the source of Stukely's extraordinary and uncanny knowledge of Indian lore, and of the ancient Peruvian language—which he had never learned—would be unfair to the reader.

But in the rough yet voluminous notes of the adventure which Sir Richard Chichester amused himself by jotting down at his leisure after his return to England, which he left to his heirs at his death, and which fell into my hands some twenty years ago, I find no word which throws the slightest light upon the subject. Yet from the time when I first skimmed through those notes I have been moved by an ardent desire to put them into narrative form, in order that Englishmen of to-day may be afforded yet one more example of the indomitable courage and tenacious perseverance that distinguished their forefathers during the stirring and glorious days of good Queen Bess. But until quite recently I have been deterred from undertaking the pleasant task, for the reason that certain portions of the narrative are of such a character as either to strain the credulity of the reader to breaking point, or to cause him to denounce the good Sir Richard as a— shall we say—perverter of the truth. And I should be exceedingly reluctant to do anything which would produce the latter result; for it seems perfectly evident, from contemporary records, that the worthy knight was held in highest esteem, by all who were brought into contact with him, as a man of unimpeachable honour and probity, whose word was always to be relied upon, and who was so unimaginative, so thoroughly matter-of-fact, and of so simple, straightforward a character generally, as to be completely above the suspicion of any slightest tendency to embellish a story by the perpetration of an untruth. Quite recently, however, I was made acquainted with certain extraordinary facts which may possibly bear upon the matter, and which, although not absolutely conclusive, appear to corroborate Sir Richard's astounding statements; and as they may perhaps prove of interest to the reader, I now set them forth.

It chanced that a few months ago I was a guest at a dinner party at which men only were present, and that I was seated next to a very brilliant young American physician who was devoting himself especially to the study of Heredity. It being his hobby, he soon contrived to turn the conversation toward that topic, and, after a few general remarks, told several very startling stories illustrative of certain contentions which he advanced. Among others he related the case of a young Western farmer whose ancestors had emigrated from the little village of Langonnet, in Brittany, to America, some two hundred and fifty years ago. They had passed through the usual vicissitudes of fortune experienced by the early settlers, and in process of time had become so absolutely Americanised that even their very name had become corrupted almost out of recognition as of French origin. The young farmer in question possessed only a very elementary education, and had never been taught French, yet almost from the moment when he first began to speak he occasionally interpolated a French word in his conversation, and the practice extended as he grew older. Finally, it transpired that certain property in the neighbourhood of Langonnet which his ancestors had abandoned as practically worthless had become so valuable that enquiries as to the whereabouts of the owners had been set on foot, the descendants had been with much difficulty traced, and the young farmer, as being the person most directly interested, crossed to France to investigate. And now comes the marvellous part of the story. The young man had no sooner arrived in Langonnet—which, be it remembered, he was now visiting for the first time in his life—than he began to recognise such of his surroundings as remained unaltered since the emigration of his French ancestors, and, more strange still, perhaps, was able to converse in the Breton dialect with little or no difficulty by the time that he had been twenty-four hours in the village!

The point which the narrator sought to illustrate and emphasise was that not only is heredity responsible for the transmission and persistence of certain peculiarities of face, form, and character, but also that in a few isolated cases it has actually been known to *transmit knowledge!*

As soon as my neighbour had finished his story and replied to several comments upon it, I put to him the case of Philip Stukely, asking him whether he thought that the uncanny knowledge manifested by that gentleman was also due to heredity, to which he replied that he had not a doubt of it, and that, if I chose to investigate, I should probably discover either that Phil had Peruvian blood in his veins, or that some long dead English ancestor of his had once been in Peru and remained there for several years. I have not yet been able to undertake the suggested investigation, and were I able to do so I am afraid that after so great a lapse of time it would be found impossible to pursue it very far; but I cannot help thinking that the story of the American physician tends to explain to some extent, if not completely, the source of Stukely's amazing and otherwise inexplicable gift of knowledge, and accordingly I offer the suggestion for what it may be worth.